BURNING
THE ICE

Also by Laura J. Mixon

Astro Pilots
Greenwar (with Steven Gould)*
Other *Avatars Dance* books:
Glass Houses
Proxies

*Published by Tor Books

BURNING
THE *ICE*

Laura J. Mixon

A Tom Doherty Associates Book **TOR**® New York

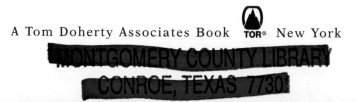

BURNING THE ICE

Copyright © 2002 by Laura J. Mixon

Edited by Patrick Nielsen Hayden

Book design by Jane Adele Regina

A Tor Book
Published by Tom Doherty Associates, LLC
175 Fifth Avenue
New York, NY 10010

www.tor.com

Tor® is a registered trademark of Tom Doherty Associates, LLC.

Library of Congress Cataloging-in-Publication Data

Mixon, Laura J.
    Burning the ice / Laura J. Mixon—1st ed.
        p. cm.
    "A Tom Doherty Associates book."
    ISBN 0-312-86903-7
    1. Space colonies—Fiction. I. Title.

PS3557.O8947 B87 2002
813'.54—dc21
                                2002025368

First Edition: August 2002

Printed in the United States of America

0 9 8 7 6 5 4 3 2 1

For Kay and Jim Mixon—
fellow siblings, fellow singletons

Part I

The Twin

Dane—dearest—

You asked me last night why I've decided to stay with the colonists instead of going on with the ship. You asked if I'd stopped loving you.

How can you doubt me? Even during the worst of the hidden war, when people were dying and things looked bleakest—when the bonds that bound us two were so strained by your unbreakable ties to Pablo and Buddy and the rest of the crèche-born—I never once doubted your devotion. How can you doubt mine, now?

You crèche-born are the colonists' *parents*. The others have refused to face that. They treat the colonists the way they were treated, back on Earth: like experimental animals. These young people need to be well away from the crèche-born, and they need a sane adult (at least, I hope I'm sane!) to provide a compass for them. To help them find their way. It's my place to go with them.

So. Yes, you're right. I've given up on the crèche-born. They'll never change. You know it as well as I do.

Goddammit, Dane, it's been a hundred and fifty years! I'm bone-weary of living that anguish day after day, of facing that failure—mine *and* theirs (though not yours, thank God; never yours). It's time for a fresh start.

I believe—I hope—I've shielded the colonists from the worst of the crèche-born's madness, enough so that they'll be able to find a new way, a different way of being. One that doesn't abnegate life, but embraces it.

I wish you could come with us. You're like a daughter to me, and the dearest of friends. I'll never forget you. I'll always grieve that circumstances force this separation between us.

Never doubt my devotion. Never.

all my love,
Carli

—from Dane Elisa Cae's private files: United Nations Interstellar Ship Exodus *archives, logged 03/03/2218.*

1

Singing the Icebrine Blues

That morning before breakfast Manda stopped by her work chamber to check her marine-waldos' night's work.

The chamber was an ugly, rock-hewn room with poor lighting and a thatch floor. In the room's center, a device that looked like a hiker's daypack hung from a wire web suspended below the rough ceiling. Already decked out in her livesuit and -hood, Manda slipped the livepack on and plugged its leads into her yoke. Her liveface appeared before her as she did so, rendered on her retinas by lasers in the specs set into her livemask. Glamour filled the room, a glowing sphere that defined her projection pod. A host of 3-D icons appeared: shiny, translucent satellites locked in Manda-static orbit.

First Manda touched her communications-cube, and it expanded into a thicket of geometric shapes. With economical movements, she checked her mail and messages, then folded the commcube up and called up her marine-waldo data. It blossomed around her in glistening bouquets and thickets of numbers, charts, and graphic landscapes, and she began to sort through it all. Her handcrafted fleet of eight marine-waldos, the *Aculeus* series, had collected a lot of information, and she had a lot of data to get through since she had taken the evening off yesterday.

But it wasn't long before fingers of cold seeped in, disrupting her concentration. Beneath all the protective layers Manda had on—layers of plastic, organic, and metallic fibers, one after another till she could scarcely bend elbow or knee—she shivered, nicking virtual icons with cold-clumsy hands and elbows. Data strands fragmented and cascaded down the inner boundaries of her projection sphere.

"Shit."

With a sigh, suppressing both her frustration and the shivers, she recovered the data, reconstructed it, and started again— dancing her marine-waldo control dance, working her fingers, arms, legs, and torso to guide her fleet of machines across the dark floor of the ocean, to read its secrets with their instruments.

She was the colony's best waldo pilot. The best. Amid the billions back on Earth, how could any single human presume to be the best at anything? For that, at least, she was glad to be one of the handful who lived on this freezing, barren world. She hadn't lost a machine yet, in almost eight seasons of piloting in some extremely dangerous environments. And she didn't intend to start now. But she was growing tired of this latest assignment, this fruitless search through the depths of Brimstone's frigid waters.

Arlene had suggested the ocean search project to Manda, while the rest of the clone geared up on Project IceFlame. Whatever secrets lay beneath Brimstone's icy crust had stayed hidden ever since the JebediahMeriwether twoclone had died fifteen seasons ago, while exploring the ocean floor in their deep-sea submersible. The colonists knew little about this world they inhabited.

When Arlene had suggested it, this assignment had seemed ideal. Manda hadn't been interested in attempting a collaboration with the rest of her sibling group—even if it would have put her at the controls of the winged waldos that would shortly be strafing the methane-laced ice at the poles. They had all the skills they needed without her, and without a twin she was always the odd one out. She wanted to carve out her own space, not simply try to fit into theirs.

But all she'd found so far was dark and cold, and she'd had her fill of those. At least her prior assignments—flying the jet-waldos up to the poles, and using land-explorer equipment to take ice and air samples there—had turned up interesting data to analyze. Even her tedious and dangerous first assignment, driving a tractor-waldo across rotten tropical ice floes, mapping the myriad island chains down there and looking for signs of volcanic activity, beat this oppressive succession of days scanning barren rock and lifeless brine.

Manda was a woman of planetshine, of air currents and ice fog and indigo sky. In her aerial and terrestrial waldos she could outrun the cold . . . or so she pretended. Down here in the ocean there was nowhere to run. The chill pressed in all about. Thousands of tons of water and ice lay overhead. Even the sounds were oppressive, the gut-deep groans of shifting floes that carried to Manda's detectors across thousands of kilometers of gelid liquid.

She'd heard sounds like that, once, in a documentary in their archives: growls both agonized and determined; the moans of a woman in labor. The ocean's cries sounded to Manda's ears as if the world itself were trying to give birth.

And the dark too, oppressed. Her fleet of marine-waldos had computer-enhanced vision; their visuals swirled with false-color images. But it was all unreal, no different than the hallucinations that swarmed behind her eyelids while she lay alone in bed at night—shivering, sweating—filled with unreasoning certainty that any minute now, she would die.

Her chest had grown constricted; through the pores of her livemask she gasped for air. With a pirouette that bordered on panic and a set of finger flicks on the translucent control icons that orbited her, Manda retreated from the waldo she rode. She wadded the whole thing up, shrinking its inputs till it was merely a shining ball of reduced data in her hands, and set it loose to float amid the other balls of compressed data at waist level. This took only a second to do. Then, with a word or two, she adjusted the livesuit settings, and bent over till the pressure eased.

Nerves, that's all, she told herself. She touched a different waldo's commandshape and the dodecahedron grew till it swallowed her, infusing her with its sensate data.

Maybe, she thought, calmer now, as a current lifted her marine-waldo, *Aculeus Quinque,* over a rise blanketed in faint, neon-green rocks—as she scanned the ocean floor with infrared skin sense and magnified-light eyes and sonar ears, as she tasted the ocean currents with her waldo's thermocouples and chemical composition detectors—*maybe it really* is *time for a job change.* Moss or bamboo harvesting, polar duty—judah shit, even baby-tending—would be better than this endless dark. (OK—maybe not baby-tending.) Maybe she *should* join the terraforming effort.

Manda pulled off her livemask and tam—and saw that Teresa and Paul had paused at the doorway.

Teresa and Paul were tall and muscular, with smooth, almond-dark skin and yellow-green eyes, and kinky, ginger-blond hair—their faces and bodies an identical, exotic mix of African and Scandinavian features. The bristles of Paul's short hair stuck up through the mesh of his livehood; Teresa's hair was longer, pulled back in a severe ponytail pressed flat under the translucent mesh of hers. Teresa had breasts and broader hips than Paul. Otherwise they were the exact image of each other—and of Manda too, other than the eight seasons of age they had acquired that Manda hadn't yet.

"Talking to yourself again?" Teresa asked with an arch smile. Manda realized she'd been vocalizing her unhappiness. And as usual, Teresa's teasing stung—probably more than she had intended it to.

"I'm trying to work. Leave me alone."

Teresa's expression went flat. Paul pointed a finger in Manda's face. "Lay off my sister."

He followed his vat-twin away.

"She's my sister too, asshole," Manda said to their backs. Then regretted her testiness. *Warm it up a therm or two. Your clone is just about the only friend you've got.*

This irritable back-and-forth between her and Teresa-and-Paul was a stupid pattern, but one Manda felt helpless to change. From childhood, when Teresa and Paul were adolescents and Manda was "the baby," they'd always fought too damn much. Teresa was always provoking her, scolding or teasing—and Manda usually insulted her in response. Which invariably brought Paul around to Teresa's defense. Which resulted in a fight between Manda and Paul, which caused Teresa to further provoke Manda in defense of Paul.

Round and round we go, Manda thought. She'd have to apologize later.

That's when it dawned on her that she shouldn't be this cold—not *this* cold. She minimized the commandball again and then disconnected herself from the livepack that hung suspended in the middle of her projection pod. All her command- , program- , and databalls shrank, flattened, and moved toward the center of her vision, and the hazy boundaries of the light-sphere that defined her projection pod vanished.

Then she noticed the rock wall, which was beaded with frozen condensate.

Frozen?

The readout above the thermostat on the wall read two degrees Celsius; that couldn't be right. Striding over to the wall, she ripped off a fleece-lined shell and nylomir mitten and her live-glove. She touched the wall's white, chalky surface with her bare left hand. It was cold. Sticky-cold, as the sweat from her fingertips froze. More like minus fifteen. The heating system had failed again.

With a sigh of disgust Manda recoiled her frizzy braid. She pulled the slick-soft mesh of the livehood down over her head and face again, dragged the tam's cuff down over her ears, pulled her gloves and mittens back on, and plugged back into the livepack. The sphere reappeared around her. She stabbed at an icon that now hovered at shoulder height, which solidified as she focused on it.

"*Damn* you, ObediahUrsula!" she snapped at the two young, round faces that materialized. "I can't work with the heaters failing all the time."

ObediahUrsulas' brows puckered and their eyes widened. So young. What were children doing in charge of something as critical as the heaters?

"It's, it's just that—" "—the thermostats are—"

"Don't. Give. Me. Another *fucking* sob story about equipment breakdown." The words darted out of Manda's mouth in explosive puffs. "Just fix it. If I lose a waldo, I'm going to put your name down as the cause."

She stabbed the com icon off in the midst of their reply, and rubbed her hands over her painfully spasming diaphragm. A knot in her throat formed, swelled, threatened to burst.

"Goddammit." She swallowed the knot, washed it down with a dose of anger. "Damn it to hell."

A pair passing by in the corridor glanced in at her and shook their heads in disapproval. They were PabloJebediahs: the twelve-clone's next-to-youngest siblings. PabloJeb and ObediahUrsula were closely allied, and Manda had probably just disrupted some sort of delicate, inter-clone power balance.

Too bad. She glared at them until they went away. Then she pulled her livehood back over her head, adjusted her specs and mic, and hooked back into her livepack. Her data- and command-balls reappeared, within the confines of her sphere of light.

All right, she admitted to herself. *It isn't ObediahUrsula's fault the heating systems are failing. But if I didn't yell about it nothing would get done, and we'd all freeze to death.*

She reconsidered and started to disconnect; she needed to

calm down, and was getting hungry for breakfast anyhow. But a glimmer in one of the dataglobes at waist level caught her eye. Probably nothing—another false alarm; *Aculeus Septimus*'s visuals might need calibrating again.

Or.

Maybe this time it was the hydrothermal vent she was looking for. The place where, if this frozen, forsaken pissball of a world had any remnants of life left, it would probably be. Shaking her head at her own optimism, Manda reached out for the little sphere, which showed a snippet of ocean floor with a bit of flickering red in it.

2

Ur-Carli Pays a Visit

Manda ate breakfast alone in the mess, later, at one of the tables nearest the galley. None of her clone was there. It was just as well, since she was still cranky and not in the mood for company. The temperature anomaly her marine-waldo had reported had turned out to be a thermocouple a malfunction. As she'd known it would be.

The young ObediahUrsulas she'd yelled at sat at one of the other tables, along with their other two vat-mates: four identical copies with the same round face, black eyes with epicanthal folds, brown, arrow-straight hair, and compact build. Manda didn't need to hear their words to know they were trading insults about her.

Her lip curled. *Bite me, infants.* The set glanced at her with identical angry glares, and then huddled together. *Well,* she thought ruefully, *at least I've got entertainment value.* With a piece of *mana* bread she mopped up the last of the gravy and chicken from her plate, then scooped up and pocketed the rationing chits still on her tray and stood. As she did so, a low rumble shook the trays and silverware.

Manda and the others looked up. Brimstone circled its mother planet once every thirty-four and a quarter hours, and being so close to a Jovian giant two and a half times the size of Jupiter meant tidal stresses produced frequent quakes. They rarely amounted to much, but several times in her life Manda could remember quakes big enough to trigger cave-ins, and a big one when she was a child had killed several people. So whenever the rumbling started she felt a prick of fear, and saw that same fear reflected on others' faces.

The quaking died away, though, and within a couple of seconds everyone had returned to what they were doing. In Manda's case, leaving.

Then ur-Carli entered. Startled, Manda stared.

The syntellect occasionally donned an avatar (a virtual projection) or a proxy (a humanoid waldo) and made an appearance, but sightings hadn't been all that common in the past few seasons. Manda hadn't seen ur-Carli at all, since it had finished helping her with the sea-mapping software last summer. She pulled up on the mesh of her livehood mask and peered out underneath it. Ur-Carli vanished.

The syntellect was projecting, then, rather than borrowing one of the colony's handful of still-functional proxy bodies. And none of the dozen others seated at the surrounding tables reacted to the syntellect's presence, which meant it must be projecting to Manda's liveface alone.

Ur-Carli's user interface was humanoid, a frail old lady with wispy white hair and pale skin and blue eyes. They were the features of Carli D'Auber, the scientist who had travelled here from Earth with the crèche-born, and then decided to stay with the colonists rather than head off to parts unknown. She—the real Carli—had disappeared within a couple seasons of landfall; she'd been killed, or chosen to end her very long life, out on the surface.

Manda smoothed her livemask over her face, surprised.

"What do you need?" she asked the syntellect.

One of the (few) things she liked about ur-Carli was that its auditory interface was better designed than most of the colony's syntellectual systems; it understood spoken English relatively well. The colony's computational jack-of-all-trades, it had been around for just about forever, since even before they'd made landfall. It had a great deal of autonomy and flexibility built into its makeup. But Manda found its human-mimic interface annoying. She kept expecting it to act like a human, and it kept disappointing her.

It leaned toward her. "I've got a secret."

There's no point in whispering. Manda thought in annoyance. Ur-Carli was projecting. If anyone else could see the projection, they would hear the whisper too. And even if the syntellect had been here in proxy or waldo, whispering would be pointless. On Brimstone, a normal conversational tone was difficult enough to hear from farther than a couple meters away, and the mess wasn't very crowded.

"Something that nobody in the colony knows about," the syntellect continued, in its growly old-lady voice. "I think it will interest you. Do you want to come see?"

Manda sighed in exasperation, then stood. "All right." She might as well get it over with; ur-Carli wouldn't leave her alone until it had achieved its end.

And, despite herself, Manda was curious. What knowledge could a syntellect possibly have that would be of interest to humans?

Ur-Carli led her away from the main colony areas, through the winding, rocky passages and stairways toward the lifts. By the time they reached the main lift station no one else was around.

A brownout had rendered the elevators inoperable, so they had to take the stairs: a seemingly endless set of ice-coated rock slabs. Manda soon got winded, and had to stop for frequent rests. Brimstone's oxygen content was higher than Earth's, twenty-five percent, and Manda was all but a native of this planet; they'd made landfall when she was barely a fire-year-old, three earth-years. But the human cardiovascular system simply didn't work that well at less than four hundred millibars, an atmospheric pressure comparable to seventy-two hundred meters above earth-sea-level—among the highest of Earth's moun-taintops.

After she slipped and fell a second time, Manda sat down on a step and leaned over her knees, heaving labored breaths. Ur-Carli waited patiently on the step above.

I hate you, Manda thought. She was starting to feel the chill, despite her exertions; these upper, unheated tunnels stayed at about minus twenty Celsius. She donned her parka hood and her mittens and shells, then activated the spikes in her boots and stood yet again, cursing herself for going along with this. The syntellect started upward once more.

"Not much farther," ur-Carli said finally. Air stirred on Manda's cheeks, and she could hear the echoing clatter of the gears and chains of the colony's heavy equipment transport loop. She pulled her hood close with a shiver. If she could feel the breeze down here, through the lock, quite a storm must be blowing. And she didn't have radiation gear with her.

But she was looking forward to a visit to the surface anyhow. One got tired of small, windowless chambers and crowded, me-andering, poorly-lit corridors—of cliques and political maneu-verings—of shifting loyalties, lies, nasty little secrets, and furtive looks. Going to the surface meant being truly alone, not just hiding out in a simile or sending your consciousness off into the ocean depths in a marine-waldo.

But at the landing twelve steps below the main colony en-trance, within sight of the massive chains and pulleys of the equipment transport loop, ur-Carli shrank to about three-quarters size, turned, and headed into a cramped tunnel nor-mally used only by the colony's maintenance robotics. It led, Manda was pretty sure, to the main equipment storage hangar. The corridor was rather too small for a human; Manda was forced to walk stooped over.

"Wait," she gasped, but ur-Carli didn't pause. Manda could no longer see a thing except ur-Carli's projection; the colony didn't waste power lighting corridors for robots that navigated solely using radio and internal maps. Manda's tool belt had a flashlight, but she'd left the belt in her locker at breakfast.

So she trudged along behind the syntellect, getting angrier and angrier. About the time she'd decided to put a stop to this and announce that she was heading back, ur-Carli halted and gestured.

"Immediately to your right," the syntellect said, "is an access tunnel with rungs set into it." Its voice, a projection directly into the speakers at Manda's ears, didn't echo as Manda's footsteps and breathing had. "There are twenty-four steps. Be careful—it may be slippery."

Manda shook her head, exasperated. "Why are you doing this?"

But ur-Carli had vanished.

"Goddammit!"

Manda stood still for a moment, still panting, sparks dancing on the periphery of her vision—on the brink of saying *fuck this* and leaving. She groped for the access tunnel, defining its shape and size with her hands. The opening was about a meter square, its top at about shoulder height. She stuck her head inside. A dim light shone above, its garnet reflections making the coarse tunnel walls glisten.

I've come all this way, Manda thought. *I might as well see it through.* She scaled the ladder and climbed up into a room with thatched flooring and ice-coated walls.

It was a long room, one that stretched back into dimness. Near this end a tall, narrow window allowed sun- and planet-shine in. Manda could tell from the pinkish quality of the light, and the fact that everything had two faint shadows, that both 47 Ursae Majoris, the sun, and Fire, Brimstone's parent world, were up.

This room was colder even than the tunnel she'd just left. Thirty below, perhaps? Maybe colder. Cold enough it hurt to breathe, even through the livehood and the fur fringe of her parka, which she pulled close to her lips. She realized she'd left her tam and neck gaiter below. Her fingers had already begun to throb, even through the gloves and shells, and her feet were starting to grow chill too.

I'd better not linger long, Manda realized. Her livesuit wasn't the only thing that might give out in this severe a cold. But she had a few moments, at least, before the cold would harm either her or the liquid nano-muscles and -transmitters of her livesuit. She touched her clock icon and set an alarm for ten minutes.

It was then she noticed her connection with the colony network had been severed. She looked around, startled. *This room is unplugged!* If so, it was the only place she knew of in Amaterasu that was.

From the window, she saw that the view looked out onto the snowy basin below the mountain range housing Amaterasu. Out on the plains, small musk oxen and reindeer herds grazed on grey lichens and pink snow fungi. She spotted a couple of shepherd clones and their dogs with the herd animals.

The main entrance to Amaterasu must be almost directly beneath this place. Manda was surprised that she had never glimpsed this slotted window from below. The window must be hidden by the promontory that overhung the entrance.

As she'd guessed, a fierce windstorm was blowing. Ice crystals struck the window with a sound like wild applause or voices shouting, at a great distance.

The sound was hypnotic. Manda pressed mittened hands to the glass and leaned close, and her breath left fractal frost trails on it. She squinted against the snowy brightness outside. Ice-laden gusts outside obscured, then revealed, the Scimitars: a jagged range of mountain peaks that rimmed the basin's far side.

She looked upward. Fire, a Jovian world two and a half times the size of Sol's largest planet, Jupiter, was faintly visible beyond the ice-crystal clouds. It hung near the horizon, dominating the western sky, subtending twenty-five degrees of arc. She remembered how once as a child she'd stood on the valley floor—staring at that enormous flame-red, white-yellow, and bunsen-burner-blue ball in the sky with its sweeping arc of a ring—watching as storms coiled like bands of gaudy smoke across its face, imagining she could reach up and touch it. It looked that close.

Brimstone orbited Fire at about 400,000 kilometers—roughly the same distance as that between Earth and its moon—but Fire's powerful pull took only thirty-four and a quarter hours to whip Brimstone around, rather than the twenty-eight days Earth's paltry gravity took to pull its own moon around. They used Brimstone's roughly-thirty-four-hour revolution around Fire—during which time the sun, Uma, rose and set as a result of that lunar orbit—as their "day," and broke this day into two seventeen-hour watches, each with its own work, eating, and rest periods. So each thirty-four-hour, bifurcated day held a total of sixteen hours of work time, with six hours for eating and relaxation, and thirteen for sleep. They wedged an extra work hour in every four days to correct for the difference. Brimstonians worked hard.

They used a five-day week and a twenty- to twenty-one day month, which made their weeks and months the same length as Earth's. Three twelve-month seasons made up a fire-year. This made Brimstonian weeks and months correspond closely to Earth's weeks and months in length, with each of their seasons lasting an earth-year.

Fire had been named for its fiery appearance, but whether the irony was intended or not, neither it nor its moons had ever had more than a nodding acquaintance with warmth. Even in Brimstone's earlier days, the moon had never been as warm as Earth. Their sun, 47 Ursae Majoris or Uma, radiated enough heat to make a band along Brimstone's equator, its "tropics," marginally habitable: comparable to the polar regions of Earth. Without its once-high carbon dioxide content, Brimstone would perhaps never have been able to harbor life.

They were certain Brimstone had harbored its own life at one time. No one argued with Manda about that. (Technically, it still did; their probes had found traces of bacteria and they'd discovered a couple native, cold-adapted versions of algae when they first landed; they'd used the native life forms as templates to modify Earth-based organisms during their early terraforming efforts.) If the high oxygen content in the atmosphere and the large reservoirs of crude oil they'd found weren't indicators enough, they had Amaterasu itself: the geologists believed the caverns' calcite and silicate structures had been some sort of rough equivalent to Earth's coral reefs, billions of years ago—though some argued that the structures might actually have been a freshwater and/or aboveground biomineral feature, rather than an undersea one. And some of the cavern's strata held the occasional two-billion-year-old partially fossilized fragment, evidence of small creatures that must once have inhabited Amaterasu.

But just about everyone besides Manda was certain that at this point, the world was to all intents and purposes post-biotic. Most of the planet's carbon was now bound up in subterranean hydrocarbon pools and vast glaciers of methane-ice at the poles, and on the ocean floor, beneath the almost-worldwide ice caps. Much of the rest had condensed out of the air gradually as the moon had cooled, forming deadly-cold, smoking carbon-dioxide pools atop the methane-hydrate glaciers at the poles.

Unless Hell had frozen over while nobody was looking, there was nothing brimstone-like about Brimstone. This world was an icy slushball on its way to becoming a frozen-solid snowball, and organic-based life couldn't survive below the freezing point of water.

Pondering this, Manda wandered around the large chamber. A desk and a set of cabinets rested against one wall. Near the desk, a spiral staircase ascended through an open hatch in the ceiling. Intrigued, she climbed the staircase into a small, dark room with metal walls.

Above chin-level, the walls of this room sloped inward toward the ceiling, creating a four-sided pyramid. The only light came from the opening in the floor. Wind pounded against the thin walls, beating them like a drum. In the room's center was a long box, a handmade affair of metal and bamboo, about half a meter square by about four meters long—the room's only feature. Curious, she groped her way around it and found a wheeled stepladder next to it, which she climbed. Near the upper end of the rectangle she located an eyepiece; she peered into it and saw nothing but a blur.

It was a telescope!

She spotted a glint out of the corner of her eye, and reached for it: a remote control lay in a basket attached to the hand rail. She picked the remote up, squinted at it in the low light, then fiddled with its levers, which made the telescope tilt up and down and back and forth.

Still powered. Good. One never knew anymore what equipment would still be working from the original settlement, and what wouldn't. The equipment that time and heavy use hadn't yet broken, the severe cold and intense UV emanating from Uma and Fire often did.

The Amaterasans had grown quite clever at fixing things that seemed unfixable, and reformulating broken parts or juryrigging stand-ins when the original equipment failed. *Exodus* had been designed as a colonizing ship, stocked with a wide array of equipment that was highly modular, powered by antimatter batteries, and intended for use in severe-environment conditions. And the crèche-born had made a little progress with nanotechnology on their way here, whose fruits the colonists had access to.

Still, it was only a matter of time before all their original technology failed. Even if the equipment itself weren't gradually failing, they had no means of making more antimatter, and *all* their waldos and robots were powered by it. Already many of the more heavily used recycling and refining equipment were on their second battery packs. And the crèche-born *hadn't* left them the means to manufacture replacements, reasoning that these would be needed at their next destination.

So the colonists had had to make do, and come up with ways to survive until they could mine enough ore and build enough infrastructure to manufacture their own technology: a process that would take centuries. According to her siblings' estimates, they only had another fifteen to twenty seasons before equipment failure and battery depletion started putting the colony at risk. They had to start warming this world up, quickly, and develop an agricultural base big enough to support them. Hence, Project IceFlame.

Manda fiddled with the remote control some more. A recessed oval button between the levers caused a loud screech when she pushed it. Something started beeping, and a red LED began flashing on a panel by the stair that she hadn't seen at first. She went over, scraped off the frost, and squinted at it. A faded, hand-printed label next to a switch said "De-icer." She flipped the switch.

The beeping stopped, and the red LED on the wall panel went from blinking to a steady glow. Manda could feel on her cheeks the warmth that emanated from a set of glowing coils against the metal ceiling. She spent the next few minutes, while the de-icer worked, fiddling with the telescope's controls, familiarizing herself with them.

A drop of icy water hit Manda on the cheek. She looked up. A faint crack of light showed. Then the red LED went off, and the screeching started again. Manda flinched as the ceiling overhead split into four triangles, which fell away like the petals of a blossoming flower, and a cascade of snow and dust fell onto her. She covered her mouth and eyes, then laughed in delight as the storm blasted her in the face, stinging her cheeks with ice crystals, stealing her breath with its ferocious cold.

Wind whipped over the upright portion of the wall. Manda pulled her hood close again. This little observatory was set on the spine of a ridge, at a wide spot that narrowed again on both sides. Nearby, the colony's lone radio tower stood, a slender, skeletal structure that reached into the sky, trembling in the gusts. The blinking red light at its apex served as a beacon for the herders, waldo pilots, and explorers who wandered Brimstone's surface.

Manda eyed it, buffeted by the wind, hunching her shoulders and stamping her cold-stiffened feet, remembering how many times she had used it to get her aerial-waldos home. She shuddered violently. She had forgotten just how cold it could get, out here in the spring winds. Even if she could tough it out, her livesuit couldn't handle it, and she didn't have her radiation gear. She should get back inside.

But first—shivering, fidgeting—she looked through the eyepiece again, and cranked the knobs until Fire came into focus. Even through the haze of ice-fog she could make out shadows cast by the white clots of cumulus in Fire's outermost atmosphere onto the crimson and blue cloud canyons of Fire's upper-middle layers. Fire's ring of ice and rock—its upper half pale gold in Uma's early morning light, its lower half invisible below Fire's night side—cast a sharp, slender shadow down onto Fire that freefell between the cloud formations like a misplaced strip of night.

Finally she acquiesced to the need for warmth. She triggered the recessed button again, and the walls came back up, screaming their rusty outrage, to shut out the two-toned light and the howling wind. Manda headed back down the spiral stairwell and checked her livesuit.

She wasn't worried about her yoke; liveyokes were bioptronic systems and much hardier, thermally, than livesuits. But livesuits used a nanobug stew of muscle-like molecules and signal transmitters that was sensitive to extreme cold. The suit's temperature warning readouts were getting jittery, and drifting down toward the danger zone. After a moment's nail-biting indecision, she decided she could squeeze a few more minutes in, to check the dark reaches in the long room's back.

Equipment of unknown function was scattered throughout, along with some machining tools. She wandered into the increasing dimness past the office, through a lab of some kind, past a small machine shop. She spotted a collection of old waldos, both big and small: ancient, broken-down models; dusty hulks that looked like bizarre bugs, monsters, and skeletons in the dimness. She really needed a flashlight to explore here. She couldn't make out much detail. Pale, purple-tainted dust mingled with snow powder had covered every surface and piled up in the corners.

Nobody knows about this place, she realized. *It's been forgotten—if anyone ever knew it was here at all.* She wondered whose space it had been, and smiled. *Well, I guess it's mine now. At least for the moment.*

Her eyes had slowly become accustomed to the low light. Beyond the lab she spied an open doorway. She made her careful way there and at the door she paused. The cold's severity irritated her eyes; she blinked repeatedly and stared into the dark room, trying to make out detail. Her shadow stretched thin, faint, and brown across the floor of a small room. A very slight change of odor reached her. She couldn't put her finger on the difference. It was not an unpleasant smell.

Against the wall seemed to be a cot, or a bed. She stepped into the room and her eyes adapted further to the darkness. It was a bed. And someone was lying on it. She yelled in sudden fear—her heart thundered and her mouth went dry. *RUN.*

But no, the figure hadn't moved when she'd cried out. And the dust was deep enough that behind her, in the faint light coming from the observatory, she could make out its peaks and craters where her feet had fallen.

She was in no danger. No one had walked on this floor in years. It was a proxy, or—

She stopped, heart pounding again. Or a corpse. Shit.

There must be a light source, she realized, *no matter how old this place is. If it still works. Which it probably does. Why are you stumbling around in the dark? Idiot.*

Did she really want to see this?

"Lights up," she said.

And covered her eyes with another shout as the lights came on full force, blinding her.

"Lights down by half!" she yelled. "You stupid shit!"

Ur-Carli had to be watching; it was probably laughing its algorithmic butt off. (Perhaps not, though; not if the room was isolated from the colony network.) Manda blinked hard, eyes burning, and finally worked up the nerve to remove her hands from her eyes and look at the bed again.

It *was* a corpse. A frozen one, to all appearances perfectly preserved. A very old woman, blanketed by Brimstone's lavender-and-snow dust. Manda released her breath through her teeth and approached cautiously. She blew dust and snow from the face, thinking it looked familiar.

And she realized. For one thing, the corpse's face shared features with Manda and some of her fellow Brimstoners—this woman was certainly a forebear of one or more of the colony's clones, including Manda's.

But that's not what jarred her. She had seen precisely this face—or rather, a somewhat younger version of it—many times. Most recently only moments earlier, in fact, on ur-Carli.

With a frown, Manda pressed the edge of her hand against her chin and looked at the corpse on the bed. *Are you who I think you are? Are you really Carli D'Auber—the crèche-borns' last and truest mother? And if so, what the hell are you doing, hidden away here? Why did ur-Carli keep you a secret from the colony for so long, and why did it want me to find you now?*

Her alarm went off. Time to leave. With a reluctant sigh, Manda trudged back on the numb clubs of her feet, through the long room, to the ladder. She climbed down and felt her way back through the dark access tunnel and down the endless, fluorescent-lit flight of slippery stairs. By the time she got back to the base of the lift station, the exertion had warmed her up enough to alleviate her worry about frostbite.

She reactivated her liveface. It booted up rather slowly, and numerous alarms began fussing at her. She'd stayed too long in the cold.

Ur-Carli was waiting for her. Manda stopped before the syntellect, hands on her hips. "Well?"

"Did you find anything?" ur-Carli asked.

"You know what I found."

Ur-Carli was silent.

"Why did you show me that place?" Manda demanded. Again the syntellect didn't respond.

"The body needs to be recycled," Manda said. "It's intact. The materials can be used."

"No." The syntellect spoke quickly. "It must remain as it is,

BURNING THE ICE

for now. I'll tell you more later. In the meantime, you mustn't tell anyone."

Manda frowned. *Don't I wish.* But she didn't dare. "I can't do that."

"There's a reason."

Her commcube chimed. With a scowl of annoyance she touched the commcube, which moved to the center of her vision and unfolded. Her eldest clone-sister Arlene appeared inside it. An old, gaunt version of Manda, she wore a livehood in place over the upper half of her face that shone like glitter-paint against her cheeks, nose, and forehead. Her throat mic was a black collar against her neck.

"Project meeting, everybody," she said. "Meet me in conference chamber delta in fifteen minutes."

Manda sent a confirmation and then turned on ur-Carli again. "*What* reason? Why have you kept this a secret for so long? She—she—" Manda stopped. A confusing mass of feelings surfaced.

She found an early memory: an island of kindness that an old woman had created for her; a dollop of safety placed squarely in the heart of a miserable and lonely childhood. *Carli.*

Manda didn't remember where she'd been or what had happened, exactly; perhaps she'd been four or five seasons old, perhaps younger. All she recalled was a loving smile buried in wrinkles, a touch on Manda's hair, a stream of comforting words that carried some childish hurt away.

Ur-Carli was saying, "I know other secrets also."

Manda collected herself. "The others will want to know. They'll want to honor her. Give her the proper ceremonies and give her remains back to the colony. She won't be able to rest till we do."

The syntellect gazed at her. "Do you really believe that? You don't go to the religious gatherings."

"I don't know. I don't know what to believe." *But I do know,*

33

Manda thought, *that if I keep this a secret, and the others find out that I knew and told no one. I'll be in serious trouble.*

Besides, it's Carli.

"This shouldn't be one person's secret," she said. "All that equipment up there belongs to the colony. *Carli* belongs to the colony. Not to me and especially not to you."

Especially not to you. A hurtful thing to say. But syntellects weren't conscious beings. They didn't have feelings to be hurt. For all its idiosyncrasies, for all its human mimicry, ur-Carli was merely a very sophisticated program, a series of instructions for processing information with no real awareness or sense of self. The human body it wore was merely its GUI: its graphic user interface, chosen in some fit of perversity by the crèche-born programmers who created it, way back when. Manda knew she needn't feel guilty.

But somehow, she felt worse about insulting this mindless computer program than she did her fellow colonists, who usually had it coming. Ur-Carli was just a dumb machine; it couldn't help being annoying.

She cleared her throat. "Sorry about that."

"I have to go," ur-Carli said abruptly, and vanished. Manda's feeling of compassion disappeared along with it.

"Fucking idiotic syntellect," she muttered.

Firste things first: Manda's livesuit was failing. She headed down to the machine shop.

CarliPablo ran Waldo Systems, in the machine shops housed in the upper chambers of Amaterasu. Livesuits weren't exactly waldos, but as an integral part of the waldo interface system, the suits were manufactured in the same area as waldos, which was where Manda had spent much of her adolescent apprenticeship. So Manda knew all the livesuit construction and maintenance clones.

She heard, and smelled, the machine shop well before she

reached the entrance: the acrid stench of burning metal; the whirring of blades; the hiss of welding arcs; the sweet smell and sloshes and bubbling of liveware vats. Manda ducked into the large chamber through a large vertical crack, faulty livesuit now tucked under her arm (it had proved impossible to walk in, and she'd finally been forced to retreat, St. Vitus-like, to a restroom and strip it off). Work crews crawled all over the big space: some welding, machining, and making repairs on their mechanical systems; some testing parts; others piloting machine-waldos through different test sequences.

Manda wove her way through, waving and returning greetings to the clones working in teams here and there. In the glassfront lounge up on the catwalks she saw part of the livesuit team, JeanTomas: two stocky women about ten or fifteen seasons older than Manda with curly red hair, freckles, and brown eyes. They were in intent conversation with a pair of older, grizzled twins, livesuit programmers from the MeriwetherMichael fourclone.

Manda headed up there. She stuck her head in the door and opened her mouth to speak, but one MeriwetherMichael drowned her out with a bark of disbelief, aimed at JeanTomas, both of whom were leaning back with looks of amusement.

"You just don't get it!" His brother picked up the thread. "We have this *fantastic* library of similes, from almost a hundred seasons of Earth's finest entertainment, that give you complete immersion in sensation—" "—and whose story lines conform to your own control!" the first one said. "How can you *possibly* prefer some ancient, bloviating *prose*?" they finished together.

"It's bad enough to waste your time with the old TV and thrideo A/V stuff," said the second, "when you can be doing similes. But prose—" "Prose doesn't even give you sight and sound, much less touch, smell—interactivity!" Both JeanTomases opened their mouths, but the brothers interrupted.

"Have you ever even *tried* any of Doryzcek's works from the 2050s and 60s?" the first demanded. "His *A New Zoroastra* transformed the way we experience the fictive simile!"

"Oh, puh-*leeze!*" the JeanTomases said in unison. One Jean-Tomas folded her arms, sitting back, while the other leaned forward to respond, "You're the ones that don't get it. Prose gives you all the sensations of the other media." "Right in here." Both women touched their temples.

"And it's all yours," the first said, "because *you're* the one that builds it, from the cues the writer gives you." "And hey, you even get to know what's going on inside people's heads! How many similes have telepathy built in?" "As for interactivity—" They shrugged, and said together, "We don't *want* interactivity." The second went on, "We want to let go of the controls and let a master storyteller give us a good ride."

"You sure know an awful lot about *I Love Lucy*, for someone who disdains everything but prose." The brothers smirked at each other. The JeanTomases stiffened.

"Oh, sure—" "We'll take in a video or thrideo every once in a while!" "But we spend our whole damn day interacting with liveware." "We want a break from it on our off-time."

The male twins looked at each other and rolled their eyes. One JeanTomas, spotting Manda, said, "Where do you stand on the subject, CarliPablo?"

"Me?" Manda didn't want to get into the middle of this argument. She'd heard it too many times. She occasionally dipped into *all* the many forms of story-entertainment they'd brought with them from Earth—from poetry to prose to video to thrideo to simile, and assorted odd variations of the above—from ancient to modern—and couldn't understand people who felt the need to stake out a claim of superiority for any single medium or form. "I don't believe in entertainment at all. There's too much work to be done. Speaking of which—" She handed her livesuit bundle to the JeanTomas nearest her. "I need a favor. My livesuit's acting up."

"Sure." They stood. "Let's leave—" "—these bozos—" "—to

their ridiculous fantasies—" "—and get you set up."

Manda and the JeanTomases headed over to an adjunct area, kept warmer than the main machining cavern, which held the livesuit-growing vats and the yoke construction and repair benches. As they walked in, three newly-grown livesuits were scrambling out of a nanojuice tank, one after the other. They climbed up to stand on drying racks above the tanks. A row of over a dozen stood there, glistening silver-grey spectors with nothing but air inside their translucent mesh.

Seeing their faceless forms, Manda suppressed a shudder. She didn't like it that what amounted to an article of clothing imitated volition. Nearby, an additional two JeanTomases, males, were remote-testing a pair of livesuits, first putting them through some martial-art kata and then having them do a swing dance.

While Manda watched this, the JeanTomas twins she'd come in with ran diagnostics on her own suit.

"Bad clone," one JeanTomas remarked after a moment. "No honey-*mana* for you." "You've been wearing your suit outside," her twin said, studying the readouts over the other's shoulder.

"Yeah. Sorry."

"We'll have it fixed in a sec." The sisters gave it an injection, activated it, and then ran through the standard tests. Manda wandered around the chamber, and lost track of which woman was which by the time the two were done with her suit. One of them brought it back to her.

"Good as new," she announced. "No more outings in it, though."

"I promise," Manda said, hand over her heart. "I owe you coup for this."

JeanTomas waved her hand in dismissal. "I-we owed you-you coup anyway, for some machining time Arlene allocated me-us the other day. Just be sure to tell her about this when you see her, and we'll be square."

*   *   *

Next Manda headed over to the Project IceFlame meeting.

"This is it," Arlene was saying, as Manda entered. "We're within the last hundred meters of substrait."

The entire project team was there. Manda's clone sat in front. The rest were all at least eight seasons older than Manda. At sixty seasons, Arlene and Derek were the eldest. Several other clones were also present, including those who, like Manda, would be providing Amaterasu-based support.

Manda seated herself between Teresa and Paul. It was an apology of sorts. Not much of one; granted. Teresa glanced at Manda only briefly, making it clear she was still annoyed. Paul also gave her a cool look. Farrah, next to Teresa, dispensed her own peevish glance, and Janice looked unhappy. Derek looked stern. Only Bart's and Charles's gazes were neutral.

Who am I in trouble with now? Manda wondered. *Oh, well.*

"The first drills are less than a day from breaking through to the mantle," Arlene continued. "All drilling has stopped until the council makes its final decision on whether to proceed with Project IceFlame. Derek will give us an update."

An nervous murmur broke out as Derek moved to stand next to his twin sister. Manda could tell from his posture and expression that the news wasn't good—at least, not as good as he'd hoped.

"I've done everything I can, but I'm afraid the council is still deadlocked. We don't have a decision."

"What are we going to do?" Charles asked, and Bart said, "We've done all the rearranging of tasks we can manage." "We can't afford to tie up the drilling equipment for long." "We're holding up the refinery folks as it is!"

Others were talking too: expressing outrage, disbelief, and dismay. Teresa and Paul looked distressed, as did Manda's other twin siblings, Bart and Charles, Farrah and Janice. Arlene held up her hands.

"Quiet, everyone! Let's hear what he has to say."

"The council is aware of the timing issues." He sighed. "The trouble is this. The colony has been splitting its excess resources between our project and PabloMichael's Project Reformation for the past six seasons, but now that IceFlame has reached the point that we need to greatly expand our effort, we'll be calling on colony resources that will put Reformation on hold indefinitely." And PabloMichael was the senior councilclone.

"I thought I-we and PabloMichael had both already recused ourselves on this vote," Teresa said, and everyone nodded. "Both JennaMara and RoxannaLuis were saying they'd support us. . . ."

Derek shrugged. "JennaMara has changed its position. It doesn't want to take a stand without full colony support for IceFlame, so it is abstaining, to force a colony-wide vote."

"We're holding a town meeting tonight to present the issue to the colony and hold a vote. Can you make that timing work on the drilling end?" he asked Bart and Charles.

"We'll talk to the refinery people," they replied, "but yeah—"
"—we can probably meet our commitments with that timing."
"Barely."

"Good. We'd better get started planning our presentation."

"Also," Arlene said, "we still have a polar expedition launch in eight days. I don't want that date to slide, or we'll have to deal with all kinds of equipment allocation foul-ups and renegotiations with the other clones. So we're going to carry forward with project planning as though we already had approval."

Eight days? Manda felt a stab of anxiety again. Once they left she'd be left alone among the others, not one of whom cared whether she lived or died.

But hey, maybe they'd lose the vote.

Derek took several members of the team over to some tables in the back to plan the presentation, including Farrah-and-Janice and Teresa-and-Paul. Manda stayed with her remaining siblings, Arlene, Bart, and Charles.

Project IceFlame had two main thrusts. The first, which had been going on for several seasons, was a drilling effort. At twenty-eight locations strategically placed around the moon's surface—primarily in the upper latitudes, where most of Brimstone's carbon dioxide was stored—drills would pierce the crust and tap into the magma, creating vast fields of lava "irrigation." These would serve as the ongoing energy source to keep the methane hydrate deposits burning, with fleets of air-avatars controlling burn intensity and burn vectors.

There were serious risks involved in piercing the moon's crust, obviously. It could set off a series of quakes that could jeopardize the colony. Or their precautionary tamps could fail and the terraforming fires would burn out of control, putting toxic amounts of carbon dioxide into the air—or melting the ice caps to the point that their coastal and island outposts would be inundated.

But their equipment was slowly breaking down around them; their population was dwindling, as dozens of colonists a year died of exposure or cold-related accidents. They needed to get out of these caves.

"Bart and Charles will give us a status report on the magma drilling," Arlene said. The middle-aged CarliPablo twins came to the front of the room.

"The first drill is scheduled—" "—to penetrate the crust and reach magma—" "—at thirty-six o'clock tomorrow night," they said, trading off with such natural ease that it didn't matter who was talking. "Assuming IceFlame is approved." "The other twenty-seven should be breaking through the crust—" "—over the next six to eight days." "Any delays in drilling will result in a delay in the polar expedition's launch."

Others raised questions and brought up technical points; the discussion continued. While this went on, ur-Carli materialized beside Manda. The syntellect superimposed itself next to Arlene, crowding Manda if only virtually. As at lunch, no one reacted to the syntellect's presence—meaning that again, it was presenting only to Manda. Ur-Carli gestured at Derek's simulations showing how the flames would spread, and how they would use burning and suppressing runs to control the blaze.

"According to my analyses," ur-Carli remarked, "the current simulations are insufficiently complex enough to predict whether the terraforming flames will die out, continue in the desired fashion, or run amok, creating a series of cataclysmic meltings and eruptions that will eventually wipe out this colony."

"Tell *her* that," Manda subvoked, gesturing with her chin at Arlene.

Perhaps ur-Carli's analysis was correct. But Manda would rather go out in a cataclysm anyway, than die slowly as their technology broke down around them—which would eventually be their fate unless they acted now, while they had the resources.

She said as much to ur-Carli. "We haven't got a lot of alternatives."

"There is one," ur-Carli replied after a long pause. By this time Manda had gotten wrapped up in the terraforming talk, and the syntellect's comment confused her.

"One what?"

"One other alternative."

Manda shook her head. "The colony has already rejected the genetic reengineering course. The uncertainties are too great. Ours has a greater likelihood of success, and a greater chance of survival if it fails."

"That's not what I meant."

"Then what?"

"*Exodus.*"

Manda scowled. *"Exodus?" What's that got to do with anything?* "Um. There's one small problem. They're long gone, and we have no omni transmitter." Omni—or instantaneous—communications had been around for a long time. The concept had been Carli D'Auber's invention, back in Earthspace. With the omni, interstellar distances were reduced to nothing. But it was a breathtakingly expensive technology in terms of construction, maintenance, and energy use, and the crèche-born hadn't been disposed toward sharing with the colonists. "It would take nearly seventeen seasons for them to receive our signal," she went on, "and much longer for them to return—even if they were inclined to, and could. For all we know, they're long dead, stranded between the stars."

Again the syntellect remained silent for a while.

"Actually," it finally said, "they're still insystem. They didn't leave immediately upon depositing the colony."

The shock hit Manda like an electric jolt. *"What?"*

Everyone stared at her. "Sorry," she said to Arlene. The halls of Amaterasu were filled with people wandering absently around, gesturing and subvocalizing into their livefaces, but it was rude to take a call during a meeting, or worse, to shout.

Ur-Carli donned an enigmatic smile. How had Manda, of all people, ended up saddled with this eccentric pest of a syntellect?

"Would you just go away?" she whispered.

It was hard to tell because ur-Carli's avatar was in the way, but Arlene appeared to be shaking her head. "You really need to learn to get along better, Manda. People are complaining. We can't shield you from the rest of the colony forever."

Ur-Carli talked over Arlene. "She's referring to Obediah-Ursula's complaint to the council over your shouting at them this morning. I retracted it over their digital signatures before it could be considered by the council."

Manda parsed out the two streams, and stared at ur-Carli, who, Cheshire Cat–like, had vanished, all but the smile, overlain on a displeased Arlene.

That explained why her clone was annoyed with her.

Syntellects didn't lie. Why would ur-Carli delete a complaint about Manda? To protect her? But why? Why bother?

And more to the point, could *Exodus* really still be insystem? It didn't seem possible. It had been an accepted reality for as long as Manda could remember that the crèche-born in their interstellar ship had left the system shortly after Amaterasu was founded eighteen seasons ago.

But syntellects didn't lie. Did they?

It dawned on Manda that she did have a way to find out. All she needed was a good telescope. In space, there was no place to hide. If the *Exodus* were insystem, it would be visible.

The colony had DMiTRI, a satellite with an optical telescope, stationed between Brimstone and Fire at Brimstone's synchronous orbit. Unfortunately, several teams were constantly competing to use it for their own projects, and Manda had no good excuse for appropriating it. If she explained she wanted to look for *Exodus*, they'd only laugh.

But she had access to DMiTRI's catalog of historical data. And then there was the telescope she'd found in the secret room. If the ship *was* still around, she should be able to see them with that. Especially if ur-Carli told her where to look. If that damnable, contrary syntellect could be persuaded to show up and cooperate for a minute or two.

At the end of the meeting, she headed over to Derek—agonizing about whether to tell him about the secret room—feeling she should; not really wanting to. Numerous others had already mobbed him, though, and after waiting several minutes, she got tired of waiting and left.

The room and the body had been hidden for years. What did it matter if she kept ur-Carli's secret for a little while? No one would be harmed.

Intersticial: the crèche-born
Pablo's Secret Meeting

Dane detected Pablo's meeting, barely in time. When she came across them, the interested parties were already gathered in one of Pablo's weird virtual realms—heads together, surrounded by virtual monstrosity, plotting something bad.

The crèche-born were not yet on their way to 70 Virginis, though the younger Brimstone colonists all believed otherwise. They had just finished harvesting the needed antimatter, and were readying themselves for departure.

They were losing the will to commit to another long interstellar journey, though. Carli's memory didn't hold the same sway over them as it once had. But Dane hadn't forgotten what they'd promised, and she wasn't about to let her compatriots forget, either.

The crèche-born were either twenty-four in number or forty-one, depending on whether you counted bodies or personalities. In the crèche-borns' case, this made a big difference, since each personality had his or her own beanlink and vote. And since their true bodies were locked safely away in their crèches, with their direct brain interfaces, it wasn't easy anymore—or even particularly useful, except perhaps during the crèche ceremonies—to distinguish who came from which flesh.

These gathered were leaders of four of the crèche-borns' seven main power groups. Pablo wielded the most power, though his leadership was not a foregone conclusion. He had to wrangle support for any big ideas, and since most of the crèche-borns' desires and will shifted with the fluidity of some of their insane virtu-spaces, the worst of his impulses often died in the planning stages.

Dane knew all this because she knew Pablo with an intimacy unimagined even by the colonist vat-mates. They shared not only the same DNA; they—and Buddy, and little Pablito, who was long gone, buried deep inside them—were born of the same psyche. They shared a body locked safely in its metal crèche, in the belly of the ship.

A body was all they shared, anymore. Pablo's ruthlessness had long since earned him Dane's disdain, and Buddy's amoral pragmatism wasn't much better. If only Pablito, the core personality who had spawned them all, would return. But he'd vanished long ago, during the info wars. Dane often thought that his innocence might remind Pablo of his humanity again—might mend things between them three. But in her more pragmatic moments, she knew she might as well wish for someone to hand her one of Fire's moons on a platter.

She eyed the conspirators from a set of spy-holes she'd hacked into this horrific landscape of Pablo's. As the conspirators walked along, she hopped in and out of the pustules and blisters of Pablo's swamp, eavesdropping with her ears and her mind. He had never been able to shield his thoughts well from her, and she knew what he was up to. He didn't want to commit to a launch to 70 Virginis. He was going to try to manipulate these others into opposing the launch.

I'm getting too damn old for this, she thought. Running interference for the colonists, as she'd long ago promised Carli she would—protecting them from her fellow crèche-borns' long-distance manipulations—had worn her down. She had little left to give.

It wouldn't be much longer now, though. Pablo had little chance of overcoming the momentum of their launch. While few were excited about the possibilities, no one wanted to defy Carli's wishes—especially not when her avatar, ur-Carli, still wandered the halls of the ship, reminding them of their promise, and when Carli's ghost haunted their dreams.

When they departed for 70 Virginis, Dane could rest.

"What are these veiled threats about?" Jeb was asking. "I'm committed to going! I've never said otherwise."

Pablo put his arms together behind his back and paced away through the fluid landscape. When he turned back to gaze at them, Dane felt the same rush of fear the rest must be feeling.

Pablo had calcified into the worst kind of idealist over the years. Life mattered not an iota to him. If you got in his way—unless you had some hold over him—your life was in danger. He was a dangerous man. But Dane had been dealing with Pablo for a long time and she knew exactly what to do.

There were other power groups besides the four. Buddy, Dane knew, she couldn't count on for anything. He wouldn't buck Pablo. But Dalia was a longtime enemy of Pablo's, and Joe would go along with her.

Trouble was, neither they nor most of their compatriots could care less whether they were going to head for 70 Virginis, or stay hidden insystem in 47 Ursae Majoris for the rest of their unnaturally long lives. Reality didn't matter to them. All they cared about were their pointless power struggles.

They wouldn't be pleased, though, to hear Pablo was trying to form a coalition behind their backs. Which, in a sense, was what Pablo was trying to do—even if not in precisely the way he was pretending, nor in the way that Dane would make it appear.

Better get to work, Dane thought, and disengaged.

More Naked Than the Day
She Was Decanted

anda got the alert at eighteen o'clock, at the start of the second-watch work shift: the town meeting would be held at twenty-six sharp in the Gather, the colony's main amphitheater. After thinking it over, she decided not to go. She hated crowds, and was well familiar with all the issues. She got Derek and Arlene's approval, and added her name to the list of volunteers available for skeleton and emergency duty. Around twenty-four thirty, she got an email request to fill in for another clone in the Fertility labs.

Manda had learned at a very early age that if you can endure intense loneliness and the scorn of your peers you have a lot more options than otherwise. Still, she wasn't above doing a favor for a fellow colony member. Especially if it gave her alone-time. Alone-time, in this crowded and insular cave-colony, was more precious than *mana*. More precious, perhaps, even than warmth.

When Manda showed up in the labs shortly before the town meeting, everyone had left except for the youngest Roxanna-Tomas twins, who stood and picked up their sweaters as soon as she entered, their livesuits flashing like a film of mother-of-pearl on their cheeks, foreheads, hands, and wrists.

The RoxannaTomases seemed nervous. Neither would meet Manda's eyes. The male was tapping the toe of his boot against the thatching, and the female fiddled with a lock of her black hair, which had slipped out from under the hood of her livesuit.

"Thanks for covering for me-us," she told Manda. "It won't be for long," her twin added. "An hour at most." "I-we just want to hear the main arguments," the woman went on, "and then I-we'll log my-our vote—" "—and our older siblings will be right back."

RoxannaTomas ran the medical branch of the biological sciences. CarliPablo didn't have much to do with biology, so the two groups rarely interacted. This pair, Jeannelle and Vance, was about seven seasons younger than Manda—barely an adult. But—though Manda remembered them vaguely from the nursery—it would be rude to refer to them by their given names, when they weren't close.

"Take your time," Manda replied. "No hurry."

The male nodded, but the female hesitated. "You sure you don't mind? It's an important meeting for your clone; I-we'd hate to put you out. . . ."

"I'll be fine. Go! I'll call you if there are problems."

"Thanks," the twins said in unison, and left, running.

Manda drew the door to and sank against it with a sigh. Alone, finally, in the warmest set of suites in the colony of Amaterasu: the catacomb of caverns and cul-de-sacs that made up the Fertility labs.

She flexed her fingers. They were rapidly warming up. The dull, ever present ache in her tendons and joints was melting away like yak butter in soup. In fact, she was getting too hot in her multiple layers. Sweat had collected under her arms and was trickling down her torso. She was suddenly conscious of how much she stank.

Manda took off her musk-oxen-knit sweater, mittens, gloves, and neck gaiter, then sat down on the stool RoxannaTomas had just vacated and pulled off her reindeer fur-lined boots and wool socks.

She reflected on the RoxannaTomases' nervousness over accepting a favor. The most obvious possibility was that their clone had decided to vote against CarliPablo's proposal. But a more subtle conflict might be at work. The two clones often ended up at odds on key resource issues. RoxannaTomas reported to and usually allied itself with PabloJebediah, CarliPablo's main rival. The young twins might be worried that CarliPablo would try to collect coup on their clone sometime.

Manda couldn't help but be amused by the notion that any clone had anything to worry about with regard to her, when it came to coup.

She wiggled her bare toes, and rubbed the balls of her feet against the floor's thatching with a sigh of relief as the warm air dried the sweat from them. Oh, yes. Much better.

And she thought, *What the hell.* This place would be completely empty (though technically it wasn't *really* empty, if you counted all the human and other embryos and fetuses growing in the Teklar vats in the various suites) for at least an hour. No one would know.

Feeling just guilty enough to make it interesting, Manda stripped off her sweater, shirt, pants, thermal leggings—and, after a hesitation, pulled off her thermal undershirt. She removed and collapsed her liveyoke and then triggered her livesuit's doff-and-fold routine. *If you're going to get naked, don't do it by half measures.*

The livesuit expanded and rippled down her form as the nano-muscles inside the mesh stretched, contorted, and contracted in a carefully choreographed sequence. She stepped out of the suit. Her gloves ballooned, inverted, and fell off her outstretched hands into the collapsing livesuit's center. It folded itself into a neat bundle, convenient for carrying.

Manda folded her clothes, picked up her livesuit package, and piled everything on the cabinet by the chemical storage locker. Then she rubbed her shoulders and arms, grateful to be free of the confinement of clothes, livesuit, and yoke.

Other than the hot springs, this was the only place in Amaterasu you could comfortably strip (and Manda was willing to bet she wasn't the first who'd thought of doing so, when alone here)—and this was about the only time you could get away with it. Usually the labs were full of people.

She passed cell-cloning and gene-splicing, and climbed down into livestock gestation, catching glimpses of trays of eggs under lights and vats with tiny wax-doll-animals floating in them. From there she entered the largest suite, human gestation.

The cavern opened before her—not one of Amaterasu's largest, but nevertheless quite respectable in size, perhaps ten meters across. A spiral staircase wound down from the entry where Manda stood, at a craggy crevice about halfway up the wall. Several meters overhead, lights, fans, and power cords dangled among truncated, shadowy stalactites. The bodies of the more massive limestone spears had been chopped off long ago, but new daggers had formed on the stumps: small stalactites that dripped cool water onto Manda's head. They'd need to be cropped back again soon, or they'd start to pose a threat to the fetuses.

As she descended the stairs, she noted the wall-harvesters. A fleet of mite-sized robots with green belly-sacs, they moved along the chamber's surfaces, harvesting slime, mold, and the eggs laid by real insects and mites. These compounds would be frozen, analyzed, changed if necessary, and reinstalled later, or perhaps moved to other locations. The gengineers never stopped tinkering with the caves' ecology. The robots' movements created a dull green wavefront that crept over the coarse stone.

At the base of the metal stairway, Manda paused to stretch, and stroked the skin of her bare arms. It was so warm! Tropical! Twenty degrees Celsius, according to the temperature strip above the door. She scanned the chamber. It'd been years since she'd been here, but it hadn't changed much. Jar- and vat-lined benches ran in crude rows on the uneven, bamboo-thatched floor, among lumpy stalagmites and rumbling utility pipes. The containers increased in size toward the rear of the chamber.

She descended into the fetuses' domain. White, yellow, and blue LCDs flickered all about; machines hummed their sixty-hertz hum; fluid dripped and flowed and swished through tubes in a hypnotic rhythm. With each step away from the staircase, the feeling grew in Manda that she was entering a sanctuary, a holy place.

She found herself wishing she hadn't stripped. She didn't care what the rest of the colonists thought, but this feeling of being out of place slipped past her defenses.

Manda slowed. Her footsteps touched down softer than snowfall on the thatch; she found herself holding her breath, remembering the decanting ceremonies she'd attended as a child, before she got old enough that they couldn't make her go anymore.

She could almost hear the children's whispers. *Outsider. Troublemaker. Singleton. You don't belong here.*

Oxshit. With an impatient frown, Manda slapped her feet hard enough on the matting for the sound to register on her ears. The pains that shot through her soles were a small price for breaking the spell of exclusion, shutting out the chorus of scolding voices.

Except for occasional hot-spring baths, Manda rarely got this naked even in her own quarters. The warm air felt so good. She would spend more time here, if only she didn't feel the press of all those tiny eyes.

This was nonsense; even if the fetuses *could* see her—and most of them were housed in smoky, one-way-see-through containers—their regard would hold no more intent than the simplest syntellect. They were unaware, and utterly innocent.

Still, she eyed them distrustfully as she passed their fluid-filled pots. *If they're so innocent,* she thought, *where does this feeling of malevolence come from? Why do they unnerve me?*

There were about two dozen labelled and arranged by gestational age. First the zygotes: clumps of flesh in petri dishes; most of the gestating humans fit into this category. Many would fail to flourish, and die. Up the next aisle were the survivors of the first stage: little human tadpoles, attached by filaments to a nutrient gel inside Mason jars. Then came the salamanders, and then a series of fetuses that were clearly mammals but could be any one of a number of species—and finally the waxy-skinned, giant-headed human forms, in various stages of growth.

They floated serenely in artificial amniotic sacs, or swam around in them, kicking off against the sides of the vats. Or sucked their thumbs, or played with their tiny webbed toes or fingers—or slept, eyes twitching behind translucent lids. Miniature, naked, preconscious merpeople in their watery Edens, breathing their amniotic fluid, simmering in their own primordial soup pots—growing, changing—preparing for emergence onto this cold, harsh world.

Hmmm. Naked, yes—but not *quite* as naked as Manda. At every stage past the early embryonic, monitoring and life-support equipment of every kind intruded through their umbilicals, emerging from bioengineered placentas: those dark, still masses hanging over their heads.

Manda on the other hand was thoroughly disconnected. Her only leads right now were those that connected her to the natural world. Eyes. Ears. Nose. Skin. She was truly, utterly alone.

Manda relished this—twirled again, feeling the whisper of air against bare skin, the brush of hair against her shoulders as her ponytail swung back and forth. She licked her lips and tasted the salt of her dried sweat, from her earlier livesuit link exertions. You *should envy* me, she thought at the fetuses.

They were all multiples: mostly twins; a couple of triplets; and one set of quadruplets in the large economy-sized vat at the end.

She'd heard that a set of twins cast from her own clone's genome—a girl and a boy—was nearing the end of their gestation cycle: the first new addition to the CarliPablo clone since Manda herself was decanted, twenty-six earth-years ago—nearly nine fire-years—aboard *Exodus*. Despite herself she was curious, and studied the vat labels as she walked along the third-trimester row.

The label on a vat told her that this was the one containing her identical siblings. (Of course, the male wasn't *exactly* identical to Manda, nor to his female vat-mate; their sex-specific genes had long ago been grafted onto their DNA from assorted different sources—but let's not split base pairs.)

Manda laid a hand on the cool Teklar of the vat and gazed at them. Both had heads capped with dark hair, waxy skin, and tiny, bony butts. They were covered head-to-toe in a dusting of white. They probably had at least another ten weeks' worth of gestating to do: they were no bigger than a child's closed fist.

So small, so perfect. *Is that what I looked like?* A sense of awe filtered through her, as she watched them. How could she ever have been that tiny?

She could imagine what they were feeling, as they rolled together and swam apart in their twin amniotic sacs, which hung in the clear fluid like a pair of baby-filled lungs. It was all deep, watery sounds for them; the clicks, ticks, and hums of the nurturing machinery that kept them alive; the bumps and hiccups that their vat companion emitted.

Vat-mates. Always there, an extension of themselves—a remote limb, another self—since before awareness stirred in their cerebral cortices, before their nerve endings began to form and send signals to their nascent brains.

Self and other: the boundaries blurred, between clone siblings. Especially you and your vat-mate. Your vat-mate was part of you. When one died, the the other committed suicide shortly thereafter. Almost without exception. No point in going on, when half of yourself had been amputated.

Or so she'd been told. Manda wouldn't know. Her vat-mate had died as a fetus, back on the starship *Exodus* twenty-six seasons ago, as they neared this solar system. An accident; equipment failure or something.

This kind of thing happened a lot. All the machines were ancient, built back on Earth long ago, and even though they'd been designed for longevity in severe environments, and even though all the crèche-born and their progeny, Manda's people, had learned how to fix just about anything, entropy always took its cut. It was pure luck that Manda herself survived.

She remembered none of it, naturally. She'd always been alone.

You'll never know the freedom of being a single, she thought at the undecanted twins, smiling. Except that it wasn't joy that coursed through her, now, but a blinding hatred, as she watched their casual intimacy: a closeness so much a part of their world they would never even know enough to take it for granted.

And a vivid vision flashed before her. The chemical locker was full of toxins. All it would take to kill these two would be a small amount of . . . something. Some ingredient that should not be a part of their soup.

It would be easy enough to edit the camera recordings afterward. No one would know.

Even as the thought came Manda jerked her hand back from the glass, and her pulse pounded in her neck. As if her anger could *ever* cause her to harm these helpless siblings of hers. Or cause her to allow others to.

"I won't let anybody hurt you," she whispered to them, and added silently, *not even me.* Her heart still raced, and her chest muscles had knotted up, tight as a fist. Unshed tears stung her eyes.

"What the hell are you doing?" Two voices, almost identical to her own, spoke in stereo.

Manda turned with a start. Her older twins, Teresa and Paul, stood scowling at her. Teresa clutched Manda's clothes and Paul held her livesuit.

Manda groped for an attitude; tried nonchalance. "Hi." She found it hard to talk. "Is the meeting over already?"

The identical, skeptical look on their faces beneath their glittering livemasks said Manda's casual facade wasn't fooling them. They opened their mouths simultaneously to say something more, then sighed in unison at her expression. "OK, what?"

Manda shook her head. "They're so vulnerable. Anybody could hurt them. It scares me."

Teresa and Paul gazed at Manda for just a microsecond too long, then exchanged a swift look. Teresa flicked the remark aside.

"No one would hurt them," she said. Paul went on, "Why would they?" "Now, put your clothes on," Teresa said, and thrust the bundle at Manda. "The others will be here any minute!" Paul added. "What possessed you?" they asked together.

The slight pause in their reaction, the brief masking of emotion in their faces, made Manda curious. *I startled them,* Manda thought. *I triggered something. An association they didn't want to share.*

But Manda didn't have a chance to interrogate them; voices and footsteps of the other Fertility lab staff echoed faintly into the cavern from the adjoining tunnel. Others were coming. Manda hurriedly started dressing—skipping the livesuit and other inner layers, donning merely the outer ones.

"You're lucky it was us who found you first," they went on, trading off, as Manda pulled on her shirt. "If one of the others had seen you like this—" "—I-we would have lost major coup." "It could put the terraforming project in jeopardy—" "—even get me-us booted off the council!"

"Give it a rest," Manda said, stepping into her pants. She snugged the drawstring tight. "No harm was done."

"No thanks to you," Paul said, and Teresa pressed her lips together with a frown.

Others entered the room, talking animatedly, as Manda bent to tug her fur-lined boots on, including the middle Roxanna-

Tomas triplets. The female, Tania, gave Manda a wave of thanks and dismissal as she and her brother crossed to the area's central monitoring station. More sets of twins and triplets entered. Clearly, people were stirred up about the meeting.

Curiosity overcame irritation. Manda stood, grabbed her cable-knit sweater from the counter next to the vat, and pulled it over her head. "So, did it pass?"

Teresa and Paul broke into grins. "Yes." "Charles and Bart already have the drills going." "We launch the polar expedition as soon as the preparations can be completed," Paul said, and Teresa finished, "We're back on schedule."

The twins lowered their voices—in Brimstone's thin air sound didn't carry far and the risk of being overheard by the other clone members was minimal; still, it paid to be cautious when discussing matters of coup—and added, once more trading off with unselfconscious ease, "PabloJebediah—" "—and KaliMarshall—" "—tried to outmaneuver us by raising some key resource-allocation issues—" "—but we were ready for them." "We demolished every one of their arguments." "And Derek and Arlene offered up several proposals for time and equipment swaps—" "—and kept them from losing too much coup. That won over enough allies to soften their objections." "The colony approved the first phase of the project in its current form." "Five-sixty-eight to five-oh-nine," they said together, as Manda opened her mouth to ask by how much.

"How many abstentions?"

"Only three," they replied.

Manda nodded thoughtfully. A fifty-nine-vote margin with three abstentions was not precisely an avalanche, but a couple of the current councilmembers had gotten their seats on a slimmer margin.

Still, CarliPablo would have to tread carefully in coming months. The project could ill afford setbacks of any kind, or their support would quickly erode.

Not my problem, though.

Then she thought about what it was going to be like without her clone around, and grimaced as she stooped to roll up her livesuit.

Teresa caught a glimpse of Manda's expression. "Can't you scrounge up just a little fellow-feeling?" "We worked hard to get here," Paul said, putting just a hint of emphasis on the *we*.

Manda straightened again with her livesuit bundle tucked under her arm. *What, are we going to dance this number again?*

The siblings regarded each other, and all the old arguments bounced back and forth between them like off-key echoes. Most of her clone thought Manda's proper place was with the terraforming team, not on her solo-effort ocean exploration project. Manda disagreed. Fortunately, in a rare spasm of good sense, Derek and Arlene, their oldest twins, had supported Manda. And they were on the governing council. Manda knew they supported her only because they'd given up trying to make her fit into the clone dynamic. She didn't care, as long as she got what she wanted. So that was that.

Except, of course, neither Teresa nor Paul was any better able to let go of their notions than Manda herself.

Their gazes remained locked a moment longer. Then a sigh escaped Teresa. She gave Paul a look, and Manda sensed his grudging acquiescence.

Half in appeasance and half in exasperation, Teresa laid an arm across Manda's shoulders, jostling her. "All right, all right. We'll save the argument for another time. Come on. It's time to celebrate."

The rec chamber was a cul-de-sac off the bamboo caverns. Arm-in-arm, Teresa and Paul led the way through the rows of bamboo stalks. The bamboo forest rustled in the cool eddies of the cave's air currents. Their trunks were as thick as Manda's thigh, and towered toward the stalactites amid calcite columns, totem poles, and mounds. Birds made the leaves flutter as they hunted insects put there for them and for the health of the plants and soil; small animals (probably rats; stowaways had come across from *Exodus*, and the biologists had been trying to gengineer them to fit into the minute ecosystem of Amaterasu's caverns ever since) rustled in the grasses and scraped in the thin layer of topsoil for seeds and bugs. The scents of wet limestone and greenery filled Manda's nostrils.

She trailed behind her siblings. Other colonists' voices filtered through the long, green blades and bone-yellow stalks. The floor was extremely uneven and strewn with manure, rocks, and broken speleothems. Numerous crevasses and pits in the floor, surrounded by fencing or natural barriers, led down into uninhabited areas below the colony.

The gleam of a feral cat's eyes in the rushes caught her glance as she strode past. *Good hunting,* she thought.

Pests were a constant problem: getting underfoot, chewing wires, getting into the food supplies. Birdshit rained down from overhead wires and formations and got into the equipment, eroding it and making everything stink. The colony's cats weren't pets; they were the first line of defense against rodents, birds, and the larger insects.

The good hunters lived. The less successful ones starved. The ecosystem engineers insisted it was necessary—for the local ecology to stabilize, predators and their prey had to reach a balance. Insects were needed for the health of the plants; rodents and songbirds kept the insect population down and controlled and shaped the plant growth; cats and the few predator birds controlled the rodents and songbirds. Human interference in that process had to be kept at a minimum. The feeding of cats was strictly forbidden.

Manda had befriended and kept a kitten anyway for a while, secretly, as a child. She had rescued him from a pit and hidden him in the bamboo forest—she'd fed him and petted him and called him Terrible Tom and taught him to do a few tricks, like she'd seen on some of the old videos from Earth. He was orange, a tiger-striped cat. One of his paws had been white with seven toes, and he'd had bright yellow eyes. He'd loved string. He would wrap himself around her fist, biting and clawing—but not too hard.

He was eventually discovered by the other kids. They'd captured and tortured the half-grown tom, and when Manda tried to stop them they tied her up, and one of the bigger kids sat on her so she couldn't move. Finally they left him for dead and he'd dragged himself, bleeding, off into the weeds before Manda could free herself and go to him. She'd never seen him again.

She could have told on them. Harming any of the colony's creatures—even the bugs, in large enough quantities—was a crime serious enough to require review by the council. But they'd threatened retribution, and she'd had every reason to believe them. So she'd kept it a secret.

She sometimes wondered if he was still around somewhere. Probably not; even if he'd managed to survive his wounds, cats typically didn't live so long. Not on Brimstone.

As Manda emerged from the bamboo forest behind Teresa and Paul, she spotted Derek. He stood at the entrance with a bulb of mead in one hand and a *mana*-roll in the other. PabloJebediah stood with him. From his age and sex, it had to be Jack or Amadeo. Jack, almost certainly: he had a small scar on the bridge of his nose.

Derek looked pleased, when they walked up. PabloJebediah turned a neutral expression toward them. Manda exchanged a glance with Derek and was then certain this PabloJeb was Jack. Something in Derek's gaze confirmed it.

Like CarliPablo, PabloJeb was one of Amaterasu's five-clone governing council, and with its substantial backing PabloJeb was the de facto leader, the first among equals. At twelve siblings, eight of them adults, PabloJeb was the colony's largest, and thus had great influence. It had staunchly opposed Ice-Flame. When the vote had turned against it, PabloJeb had lost coup on the council, while CarliPablo had gained. Despite whatever concessions it had been thrown, it couldn't be very happy right now.

So, that PabloJeb was here almost certainly did *not* mean it was being gracious in defeat. It must hope to pry some additional compromise out of CarliPablo, some under-the-table concession or change in approach. Perhaps PabloJeb intended to force its way onto the project in some capacity, now that forward progress was inevitable, so that it wouldn't be seen as irrelevant to this major new effort.

Just have to piss in the pot one way or another, don't you? she thought.

Derek's eyes glittered sidelong at Manda, through the specs set into the half-face mask of his livehood; he knew all this, and saw she knew it too. His gaze lifted then, and she followed it to Derek's twin Arlene, who was eyeing them from across the chamber. She was in the midst of some other small knot of influence, soothing another important clone's bruised ego.

Good luck, Manda thought wryly, *to you both,* and touched Derek's arm in passing. Manda hated colony politics. She didn't know how Derek and Arlene stood it.

Derek gave Manda a hint of a sardonic smile, and pulled Teresa close as Paul moved to his other side. Teresa folded an arm around Derek's waist and uttered some witticism to Jack as Manda moved on past—Jack ignored her as thoroughly as she did him, which suited her just fine. Let Teresa and the others play at coup. She entered the damp, cool chamber.

Three dozen or more people were crammed into the cul-de-sac. Nearly all of them had at least throat mics and livehoods on, if not an entire suit—and the several people talking to the air made clear that others were telepresent, as well. She was glad not to be conscious of them. The press was bad enough as it was.

As she worked her way inward, Manda spotted most of the rest of her clone—Charles and Bart, and also Janice—in conversation with councilclone JennaMara and some of its associates. She saw that Janice was alone.

Where's Farrah? Manda felt a shock of apprehension. *Is something wrong?*

She decided she was overreacting. Farrah was almost certainly telepresenting here from the head, or while dealing with a minor emergency in the machine shop, or something. Though she sensed some other energy too—some tension that felt sexual. Manda's gaze was drawn again to Janice, who was talking to a female JennaMara perhaps Manda's age.

Oh-ho, Manda thought. *Trolling for an exo-bond, are we?* Janice met Manda's gaze over the other woman's shoulder, and gave her a subtle flicker of the eyelid. Manda looked around and found her other siblings' eyes on her—Charles and Brat's, Derek's and Arlene's, Paul's and Teresa's.

They were worried about Farrah, and worried about Janice. *An exo-bond with JennaMara could mean trouble. Trouble for the clone; trouble in council.*

Which explained why Farrah wasn't here. She was off sulking somewhere. Manda felt a twinge of annoyance at Farrah and the rest of the clone.

Let the woman have a little fun, she thought irritably, and gave Janice a minute nod.

This silent interplay between Manda and her siblings wasn't telepathy; or if it was, it was a very organic sort, born of essentially identical genes and as similar an upbringing as their crèche-born forebears could muster. And though Manda had lived with the effect all her life, she had never been totally comfortable with it. It felt a bit like living in an echo chamber.

She moved on. It seemed as if half the colony were there. Most members of the other ten team-clones, as well as assorted supporters, well-wishers, and hangers-on, all chatted noisily about the town meeting and the terraforming effort. Manda dodged through the social gauntlet, grabbing a bulb of mead along the way, to RoxannaTomas, whose eldest and youngest twins sat on a set of big pillows in one corner of the chamber.

One of it gave Manda a smile and a wave: the young woman Manda had relieved in the fertility center earlier, Jeannelle (it had to be her; RoxannaTomas didn't have two female siblings near Jeannelle's age). Her siblings were arguing with a set of triplets from another clone over a *Three Stooges* episode. Manda didn't pay much attention; of the twentieth-century 2DTV comedy classics in the colony's entertainment archives, she preferred Charlie Chaplin and *M*A*S*H*.

The young RoxannaTomas lifted her drink bulb. "Manda—hi!"

I guess we're on a first-name basis now. Manda made the mental shift. "Hi, Jeannelle."

"Here's to IceFlame."

"To global warming," Manda replied. She touched Jeannelle's bulb, and Jeannelle's twin Vance joined the toast. Manda took a long draught of mead, and Jeannelle and Vance gestured for Manda to sit next to them.

"Thanks for covering me-us in the labs," Jeannelle said, as Manda squeezed onto the cushions next to her.

"Sure. What did you make of the town meeting?"

Jeannelle and Vance both rolled their eyes. "It sure got hot in there. Speaking of warmth." Vance added, "You-you have made some enemies, you know." An attempt to buy back coup with information, perhaps? Manda shrugged.

"That's not my problem."

Jeannelle and Vance arched eyebrows. "Isn't it?" "Well, just watch you-your back for a while." "Tell your clone." "I-we've heard some angry talk."

Manda had no use for dark hints about possible repercussions that later fizzled into the void of improbability. But the remark triggered a thought. "Listen, I'm curious about something. How do you guys in the Fertility labs make sure the fetuses and genetic material are protected?"

Jeannelle's and Vance's faces mirrored shock. "That's an odd question."

"Is it?" Manda mimicked Jeannelle's earlier remark. "I just wondered. They're always arguing over which genome gets replicated next. Somebody with a grudge could do serious harm."

"That's a creepy thought, CarliPablo." Jeannelle's switch to Manda's clone-name, and the twins' expressions, said that they thought *Manda* was creepy for even suggesting it. "No one would dare," Vance said.

"Why not?"

Jeannelle and Vance replied, "If one clone started tampering—" "—there'd be no stopping it." "Everyone would do it. Everything would fall apart." "It would be insane to even think—" "—of doing such a thing." After an awkward pause, the pair came to their feet. "We see someone." "Excuse us."

" 'Bye." Manda lifted her drink at their retreating backs. Their older twin brothers shifted subtly, shutting her out of their discussion.

Another smudge on my social standing, Manda thought, standing. But Jeannelle and Vance—*or should I call them RoxannaTomas again?*—whichever—neither the twins nor their clone interested Manda all that much. For that matter, neither did this party. She decided to call it a night.

Escape was easier conceived than achieved. In the short time since she'd entered, a new tide of party-goers had crammed into the room. She caromed, squeezed, and maneuvered her way

Laura J. Mixon

through until—teetering on the brink of an agoraphobic shriek—
she caught a glimpse of the exit. Only two shifting knots of people stood in her way.

As she neared, a slim crevice presented itself between the two groups, and she made for it. But someone on the outer edge of one of the groups backed up, making an effusive gesture with his arm as she accelerated into motion, and caught her on the chin. She went spinning into the other knot of people—and knocked someone's drink into someone else's face.

The someone else was Amadeo PabloJeb, Jack's vat-mate. Who-whose pet project had just been defeated in a colony-wide vote by Manda's clone.

Behind Manda, the man who had hit her was trying to apologize, but the implications of what had just happened sucked attention away from him and toward the tableau between Manda and PabloJeb. Silence collapsed around them, and spread outward to the edges of the room. Manda felt her clone's gaze on her neck and back.

Anger had darkened PabloJeb's face. Someone handed him a cloth and he wiped the liquid off. "As clumsy as she is maladjusted, it seems." Laughter rippled outward, disrupting the charged silence.

The insult was made worse by the fact that he presumed to refer to Manda directly, as an individual, and not as a member of her clone.

Because of IceFlame, the balance of status between her group and his was delicately poised right now. Her clone was losing coup at this very instant, and the longer she took to respond, the more it would lose. If she apologized, her clone would lose coup. If she didn't, she turned a member of the council into an enemy. Someone with a grudge against her personally.

Apologize? To that flaccid excuse for a man? Oh, please, she thought. *Besides, it wasn't my fault.*

"At least I have the good manners not to insult someone without understanding the circumstances," she said. "It wasn't my fault." With that, she turned on the one who had knocked her down, intending to lay into him for his clumsiness.

But she saw it was one of the very few clones outside her own that she actually *liked*—LuisMichael, the threeclone in charge of the refinery. It had always treated her kindly, and Jim, the geophysicist, had given her a lot of assistance launching her ocean-mapping project three seasons ago.

The LuisMichael in question looked chagrined, as did his vat-mates, who stood just behind him. She thought it might be Jim, who had struck her, from the black braid that snaked down his back. His clone-brother Brian usually wore his own long hair in a tight knot at his neck. But she wasn't sure.

"She's right," LuisMichael told the offended PabloJeb. "It wasn't her fault. I knocked her down as she was passing behind me." All three siblings gave PabloJeb a rueful smile. "Too much exuberance and mead, I fear," the brother said. "You should be laying the charge of clumsiness at my-our feet," the sister said, "not hers."

PabloJeb gazed sourly at the threeclone and then at Manda. "LuisMichael takes the blame for CarliPablo's action. How convenient. I hope it rewards you-you well."

He turned and stalked off.

Manda caught Derek's gaze across the way, as the LuisMichael who'd hit her said, "I'm so sorry." Derek flicked a hand; Arlene gave her head a minute shake: *don't worry about it.*

Manda waved LuisMichael's apologies away. "It was just an accident. If he's too stupid to figure that out, too bad."

After that, there was nothing to do but make a hasty retreat, leave the partiers to their gossip, and hope that the rest of her clone was still talking to her in the morning. Manda walked away, feeling people's stares on her back and imagining (probably rightly) that all their laughter was at her expense, until she entered the screen of bamboo.

Laura J. Mixon

Once alone, she wandered into a clearing and sat on a bench. For some reason, she felt sad—as though she truly had done something wrong back there. The feeling confused her.

Someone cleared their throat from the edge of the clearing.

She looked up. It was the LuisMichaels again.

"Thanks for backing me up," she said. The triplets joined her. One brother—not the one who'd struck her—she wasn't sure yet whether it was Brian or Jim—sat next to her. Amy, the female, sat on her other side, and the one who'd hit her squatted in front of her.

"Did I hurt you?" the one squatting asked.

She fingered her cheek and jaw. They felt fine, hardly sore at all. All the energy of the impact had been turned into kinetic energy. "Only my pride. Really, don't worry about it," she said.

"You looked pretty furious with me-us, there for an instant," his sister said, and his brother added, "I-we thought you were going to rip his face off."

She laughed. "I considered it. But I realized, if I had to spill a drink on someone, PabloJeb is just the clone I'd like to do it to. I'd never have had the nerve to do it on purpose, so I actually owe you-you coup for giving me the opportunity."

All three threw their heads back and laughed, an infectious, three-tone belly-laugh. "I-we hope—" "—it doesn't mess up—" "—your clone's plans."

"They're used to dealing with my messes by now." She shook her head with a rueful smile. "Really, Derek and Arlene didn't look all that upset. I suspect they have coup to spare right now."

"It was obviously not deliberate," the brother on the bench said. "I think Amadeo hurt his own clone in there—" "—a lot more than he hurt you-you," the sister, Amy, added, "—or me-us," the one squatting finished, and his siblings nodded agreement.

Manda chuckled. "We can hope. So," she said, "what are you-you doing back in town? How long are you-you here?"

66

All three shrugged. "Not long." "I-we had some refinery business with the council this afternoon before the meeting—" "—and a couple of errands to take care of." "I-we head back tomorrow morning." "How is your work coming along?" the one squatting asked. "Found any worms yet?"

So the one who had struck her *was* Jim. Brian wouldn't ask. "Nope. Not a worm, not a benthic organism, not a bacterium—not even a temperature fluctuation worth a rat's droppings. To tell you the truth, I'm getting discouraged."

"Don't be." He said it with emphasis, and his siblings nodded. "There's definitely something down there." Down below the ice layer, she meant. Down in the watery depths Manda was exploring.

She perked up. "What do you mean?"

Jim glanced at his siblings. They shrugged. He said, "Well . . . I don't know exactly, but I'm picking up some odd seismic readings in Brimstone's crust."

Manda lifted an eyebrow. "So?" Quakes and tremors were a biweekly occurrence on Brimstone. They were one of the main reasons Amaterasu had few of the more intricate stone structures—the soda straws, popcorn, flowers, and coiling tubes—that Earth's calcite caverns were famous for, despite that it was bigger than the largest of Earth's. Eons of quakes and tremors had prevented their formation. But its larger structures—rippling draperies, cascades, falls, lily pads, and totem poles—were so plentiful and of such appealing shapes and forms that Manda sometimes got lost, just staring at them as she walked from one place to another.

Jim leaned forward, intent. "No, these readings are different. I'm picking up seismic activity that isn't tidal, tectonic, *or* volcanic."

How could that be? There weren't any other kind of tremors. Were there? "So what are they?" Manda asked.

"Well . . ." He twirled a lock of beard between thumb and fore-finger. "What they resemble most are explosions."

She stared. *"What?"*

He nodded, and his siblings mirrored the gesture. "Big ones. Or some kind of compression event, anyway. A periodic gas buildup and ignition sequence, I'm guessing—a complex geologic process of some kind."

"They've been going on—" "—quite a long time," Brian and Amy interjected.

"Really?"

"Really," the threeclone replied.

"Now that I know what to look for," Jim continued, "I've been going back and checking the historical data. They've been around for as long as we've been recording seismicity."

Manda's eyebrows floated up. "Did you report them to the council?"

"Of course," all three replied. Jim said, "They told me to fill them in if I find out anything else—" "—but I-we think they were too absorbed in the IceFlame/Reformation debate—" "—to consider the implications."

Manda rubbed her lower lip with her thumbnail. If there *were* ocean thermal vents, and if there *were* life there—even an utterly primitive kind of life; a single-celled organism or two—it would be big news. "Any idea where these 'compression events' are coming from?"

Jim shook his head. "I'm having a hard time pinning them down. Brimstone's lithosphere has some odd complexities that make the data hard to interpret, and I don't have enough seismographs. There may be more than one source—or geologic structures in the inner mantle may be setting up echoes and muddling the data. But"—he held up a finger—"this is just a hunch, but—I'll give you coup they're coming from your hydrothermal vents."

Manda's eyes widened. He grinned and she chortled. "You've just done me another favor, LuisMichael."

"Oh?"

"Oh, yes. I've been at these searches for so long I was starting to get bored. But you've gotten me interested again."

"At least I've done *something* useful for you tonight." This was Jim.

"Tch. Don't be an idiot. Stop worrying about Amadeo! Just send me your data on possible locations for your explosions and I'll be happy."

"All right, all right," he said, holding up his hands in mock defeat. Brian picked up the thread. "You're happy;" "I-we am happy," Amy added. "And"—all three finished in unison— "PabloJeb is all wet."

anda had her own little space, separate from the rest of her clone. It wasn't supposed to be like that but she'd held out against all the recriminations and insinuations, back when, and eventually people had stopped making a fuss about it.

In the morning, she awoke to find Paul and Teresa at the craggy entrance to her nook. Manda's first thought was that they knew, somehow, about the secret room, and her heart thumped painfully. But how could they know? She was being paranoid.

"You OK?" Teresa asked with a frown, giving Manda a penetrating look.

Manda forced herself to stay calm. *It's been hidden for years, with no harm to anyone. I'll report it in the next few days. As soon as I've had a chance to use the telescope to look for* Exodus.

"I'm fine," she said. "Lights up."

A bulb burned out with a flash and a pop. Manda swore. Finding a replacement was going to be tough. She wrapped the fur about herself, and eyed her older siblings in the dim light, trying to make out their expressions. "What's going on?"

Paul held out a data crystal, which she took. "Here's some stuff Arlene wanted you to look over." "Inventory and loading schedules." "They'll need you in Stores tomorrow, to double-check everything."

"All right." She stood and tucked the crystal into a pocket of her pullover, which hung on a hook by the head of her sleeping mat. But the data could just as easily have been transmitted online. Something else was up. She sensed a confrontation coming.

Teresa started to speak, but Manda silenced her. "At least let me dress first." She triggered her livesuit's don-routine and stepped into the footprints that formed in the suit's center. It rippled up her form, and she pulled her long johns on over it. With a deliberation that bordered, she knew, on insolence, she lowered the yoke over her head, plugged it into the livesuit, slid on her gloves, and fitted them to the sleeves' leads. Finally she turned with an exhalation, bracing herself.

"All right," she said. "Go ahead and break it to me."

Teresa started: "We want you to—" "—stay with us tonight," Paul finished. "For a while," they said together. "We're holding a covalence ceremony," Teresa explained. So someone had a new exo-bond—a sexual pairing.

It had to be *really* important for them to be here. She'd refused to participate every single time they'd asked in the past ten seasons, since her disastrous experience with KaliMarshall. Curiosity overcame her initial impulse to simply refuse and kick them out.

"Who?"

"JennaMara," they both replied. One of the other clones on the governing council. Manda remembered Janice's flirtation the other night, at the celebration. So she had gone through with it. "For real?"

"For real."

Wow. Major coup is in play. She started to ask, *who?* Paul anticipated her. "You know Charlotte?" Manda shook her head. She didn't really know JennaMara, except for its prime, Lawrence. He was OK.

Manda worried a hangnail. "How is Farrah handling it?"

"She's handling it," Paul said, tersely. "The hell she is," Teresa replied.

Manda looked from one to the other. Paul and Teresa had never quite gotten over their one experience with exo-bonding. About ten seasons ago there'd been a pairing between Teresa and a ByronMichael. It had been really hard on Paul. And all his anxiety and anger over it, Paul had taken out on Manda when she'd refused participate in the covalence ceremony. Teresa had somehow gotten Manda off the hook with Byron-Michael, Paul had eventually forgiven Manda, and the exo-bond with ByronMichael had dissolved not long afterward.

But in return, Teresa had extracted a promise from Manda to attend the next covalence she asked her to, and Manda had agreed. Until now, Teresa had been careful to avoid calling her on it—which had only increased Manda's indebtedness to her.

Manda couldn't get away with a flat refusal. Still, she gave Teresa a pleading look. "Can't you—"

"No." Teresa's tone was sharp. "Charlotte has asked for you."

Manda was surprised. "She did?" Paul and Teresa both nodded. "Why?"

"We don't know, but it wanted us all to be there." "JennaMara really put its coup on the line for Project IceFlame."

"So *that's* what this is about."

Paul frowned. "It's not just that. Don't be so fucking cynical, Manda." "Janice really has a thing for Charlotte." "She needs you to help make it OK." "If you're there, it'll mean major coup for us. Everybody knows—"

—*how you are.* Manda heard it without Paul saying it, and glared, but he stared steadily back.

"Farrah needs you," he said, and Teresa nodded. "She's taking it hard."

"She is?" Manda felt a twinge of sympathy. It hurt—she was told—when your vat-mate took a lover. The covalence ceremonies were supposed to salve anxious feelings and resentment between the unpaired siblings on each side.

Then she thought, *at least she* has *a vat-mate. Farrah doesn't give a shit about me. None of them do.*

Try not to be a bigger asshole than you can help, Paul's gaze said. And, *you owe me,* said Teresa's. *You promised.*

Manda's heart fluttered painfully. No clean way out.

It was just a formality. It wouldn't take too long. She'd participated once or twice when she was younger, before she'd worked up the nerve to refuse. And at least Janice was showing good taste.

Manda sighed heavily. "All right. This once."

Relief spread onto their identical faces. Teresa hugged her and Paul gave her shoulder a squeeze.

"Thanks," they said in unison.

"When and where?"

Paul said, "Arlene has prepared—"

"—a meeting space on the Mound," Teresa added. "See you there," they both said, and finished, as Manda opened her mouth to ask when, "at twenty-seven o'clock."

Everyone had to give fourteen shifts per month—about a third of their worktime—to colony-support chores such as tending the forest and gardens, doing repairs and maintenance on colony equipment, tuning the recyclers, or herding livestock. So Manda spent both watches that day doing gardening chores for UrsulaMeriwether, the threeclone in charge of Hydroponics.

Manda had always been intimidated by UrsaMeri. It seemed to have some secret knowledge that gave it authority. The clone was short and stocky, three of the oldest colonists, with milk-white eyes, iron-grey hair cut in a short crop, creased, coppery skin, and bad feet: Helen, Rachel, and Jessica.

None of the three said much. Its manner was calm. Reserved. Manda never saw any of it laugh, though occasionally she caught it smiling, sharing quiet jokes as it worked: weeding, watering, checking nutrient influx and effluent, instructing the apprentices, tending its plants with a triad rhythm so precise and finely tuned it might have been a three-souled old *bruja* working an enchantment.

It was blind. Manda didn't understand how this had happened—whether it had been a genetic flaw (and if so, *why* it had been allowed to happen—though she'd heard rumors that the crèche-born's early attempts at cloning had led to some odd mutations, and UrsaMeri was among the first, if not *the* first clone) or a accident that had somehow damaged all three at once.

Blindness didn't seem to slow it down. UrsaMeri seemed inexorable. A force of nature. Coup games never touched it. It rarely spoke up in town meetings, but when it did, everyone paid attention.

And Manda admired it. This was one of the reasons she enjoyed Hydroponics chores and worked there every time the chore rotation schedule gave her a choice. She watched the trio now out of the edges of her gardener-waldos' camera-eyes, as she guided the small fleet of harvesters over the rows of hydroponic tanks, and she pondered what magic the old sisters possessed that gave it such selves-confidence. As if its blindness had freed it to see other things.

To Manda it seemed that UrsaMeri could see with fingers, nose, ears, and feet. Though able to read any label or sign with liveware, it had also taught itselves a written language from Earthspace that they called Braille, and had built a Braille interface for itselves, after a power outage soon after landfall had nearly caused one of it to plunge to her death.

UrsaMeri had erected virtual signposts and labels in Braille all over the caves. The labels were installed on the clone's own internal systems, and was not dependent on the colony's nets. Once, in her adolescent curiosity, Manda had copied the software and spent hours trying to teach herself Braille. She'd eventually given up, after learning a few simple words and phrases. But she'd kept the software, and even now occasionally used the Braille signposts to navigate the caverns. This had paid off a couple of times during outages.

But most of all, she envied UrsaMeri its serenity. How could it be so calm, so comfortable inside its skins, bereft of a sense so crucial as sight? Without sight, how had it found the resourcefulness to achieve what it had, on this unforgiving world?

Her scheduler gave her a heads-up. Twenty-six-fifty. Covalence was about to start. With a grimace of distaste, she disengaged from the Hydroponics waldos, checked out on the colony's chore scheduler, then sifted through her commandshapes and put them away.

Gift. I need a gift. She remembered while hurrying toward the bamboo forest, and reversed her direction. The gift had to be something valuable. Something with personal meaning.

At her cubby, Manda picked hurriedly through her belongings, set in the niches around the small room's perimeter. Then she spotted her rock collection. Perfect. She'd gathered all sorts of interesting specimens over the years.

She picked up a small geode she'd found once. The geode's crystal interior caught the light in its many rosy prisms. She remembered how when she'd broken the egg-like rock open, she'd exclaimed with delight. How could such a rough, ugly exterior hide such inner beauty? She'd spent many a time gazing at the rock, imagining she had discovered a tiny fairy city in its depths. She loved it.

Then there was her lichened shale. She fingered the pale, grey-green, lacy growth that covered the rock. Bits of lichen and rock flaked off onto her fingers. She rubbed her fingers together, smelling its dust—imagining the rich topsoil the lichen was building, molecule by molecule.

As a child, while helping the herders with their yaks, Manda had discovered a small outcropping blanketed with the stuff. The lichen growth was a volunteer—not planted by the colonists and not expected. Everyone had gotten excited. It was one of the first indicators that their early terraforming efforts were taking hold. The geologists she'd reported her find to—LuisMichael; the current threeclone's two older sisters, back when they were still alive—had given her this small piece in thanks.

It was that incident as much as anything else that had filled Manda with a desire to explore this icy moon they inhabited. They knew so little about Brimstone. Though several efforts had been made to explore overland and aerially—in which Carli-Pablo had featured prominently—the colony's early efforts to explore the ocean floor had ground to a halt, back when Manda was little, when the JebMeri twins had died.

Manda hesitated, then put the lichened rock back onto her shelf and took the geode.

She didn't want to lose her lichen. The stuff was all over the place now, and the geode was her rarest and prettiest stone—unusual enough to buy plenty of coup, at the upcoming ceremony. But to Manda, the lichen and the memory it stood for was worth more.

The Mound lay in almost the exact center of the great cavern that held Hydroponics and the bulk of the bamboo forest: the lowest inhabited level of Amaterasu.

The colony's bamboo forest grew in a series of twenty interconnected large chambers, each in different stages of growth or harvest. These crop chambers surrounded a single, vast chamber—the third biggest in all of Amaterasu, after Hydroponics and the Majestic—that had a naturally-formed low hill in its center.

The engineers had worked hard to grow a meadow and forest there, out of the barren, metal-salt-laden dust of Amaterasu. They'd been reasonably successful. Though marred by bald or sickly patches, if you squinted hard enough it was a lovely spot: a big, gentle hill shot through with wandering stands of ash and birch and black spruce (albeit dwarvish and spindly compared to the virtual specimens in their Earth archives), covered with cold-resistant, drought-resistant, metal- and salt-tolerant grasses, and spritzed with pink, gold, and white wildflowers (-resistant, ditto) pollinated by bees and butterflies.

The lights set way overhead created a soft, shadowless twilight—a dim evening setting, which left enough light to see by but gave the nocturnal animals their time to come out of their burrows, to mate and graze and collect seeds. The acoustics were excellent here: bamboo leaves whispered; birds chirped and cats yowled; distant machinery in the hydroponics and machine-shop caverns echoed their arrhythmic, dissonant clanking; the soft lowing and yipping of the domesticated animals in their stables up and down the cavern walls wove a unifying harmony through the other sounds.

In the Mound's center lay the ceremonial circle where many of the colony's major harvest rituals were held. The circle was defined by a ring of carved stalagmites and rocks. She'd been told its design harkened back to some ancient sacred places on Earth. The carvings were geometric patterns, some of them, while others sported an assortment of caricaturish faces.

From the forest's edge, Manda saw that everyone else from both clones was there: CarliPablo seated on the far end of the circle, and JennaMara, an eightclone, seated on the near side. Farrah and Janice both wore long white gowns, as did Paul and Arlene. Of Janice's clone, Lawrence's vat-mate Donald and Janice's two vat-mates were also gowned. There must have been a drawing to see who would be the main participants. Manda felt a twinge of gratitude that they had left her out of it. Her role would be minimal.

Teresa held bamboo claves in her hands and one of Janice's younger siblings had a multi-reed flute. Stacks of blankets and large cloths lay around the circle, behind the main participants. Both clones had arranged themselves by age.

Manda stepped between the tall stones and crossed over to

where her siblings sat. As she passed around the outside of the circle, Bart and Charles were whispering to Derek in excited tones, "Drill eighteen has broken through, eleven hours early!" "Fourteen and one are scheduled to hit magma in the next few hours."

"Excellent," Derek replied. "Great news."

Manda pressed her hands on her stomach.

I don't need them, she told herself. *I don't need anybody.* She only wished it were true.

"Any tremors?" Derek asked.

"A few small ones. Nothing serious so far." "We're keeping a close eye on things."

"Good. Good. I'll let Arlene know after the ceremony."

She passed behind Janice, Farrah, and Paul, and sat cross-legged at the end of the line next to Teresa. Janice was holding Farrah's hand but looking across at Charlotte, who gazed back at her as if no one else were present. Farrah's face was stiff. Manda thought, *that's not an auspicious start.*

At a glance from Arlene, Teresa started a syncopated beat on her claves. The wooden sticks *clack-a-clacked* a short, repeating pattern, while the JennaMara flutist played a little tune. Manda winced. JennaMara apparently didn't have much native musical ability.

Arlene, taking prime for CarliPablo, and Donald, prime for JennaMara, both stood and came to the center of the circle. Arlene carried a huge, handled bowl of mead, and Donald carried a burning taper and a meter-long water pipe filled with mixed tobacco and cannibis.

Arlene held the cup up. "I-we bless the joining of Janice and Charlotte." Then she took a sip of the liquor and dabbed at her lips with a long cloth napkin she had draped over her arm. From his seated position near her, Derek mimicked her gestures in miniature, moving his lips in synchrony with her words. So did the rest of her clone. Manda knew they weren't conscious of it.

She felt that familiar pang of mingled deep affection for and painful isolation from her clone.

Donald lit the ceremonial herbs and sucked on the pipe till tendrils of smoke curled upward. The air above the water in the bulb filled with smoke. He lifted the pipe. "I-we celebrate this union of JennaMara and CarliPablo." Then he inhaled deeply. After this, he ground the taper out in the dirt and then exchanged pipe for bowl with Arlene, as twin streams of smoke trickled from his nose.

"My-our thanks to CarliPablo for this drink," he said, and took a deep draught of mead from the ceremonial cup. He coughed a bit, and wiped his mouth on his sleeve.

"And my-our thanks to JennaMara for this smoke." Arlene put her lips on the mouth of the water pipe and inhaled. Then they traded back. Donald brought the pipe of herbs over to CarliPablo while Arlene went to JennaMara with the liquor. Manda watched while Donald, an older man with black skin and hair and a cordial gaze, handed the pipe to each of her siblings. Her turn came last. Donald gave her a nod that made her skin flush as he held out the pipe. She drew a deep breath, and coughed, as the cool, sweetish smoke scoured her throat and bronchia.

Arlene had finished sharing mead with the youngest of JennaMara, adolescent male twins perhaps fifteen seasons in age. Manda guessed they'd never attended a covalence before; they were barely old enough. Children, for obvious reasons, weren't expected to participate.

Now Arlene came across to Manda and knelt, putting the bowl to Manda's lips. Manda took a big swallow, and managed to keep from sputtering as the liquid scorched her throat.

"Thanks," Arlene whispered, as she dabbed Manda's lips. *Thanks for coming.* The remark only made Manda angry.

What the hell am I doing here?

If only she'd had the nerve to renege on her promise to Teresa. She didn't believe in any of this mystic shit. It was all a big lie.

Nobody really cared about anybody. They just wanted her to pretend. Don't make a scene. Pretend to be like the rest.

The gift exchange came next. Manda presented her geode to the youngest JennaMara vat-twins, who thanked her nervously. One of them gave her a framed photo of a dog, and the other gave her a bamboo boot-horn he'd made. She muttered thanks and tucked them into her pockets, but instead of sitting next to the young JennaMara twins, she went back over to her original spot, and ended up next to Teresa, who was chatting with her own JennaMara counterpart.

I'm acting like a nervous adolescent myself, she thought. *What's the big deal? They're certainly cute enough, and I could teach them a thing or two.* (Not that she was all *that* experienced.) But she didn't get up and go over.

Several more passes were made of liquor and smoke, and Manda was getting dizzy. The music seemed to be getting better. She listened for a moment. Yes. Definitely improving. That was something, at least. But the rest of it still infuriated her. People were talking in whispers, laughing. Manda merely sat there, arms folded. The twins were eyeing her. She studiously avoided their gazes—looked instead at the glistening stalactites, and the bamboo stairways and bridges that conjoined the holes along the walls, along which distant human and animal figures moved.

Bowls of curried ox-steak with bamboo shoots were served with *mana* bread, and afterward, more alcohol and smoke was dispensed. Some sweets went around. Manda relaxed a bit, and chatted with Teresa and Paul, and with the two young men, who had moved over at some point. They seemed nice enough, and eager to please. They made a big deal over the geode and asked her where she'd found it. She told them the story, and they shared anecdotes about their own experiences upside.

After a while, Arlene and Donald called for everyone's attention. Janice and Charlotte came to the center and kissed each other, lingeringly. Everyone whooped and clapped. They looped strips of leather over each others' wrists. Meanwhile the other active participants stood up and came to the center as well. Everyone was a little drunk or a little high, or both, and their gaits weren't too steady—except for Farrah, who looked stone-cold sober, and a lot like she was going to explode.

I know just how you feel, Manda thought. But she didn't, really. She wasn't angry about being here. Just anxious, and—for some reason—sad.

Arlene joined Farrah's left wrist to Charlotte's right with the leather strap, saying, "CarliPablo embraces JennaMara through its member Charlotte. Share you-yourself with each of me-us as you have with one."

Donald JennaMara joined Janice's wrist to one of Charlotte's vat-mates', the male one. "JennaMara embraces CarliPablo, through its member Janice. Share you-yourself with each of me-us as you have with one."

Next Arlene gestured at Paul. "Since Janice is a two-mate and Charlotte is a three-mate, Paul has agreed to covex with Martha for CarliPablo." She joined his left wrist to the right wrist of Charlotte's female vat-mate, saying, "CarliPablo embraces JennaMara through its member Paul. I-we share ourself with you-you through you-your member Martha."

The bindings were only ritual, and fell away as Charlotte reached up to kiss Farrah. Manda watched some of the tension leave Farrah's body as she released herself to Charlotte's passion. Everyone applauded and laughed. When the kiss ended, Farrah bowed her head, dashing away tears.

With a tender smile, Charlotte put an arm around her, picked up a blanket, and led her away from the circle. Janice watched them go with an expression of relief and approval. Then she kissed her own partner, Charlotte's triplet brother, while Paul kissed Charlotte's triplet sister Martha, and both couples got much appreciative applause. They also took blankets and left the circle.

More food, mead, and smokes went around. Manda got woozy. A while later, she found her head in the lap of one of the youngest boys. His twin was stroking her thigh while the first fondled her breast, smiling down at her. A very pretty young man, whose eyes were as dark and friendly as those of Donald and Lawrence.

Terror lanced her, sharp and hard as a knife blade, dispelling the pleasant ache of desire low in her belly.

Shit.

She sat up and pushed them away, and staggered to her feet. Concerned and confused faces swarmed around her—*what's wrong? are you OK?*—as she stumbled out of the stone circle and off into the bamboo forest.

Teresa came after her.

"You promised!" she said. Her voice was a bit slurred but her tone pierced.

"Leave me alone!" Manda threw off her grasp.

"You owe me this."

"I don't owe you a fuck with strangers. They aren't *my* exo-bond."

"You don't have to do anything with them. Nobody made you. But you shouldn't leave alone like this, before we do the wrap. It's rude."

Manda shook her head slowly, confused. She heaved deep breaths, trying to clear her head. Her heart was thumping, striving for her attention. Somewhere off to her left, one of the couples was engaged in lovemaking. Their moans and rustlings made her aware again of the ache low in her belly.

"I don't belong here," Manda said, wiping away tears. "This is hurting me." She grabbed Teresa's hand. "Please release me from the promise. Please."

Teresa glared at her, and snatched her hand away. She stalked back toward the circle, with a "Go, then," flung over her shoulder. Manda lifted a hand after her, then dropped it. She turned and made her sad and drunken way back to her cubby, where she relieved her unrequited desire with her livesuit and a sex syntellect, thinking of those two lovely young men she couldn't bring herself to covex with.

Late-Night Hacktivity

rimstone nights were all too long. Manda woke up at thirty-one, a good three hours before rising time. For a while she stared at the inside of her eyelids, trying to drift off again. The effects of the alcohol and cannibis had mostly worn off, but the events at the covalence churned in her thoughts, undigestible, refusing to release her to sleep.

Finally Manda gave up. She donned her livesuit, brought up her liveface, and broke open her entertainment nonahedron. Its icons spread out before her.

She browsed restlessly through the entertainment choices—similes, video, thrideo, books, and so on, from several hundred years of Earthspace storytelling and storyplaying. It all left her cold. Most of the Earth stories in the colony archives concerned themselves with heterosexual exo-bonds (heavily mythologized, cloaked in sentimental trappings; *Jeez,* she thought, *it's just sex; get over it*) or friend-to-friend bonds, or parent-child relations, none of which had much to say to Manda.

Who needed friends, when you had your clone? Who needed parents; progeny; lovers?

OK, she amended, *maybe lovers.* The colonists liked getting laid as much as folks back on Earth apparently did, and fooling around with your sibs just didn't cut it. It was too much like masturbating: you could get yourselves off, but it just didn't quite satisfy. Do this, don't do that: everything was a foregone conclusion. Attraction to the strange—the exotic—was hardwired in, however the crèche-born and the colony founders had tried to engineer it out.

Manda sighed. She could do with a lover. But she didn't have a vat-mate to join her with another set of twins or triplets. It was rather overwhelming to have two or three people focusing on just little old *you*. True one-on-one exo-bonds like Janice's with Charlotte were rare; it was almost impossible to get somebody alone without his siblings hanging around, getting in the way. She sighed. *Virtu*-sex was much more convenient.

But at the moment, Manda realized, she was more interested in Carli and the crèche-born. Until she'd found the secret room they'd simply been a feature of her young childhood—unexplained and inexplicable—and over the seasons, her memories and interest in them had faded. But recent events had rekindled her interest.

When she was younger, she'd often wondered why the colony hadn't remained in contact with the crèche-born, after they'd left. She'd known that *Exodus* had an omni field generator, which allowed for instantaneous communication between two distant points, and the colony had plenty of omnilink transceivers. To satisfy her curiosity she'd once read up on how the omni worked and figured out the answer. In the presence of a large gravitational mass, or under a high enough acceleration, an omni field generator created a sphere within which instantaneous communication could occur. Omni transceivers could communicate instantly inside that sphere—or with omni transceivers inside the sphere of other omni field generators. So anyone within range of a working generator could instantly contact anyone else within any omni field, no matter how great the distance between them.

But the size of the omni field was determined by how strong the triggering gravitational pull or acceleration was. The colony didn't have its own omni field generator, and even if *Exodus* was still insystem, as ur-Carli said, the colony would be well outside the range of the ship's omni field. So the only way to reach *Exodus* would be visually or by radio.

Right now she wasn't so much interested in contacting them, though, as she was in learning more about them. She brought up background documents on Carli D'Auber and the crèche-born, and pored over the titles in the archives. The records were a mixture of text, still images, video, thrideo, and audio, some with arcane lettering and numbering systems, others with brief descriptions. They were cross-referenced, both chronologically and by subject. There was so much material Manda couldn't sample even a meaningful fraction of it. Where to start?

Then she noticed something odd. Documents got sparse starting when the ship was approaching 47 Ursae Majoris, and extending to when the colonists made landfall—even bearing in mind that the infowar forty earth-years before had cut off their omnilink to Earth. She wondered if there had been some kind of file purge. The older colonists rarely talked about those times.

But there was still plenty to choose from: files logged during or about the info war, itself; files about their departure from Earth and their early years en route here; and plenty of files about KaleidoScope, the top-secret project launched in the mid-2050s that had taken twenty-seven infants and toddlers, implanted beanlink technology in their heads, and permanently sealed them in sensory deprivation tanks, or crèches, dooming them to lives lived through an interface (or freeing them, depending on who you talked to, to be the world's best virtuality navigators and hackers). The crèche-born.

She chose one that looked interesting:

Radiolink meeting: Dr. Patricia Taylor & Sen. Chauncy D'Auber.
w/ video and hypertext attachments.
TOP SECRET: Progress Report #353, Project KaleidoScope
—*from United Nations Interstellar Ship Exodus archives,*
04/18/2060.

Manda vaguely recognized the names. Dr. Taylor was the scientist who'd first launched the crèche-born project, back in Earthspace long ago. The crèche-born had practically worshipped her. Manda queued the recording, and a lovely young woman-proxy stood before her, looking poised and friendly. But either the proxy technology of the time had not been sophisticated enough to reproduce the proper muscle responses in the woman's face, or she wasn't truly feeling as beneficent as she looked, because there was an intractable look to her. Like silk over steel.

A middle-aged man with chiseled features and an old-fashioned sheath suit entered the room. Manda spotted a resemblance between him and Carli. This must be Senator D'Auber, then. He too had been involved in the crèche-born project. Manda had heard mention of him before, but never seen a video or still. She called up his bio in a sidekick globe and saw that he was indeed Carli's father. Since Manda's genes were half Carli's, this man was—in a sense—Manda's grandfather.

That brought her up short. She actually had relatives back in Earthspace. And not just relatives, either: *ancestral* relatives. Biological, non-sibling family. Non-clone kin. Just like the characters in the entertainment archives. If you went strictly by genetics, in fact, she had everything: a biological mother (Carli), father (Pablo), grandparents, aunts, uncles; the works.

She'd never thought of that. It made her skin crawl. Gross.

Both participants were white. To a race-blended, gene-spliced Amaterasan, their pale faces and eyes and their pointed, narrow noses were bizarre—anachronistic.

"Senator," Dr. Taylor said, "my engineers tell me we have a three-second comm-lag—it looks like they're bouncing our signal around a bit. So I'd like to give you my report first, and then record your questions for response."

A pause, while he awaited transmission of her signal, then the senator said, "You have five minutes. Proceed."

87

Another pause. Taylor nodded once. "We've made excellent progress in the past few months introducing the second group of children to their beanjacks." She lifted a hand: behind her a projected image expanded. Within it, numerous piloted proxy bodies, machines that looked like adult humans, crawled around the floor, or chewed on their toes, or played with bright toys.

The proxy bodies were those of fully-grown adults; the behavior of those piloting them was that of infants and toddlers. More disturbing still, one was banging her proxy's head rhythmically against the wall, and another gnawed determinedly—almost desperately—on his forearm, tearing at the plastic flesh. A third was spinning, hurling herself against the padded walls, knocking heedlessly into other proxies, catapulting through the low-gravity room, till one of the true adults there, a young man *in corpus*, shot up and caught hold of her, and carried her flailing and screaming out of the room. A few sat staring at empty air, not even responding as their playmates crawled past or waved toys in front of their faces. All of this went unremarked by Dr. Taylor. Senator D'Auber wore a troubled look, but said nothing.

Taylor spent the next few minutes going down a detailed list of test results and whatnot, but Manda didn't really listen. It was slowly dawning on her that these children, these damaged infants were the people who had cloned and decanted Manda and the rest of the colony's older clones. The crèche-born. If the colonists had any true parents to speak of, it was these damaged children. She shuddered.

"You'll note that we've abandoned the use of proxies targeted to their actual ages," Taylor said. "We found the manufacture of child-sized proxies prohibitively expensive and complex due to their small size, so we've replaced most of the proxy piloting exercises with similes that give them exposure to developmentally-appropriate childhood experiences. They've really taken to it and spend most of their time now *in virtu*. I'm now downloading a full report for you to study at your leisure."

Senator D'Auber was watching the children, and looked uneasy. "We're going to take some heat this budget round. Chairman Torquilstone is still raising questions about the briefing. He's uncomfortable with the direction your research has taken in recent months."

Long pause. Taylor sighed. "Senator, it's too late to turn back now. These kids can't return to a normal life. Especially not the older kids. We're committed."

Pause. "I recognize that. But in this political climate, we don't have a lot of support. Budget cuts are inevitable."

Pause. Taylor bristled. "My telepresence research has been extremely profitable. Waldos, Inc.'s board of directors is fully behind me. Cutting off the government share of our funding now would raise all kinds of issues for them. I'm sure the president doesn't want a major transnational manufacturer breathing down his neck, demanding to know why the US is reneging on its commitment to beanlink research."

Pause. Annoyance crossed the senator's face. "The country's in the middle of a seven-year recession, Doctor. Congress is filled with a slate of freshmen this term, all desperate to find cuts that will make them look good. If anyone scrutinizes our climate-adaptation research too closely at this point, or if they dig too deeply into the small print of our agreement with the Department of Defense, the precise nature of your research will start getting around the Hill and the press may get wind of it. And if that happens. . . ." He left the sentence hanging, with an eloquent shrug.

Pause. Taylor's lips went gash-thin. "My research is perfectly legal."

Pause. D'Auber snorted. "You're experimenting on human children, Doctor. Homeless and orphaned refugees. Sick kids." Taylor broke in: "Sick refugee children whom nobody gave a *damn* about until I stepped in! They'd be dead now, if not for me!"—but the senator kept talking: "You know what the media would do with that. Ever heard of tar and feathers? No one will give a shit that we've got the signature of a president no longer in power, based on some arcane legal document dating from the martial-law years, saying it's OK."

The pause that ensued went on far longer than three seconds, while Dr. Taylor regarded him, hands on her hips. "Just what are you saying, Senator?"

Pause. "I'm saying that you'd better keep a low profile during the budget negotiations. I'll do my best to keep your project out from under the knife—but the fact is, you'll have to take a hit, a cut of at least seven hundred fifty million this year."

Taylors expression hardened, but she said nothing.

"Let me be blunt," D'Auber continued. "You had better not stir up your cronies on the board of directors at Waldos, or draw any other undue attention to yourself. Not if you want your project to stay alive."

Pause. Dr. Taylor's glare by now had grown so fixed, so angry, that Manda had to remind herself she was watching a virtual recording and at no risk.

"Senator, I'm sure you don't need me to remind you that if Congress does cut my funding, I'll be forced to seek other sources of income. And that means, inevitably, more people will know about KaleidoScope. The more people who know, the harder it will be to keep this project secure.

"And I'm sure you're also aware," she went on, "that if word on our project does get out, try as I might to protect you, all the evidence detailing your own involvement is bound to come to light." She paused, and a thin smile spread across her lips. "As I'm sure you see, it's in both our interests to make sure that KaleidoScope remains fully—and discreetly—funded."

The senator's own expression went cold. More silence stretched between them. When he spoke, his voice was hoarse. "I'm well aware of that."

"But perhaps it won't come to that," Taylor said.

"Perhaps not."

"Well then. I'll trust you to do your best to keep the project from under the budget-cutters' knives," Taylor said, and the recording ended.

Now that *was coup-slinging,* Manda thought. Then, thinking about the origins of the crèche-born, she shuddered again. *And I thought* my *childhood was rough.*

Intersticial: the crèche-born
Confrontation

"About another two weeks," Ferris, a DaliaMichael clone, told Dane. He meant two weeks before they were ready to launch for 70 Virginis. "My crew starts disassembling the solar collectors tomorrow."

Dane felt a thrill of anticipation. Two weeks before we leave! "I want the crews working double-time. I want the ship launch-ready in eight days."

He bowed, and Dane saw that old flicker of fear in his eyes, that all the ship clones felt for the crèche-born. She wished she could comfort him, but she didn't dare act too kindly, or it would weaken her position among her fellow crèche-born.

She couldn't afford to appear weak.

The crèche-born had grown a few more clones, after the colonists had left for Brimstone. They were cheaper and easier to maintain for certain kinds of tasks than syntellects. The ship housed about three dozen. Dane worried for them. There'd been talk of culling the clones after they launched, to cut down on resource consumption.

Pablo appeared in her face. "A word with you," he said.

"Of course."

"In virtu."

"I'll be right there."

Distantly, she felt her heart thumping as she plugged in the coordinates he sent her. She materialized in his virtu-space. Pablo loomed threateningly.

"Don't fool yourself that I don't know what you did," Pablo said. She stared at him impassively, though she was certain he could detect her fear. "I can smell your interference from two worlds over."

"What are you raving about?"

"You know exactly what I mean. You tricked Joe and Dalia into cracking my face and interrupting my planning session the other day. I tracked your signals." Dane knew that had to be a lie. She'd carefully deleted all recordings and rehacked them. He was guessing. Or Buddy had figured it out and told him. "You could have cost us weeks of preparation time."

Pablo was still pretending that he was in favor of leaving—he wasn't prepared to visibly violate his sacred vow to Carli, a vow made just before she'd left, to keep his hands off the colonists and move on. He intended to make it look like others' doing.

Carli was the only person Pablo had ever cared about: the only chink in the armor of his indifference. If Dane confronted him directly over his attempts to undermine his vow, she might push him over the edge. It took a careful balancing act.

"Oh, stop acting the fool," she said. " 'Planning session,' indeed. I know what you were doing in there with Mara and Kali and Jeb. You were trying to organize them against the rest of us."

He stared at her, and she mentally dared him to call her a liar.

"Take care, Dane. You have no special hold on me. I won't have you interfering."

"Get a grip! You're getting paranoid. Maybe you'd better have a chat with ur-Carli."

"I could lock you away," he said. "I'm the dominant one. I could trap you in darkness forever. . . ." the way I-you did Pablito. A rare, conjoined thought.

"Do it, then. What are you waiting for?"

She felt as if the words had come from somewhere else. The world spun and she felt as if she were falling.

You used to care about me, *she thought;* you used to care at least for your fellow crèche-born. Once you were something akin to human.

Maybe he heard her. It only made him angrier. They trembled under an onslaught of rage-fear: their hands balled, their heart raced. She'd seen him kill before—one of the new clones, just recently, who had pushed him too far.

He was the dominant one; she had little defense against a direct mental assault. She braced herself, wondering remotely what it would be like to be obliterated. She realized that on some level it would be a relief.

It was only moments later that she realized Pablo had left. Dane sank to the floor and rested her arms on her knees, shaking, trying to calm herself.

"Why do you taunt him?"

Dane looked up. Buddy was there, in virtu, *hands planted on hips.*

"You told him, didn't you?"

"I had to. I'm not the idiot you are."

Dane growled. "Why do *you go along with him? Look what he's become!"* Look what we've all become. *"You know what he's trying to do, Buddy. You better than anyone. He's trying to go back on his word to Carli."*

Buddy shrugged. "We made that promise decades ago. Times have changed. Why should we spend hundreds of years in transit to another solar system when there's one here, even now being made habitable for us?"

"It's their world. We gave it to them. We promised Carli." The crèche-born knew they had to stay away from the colonists. Carli had forced them to see it. Her love for the children they'd cloned had infected all the crèche-born, just enough for them to send them away—to resist consuming them.

Buddy's gaze flickered and Dane could tell she'd scored a hit. He'd loved Carli too.

"You know that means something to me, Dane," he warned, "and maybe it means something to the others, but it doesn't mean squat anymore to Pablo."

"I don't believe that."

"Her hold on him is weak. He's still angry that she left him."

"He's one," she said, "and we are many. He can't vote us all down."

"No, but he can manipulate. He can persuade. Another long journey is daunting."

I'm not going to let him go back on his words, she thought. Buddy merely shook his head.

"You're a fool."

"If caring makes me foolish, so be it." She paused. "She was right about us, Buddy. Look what we've become."

He frowned, and vanished. Dane slumped over her virtual knees, and hugged them, feeling as clumsy and vulnerable as a child.

Eight more days, she thought wearily. I can do this. Eight more days.

When Manda woke in the morning, the covalence had taken on, mercifully, a dreamlike vagueness. The absence of her clone in the crowded, noisy mess hall at breakfast—they were probably hungover or sleeping in with their lovers or something—anyway, their absence, and the absence of any Jenna-Maras, made it easy to put it all out of her mind. Besides, she had a lot of work to do. And maybe tonight she could spend a little more time exploring the secret room and even track down the crèche-born's ship.

She called up her faceware and looked over her to-do list while waiting in line to select her meal. Then she sat down to eat, tuning out the murmurs and clinking diningware of the other diners.

Nearby a commotion started. She looked up just as one of the food-serving robot arms hurled a glop of barleymeal porridge in her face. Suddenly food was flying everywhere—the robots were running amok, grabbing ladles-full of food and flinging them about.

People ducked for cover. Food flew in great arcs that smacked against the rocks and bamboo supports of the walls and ceiling, that splatted on bamboo tables and bamboo-and-thatch chairs, that splashed on clothing and faces and the floor, causing fleeing diners to slip and fall.

Manda leapt up onto the counter into the worst of the barrage. She whipped out a screwdriver—and as she did, caught a glimpse of two young adolescents, perhaps eleven or twelve seasons old, dashing out the door, giggling. Dodging vegetable and animal and reconstituted-whatever matter, she removed a panel in the back of the robots' control box, while yanking cords from pockets in her liveyoke. She plugged into the unit, then pulled up and unpacked the unfamiliar commandface.

This had to be a prank those kids had somehow pulled. She knew them; they were the younger twins of the ByronDalia six-clone. Their older quadruplets were hackers. Good ones: some even said ByronDalia could give the crèche-born a run for their coup. She'd also heard that they were troublemakers.

Well, it looks like the younger two are well on their way to joining their older siblings in the shithouse.

Somewhere in here, then, was viralware: a liveworm or pop-can or some other system hack overriding the robots' regular command processes. Furiously she began sorting through and opening candidate programballs—but found no clues to the problem. Then she touched a suspiciously blank-faced cube—which sprang open to reveal a leering jack-in-the-box. She nearly fell off the counter as it lurched into her face.

"Food fight!" it screamed, and laughing maniacally, it faded away, leaving Manda scrambling to grab traces of its dispersing algorithms and data bits. (She knew the council was going to want to know how they did it, to prevent a recurrence.) All she caught was a few dregs: garbage data.

Disgusted, she unplugged. The cleaning robots and several kitchen staff, a fiveclone, were already cleaning up the mess, and the robots were replacing the ruined trays with new ones. The triplets who headed up the mess team came over, wiping hands on their aprons.

"Thanks," one said. Another dropped some ration chits in her palm by way of thanks, and the third handed her some damp towels to clean up with. As she wiped herself off, the second triplet said, "I-we owe you."

"The council's already been alerted," the first said. The second went on, "They've requested a debriefing as soon as you're available, in *virtu*-conference epsilon."

"Might as well get it over with," Manda replied. "Do you mind if I borrow a table and tune out for a few minutes?"

"Be our guest," the triplets replied in unison.

Manda brought up her liveface and activated immersive-conference mode. Her wardrobe of five avatars stepped out of the conference-interface cube as it unfolded, and stood silently before her in their characteristic poses. Three were fanciful creations: there was the bitch-queen-in-leather-and-chains; the predator-cat-the-size-of-a-horse; and the translucent-silver-banshi. The other three were stylized versions of her, physically identical but each with its own emotional affect-settings (one transmitted all her facial expressions and body language with no filters or add-ons; one transmitted none; the third exaggerated her expressions somewhat). All of them had emblazoned across their chests Manda's name and digital signature: a secure-systems tag that all *virtu*-avatars had.

The founding colonists didn't often wear avatars that diverged from the human norm. Apparently the crèche-born were inclined to wear fanciful avatars and the association was unpleasant for them. But like most of the, younger colonists, Manda thought of her avatars as clothing—wearable art—wearable attitude. The colonists didn't have resources or time for making much in the way of jewelry or colorful clothing. So why not have a little fun *in virtu*?

She knew her siblings would prefer she wear something more conservative for this meeting—but she preferred her predator cat. It let everyone know that she wouldn't be intimidated.

She touched the nose of the cat, which turned its back to her. When she stepped into it, the cat fitted itself around her consciousness like a glove folding itself around her. She-cat bounded through the neon-and-crystal strands and plates of the colony's virtual spaces, her own liveface icons swarming after her like a cloud of large, colored-glass insects, till she came to the conference-room icon: a pane of blue glass than hung amid the other conference-room panes.

As she-cat neared the room icon, it grew and tilted toward the horizontal till it appeared to be a mirror-smooth pool of water; beneath it, the image of the conference room wavered like some undersea tableau. Manda-avatar dove in, sank through the interface, and landed on a marble floor, and her cloud of personal icons arranged themselves around her in an unobtrusive configuration.

The council were all there: PabloJeb, JennaMara, Roxanna-Luis, PatriciaJoe, and of course, Derek for CarliPablo.

Protocol required that a member of all five clones be present when the council met. In theory, any one of the clones' siblings could represent their clone on the council, but in fact only the eldest vat-siblings participated—and except in emergencies, only one of each came. Jack, Lawrence, Anne, Victoria, and Derek were the day-to-day councilmembers, while their vat-mates ran the major functions that supported the colony. PabloJeb ran medicine and the bio-sciences; CarliPablo took care of robotics, waldos, and computers; JennaMara ran food production and distribution; RoxannaLuis ran equipment maintenance and the refinery; and PatriciaJoe was in charge of facilities, general services, and agriculture.

Because of their leadship roles, the council members were forced into a separation from their clones that felt very unnatural to the colonists. Manda knew how they were able to tolerate the frequent separation from their vat-mates; she'd seen Derek and Arlene do it often enough. They all maintained a live telepresent contact on a private channel, their voices a constant murmur in each others' ears. That, and years of practice and self-discipline, she supposed. Still, seeing all the singles sitting there, it was like looking at a collection of amputated limbs. It made Manda very uncomfortable. Times like these, she understood best why everyone thought her a freak.

All five councilmembers wore avatars that resembled their real bodies—with minor tweaks here and there to remove flaws and enhance desired traits. Derek-avatar gave Manda-cat a subtle nod. Then the elder ByronDalia quadruplets appeared next to Manda-cat in a flash of fireworks.

Nice trick, she thought. Most people used the regular, preset entry routines. Their avatars were assorted versions of fey and puckish creatures, and their-avatars' smiles were vaguely reminiscent of the jack-in-the-box's leer. She had the feeling they wouldn't *entirely* disapprove of what their younger siblings had done.

In the conference room's center played a rerun of what had happened. The councilmembers watched closely as people dodged food and Manda scrambled up and disabled the food-fight virus.

Manda noticed that the young ByronDalia twins were nowhere to be seen. They'd gone in and hacked the recordings already (doubtful)—or (more likely) set up some judicious illegal hacks ahead of time. Clever. Then she glanced over at the elder ByronDalia foursome's avatars, who were watching it with deadpan expressions, and she wondered whether the twins had edited *themselves* out, or whether they'd had some help.

"Run it back to several hours before the event," Derek-avatar told the room's syntellect, "and replay it at ten-ex speed. Let's see if there's any evident tampering prior to the event."

They watched, then, as several waves of people minced in, chowed down at warp speed, and rushed out. No sign of tampering appeared. When the food fight began again, they had the scene frozen, and spoke in low voices, then turned to Manda-cat and the ByronDalia avatars.

"Did you see anything when it happened," Jack-avatar asked Manda-cat finally, "that might give you an idea who was responsible?"

"None," she-cat said, and hoped she was fooling Derek as well as the others.

She wasn't at all sure she was doing the right thing, but couldn't bring herself to turn the twins over to the council. She'd had a few run-ins with the council, herself, and wouldn't wish them on anybody. Derek-avatar's gaze pinned her. She hadn't deceived him.

"I hope you appreciate what a serious infraction this was," he said. She-cat toughed it out with a blank stare, and he-avatar sat back, letting it go.

"What access did the perpetrators have to the food-serving units?" RoxannaLuis-avatar was asking the ByronDalias. "Would they have had to plug directly in, as Manda did to disable the prankware?"

"Not necessarily," ByronDalia-sprite replied. ByronDalia-pan said, "All waldo systems are tied into the nets. They might have cracked the units' I/O systems and downloaded their prankware that way."

The councilmembers conferred among themselves again.

"How can we prevent this sort of intrusion in the future?" Jack-avatar asked the ByronDalias.

"We can further tighten security, but—" "—the colony computer systems are extremely complex." "It's not possible to come up with something absolutely secure." "Security and anti-security measures evolve in a basically Darwinian way." "For every solution we might come up with, someone persistent and clever enough will eventually find a way around it."

Victoria-avatar said, "You are our best coders. We're counting on you not to let that happen."

"And we're counting on you," Derek-avatar added—and his gaze flicked briefly to Manda; *you too, little sister*—"to find the perpetrators and inform us so we may deal with them. The colony computer systems are critical to our survival. Even a childish prank could do grave harm."

"We'll do our best," all four ByronDalia-avatars said.

And Manda silently replied to Derek's stare: *I'll deal with it. In my own way.*

"We believe we can prevent a recurrence of this kind of incident," ByronDalia-Pan finished. "We just don't want to give you unrealistic expectations about our systems' security capabilities."

"Very well," Jack-avatar said, gruffly. "Get to it."

"A word with you," Manda-cat transmitted privately to them, once the meeting had dispersed. "Meet me ex-face right away, in the mess."

"Why should we?" the sprite-avatar asked her.

"I know who cracked the mess robots," she-cat said. All four ByronDalia-avatars' gazes went to her.

"Ah," the Puck said, and the brownie said, "We'll be there."

When she disengaged from her liveface, the mess was clean once more. While waiting for ByronDalia-the-elders, she served herself some tea and porridge and a *mana*-honey roll, and looked over her to-do list. The cryptic note she'd left herself—*E. insystem? explore astronomical detection methods*—brought back ur-Carli's wild assertion during Derek's meeting, about the crèche-born still being around. Manda called up the colony news site and looked over the weather report. The storm she'd witnessed yesterday was still raging. No way to use a telescope in that mess.

It was just as well, since she'd had her marine-waldos scanning the ocean floors for most of a day now, unsupervised. With eight of them out there collecting sonar soundings, current flow, water temperature, salinity, and assorted chemical composition screens, it didn't take much of an absence to put her behind. She would need to dedicate a few hours to dealing with Project IceFlame too, and needed to donate the day's second watch to colony chores. Her work-hours today were pretty much booked up.

She'd save the sky search for tomorrow. Or maybe late tonight, if the storm let up and she wasn't too tired after chores.

The ByronDalia quadruplets pulled chairs up and sat down, surrounding her. Two were male, two were female, and all four were striking: muscular, tall—even taller than she was—with big, laughing eyes and mouths that lingered somewhere between piquant and sarcastic.

They were perhaps four seasons older than Manda, and had grown up in a different dormitory, so she didn't know them except by reputation. She should probably dislike them but their cockiness was tempered with enough playfulness and charm that she couldn't help liking them, just a little.

That was probably why she'd let the younger twins off the hook. To rebel against the tight constraints imposed by the colony took a kind of courage—a stupid kind, perhaps, but she couldn't help but admire it.

"So," said one of the males, "what do you want for keeping silent?" They weren't only concerned for the well-being of their younger siblings; they were worried about the hit their coup might take, if word of this got out. Manda had them by the short hairs, and they all knew it.

The corners of her mouth twitched as she studied the four pretty copies of their face.

"Tell you what," she said. "I'm going to hoard some coup. I want you to be available to help me with coding—a big job—

and you'll make yourself available when I ask. With no preconditions. At some point in the future that I will specify."

Glances shot back and forth among them.

"Agreed," one said. They started to stand.

"And," Manda added. They all sat again, stiffly, giving her suspicious looks. "Don't get your long johns in a twist," she said. "I'm not about to extract more favors. But I do want your assurance that you'll keep a closer watch on"—she hesitated—"the perpetrators. No serious harm was done, but they did waste food. If our stores weren't fairly well stocked right now, people might go hungry. And my older brother is right that messing with our computer systems like that could hurt people. Those food waldos were out of control."

"Since when do *you* care?" one of the females asked, arching her eyebrows. But her siblings gave her quelling looks, and she subsided.

"Of course we'll take steps," one of the males said, and the other female went on, "We'll make sure the . . . um . . . offending parties are kept on a shorter leash." The second male added, "We didn't need you to tell us that."

"Good."

The four got up to leave in a single motion, and circled the table close behind her, their manner either seductive or contemptuous; Manda couldn't decide which. She rested her chin on her interlaced fingers and watched them go with a little frown on her face. Maybe she didn't like them so much after all.

Despite the fact that she'd come off pretty well, the exchange left her feeling grouchy and she ended up insulting one of the mess staff, an ingratiating young man who got on her nerves as she was sorting her leftovers and her carved-bamboo dishes into the recycler and cleaner bins—thus blowing away the coup she'd just gained with the mess folk.

Oh, well. Easy come, easy go.

*   *   *

After breakfast Manda headed to her work station and called up the projection pod. Immediately she saw that Jim's seismic data had come in. She set it aside for the moment, because one of the waldos was reporting another temperature anomaly. It was *Aculeus Septimus*, though—the same one that reported the last two false anomalies. The stupid thing was malfunctioning again. Time to haul it in for a tune-up.

Don't jump to conclusions till you've checked the data, dipshit, she thought irritably, as she slipped into the liveface pack. She buckled it swiftly, and hooked up the leads, and her liveware interface instantly reconfigured itself to a higher-resolution, more sensorily-based mode.

Her icons floated around her in the middle distance. She pivoted until she located the dodecahedral commandball from the signalling waldo, gestured to bring it closer, and when it was in range, reached out to touch it; instantly, its data exploded into assorted complex shapes that moved to the periphery of her vision. A faintly-visible model of the waldo fitted itself to her, and she-waldo became surrounded by the cold, deep, false-color sea. Her arms had become a rotary blade and a sampling fixture, her fingertips the key sampling and communications controls, and her feet the steering and speed controls. She was Manda-*Septimus*.

First she noted that both of her-*Septimus*'s thermocouples were reading higher than normal this time, not just one.

Not much higher. Nothing to call the council about, but there was one other thing: the current's tug felt just a tad stronger than usual against her-*Septimus*'s skin. It was nothing her engines couldn't easily handle, but the two of these factors together *could* mean that undersea volcanic activity somewhere in the vicinity was creating convective cells of warmer water within the trench. Her heart started beating a little faster.

Easy, Manda; don't set yourself up for disappointment. Confirm it. Her-*Septimus*'s rotors hummed, keeping her-it in place, as she disengaged from the view of the ocean floor and brought up the marine-waldo's assorted datashapes.

The data she brought up was several hours old. Her marine-waldos were hundreds of kilometers away—or more—beneath a kilometer and a half of ice and many kilometers of water. The reason they'd done little to explore beneath the ice layer was simple: all their vehicles and robotic devices could only be operated by either radio or by instantaneous omnilink. Since the omni field generator had left with the crèche-born and radio signals didn't penetrate ice or water, they hadn't had many alternatives—until Manda had come up with one.

Radio didn't penetrate water or ice, but sound did; quite well, in fact. So Manda had created a sonar interface. Her commands were processed by the colony computers and broadcast via radio to an exploratory drill site near the colony's petroleum refinery, which squatted in a valley three hundred kilometers east of Amaterasu, near the mouth of Maia: the largest glacier on Arcas, the larger of Brimstone's two major continents. From there, the signal was piped down an abandoned offshore drill hole and transmitted to her waldos via a series of phased-array sonar transponders. It was a crude link, compared to some of the elaborate computational setups she had used with other explorer waldos in the past, but it worked.

Its main disadvantage was that sonar was not an information-dense medium. Even a phased-array setup—and even with the signal-boosting buoys she had planted here and there—didn't allow for a lot of information to be transmitted at once, since the frequencies she had to use were low ones. The link between Manda and her marine-waldos was a mere trickle of information across a very large expanse, and the inevitable errors and interruptions in transmission slowed things down even more. When she issued a command—to sample salinity, for instance, or descend or turn—her waldos might receive those commands several minutes—or even an hour or more—later. But her software compensated as best it could for this very long lag, and Manda's doggedness and ability to anticipate had served her well.

Manda called up some empty, transparent boxes, then grabbed the datashapes orbiting her-*Septimus* and dropped them into the boxes. Three-dimensional, brightly colored charts unfolded inside the boxes, positioning themselves around her.

The data appeared as a series of jittery, gritty surfaces—like satellite photos of mountains. Manda disengaged from the marine-waldo, and walked through and around each chart, studying the past several days' data from *Septimus*. Faint, complex strains of sound played, shifting in pitch and tone like a discordant whale-and-dolphin chorale as she moved through each chart—listening, running her fingers across the surfaces, seeking patterns. Nothing unusual struck her eyes, but there did seem to be an unexpected variation in tone at certain spots. Some harmonics that suggested a pattern.

She massaged the data, quite literally, moving variables and re-charting them and changing the axes around in a flurry of motion, then stepping back to eye the bright datascape around her. She ran her fingers over the results, listened to the harmonics that fluctuated as she moved, and made further adjustments.

And as she moved through one node, all the anomolous data aligned almost perfectly in position and time. The sounds came together in a tuneful chord.

Yes!

Over the past half hour, the waldo had wandered in and out of currents a few hundredths of a degree Celsius warmer, and about a twentieth to a tenth of a knot faster, than ambient. Sonar soundings of the vicinity revealed nothing new, merely a rocky bottom with some silting, and a fairly featureless cliff face to the west—but the chemical screens showed slightly elevated concentrations of manganese and particulates in the warmer, faster-moving eddies.

This was all very suggestive. Still, she couldn't bring it to the council until she had something more substantial to show them. They wouldn't care about some bumps that lined up. She needed more.

Manda called up a map of the region she was currently exploring, and checked the locations of all her marine-waldos. They were spread out over almost five thousand kilometers, at varying depths but most within thirty meters of the ocean floor. *Aculeus Septimus* had been exploring a deep sea trench extending roughly north-to-south, several hundred kilometers to the east of the coast. Its precise location at the moment was—*how interesting!* She increased the map's resolution. *Yes, it's just south of the equator.* According to Jim, the equator was a highly likely location for geothermal activity, due to rotational and tidal stresses on Brimstone's crust.

She noted that the bottom of the trench had been increasing in depth as *Septimus* proceeded southward; in this vicinity it went down to about four kilometers below sea level. *Septimus* had been exploring along the lower eastern edge of the trench, cruising near the bottom of its design depth of four kilometers below sea level. The drop seemed to continue to the south, at about two degrees per kilometer.

This posed a difficulty. If the source of the thermal activity lay much further south, and the trench continued to increase in depth, the heat source would be below the range of her marine-waldos' detectors. Meaning she'd either have to risk losing the waldos to implosion, or give up the search.

Give me time, she thought; *I'll come up with something.*

When she overlaid her search grid onto the global ocean-floor map she'd been building, she saw that *Septimus* had entered a large, virtually-unmapped section of sea floor that extended south from the equator.

She called the four closest waldos, *Aculei Duo, Tres, Quatuor,* and *Octo,* to assist *Septimus*. It would take a day for the nearest of them to arrive; in the meantime she needed to come up with a good search pattern. This was no time to get sloppy. And she should let someone know what was going on.

When she expanded her comm unit, Jim's message was still waiting for her. She opened it up. It was text:

To: Manda@Amatera
From: Jim@Petrol
Re: Booms
I'm guessing the boomer is at −9 to +7 degrees lat. and either 45 to 55 or 135 to 145 long. Updates as I have them.
PS − I =think=. Don't quote me.

And *Aculeus Septimus* was inside one of those ranges.

She smiled fiercely into her livemask. Success was finally—if not yet hers—at least flirting with her for a moment or two.

Manda put a call through to Jim. He materialized, grinning through his bushy, black, ice-encrusted beard. His eyebrows and nose hairs were also iced over, and his eyes invisible behind a pair of small dark goggles. His radiation tag, a green LED, glowed at his collar. He must be using a wristband video transceiver, since his forearm, huge and near; faded into nothing at the periphery of her vision on the left, and the outsized tip of his mitten appeared at the periphery on her right. She felt like a mote standing on his arm. In the background she could see pipes, distillation columns, and a portion of a petroleum storage tank.

"Manda!" he shouted over the wind. "What can I do for you?"

"I need your help refining my sea-mapping searches. Are you available to give me a hand?"

"Not right away. I'm out at the refinery. Won't be back for several days. I-we am finishing up some repairs out here, and then I'm going to be following up on those seismic abnormalities I told you about. Can it wait till I-we get back?"

Manda gnawed her lip. She hated the idea of sitting idle for even just a few days, this close to her goal. But without his help developing a good search based on the geology of the area, she'd be wasting her time. "Not if it can be avoided. Could you link in tonight, after sunset? Just for a little while?" She hesitated. "I think I'm onto something, Jim."

His eyebrows rose. "Oh?"

"Oh, yes."

"Hmmm." He nodded. "All right. I'll try. Depends on how repairs go."

As he was talking a deep rumble came up through her soles and rattled her chest cavity. It went on longer than usual, and rather than fading it built in strength, in a series of jerks that knocked her to her knees, jarred her bones and joints, shook the breath in her chest.

"What is it?" Jim asked.

"A quake," she gasped, scrambling for purchase on the thatching. "Hang on."

The jerking seemed to last forever, though it must have been less than a minute. As the quake began to finally subside, a muffled *crack* shook dust off the walls, followed by a loud *whooomph*.

Shit. It's big—and close. She scrambled to her feet, yanking her livesuit connectors loose, and struggled out of the livepack. Jim's image depixilated to a lower resolution. He must have heard something, or read her expression. "What? What's wrong?"

"Cave-in. Big one. I'll call you back." She cut the connection as she ran down the corridor, and called the colony's support systems syntellect. Its icon appeared before her.

"Where is the cave-in?" she asked.

"Specify cave-in."

"The cave-in that just happened, you idiot!"

After an unusually long pause, it gave her the coordinates. The collapse had happened in a bad place, logistically: in the main traffic corridor at the colony's lowest level, which led to two of the colony's three major agricultural caverns. The livestock area hadn't been affected, but the bamboo forest or Hydroponics might be. As well as the Fertility labs and the nurseries and Child Rearing.

Abruptly everything went dark but her liveface, which flickered as it switched over to battery and to an even lower-rez, 2D mode. The livesuit was now running from its own processor, no longer hooked up by radiolink to the Amaterasu net. Power and communications were down. All her icons had become crude, cartoonish shapes. The air grew thick with dust. Manda coughed.

Someone collided with her. Manda pulled her flashlight from her belt. Other flashlights flicked on. The array of bouncing, caroming lights added more confusion, not less. Work-waldos now unpiloted milled about, crashing into the humans, or froze, blocking passages. The crowd pushed her along a set of corridors and around turns till she wasn't sure where she was.

The Braille posts! Manda called up the software UrsaMeri had designed. A textured map bumped against her knuckles, and the software's syntellect asked her to touch her approximate location, if she knew it. Then she peeled her livehood down and waited while it used the speakers set into the hood to do some soundings based on her guess. When the software gave her hands a *ready* squeeze, she put the hood back on, and the syntellect asked her a couple more questions.

An invisible *virtu*-cord touched the back of her hands. She felt her way along the cord to a post. The post had Braille lettering on it with the software's best guess as to her location. It also had virtual cords attached to each end, and she followed the line she wanted, bumping into stray people and equipment that fell across the path of her guide rope, until she caught a glimpse of a large staircase ahead and recognized her surroundings.

She and others crowded down the spiral staircase into the catacombs on the level below. A crowd was gathering at an intersection ahead.

She rounded the corner there. In the bouncing, crossing flashlight beams she could make out several adults herding children this way. People were shouting. Everyone and everything was coated in dust. Two lines were forming—rubble-clearance brigades—while through the middle of the corridor other adults and teens were helping the survivors—most of them kids—out.

The children looked confused; several were crying; a couple were injured—she couldn't tell how badly; she could only catch glimpses in the poor lighting—and being carried out. She sneezed: the dust was even thicker here, and a solvent mist stung her nose and throat. Steam, rubble, and poor lighting obscured her view, but it looked as if the collapse had occurred a few meters ahead, just beyond the child-care area.

About ten meters beyond the children's suites the corridor branched and opened up onto the caverns containing the Hydroponics gardens and the bamboo. The Fertility Center was in a set of caves off of the bamboo fields. If any of the three areas had been badly damaged, the colony was in trouble.

She strapped her flashlight to her head with a strip of cloth torn from her shirt hem, and then joined the brigade. It was filthy, mindless work: take the boulders and dirt and buckets of rubble from the person ahead of her, hand them to the person behind. Some of the rocks started coming out stinking and slippery, and she realized it was blood. Or worse.

Manda grew dizzy and her vision blurred—from the shock, from the effort, the smell, and the damp heat slowly building up in the corridor from the steam-line leak. But she kept going, doggedly, passing rock after bucket after rock. Her arm muscles shrieked their agony. She hurled the fury that filled her into her brigade work, grab and pass, grab and pass, snarling at the others in the line—*hurry it up, you lazy shitheads. Move it.* She knew she shouldn't, but she couldn't help it. The rage was just there, boiling inside. It had to go somewhere.

A couple of mangled corpses came through the line, bundled in blood-stained sheets. Their faces were partially exposed and she knew them; everybody knew everybody. The first was a young JoeKali, who worked—had worked—in Child Rearing. The second was Teresa.

A tingly feeling spread through Manda. She took her sister's torso and looked at it, trying to make it be someone else. But the features of the dead woman in her arms refused to change. She could tell by the way her fingers sank in at the back of Teresa's head, even through the bundling, that Teresa's skull had been crushed.

Bile rose in Manda's throat. Teresa's body was so terribly battered that Manda was grateful for the bundling.

She hugged the body tight, spasmodically, trying to ignore the odd contortions and parts that weren't where they should be beneath the sheet. Then she looked at the face again, stroked the corpse's torn, bruised face. It was like looking in the mirror and seeing herself as a corpse—but at the same time it didn't even look like *Teresa*, much less a carbon copy of Manda.

"I'm sorry," she whispered, remembering their argument this

113

morning. She felt dizzy. The world receded to the end of a long tunnel. She looked around, confused, half-forgetting where she was.

The man directly behind her was looking at her with a pitying gaze.

"Take it! What are you staring at?" She forced the body into his arms. Then she tried to rub the brown, sticky stuff off her palms and face before the next load came down the line. She didn't know what the sticky stuff was. She couldn't breathe. Several drops struck her hands. A stream of tears was flowing down her face. She remembered with a fresh shock that the body had been Teresa's.

Where's Paul? Does he know? Oh, God. Oh my God.

She found herself sitting down. A woman was giving her oxygen from a portable unit. Somehow she'd been dragged out of the brigade without her noticing. The woman was a young RoxannaTomas. Manda took several deep breaths into the mask, then signalled *enough* and struggled to her feet. The other woman, she realized, was Jeannelle.

"You gonna be OK?" Jeannelle shouted over the din. Manda stared at her. She couldn't find the words or even the thoughts to reply, and only turned away, returning to her place in line.

Gradually, the rocks began to come out clean and hot and wet: steam-blasted. Communications came back online.

A numbness had settled over Manda. Her thoughts came more clearly. She remembered the extra waldos and spare parts sitting in the equipment hangar. She should check, see what kind of equipment she could throw together. The digging could go much faster. Lives could be saved.

"Who is the rescue coordinator?" she asked those coming out, repeating the question until someone finally answered. It was Arlene. She spotted her up ahead, just this side of the cave-in.

Manda left the brigade and pushed through the crowd till

she reached Arlene. Her older sister was directing people who had crawled into the makeshift tunnel with beams and small waldos to stabilize it. The steam leak had been fixed, or the line closed.

They looked at each other, and Manda saw Teresa in Arlene's face. As Arlene looked away, Manda lowered her own gaze, squelching the horror and nausea that tried to muscle its way up. She heard Arlene murmuring to Derek across her liveface—giving him the news. Manda could hardly bear it. *Teresa. Please no. Make this be a dream.*

"I can bring some machines in," she said.

"What?" Arlene squinted at her, distracted.

"I can slap some construction-waldos together to help with the digging."

Arlene frowned. "We're too cramped already. Your waldos are too big for this work, until we get into the caverns." She paused, thinking. "But we'll need the heavy equipment soon enough. Go see what you can come up with. Get help from the machining crews."

Manda turned to go, but someone up ahead, someone inside the hole, shouted, "We're through! We're into the caverns!"

Word traveled back along the line; everything grew hushed. Manda strained to get a glimpse; it was impossible to see what was going on in there, with the dust and dancing lights and workers obscuring the view.

The word came through: "The bamboo is intact!"

A murmur of relief rippled around them.

"What about the babies?" someone shouted, and someone else said, "What about Hydroponics?"

Arlene put in a call. Twin GeorgJeans appeared in front of them, crouching, out of breath, broadcasting on a public channel. Manda and several other people gathered around. Dust motes drifted around the GeorgJeans. They spoke loudly to be heard over the digging and shouting going on around her. "Fertility Center is cut off by rubble but we're talking to them through the vents." "There are no adult casualties yet." "We're confident we can get them out."

"The fetuses?"

Both shook their heads. "The main power unit was smashed and a lot of the fetal-support equipment has been damaged as well." "Most of the vats are intact, but they have no working life support, and it's getting cold in there without the heaters." "The workers are trying to save the ones closer to term—" "—but it looks like we're going to lose most of them."

Arlene wiped a weary hand across her brow, leaving a smudge. Manda remembered her undecanted siblings, her resentment of them. A sharp pain lanced her through the midsection, briefly piercing the numbness.

Please, she thought. *Please.*

Arlene asked, "What about the gardens?"

The GeorgJeans grimaced. "We've got a lot of damage in Hydroponics." "But the power plant took a hit too. We've got power out everywhere—" "—and we're not in communication with any survivors." "We won't know exactly how much damage there is for a while."

Arlene sighed and exchanged a grim look with Manda.

"OK," she told the GeorgJeans, "the Fertility Center becomes our top priority. Give me regular reports. Manda," she said, as GeorgJeans' images dissolved, "once we get the Fertility labs cleared out we'll need your waldos for the Hydroponics cavern."

"On my way." Manda started to go, then looked back. "Was it the terraforming drilling? Is that what triggered it?"

Arlene stared at her. They both knew. There was no way to be sure. But probably.

Rage flooded Manda: rage at Arlene, at Derek—at all her clone. *If not for your fucking IceFlame, Teresa would still be alive.* Manda stood staring at her eldest sister, shaking with the need to scream at her. To accuse. To denounce. Only the anguish twisting Arlene's face stopped her. Finally Manda turned, with a smothered cry, and hurled herself down the corridor toward the lifts to the machine shops.

The team managed to rescue all the Fertility personnel, and those of their fetal charges still hanging onto life, within a few hours. Manda didn't ask about the CarliPablo babies right then. She couldn't handle losing more siblings yet.

Instead, she and the rest of the team got started clearing away rubble, building makeshift tunnels and valleys through the great mounds of debris that had dropped onto the gardens in the Hydroponics cavern. Power and the local network were brought back up after a while, which made work easier. Still it was tedious and gruesome work—there were too few living and too many dead. The fact that she was only present in proxy, piloting a team of three construction-waldos, didn't make it any less dreadful. Still, she pushed herself—and the others—very hard.

As long as she stayed busy, she didn't have to think. Didn't have to remember.

She and two other waldo pilots did the heaviest work with their six big, lumbering machines, aided by almost three dozen workers present *in corpus*.

Very early on the second day the council appointed KaliMarshall to replace Arlene as leader of the rescue effort, who joined Derek and the other council-vat-siblings in emergency planning measures. The KaliMarshall fourclone spread out, taking charge of rescue and cleanup. Manda's crew leader was Abraham KaliMarshall, a large, bluff man two or three seasons older than Manda.

Abraham and his vat-twin Robert had been among her worst

tormentors, growing up. Sneaky, vicious, backbiting bullies. The rest of their clone was no better.

But this was no time for old grudges. So she worked with him. And her focused intensity caused the other workers to turn to her for guidance and ideas at least as often as to KaliMarshall. When they grew discouraged or talked of quitting, she harangued them, reminded them that there could still be survivors—asked how they'd like to be trapped in the rubble, knowing their fate depended only on the perseverence of the rescue team? For once, no one argued with her or told her she was being rude.

The LuisMichael triplets soon returned from the refinery and pitched in, using their sounding equipment and Jim's seismology expertise to listen for sounds coming from any survivors. With the LuisMichaels' help they located ten people trapped alive under the rubble. But afterward, more than eighteen hours passed and several tons of rubble were cleared with no other survivors found, only scattered remains.

Finally they uncovered a cache of dismembered bodies. They shipped as many of the remains as they could to the genetics people, who were getting the Fertility labs cleaned up, and they also did swabs everywhere they saw a speck of blood or other apparent animal matter. Genetics reported back early on day two that they'd identified four different DNA signatures. Since two of the DNA sets were for two different pairs of clone-twins on the missing persons list, this meant that between four and six more people were accounted for. Probably six, since both sets of twins were probably working together when the cave-in had struck.

In which case, all but three people were now accounted for: the UrsaMeri threeclone, Helen, Jessica, and Rachel. The heart—and brain—of the Hydroponics effort.

Manda-Crane looked out across the wreckage of the gardens, mottled by fragmented beams of light from the searchers' lamps.

Shattered, bone-colored remains of stalagmites and chunks of shale-like rock—a stifling, multi-ton blanket—lay over the shattered trays and tubes and wilted vegetable matter. She had to admit, if only to herself, that there were probably no more survivors. UrsaMeri was dead, too.

Manda sighed, and wheeled Mole and Crane over to join Scaffold, whose rear right tire had gotten stuck in a hole. The workers building a permanent embankment there needed the scaffolding waldo out of the way to finish their task, and her efforts to unstick it under its own power had failed. She-Crane lumbered up, latched onto her-Scaffold with her-its hook, and lifted her-Scaffold up and out of the way. The workers below waved weary thanks as she-Crane set her-Scaffold down. Meanwhile, she-Mole caught a glimpse of the hole she-Scaffold had been stuck in. It was a floor drain whose grating had buckled under the bulky waldo's weight.

A floor drain? A floor drain. Back in her projection pod, Manda frowned, and detached from her livepack leads for a moment. Her liveface once again diminished in scope to a simpler display. She stretched with an enormous yawn and took a long drink of water from her bottle, then sat down on the floor and did some stretches to invigorate herself.

She was so tired it was hard to think, but there was something important about this. The drains.

A floor drain, she realized suddenly, meant that there were conduits or trenches under the floor. Tunnels, perhaps big enough for a human to crawl into and avoid being crushed, if that person were a quick thinker. Which UrsaMeri was.

KaliMarshall—Abraham's vat-twin Robert, she guessed—showed up in her workstation as she was calling up schematics for the lines under the gardens. His eyes were sunken, dark with fatigue, and his face was dirty and gaunt. Manda stood, and stiffened when she read his expression. She knew why he was here.

"Manda . . ." He sighed at the look on her face, and started again. "It's time to give it up. We've done all we can."

"I have an idea," she said. "I think I know where UrsaMeri might be."

He groaned. "Not another one."

"Listen to me—there's a drain—"

KaliMarshall talked over her. "Look, we've chased down two of your possibilities already and hauled tons of junk for nothing. It's been too long. They're all dead. It's time to quit."

No one cared about UrsaMeri. They'd accounted for everyone else. They were giving up because UrsaMeri was old and blind.

She trembled with rage. "*You* give up, then. UrsaMeri is still unaccounted for. I'm not stopping till we find it—alive or dead."

"You are fucking *impossible!*" he exploded. "Abraham's right about you."

"And you're a coward," she said. "Afraid to finish the job you-you started. Why the council would put your clone in charge I have no idea."

He went pale and his lips thinned. "I-we am pulling the crew. You do whatever the hell, you want. And the council will hear about this."

"Fine. Give them my love."

He gave her the fist of contempt and stalked out. Manda slumped against the wall and laid her forehead on her arm, feeling quivery and empty.

What am I trying to prove? she thought. She was exhausted too, and sick at heart.

This one last time, she thought. *I'll check this one last thing.* She dragged herself back to her feet and jacked into her live-pack, and the full-sensory interface bloomed around her. When she faced into Mole, KaliMarshall, all three others of it, was overseeing the equipment cleanup. Most of the workers were already leaving. The other three big machines were gone.

A hard pain squeezed her chest. "Stop! We haven't checked the drains!"

No one listened.

"Go, then!" she yelled. "Give up when there may still be people alive in there! Cowards! Go ahead and go."

She split her liveface into three and faced into Scaffold and Crane as well as Mole. Turning her-waldos' backs on the departing workers, she switched on her headlights and sent the three of them lumbering clumsily and faithfully back into the rubble mounds.

To her surprise, one of the LuisMichaels followed her. It was Jim! It must be. Amy and Brian hesitated for only an instant before following as well.

Once they reached the end of the tunnel, Manda-Mole called them over. The triplets crouched around Manda's waldo in a pool of light cast by Manda-Scaffold from overhead.

Manda-Mole wiped the dust and debris from Crane's belly screen and Manda threw a schematic up of the Hydroponics cavern, pre-collapse. Then she superimposed a rough sketch of the rubble; it blanketed the schematic like a foul mirage. The mirage had red, angular veins running through it, which she-Mole traced with her-its claw hand.

"We've dug tunnels and set up listening equipment here, here, and here," she-Mole said. "But this large section over here, near the offices where the worst of the collapse was, is still mostly unexplored. And it's also most likely to be where UrsaMeri was."

LuisMichael frowned at the schematic. It shook its heads.

"The offices abut the bamboo caverns right here, see?" Jim told her. "I've listened on the other side of the wall. I didn't detect any sound, not even breathing." "And our seismic tests of that area made it clear that there are no air pockets of any size in that vicinity," Brian pointed out.

"Not in the offices, no. But see this subterranean line right here? It's a floor drain and see?—there's grating on the floor just outside the office. The quake lasted for several seconds before the cave-in occurred. It's possible they had time to make it to the drain."

"In which case they'd have run out of air by now," Amy said.

"Not necessarily. Not if they belly-crawled through to here." She pointed.

"The catchment sump?" Amy asked, dubious. "That's a good twenty-meter crawl, with two grated openings between the office and the sump," Jim pointed out. Brian said, "The drain would be blocked by debris."

"I don't think so," Manda replied. "At least, there's a possibility it wasn't. A lot of the rubble has been larger than the grating gaps. And they could dig some, if they had to."

Amy said, "They're blind!"

"They're resourceful," Jim replied, and Brian and Amy eyed him, seeming surprised.

Jim gestured for Manda to continue.

"Look." Manda changed the overlay to a schematic of the level just beneath the floor. "All these utility pipes run on top of the sump. They're undamaged and some are still operating. Adding up to lots of vibrations from fluid flow and transmission of engine noises. They would mask any sound the survivors might make, if they were down there."

Brian and Amy shook their heads, but Jim nodded, slowly, after a moment. "It's worth a try. Where are we, in relation to the sump?"

Manda-Mole pointed straight down between its tractor treads. "Almost directly above it, according to my calculations."

The threeclone considered. Manda held her breath.

Brian jumped up. "We'll get the utilities shut off—" "—and bring plumbing equipment back with us," Amy finished. They ran off, while Jim started setting up his sounding and seismic detectors.

Let this work, Manda thought. *If it doesn't, I'm out of ideas.*

It didn't take long for Manda-Mole to tear through the thatch floor and the dust and rock layers, to reveal the utility pipes that overlaid the drainage conduit about a meter and a half below the floor.

"There it is," she-Mole said. In the dimness, numerous utility pipes ran on top of the concrete floor drain, both parallel and crosswise to the drain. She saw no indication that the floor drain discharged into a sump within the confines of the large hole they'd dug. "We're not as close to the sump as I thought."

"That's OK. If they're down there, anywhere in the vicinity, with the utilities turned off I should be able to hear them." Jim scrambled down into the hole, aided by Brian, while Amy loaded the seismic and other sounding equipment onto a pallet.

Back in her workstation, Manda disconnected from her livepack and then made her way to the caverns. She could be more use *in corpus* for the finer-scale work, and if more heavy work was necessary, her lower-rez interface was adequate for controlling her waldos on-site.

She wanted to be there in person, when—if—*when* survivors were found.

By the time she arrived, Jim had climbed down among the pipes and was brushing away soil. Amy and Brian were lowering equipment down on a rope.

"I'll need more light," he said. Manda-Scaffold shuffled over to shine lights inside the hole. A rumbling started. Terror knotted in Manda's throat. She looked up at the cave ceiling with her own eyes and with Scaffold's—then around at the swinging lights, at the choking clouds of fine dust that filled the air with the smells of dirt and ruined vegetation. Small rocks pelted the ground here and there, with a sound like hail. LuisMichael's gazes met hers, its own six eyes wide with fear.

But these were just the usual small-scale tremors, and died away in seconds. Amy and Brian continued lowering the equipment. Manda-Scaffold adjusted the lighting at Jim's direction. Then they waited, while Jim placed leads among the pipes.

"Turn on the detector," he said finally. Amy squatted next to the sound detector and turned it on. Lines appeared on the screen. "I want everyone to be very still." The lines on the screen peaked and bounced in response to his words. "No talking, no shuffling, breathe as quietly as possible."

They fell quiet, and the squiggles died down to small, occasional wiggles. Manda resisted scratching a sudden, fierce itch on her leg. Her heart was beating harder than usual, a response to the tremors as well as the thought of finding UrsaMeri. The noise was loud enough that Manda half-expected the detector to pick it up.

"Nothing unusual," Amy said after a few moments. "You want to come check it out?"

"No. You know what to screen for. I'm going to move the leads. Any idea which way the sump might lie from here?" he asked Manda. She checked her maps once more, and leaned over the edge of the hole to check the pipes. It was too hard to tell precisely where they were, in the midst of such ruin, but the sump *should* be almost directly below. Somehow, her calculations were off.

She chewed her lip, then pointed. "Let's try that way."

Again Jim set the leads, this time at the edge of the hole where she'd pointed, and again asked for silence. After a moment, Amy exclaimed, "I think we have something!"

Jim climbed up out of the hole and hurried over. All four crowded around the readout screen.

"See here?" Amy whispered, pointing at one set of squiggles. "And here."

"I see. Shh." Jim studied the lines, wearing a deep frown. "Well, it's something. Hard to say what. It could just be aftershocks. Manda, do you think you could clear away that section of flooring there?"

Things proceeded like this for some time, with Manda digging and scraping, and the other three moving the sound equipment and listening, with equivocal results. They couldn't seem to locate the sump. They were all so exhausted that the mere act of lifting an arm or speaking had become too great a chore. The hint of sound Jim had detected never panned out into anything. They were all growing discouraged. Manda suggested they take a short break, and volunteered to bring back food and water for everyone.

The mess was full of people, but no one said much. She tossed two decachips onto the counter next to the cashier syntellect. The syntellect told her, "The colony is on emergency rations. No one may have more than six chips' worth of dinner."

So rationing had started already. She shouldn't be surprised. "I'm collecting for LuisMichael, also."

"How many people total?"

"Four."

After a brief pause, the syntellect approved the additional purchases. Manda looked at the food on the tray. *Going to be a lot of hungry people around here.* She took the water bottles, fruit, and crispy-duck-and-bamboo-shoot *mana*-rolls the robotic arms had assembled and headed back to the dig.

Her companions took the food and ate greedily. It was all gone too quickly. After a few moments of silence, Brian took a slug of water and then said, "I-we've been mulling it over, Manda." "It's almost fifty hours since the cave-in." Jim. "We can't locate the sump, and even if they made it there, they've probably run out of oxygen or died of exposure by now." Amy.

All three LuisMichaels looked so tired. And her own limbs had no strength left.

It was all too much. Too much for such a small group to do alone. "The others should be here helping," she said, and slumped over her knees. "It's a big sump. There could still be some air left."

LuisMichael stood and brushed itselves off. Jim said, "Come on, Manda. Time to call it quits."

The pause lengthened as she looked up at the threeclone, its identical three faces staring back.

Time to quit, Manda. You know they're right. She didn't have the strength to deny it, anymore. She really had given it everything she had. With a sigh, finally, she opened her mouth to say so.

Then closed it.

Then shook her head.

"I can't quit. Not till I find the sump."

The others exchanged glances filled with depths she couldn't read. When Manda next looked up, Jim was still there, his face weary and eyes shadowed. The other two had gone.

"Till we find the sump," he said. "And that's it."

She stared, opened her mouth. Her heart gave a little lurch. It would be Manda Amy and Brian would blame for this little rebellion of his, this separation. Not him. But she couldn't bring herself to protest. She needed him here.

"Thanks," she said hoarsely, and blinked away tears.

They did extensive sonar soundings along all sides of the trench they'd dug, and Jim finally reported that there *might* be an air pocket not beneath *this* floor drain, but beneath the one on what would be two aisles over. *"May,"* he emphasized. "I could just be picking up empty piping or a crack that formed in the floor and didn't get filled in."

This meant excavating several cubic meters of rubble before they even got to the floor. Manda eyed the mounds she must move—mounds of dirt even higher now than they had been before she'd started—and a feeling of futility rose in her chest. The fucking sump could be anywhere.

But if it were one of her own siblings, she'd work till she collapsed. Would she do less for UrsaMeri?

"This will take a while," she told Jim. "Why don't you get some rest, and I'll call you when I reach the pipes." He gladly took her up on the offer.

She first made another careful study of the maps. Then she started digging.

Those next four hours she worked alone in the enormous cavern were the longest of her life. She felt more tired than she ever remembered being—it took all she had to remain awake, huddled in the rubble surrounded by shattered Hydroponics equipment, in a dusty, fragmented pool of light, while Mole and Crane and Scaffold's grinding, hammering, clanking chorus echoed against the dark upper reaches of the cavern, and returned to her in wobbly, staccato mimicry of itself, as little by little she-they moved the rubble and dirt aside.

She found a certain peaceful rhythm to the task. This wasn't necessarily a good thing: several times she dozed off and reawakened to find her waldos standing lifeless nearby. Manda got up and paced as she worked, shaking her head, slapping her cheeks—willing herself to stay awake as she danced her waldo-control dance, and her three massive machines clanked and rumbled and bucked, first one, then two in concert, then the third. And finally she reached the floor, one aisle over.

She-Mole drilled through the thatch and rock and dirt, and she-Crane lifted the chunks of debris away, and now she was down to the piping. She was tired enough that she misjudged the depth and marred the pipes, rather than just skimming dirt from them. *Fuck it*, she thought. *It's a small price to pay.* The debris she had moved to get there made a dark mountain beyond Scaffold's stick legs. She called Jim.

"I'm ready," she said. He rubbed his eyes and sat up, blinking blearily, in his quarters.

"Be right there." His words were slurred by fatigue.

Jim came, and so did Amy and Brian, and as they were setting up, some of the other rescue workers who'd left earlier trickled in. And Derek and Arlene. Word had apparently gotten around.

"LuisMichael told us about your idea," Derek said, at Manda's curious glance, and Arlene said, "It's worth a try."

Jim climbed into the hole and squatted on the piping. Beneath his feet, the curved, white sump lay. He took out a wrench, reached down between the pipes, and tapped on the plastic. It thumped hollowly. Everyone waited. Nothing. After a long pause he tapped again. And there was an answering thump. And more thumps. And muffled voices.

Cries of excitement went up. Several people jumped into the hole and began trying to pry the pipes out of the way, while others started hammering and banging shovels on the floor drain. Manda whistled for attention, and she-Crane lumbered up.

"This will be quicker," she said. "Everyone out of the hole."

Jim shouted, as much for the sump's occupants as the workers, "Stand clear!"

Manda-Crane grabbed the pipes and floor drain with her-its claws and tore a two-meter segment of conduit away, with torn pipe segments trailing streams of fluid. When she-Scaffold rolled over to the hole and shone her-its lights back into it, the sump had an opening in its top, which had formerly been connected to the concrete floor drain. Manda left Crane there and jumped down into the hole with the LuisMichael triplets. She and Jim climbed down among the severed utility pipes and shone their flashlights into the sump, and their beams glinted off the up-turned faces of three very dirty, shivering people: two of the UrsaMeri sisters, and a JennaByron—one of the clone-siblings presumed dead.

Manda stumbled over to Arlene and Derek, while others moved in to help the survivors out. She couldn't bring herself look over at them as they were ushered past and laid onto stretchers. None were likely to thank her for this rescue—they were probably all three wishing they were dead.

Derek opened his arms and she walked into them; they gave each other a long, wordless hug, and Arlene wrapped her arms around both of them. Finally Manda pulled back.

It was time to ask. "The twins?"

Both his siblings drew a breath. "We lost the girl. The boy is hanging on. They have him in intensive care. It . . ." His voice broke. Arlene finished in flat tones, "It doesn't look so good."

Manda pressed herself against them again, and hung on tight. She felt as if the world were coming to an end. Perhaps it was.

Part II
The Other

Early hominids were social creatures, and like other higher mammals their relationships were *radial* in nature: that is, they perceived themselves as being at the center of their universe, connected with others in their social network in a sort of spoked wheel, with all others at the far end of each spoke.

In a radial relationship, the *I* is implicit: "if a strange male beats his chest, [I] feel intimidated"—"if this baby cries, [I] pick it up and suckle it." It wasn't necessary to know who the *I* in the equation was; all one needed to do was act on instructions programmed in by prior experience and genes. The *I* in early hominids' mental behavioral models was, in other words, a *constant*, hardwired into the system. To maintain radial relationships, they had no need for anything more complicated. The self remained unrecognized.

But at some point, hominids who had some inking of *circumferential* (i.e., third-party) relationships became better able to understand the motives underlying others' actions—*even when they themselves were not involved*—and thus better able to predict behavior. These individuals who could predict social outcomes were more successful at recruiting assistance and avoiding trouble, and over time this emergent ability became more pronounced and generalized.

Consciousness, then, is inextricably tied to relationship. *Without others, there can be no self.*

—From The Variable I *by Charles Erasmus (copyright 2020): United Nations Interstellar Ship* Exodus *archives, logged 08/20/2067.*

anda went to bed after the town meeting. She was more tired than she had ever been, but couldn't sleep. She couldn't stop thinking about Teresa, UrsaMeri, and the little CarliPablo girl baby who had died. And the little boy still clinging to life.

She thought about how quickly and irrevocably life could take a sudden turn, and be nothing like you had ever thought it would be. She felt as if the ground had dissolved beneath her feet and she was falling into a huge, black chasm.

Finally, after shivering beneath her thermal layers for hours, staring into a darkness punctuated here and there by tiny flecks of fungal luminescence, she dozed off. When she awakened— from a nightmare about dismemberment and explosions and fire, and searching for something (she couldn't remember what) amid enormous, putrescent mounds of shit—the lighting was a rosy mid-morning glow, and the clock above the door told her she'd slept for fourteen hours. She felt like shit.

After washing up, relieving her bladder, donning her livesuit, and putting on some clean clothes, she ate a meal, then paid a visit to the Medical Center. They showed her where her prematurely decanted clone-brother was. She gazed at him through the glass window. He lay alone in his incubator, so passive under the warming lights, so still: eyes closed, tubes in his nose and hair-thin needles in his ankles, his breathing fitful.

How could he possibly survive? He was too small, too spindly. Too unformed.

She placed both hands on the glass. *I've been where you are now and I know you can make it.*

"Hang on," she whispered. "Hang on."

He moved then, slightly, almost as if he had heard her. She chose to believe he had. She leaned her head against the glass and cried some more—then quickly dashed tears away, when some medical staffers walked past. She went back to her quarters and slept again, then woke and ate, went for a walk in the bamboo, went to the stables and fed grass and mosses to some of the animals, cleaned stables for a while, then went back to her cubby and slept again.

The next morning she felt more rested—though groggy from so much sleep in so short a time; she'd slept much of the prior thirty-four-hour day away. But still the world was blanketed in invisible layers of batting.

She had a message from Arlene, but found herself reluctant to listen to it. She didn't want to face any of her siblings right now. Instead she got a report from the news syntellect.

"Funeral services for those killed in the cave-in," it reported, "are planned for twenty-six-thirty tonight." That was a half hour after the day's second-watch workshift ended. "Cleanup and rebuilding of the damaged areas are now the colony's top priority. All other tasks, except those designated as crucial by the governing council, are suspended until further notice. Colony members are to report to Hydroponics for assignments. To apply for an exemption, facemail the council. A Town Meeting is scheduled for ten-thirty." Right at the end of the first-watch workshift. "All colony members are urged to attend." And so on.

She listened with only half her attention as she dressed. The colony risked starvation if they couldn't rebuild the gardens quickly—they couldn't live on bamboo alone, and with their vat-gestating capabilities now greatly diminished, they couldn't afford to eat all their herd animals, or they'd be left with nothing.

And with one UrsaMeri down, the other two would be hindered, at the very least. If they could be persuaded to live, at all.

Under normal circumstances she would be irritated that her ocean-thermal-vent search was now, summarily and indefinitely, put on hold. But not now. She reported to Hydroponics, where at least thirty people were already digging in the mounds and sorting out pieces of equipment.

She noted from the duty roster that KaliMarshall was in charge. *Shit.* It stood nearby, giving assignments to small groups of workers. She went up to one of them.

"Reporting for assignment," she told him.

"No, you're not," he said. "Get lost." His three clone-brothers gathered around.

She gaped. "What?"

"Go away," one of them said. "You're not on the recovery crew."

For a moment she could think of nothing to say.

"Why not?" she asked finally.

"Because you're a pain in the ass, Manda," another one said. "Nobody likes working with you. You're disruptive, insulting, and insubordinate, and I-we refuse to have you on my-our team."

The fourclone turned its backs on her to talk to some of the other workers, several of whom were eyeing her, a few with open smiles. She looked from one to the other KaliMarshall, thinking about all the manifold cruelties Abraham had heaped on her when they were young, and anger surfaced through the numbness. She grabbed Abraham. "How dare you? I saved—"

He shoved her away. "Yeah, yeah, you saved part of UrsaMeri, and you're the hero of the day. Hooray for you. Now get out of my-our work area."

Ignoring the privacy warning above the door, Manda burst into the governing council's meeting chamber. All eight of those present gawked at her: Jack and Amadeo PabloJeb, Lawrence and Donald JennaMara, Anne RoxannaLuis, Victoria and Shannon PatriciaJoe, and Derek.

"What's the meaning of this?" PabloJeb demanded. "We're in session; didn't you see the privacy notice?"

"Who authorized my removal from the Hydroponics recovery team?" she countered.

"You are *way* out of line," RoxannaLuis said, and both PatriciaJoe twins spoke at the same time: "How dare you?" "Who do you think you are?"

"I think I'm the person who rescued the only clone who can keep this colony from starving, over the objections of the clone now in charge of cleanup. And I want to know why I've been booted off the recovery team."

A moment of silence sank down. The councilmembers looked at each other: weighing the state of their coup, deciding how they might respond, and what it might mean to the others. Everyone ended up looking at Derek—who was watching Manda, his face affectless.

Why aren't you sticking up for me? she demanded silently. His expression didn't soften. He didn't like the fact that she'd done this. Well, screw him, then. She deserved answers.

Jack spoke. "Manda CarliPablo, we have not forgotten that we owe you a debt of gratitude for saving two of UrsaMeri, but that doesn't give you the right to ride roughshod over others. We received numerous complaints about your behavior during the rescue effort and you are only making matters worse by bursting in here."

Derek lifted a hand, silencing Manda before she could retort. "Let me handle this," he told the rest, and took Manda out into the corridor.

She folded her arms. "Well?"

"Have you lost your mind?" he asked. "What the hell do you think you were doing, bursting in on us like that? Why didn't you come to me or Arlene privately?"

Manda glowered at Derek, but finally sighed. "I probably shouldn't have. I was angry. But dammit, Derek—UrsaMeri is all that stands between us and starvation! If it weren't for me we wouldn't have a chance. And then, to put that . . . that *moron* KaliMarshall in charge—it was too much! The idea that *it* could have *me* pulled from the recovery effort after it did practically nothing to help, and after all my hard work—" She growled in frustration.

"Look—Manda—" Derek rubbed at his brow with a sigh. "You know you don't like working as part of a team. Why not view this as an opportunity to continue your own work? Do you honestly want to spend the next three months doing grunt work while your own projects languish? Let it go."

Manda fell silent. *You're as bad as the rest of them.* But the look in Derek's eyes stopped her from saying it.

"I've already demonstrated that I can contribute a lot to the effort," she pointed out. "How can they choose to put a bunch of jerks like KaliMarshall ahead of the colony's well-being?"

"I'm not so sure they are."

"What is that supposed to mean?"

His gaze grew vacant for a moment, and then he nodded, folding his arms. "OK. Arlene says to tell you that you get on the wrong side of everybody, Manda. You're difficult to work with. We get tired of dealing with all the complaints."

"So you'd rather lose coup by letting them keep me off—"

"Manda, *I'm* the one who recommended keeping you off cleanup."

She stared at him, stunned. Then she started to turn away. Derek laid a hand on her shoulder. "Let it go, Manda. We're telling you. Let it go."

Manda threw off his touch. "If you want me off the cleanup effort, then fine. I'll do my own work. But don't patronize me."

"And I think you should also apologize to the council for intruding." He jerked a thumb toward the closed door.

"Don't push your luck." She stalked off.

Really, she thought, as she approached her workstation, she *should* be thankful that she could continue her own work, rather than having to do months' worth of grunt work. But somehow it mattered.

Was it merely pride, that made her feel so insulted by their act of exclusion? Or was it the pain they inflicted by demonstrating just how meaningless her contribution was: that they didn't want her helping, even when the colony's very future was at stake?

A LuisMichael was in her work room when she got there. He had on his own livepack, a twin to hers, which he must have hooked up to the overhead leads himself. When she entered the room he was moving his hands over displays she couldn't see and walking around, talking to himself. Then he saw Manda. His eyes glinted through the faint shadow of his livemask goggles, and his teeth flashed white in his beard.

"You weren't kidding you were onto something," he said. "I've been looking at your earlier data and, wow!"

"Jim?" she asked even though she knew it was. It had to be, even though his hair was down, not giving her any clues.

He nodded.

"What are you doing here?" What are you doing here alone, she meant; without his siblings. But he must be teleconnected to them.

He either misunderstood her, or chose to misinterpret her question. "The refinery's operation is considered crucial so we petrol clones have been given an exemption. But the team just finished a major maintenance and equipment overhaul and I-we don't have to run any more checks till late tomorrow. I-we thought I-we'd stay in town for an extra watch. And that being the case . . . I wanted a chance to check out your data. As promised."

She opened her mouth, closed it. "I—I don't know what to say."

"How about, 'say, thanks a lot!' "

She assayed a smile, albeit a fleeting one. " 'Say, thanks a lot.' " She said it with the same inflection he'd used, and he barked a laugh.

Manda struggled into her livepack and hooked up while he murmured a few comments to his siblings across the facelink.

The data she'd studied three days earlier, just before the cave-in, appeared all around the interior boundaries of the projection sphere.

"Yeah, I see it, Amy. Hold on.—Now, look here," Jim said to Manda, and snapped the oceanic data displays closed like fans, opening up her maps of the area. He ran his finger along the bottom of the trench *Aculeus Septimus* was exploring. "I've taken the liberty of running some projections of possible areas of volcanic activity in the unexplored sea floor, to the south and west of your waldo. I don't have any triangulating data from the other marine-waldos—I didn't know how to operate your waldos and didn't want to screw up your work—but look at this. I drew these from your earlier data."

He pointed at some shadowy boundaries that hadn't been there the other day. Two arcs pulsed a dull green color.

"What are those?" she asked.

"Areas of possible activity. I figure that your *Aculeus Septimus* is within a hundred kilometers of major volcanism"—he pointed at one of the pulsing arcs—"or within ten kilometers of lower activity"—he pointed at the other. The two arcs blended together in a green pie wedge with a bite taken out of the point: the point at which *Aculeus Septimus* now sat.

She eyed the map in mild dismay. The mapped area covered

a lot of surface. It would take several weeks—maybe longer—to pinpoint the area of highest activity.

She said, slowly, "*Aculeus Duo* and *Aculeus Quatuor* should have reached the vicinity two days ago. In the absence of any instructions from me they would have simply begun their standard search patterns at the new coordinates. So we may have a good seventy to eighty hours' worth of triangulating data by now. . . ."

"Let's have a look!" Jim said cheerfully. At his tone, Manda gave him a glance, and a sardonic shake of her head.

"What?"

"Nothing." After a pause she said, "I fought hard to have my own project, my own private work space, and I—"

"I'm in the way?" He looked chagrined. "I do apologize for making free with your equipment—"

"No, no." She flicked his objections away. "That's not it. I invited you to help me. I just can't figure out why you don't get on my nerves—" Then she broke off.

"—like everyone else does?" he finished.

Manda gave him a sharp look, but his expression held no ridicule, merely amiable amusement. "I guess."

Jim grinned at her. "Well, if it's any consolation, Manda, you don't get on my nerves much, either."

"Thanks," she said gruffly. "I think."

He laughed loud and hard. A smile rose up onto her face again. She pulled up her waldo controls. The balls sprang up and hovered, translucent, expectant: awaiting her input.

"Let's see what you guys have been up to," she said, flicking *Septimus*, *Duo*, *Quatuor*, *Quinque*, and *Octo* open.

They spent the next several hours downloading and reviewing the mounds of data the *Aculeus* waldos had collected—through lunch, with only brief breaks for toilet and food. It felt good to lose herself in her work. But of her disappointment, no further anomalies emerged.

At the end of that watch, muscles aching, eyes blurring from staring at charts and numbers, they agreed to meet back here at the beginning of second watch to finish the data distillation. Out in the corridor, Jim clapped her on the back.

"Don't lose your momentum, Manda," he said. "You're on the right track."

"I hope you're right." She knew she should be excited. But it was hard to generate any enthusiasm. "Thanks for the help. And the vote of confidence."

As he turned to go, murmuring through his livelink to his siblings, she noticed that it was almost time for the town meeting. "Um," she said, with a nervous flutter in her stomach.

He turned back, eyebrows raised.

"Are you going to the town meeting?"

"Are *you* going?" he countered.

Manda's mouth twisted. "If you go."

He thought it over. "What do you think, Brian, Amy?" He paused, his head cocked, and then smiled at Manda. "Sure, why not? It's bound to be an important one, for a change." Jim held out his elbow. "Let's."

What the hell, she thought, eyeing the proferred limb. *It's just an elbow.* And she took it.

The Majestic was jammed with people and sound. Manda had never seen it like this. Not only were all the seats taken; people sat in the aisles, on the rough-hewn steps, and on the floor. Nearly two thousand of the colony's members must be here.

The Majestic was the first major cavern the colonists had discovered, and one of the few with ornate formations. A natural amphitheater, it housed vast arches, rippling stone draperies, and coils and tubes of rock the color of eggshell winding through it.

This cavern spanned an even larger volume than the complex far below that housed Hydroponics, the bamboo forest, and the livestock, but its space was not as usable; its "floor"—if you could call it that—was riddled with holes and that revealed the lower chambers of the colony. From several of these, spiral staircases emerged.

Near the back of the vast hall, beyond easy reach, the fuel and equipment tankers rose and sank, clinging like bugs and lizards to the heavy transport chains. Near the front, in a large, relatively uppitted grotto they called the Gather, they held their town meetings. The Gather had room enough for the entire colony to meet—but only just. Stalagmites and totem poles rimmed it, and in its center were many lilypads—flat-topped formations of various sizes that could be used as seats and tables.

Jim and Manda scaled down into the Gather, and then he released her elbow and with a parting smile, went over to join his siblings. Manda hesitated.

The rest of her clone sat huddled together on the lowermost cluster of lilypad seats. She sensed their pain over the loss of Teresa and the girl-baby in their hunched shoulders and drawn faces.

How can they bear to be together? she wondered. It hurt her as much to glimpse their loss as it did to confront her own.

Instead of joining her siblings she went over to Jim and his two siblings at the back on a low stone mound. All three LuisMichaels gave her a surprised look, then moved over, making room for her to squeeze between Jim and Amy. She wondered if the resentment she sensed from Amy and Brian was real, or just her own anxious imaginings.

The five councilclones, including Arlene-and-Derek—eleven in all, four sets of twins and one set of triplets—sat at a large lilypad in the sunken center that served as a table. Small children played among the stalagmites in the aisles; babies were slung on people's chests. The adolescents and older children looked anxious; the adults, downright grim.

The PabloJeb twins stood and held up their hands. "Quiet, everyone! Quiet!" Jack shouted. His voice echoed. The noise level dropped. "First, the council would like to congratulate the rescue and recovery crews who have worked so hard over the past four days." "Lives were saved that would have been lost," Amadeo said, "if not for all your efforts." "Thanks," Jack went on, "to KaliMarshall and its crew for all their hard work." Applause interrupted them, and they waited for it to die down before continuing. Meanwhile Manda felt her face go hot, and Jim gave her a significant look. So KaliMarshall would be the heroes of the day.

"And," Jack added, after a slight pause and a glance at his twin, "our special thanks go to CarliPablo and LuisMichael for persevering until they located UrsaMeri and JennaByron."

More applause. People turned to look at them and nod.

Manda felt her face grow warm again, this time for misjudging PabloJeb—or at least Jack.

"Unfortunately," they continued, switching off, "we have little other good news to report." "We lost thirteen colony members to the cave-in—" "—and while we lost no children—" "—we've lost all but four of our fetuses." "Some vital equipment in the Fertility Center was irreparably damaged." "IanTomas is going to give us a status report."

The PabloJebs sat. IanTomases—stout, elderly triplets from the nineclone in charge of Fertility; from their age, it had to be Aramis, Shamus, and Seth—came down to the center of the sunken area. "We've lost all our artificial wombs," they announced, "—and all but four of the fetuses in them—" "—a triplet LawrenceByron and a single CarliPablo."

Murmurs arose; several people glanced at Manda. She could almost hear their thoughts: *another CarliPablo single; oh great.* She suppressed a smirk.

"We lost all our embryos and zygotes," the IanTomases went on, "as well as much of our gene-bank material—" "—and almost all our zygote conditioning and implanting equipment." "It appears that, for the foreseeable future, we will no longer be able to rely on vat gestation with recombinant cloning, as we have in the past—" "—to alleviate the physical burden of pregnancy."

A murmur broke out. Manda could guess what this meant. Genetic reproduction, the old-fashioned way. The discomforts of pregnancy, the risks of childbirth. Uneasy, she wrapped her arms about her rib cage.

IanTomas held up its hands for silence. "Our colonization plan calls for an annual growth rate of four percent—" "—which translates to sixty-eight decantings a fire-year—" "—to offset our death rate."

People's eyes were beginning to glaze over at the parade of numbers. "Get to the point!" Manda said loudly. IanTomas frowned up at her, as did PabloJeb and the rest of her own clone. Manda shrugged at Derek, who was glowering. *Somebody had to say it.*

"The point is," IanTomas said with exaggerated patience, "that we will need to initiate a pregnancy lottery once Hydroponics is rebuilt—" "—and all women of childbearing years will be expected to participate."

The eldest PabloJeb twins interrupted, raising their voices to quiet the outburst that erupted. "Slow down! A pregnancy lottery may be necessary at some point—" "—but for now we have much more immediate problems. Speaking of which"—both brothers gestured at the two old women who sat near the front— "UrsaMeri will give us a status report on the Hydroponics effort."

The two UrsaMeri sisters hobbled over to the council table, helping each other over the rough ground. One had a bad cough, and they both looked haggard and tired. Understandable, after spending fifty-five hours buried under several tons of debris, squatting in a puddle of cold water. They turned their inward-turned eyes to the colonists.

"We have lost about a third of our food stores," they said, "as well as the means to grow new food." "With strict rationing, our remaining food will hold us for about three months—" "—and our expendable livestock, recycling processes, and bamboo will give us perhaps another two." The sisters waited while people took that in. "According to our assessment of the Hydroponics damage, very little of the existing equipment is recoverable." "We'll need to heavily cannibalize other operating systems—" "—in order to make Hydroponics even marginally functional."

Manda exchanged looks with the LuisMichaels. Without Hydroponics, the colony would starve.

The PabloJeb twins stood again. "We'll need a complete inventory of all materials—" "—both available for use and currently in use, everywhere in the colony." "Every section leader must prepare these lists and send them to UrsaMeri within three days." "UrsaMeri, anything else?"

The UrsaMeris looked as if they wanted to say more, but then shook their heads. Manda had the feeling it would only be more bad news.

The LuisMichaels whispered together, and then Jim stood.

"Can the recycling system be modified to handle hydrocarbons?" he asked loudly.

UrsaMeri turned its blind faces toward him, appearing startled. "I don't know." "GeorgJean?—" "—Is it here?"

GeorgJean, head of Recycling—a pair of sour-looking stoop-shouldered women—stood up near the back of the room.

"I'm afraid not," one said, and her sister went on, "Brimstone crude is made up primarily of straight-chain, branched hydrocarbons and some heavy aromatics." "It doesn't have the right amino acids and other components our bodies need." "The recyclers have *some* reconstituting and reforming capabilities—" "—but crude oil is too far outside its operating parameters." "And we don't have the technology or resources to modify them." They shrugged with a glance at each other. "So our systems could probably make some sort of *mana* from crude oil—" "—but we'd still starve to death, eating it—" "—if it didn't poison us first," they said together.

"It was a good thought," Manda whispered. Jim gave her a grateful look.

After the meeting, Manda tried resting in her own private cubby, but every time she closed her eyes she saw Teresa's body. So she got up and wandered the tunnels, stairs, and crevices of the colony. They were uncharacteristically busy for a sleep period, and she was forced to dodge people and waldos and robots of various sorts, rushing about on errands, lugging materials, and so on.

Manda found herself near her siblings' sleeping quarters, and paused for a long moment, heart pounding a dull complaint. But she didn't hear anything inside, and couldn't bring herself to actually look in. Instead she backed quietly away, and returned to her work space.

A routine check of the marine-waldos she hadn't yet summoned to the trench in question—which in a spirit of almost desperate optimism she had dubbed Rima Optabile, or "Desirable Trench"—revealed that *Aculeus Quninque* had gotten confused and spent the last couple hours bumping up against a rockfall on the ocean floor; *Octo* was now out of contact. She first reset *Quinque*'s programming; sent it, *Duo*, and *Quatuor* around to come in on *Septimus*'s position from the east and northwest; and then spent an hour or so trying to locate *Aculeus Octo*—with no success.

To be tantalized as she had with a glimpse of success, and then interrupted and frustrated in her efforts—it was demoralizing. She didn't have the heart for this right now. She needed a break, and had an idea of what she might do with the several hours remaining before the funeral services.

The colony needed help more than ever, and the crèche-born had the means. *If* ur-Carli had been telling the truth, *Exodus* could be the answer to their prayers.

L ights up," she said as she climbed into the secret chamber, and sputtering fluorescence dispelled the shadows.

The cavernous room was as cold as the last time Manda had been here, but she had prepared for it, this time: she'd replaced her livesuit with a warmsuit, borrowed from the herders' supplies. They were battery-powered, heated suits: a wonderful invention. The colony only had a few working warmsuits and she couldn't use this one for long. Other than the warmsuit, she retained only specs, a mic, and a wrist kelly hooked up to her linkware yoke.

She'd also made a copy of DMiTRI's star catalog, which contained about five million observations over a twenty-six-season period, and an astronomy syntellect to help her interpret the data. This time she'd brought her tool belt, strapped on over her parka. And she had her radiation gear: a dosimeter that gave her both instantaneous and cumulative readings of her exposure, and the auto-alert liveware that would warn her if a bad storm on Fire or a flare on Uma were about to cause radiation levels to spike to dangerous highs.

Like Earth, Brimstone had an ozone layer and a spinning iron core that generated a magnetic field, both of which helped filter out the life-damaging radiation produced by Fire and Uma. But Brimstone's thin atmosphere didn't have anywhere near the stopping power Earth's did. *Most* days you could spend several hours outdoors without significant risk. But some days you could only go out for a few minutes at a time.

First Manda looked out the tall slot of a window. The storm outside had passed. Golden Uma hung near Fire, which was now a large, pastel crescent with its ring a glowing arc above its belly. Several moons were up. Fire's retrograde moon and Brimstone's nearest sibling, Dante, a half-sphere, crept upward toward zenith; Heaven's Gate, Fire's second biggest moon after Brimstone, was a faint crescent setting near the lower limb of Fire. The Host (a dozen lumpy moonlets in a loose cluster) also dotted the sky overhead.

Manda headed back up to the telescope in the little shack and walked around it, studying it.

She remembered *Exodus*, barely: once she'd bounced weightless down a corridor, playing some chase game with another, older child; perhaps it had been Paul. (Paul: who hated Manda as much as he loved her. She was almost more afraid to think about him and what he was going through right now than she was to remember Teresa.) Another time she remembered watching a large viewscreen, and Derek pointing at a ringed planet, a fiery, orangey-blue ball that hung amid pinpricks of light. "Our new home," he'd said. She'd thought he meant the big ball itself.

Things had been better aboard *Exodus*, before landfall— before Derek and the rest of her clone (all but Teresa) had abandoned her to the rough mercies of the other children, and the harried, short-tempered neglect of the caregivers.

Teresa . . .

Manda shook off the gloomy direction her thoughts were taking. Using her liveware, she called up from the network a series of technical specs for optical telescopes, and displayed them across her vision. This one was a reflector type. She spent a few more minutes re-familiarizing herself with the operation of the telescope. One lever raised and lowered the telescope's viewing end; the other rotated it back and forth and right to left. Neither lever moved the telescope very fast or far. The recessed oval button in the middle caused the walls and ceiling to fall open—she didn't bother to reconfirm that. There was also a numeric keypad and an LCD display, and three buttons: one labelled **RASC,** one labelled **DECL,** and one labelled **ENTER. RASC** and **DECL** must be short for right ascension and declination, the equivalent of an object's longitude and latitude, cast onto the heavens. When she pressed **RASC** a cursor appeared in the LCD display. She typed in some numbers and hit **ENTER.** The LCD read —**error**—. With a shrug, she laid the remote back down.

To find *Exodus* visually, Manda had to know where to point the telescope. That meant she needed to know *Exodus*'s orbit.

Time for direct measures, Manda thought. Time to find out whether this room really was sealed off from the colony's monitors and commlinks. She got up and went into the room where the body of Carli lay.

"Ur-Carli," she said, "I know you're monitoring me. I need to talk to you. I want to know where to find *Exodus*."

She waited, but there was no response.

"If you want me to continue to keep this corpse a secret, you'd better cooperate."

Nothing. She shook her head. "Have it your way, then. Say good-bye to Carli's body. I'm about to destroy it."

Manda dragged the body off the bed by the armpits. Its upper body seemed a bit too light, the weight oddly balanced. She wondered if it had anything to do with having been frozen for so long.

She deposited it on the floor, then dug through the dresser drawers and piled old clothes and rags on top of the corpse. Next she went out into the machine shop and located a tin of lubricant. *Extremely Flammable!* the label warned. She carried it into the room and dumped the liquid lubricant all over the rags. Then she pulled a flame starter out of the tool pouch and held it up.

"Here's your last chance, ur-Carli." Still ur-Carli didn't respond. Manda shook her head regretfully. "I suppose if we recycled you," she told the corpse, "it would only give us another meal or so anyway." And she struck a spark.

It took two or three tries for the rags to catch fire, but they finally began smouldering and flames darted up. Black smoke billowed out. Immediately, automated sprinklers sprayed a chemical foam onto it. Manda retreated, cursing and coughing. She'd forgotten about the fire systems. When she came back in a moment later, the fire was out and the corpse and rags were covered in frozen foam.

"Shit. What a mess." Manda hurriedly pulled the pile of rags off of the corpse and dragged the corpse back to the bed. The fire's heat hadn't reached it; it was still stiff, a sixty-kilo lump of ice.

The effort left Manda panting. She sat down beside it and propped her chin in her palms.

So much for that. Either ur-Carli really couldn't monitor her in here, or it didn't care about the corpse.

There you go, anthropomorphizing a computer program again. A syntellect was nothing but a set of digital processes. Algorithms. It couldn't *care*, even if some of its outputs—its actions—led you to think it did. Caring required self-awareness. Empathy. An awareness of the existence of one's self, and of other beings as selves too.

She headed back into the main room. If she couldn't get the information from ur-Carli, there must be another way to find *Exodus*'s location.

There were a zillion stars in the sky. Any one of them could be *Exodus*. She had to know where to point the telescope.

She turned her liveface back on. As before, it was offline. She called up her own library system.

"Access astronomy syntellect," she said.

"OK," her linkware replied.

"Syntellect, attend."

"OK."

Manda thought for a moment. "I want to locate an object—a

possible object—in orbit about Uma. Would such an object show up in your star catalog?"

"Yes, if it is bright enough."

"How could I identify it?"

"Over time it would be recorded as a series of false stars of approximately the same brightness as the object you seek."

"Oh, really?" She pondered this. "How could I tell such an object was a false entry, rather than a true star?"

"I can locate it for you if you input the correct parameters."

"What parameters?"

"I must know the orbital radius. I must know the orbit's angle with respect to the plane of the ecliptic. I must know the orbit's shape. I must know the object's phase angle."

"What's a phase angle?"

"The object's position along the orbital path at a given time."

She sighed. "All of these parameters are unknown, I'm afraid. What would be some good simplifying assumptions?"

"Unknown."

Manda sighed. To get syntellects to work for you, you had to ask the right questions. And she didn't know the right questions to ask.

So she called up an image of *Exodus* and put it into orbit around a simulated Uma. Then she added the Fire system, out at two AU. *The sky is huge. Where do I start?*

"Here," she said, "let's see what I can make of what I know. If they're sticking around, it's supposedly to manufacture anti-hydrogen. So . . . they would want to use their solar arrays to absorb as much sunlight as possible. A circular orbit as close as they can get to Uma maximizes the amount of light they can absorb, right?"

"That is correct."

She walked around the simulation, studying it. After a moment, she told the syntellect, "Use a circular orbit within the plane of the ecliptic. What else do we need to know?"

"I need to know their orbital radius. I need to know their phase angle."

"Orbital radius means how far they are from the star, right?"

"Correct."

"And remind me what phase angle is again. . . ."

"This number describes where they are along their orbital path at one point in time."

"Hmm. As for orbital radius, I know they've got to be fairly close to the star. But I'm not sure how close," Manda said. "Maybe a third of an AU, maybe less. And I haven't got a clue how to come up with the phase angle."

"I don't understand the inputs. Please rephrase your request."

She suppressed a sigh. Where was ur-Carli when she needed it? At least it was easier to talk to. "I don't know the orbital radius or the phase angle."

"Without more precision in those two parameters, I cannot complete the calculation to any useful degree of probability," the syntellect said.

"Dammit!"

"Please rephrase your statement."

"Never mind." She thought a moment longer, pacing, leaving smudges in the purple dust. The faceware objects all moved along with her until with an impatient tweak she sent them sweeping back over toward Carli's old desk.

Think, Manda. Think. The colony's satellite telescope had been sent originally as a probe, and had been collecting star-mapping data since well before the ship had entered the Uma system twenty seasons before. Sightings of *Exodus must* be in the database of star observations over the past eighteen seasons, after they'd dropped off the colonists. If she could just figure out a way to extract the information.

She turned to face the syntellect whose icon hovered over Carli's desk. "How do observations of planets and other orbiting objects differ from observations of stars?" she asked. "How can they be distinguished from each other in your database?"

"True stars do not change position with respect to each other," the syntellect replied, "from a stationary observer's viewpoint. Over time, however, orbiting bodies such as planets do change position relative to the background of stars. This is how the ancients originally discovered the existence of planets.

"In terms of the observation database," it went on, "since an orbiting body's relative position changes, it is thus incorrectly identified as a different star with each observation made. This leads to many 'false stars' being entered into the observations database in the area of sky through which the orbiting body passes.

"Therefore, a statistical distribution of star count versus brightness, or magnitude, along the plane of the body's orbit, as compared to the same distribution of star count versus magnitude throughout the whole sky, should produce an anomalous peak at the magnitude of the orbiting body."

"What? I mean, please rephrase."

"For an orbiting body of a given magnitude, a plot of the number of star observations at that magnitude will reveal an improbably high number of stars of that magnitude along the plane of that body's orbit."

Manda closed her eyes, trying to picture the concept. "OK. I think I get it."

"But to compute this," the syntellect added, "you must know the area of sky in which to look for anomalies. The effect is dampened across the sky as a whole."

"What if we assume the body is within two degrees of the plane of the ecliptic, and within a third of an AU of Uma?"

"You can then request a distribution along that strip of sky. The false stars recorded in the database will create a peak that the whole-sky plot will not have."

"Then do it."

In a few seconds, two graphs appeared before her: one labelled OBSERVATIONS: WHOLE SKY and the other labelled OBSER-

VATIONS WITHIN ONE-THIRD AU & 2° OF ECLIPTIC. Along the vertical axis it said *STAR COUNT* and along the horizontal axis it said *MAGNITUDE.* Lines jiggled across each of them, and the peaks and valleys across the two graphs were virtually identical—with two exceptions. The strip-of-ecliptic graph had two spikes the whole-sky graph didn't: one at about magnitude ten and one at magnitude fifteen.

"So there are *two* uncharted objects orbiting close to Ursa Major in the plane of the ecliptic!" she exclaimed. "Could either of those be planets, or asteroids, or something?"

"No. I automatically removed all mapped planets and plane-tesimals from the observations database. This star system has been thoroughly mapped during the past fifty fire-years, starting long before *Exodus* left Sol."

She studied the graphs. "Can a sixteen-inch reflector telescope see a magnitude-fifteen star?"

"A space-based telescope that size can detect a magnitude-fifteen object."

"What about a telescope on this world's surface?"

"No."

"Could it see a magnitude-ten star?"

"Usually, as long as atmospheric conditions are stable and none of the larger moons are out."

She sighed. "Well, I guess I'll just have to hope that the magnitude-ten anomaly is the one I'm looking for. Syntellect, how many degrees of arc across the sky is a third of an AU?"

"Approximately twenty degrees of arc."

"Hmm. Give me a keyball and a visual interface for the star-map database."

"OK."

A keyball inset with keys and buttons on either side materialized under her hands, and a star-map databall appeared beyond it. On the databall's face was summary information on tens of thousands of stars. Using the keyball, she set up a filter that sorted out all except tenth-magnitude stars whose current position would lie within two degrees of the ecliptic and within twenty degrees on either side of the sun. The number of records in the database dropped to one hundred forty-eight.

She asked the syntellect, "how can I tell which of these entries are false stars?"

"You must look for each star through the telescope and verify its location. My calculations predict a star's position based on prior observations. Since the object you seek is moving with respect to its surroundings, you will find that, unlike true stars, it does not appear where it is supposed to be."

"But that doesn't tell me where the object is; it only tells me where it *isn't*."

"Correct. However, if you provide six false entries, I can use those, along with the times that each observation occurred, to compute the orbit and phase angle of the object. I can then predict where it will appear in the sky at a time you specify, and you can do a sighting to confirm its existence."

"Yes! That's what I want." She thought for a minute. "OK, let's do this." She first filtered out all stars that weren't out right then. That took the number down to eighty-nine candidates. Then she touched the databall that represented those eighty-nine observations. The ball lit up. "Give me continual updates on all these stars' predicted current positions in the sky."

"OK."

Manda headed up the ladder with the databall trailing her, sealed the manhole to keep the room's light from streaming out, and opened up the observatory ceiling. Still, stringent-cold air burned the patches of exposed skin on her face.

It was dark now: Uma had just been eclipsed by Fire. Faint crepuscular rays streaked Fire's ring with violet. Stars fanned out across the heavens like a blanket of shining crystals. Heaven's Gate had set, and the Host mostly had. God's Wrath was eclipsed by Fire's shadow. Dante was setting in the east.

156

Archangel and Demon were still up, but both were small, and waning; they shouldn't create much glare.

At the top of the stepladder, Manda opened up the databall she'd created of the magnitude-ten stars that were supposed to be out right now, and spread it out around the telescope's eyepiece.

"OK."

She locked her virtual display to her view of the real world. Next she chose a tool from her toolkit octagon, and used it to trace the outline of the telescope's eyepiece lens, creating a virtual outline of it, and brought the selected area to the foreground. The virtual—and thus, the real—eyepiece blocked out her data fields. This way the virtual data wouldn't interfere with her vision while she was looking for faint stars through the scope, but when she lifted her gaze from the eyepiece, the data would be where she expected it to be, waiting for her to easily peruse.

"Create a new field for the database," she ordered. "A single, logical field. Label it 'False Star.' "

"OK." A blank column appeared to the right of the two star data columns.

And she started.

The process wasn't difficult. From the table she got the values for right ascension and declination for a magnitude-ten star. She plugged in each of those sets of numbers into the keypad on the remote, waited while the telescope's rotors adjusted its viewing angle, and then stared into the eyepiece. A few stars were obscured by clouds, but a bigger problem for her, other than the dimness of the target stars, was the severe cold: her hands and feet and cheeks and nose had gone numb; her nasal passages felt aflame despite the filters; her breath caused the lens to ice over; her eyeballs ached and her vision blurred.

She could wipe the frost from the lens, but the vision blurring was a more serious problem. She couldn't use goggles with the

157

telescope, and blinking only relieved the problem for a few seconds. But she persisted.

Manda verified the existence of eighteen magnitude-ten stars before coming across her first anomaly. She strained, blinked, and strained some more, peering through the eyepiece: looking for a faint star, or a trace of cloud that might be obscuring it. But there was nothing there. A *nothing* where there should be a *something*.

Gotcha. Exultant, she marked an *X* next to that star's entry in the database's FALSE STAR column, and moved to the next star on the list.

An hour and a half later she had identified five more anomalies: enough for the syntellect to do its thing.

"Syntellect," she said, "use the six entries marked 'false star' in this database to calculate the orbit of an object about forty-seven Ursae Majoris."

"OK," it said.

Then she waited. And while she waited, she worried. Uma would soon move out from behind Fire and wash away the stars. Besides, it was after twenty-five o'clock, and the funeral services were at twenty-six. And even with the warmsuit, her joints had stiffened from the cold. But quitting now, so close, was unthinkable.

Her persistence paid off. Moments before Uma was due to emerge, the results came through. The syntellect gave her a three-dimensional model of Uma's solar system, with its gas giant, its four smaller, rocky planets, its asteroid belt and Oort cloud and all known planetesimals . . . and a tiny, high-albedo object, projected size a kilometer-and-a-half, plus or minus half a kilometer, in a circular orbit right in the plane of the ecliptic, at 0.32 AU. A little more than two kilometers was *Exodus*'s diameter.

Manda danced from foot to foot, breathing ice crystals. Her sinuses burned, her feet ached, and her face was numb. But she barely noticed. "Is the—object—visible right now, from this location?"

"No. The object is occluded by the planet Fire."

Shit. "How long before it moves out from behind the planet?"

"Two minutes."

Aha! "Give me the object's projected coordinates, at that moment."

The syntellect gave her a right ascension and declination and she plugged them into the remote. The telescope turned and angled down, till it was pointing at the lower rim of Fire, perhaps five degrees above the horizon—about where Uma would reappear, just before it set.

"Give me a countdown," she said, and waited. The seconds ticked away.

As the time neared, she climbed up. The ladder was too short, so Manda scrambled up onto the first rail and—balancing there, trying not to jostle the scope—squinted into the eyepiece. She stared and stared. She could see several stars above and through Fire's upper-cloud layer, but she didn't see one that looked like the other magnitude-tens she'd been gazing at. She wasn't sure.

And then—there! Below a blue-green giant! A small white dot, twinkling just above Fire's highest clouds. She threw back her head and laughed.

"Nailed you, you fucker," she muttered, and took a digital snapshot.

"Unable to translate the phrase 'nailed you fucker,'" the astronomy syntellect said. "Please rephrase."

By the time Manda got back to her room it was past twenty-five-thirty. Talking to Derek and Arlene about her discovery would have to wait: the ceremony for those who died in the cave-in started in less than half an hour.

Manda didn't do funerals. Nor did she attend harvest festivals, baby blessings, or any other of the colony's quasi-religious gatherings.

But Teresa would want her to come.

Teresa.

Manda stripped and took a quick sponge bath in the sulfurous waters piped up from the hot springs. Then she donned her live-suit and dressed in her formal outfit: a floor-length gown atop thermal long johns. She tied up her hair and slipped on fur-lined boots, and then took out her only piece of jewelry, a string of beads Teresa had made for her when she was a child. The beads were made from odds and ends: washers and nuts; painted vertebrae from some small animal; broken screws; a couple of burnt-out LCD bulbs. It had been a birthday gift when she was nine. That was just after she'd lost Terrible Tom. Teresa hadn't known why she was sad, but she'd wanted to cheer her up.

Manda looked at it for a moment, fingering the beads, then lowered the necklace over her head. Her veneer cracked, and she sat down on her bed and clutched the necklace against her chest, struggling to suppress sobs. Tears created cool tracks on her cheeks and chin.

Teresa. Come back. Please come back.

After a few moments, Manda drew a deep breath and dashed tears away. She managed to finish her preparations and then headed up to the Gather. Her siblings were already there when she arrived, all but Derek. Several other clones were also present. Everyone was carefully avoiding meeting anyone else's gaze. On the big lilypad in the center was a ring of burning candles, each with a placard behind it. Most also had a collection of items in front of them: knickknacks and mementos. A line of people filed past, lingering at certain spots.

She got in line and shuffled past the names of the fallen. Her baby sister's spot was bare, except for the nameplate (*Baby girl, CarliPablo*). Manda laid her lichened stone in front of the candle. After a moment of wordless regret and a silent good-bye to the sibling she'd never know, Manda moved on.

Teresa's candle was near the end. Beside the name card was a short, jellographic looping clip. Seeing Teresa break into a smile and say something trivial to the person filming sent pains shooting through Manda's chest. In front of the jello stood a crudely-made clay figurine, a rock, a hand tool of some kind, and other odds and ends. Manda hesitated, then took off her necklace and laid it in front of the photo. She brushed tears away. The flame flickered as Manda's arm moved near it, and a shadow passed over Teresa's face in the image.

Manda looked up at her siblings. Once again she sensed their anguish in the stiffness of their backs, in the arch of their necks. Janice and Farrah held hands and stared intently at the nearby stairwell, where the ceremonial leaders would emerge. Arlene was crying quietly, eyes swollen and red. Twins Bart and Charles looked stoic. Teresa's twin Paul wore no expression at all. His eyes were dead: chips of malachite. No one home. That scared the shit out of her.

Manda wanted to sit away from her clones. She didn't want to share their pain. But Teresa would want her to join her family. *You're too isolated, too antisocial. You should be more involved.*

She couldn't bear to sit next to Paul—they'd never been close. She wouldn't know what to say. (*Hey, welcome to the club!* wouldn't do.) So she sat next to Charles. To her surprise, he took her hand and gripped it tightly. The pain welled up again. This time she surrendered to it, and let the sobs come. Bart hugged her, and his own tears created a cool stain on her shoulder.

Charles and Bart had always kept to themselves. But for this reason she felt safest with them. She'd felt the sting of her other siblings' rebukes before, but Bart and Charles had never judged her. She'd always assumed it was more because they didn't care about her than out of any acceptance of who she was—but she thought now that that was unfair. Anyway, she would take what comfort she could from them.

She noticed then that Derek was standing behind them; at some point during her bout of tears he'd entered. His expression was as unyielding as a cliff face. Manda noticed distractedly that the Gather had grown a lot more full than it had been a few moments ago. The service should start any moment.

"What is it?" "What's wrong?" the others asked Derek. Arlene already knew; Manda could tell from her determinedly blank expression.

Derek exhaled sharply. Manda had assumed his tension had been because of Teresa, but she saw now he was angry about something else.

"I've just come from a council meeting. The terraforming project has been put on hold. Until the gardens are functional, the colony can't afford the resources." He spread his arms, palms upward, pleadingly. It was as much as though he were trying to convince himself as the others. "There's no way around it. Every possible resource and skill is needed to rebuild the gardens."

Every ounce of effort except mine, Manda thought. *How they must hate me.*

"What about the drilling?" Bart and Charles spoke together. "We were gearing up—" "—to finish drilling." Drilling into the mantle had been put on hold after the cave-in.

Derek shook his head. "Can't afford the manpower, nor the materials. The drilling team is dismantling the equipment. They'll be returning as soon as they can get things torn down and transported back here."

"Shit," said Charles, and Bart said, "Bloody hell."

"I'm sorry," Derek said.

"We knew this was coming," Arlene said. Derek made fists. "We were so close. We were right there. In the next few days we'd have broken through on several others, and then there would have been no turning back. We would have been committed to IceFlame."

"Without Teresa on the simulators we would be hamstrung, anyway," Arlene said. *Paul* would be hamstrung, she meant. Everyone avoided looking at Paul, who stared off into space. "Paul can't do it all himself, and nobody else has her expertise. We'll have to restrategize."

"There's a Teresa-shaped hole in the world now," Farrah said softly. The rest of them looked at each other.

Derek caught Manda's gaze. His brow furrowed more deeply. "A word with you."

She followed him to a spot near the stairwell, nauseous with guilt and fear. *He found out about the room. Shit! Why did I delay telling him?*

But instead he said, "I want you to start training right away to take Teresa's place on the terraforming team."

"*What?*" She blinked at him.

"You heard me."

"I thought—but you said—but the project is on hold."

"It is. But *you're* not on Hydroponics recovery, as the rest of us are. That gives you ample time to retrain."

Manda's eyes narrowed. "That's why you did it, isn't it? That's why you kept me off Hydroponics detail."

"Don't flatter yourself. You know exactly why you're not on

the recovery team. I'm merely trying to bring something good out of this."

"But—what about—" She wanted to say, *what about Paul?* Derek could hardly expect Manda to step in and fill Teresa's position with him. They didn't even know if Paul would be able to handle the loss of his twin, much less accept any replacement for her—especially Manda. But Paul was nearby, and she didn't finish her sentence.

Derek understood anyway. "He'll be fine. He has to be. We need him. And now we need you."

"What about my undersea project?"

"It'll have to wait."

She shook her head. "We've been over this before. I work better alone. You've said yourself I don't make a good team member."

"Then you'll have to learn to be."

"Derek . . ." She sighed and tried again. "I'm on the verge of a breakthrough. I'm picking up temperature and other anomalies and I'm closing in on the source."

"Oh?" That got his attention. "What have you got?"

"Only hints so far, but I know I'm not far from the vents. All I need is a little more time."

His gaze was skeptical. "How much more time? A day? A week? More?"

She chewed her lip, tempted to lie. But he'd know. "It could be up to six to eight weeks before I have anything definite."

He cut her off with a sharp gesture. "That's too long."

"Maybe this isn't the best time to discuss this, Derek," she started; "we're all upset about Teresa," but he interrupted again.

"No. I'm tired of coddling you. I'm tired of cleaning up after you when you make trouble."

"Now wait just a minute. The council approved my undersea project—"

"Shut up. Just shut the fuck up." Trembling with anger, he

stuck a finger in her face. "For once, I swear, you'll do what the colony needs for you to do and quit complaining."

She stiffened. Anger erupted. "The colony needs me? *You* need *me?*" Her voice rose in pitch and volume. "Where were you—any of you—when I needed you?" She flung her arm at the others present, who all stared. "You were always too fucking busy with all your important work to give me even a single glance, a single minute of your time. My entire childhood was *hell*—they treated me like shit!—and you did nothing to protect me."

It had been over a decade, but she hadn't forgotten the other kids' endless taunts—how they'd ostracized her, tormented her, ambushed and beat her up, repeatedly destroyed her few personal treasures—because she was the only single among them.

Some of those seated here were among her childhood tormentors. And when she'd gone to the adults, the caregivers were always too busy to help. They would tell her to stop complaining and work it out with them herself—as if what was happening was a simple misunderstanding, rather than active brutality.

Never once did her own clone stick up for her, or even take note of what was happening. Except Teresa: she and Paul had still required schooling and were around more, in the early years. Paul hadn't gotten involved—unless Teresa got herself into trouble defending Manda, which had happened once or twice—but Teresa did. She would routinely punch the other kids out, if she found out about something they had done—and then yell at Manda for provoking them. Still, it was more than Derek or anyone else had ever done for Manda during those years.

"And now," she said, "I'm supposed to meekly comply with your commands for the good of the colony." Everyone was watching. She couldn't care less. "*Please.* Sing me another sad song."

With a roar of rage Derek hit her. She reeled, caught herself on a totem pole, and stared at him with a hand on her stinging cheek, stunned. Derek's expression crumpled into lines of shock.

"I'm sorry," he said, reaching out. Arlene and the rest of the clone came to their feet. She jerked away from Derek.

"Fuck off."

She went over and sat next to Charles again. None of her clone would meet her eyes. *Cowards.* Her innards felt carved from ice.

The celebrants in their white woolen robes had begun filing up from the lower staircase. Manda disregarded the whispers and stares, and the pain that spread across her cheek, and dabbed at the tears, and the blood trickling from her nose. *I won't let them chase me away, Teresa.*

Derek's gaze heated the back of her neck. She ignored it.

A Little Healing, a Lot Late

By the next morning Manda's eye had swollen nearly shut, and the bruise was impressively colorful. She fingered the area gingerly, despairingly, looking in her little mirror above the washbasin. Without Derek's support, how could she continue her work? And who could she go to about her discovery of *Exodus*?

What the hell was she supposed to do now?

She dressed, then took her two weeks' worth of dirty clothes to the laundry. Three others were in the cul-de-sac doing their clothes, but they all ignored Manda. She returned the favor. While her clothes tumbled in soapy water in the washing machine, she sprawled in a chair and to cheer herself up, indulged herself in a mid-twenty-first-century romantic comedy simile called *Jester's Passion*. She played the female lead for a while, then the male. But her thoughts kept taking her down saturnine paths, and the simile threatened to turn darker and more dangerous than it was supposed to. She finally saved her place and put it away.

A few moments later she heard a noise and looked at the washer—then looked again. Ur-Carli, miniaturized, now floated above it, sitting cross-legged on the air like a levitating Buddha.

"What do you want?" Manda asked.

"I received your message that you found *Exodus* yesterday evening," ur-Carli said.

"Yes. Where were you? You could have saved me a lot of trouble."

"All my system resources were tied up and I didn't process the signal in time to respond."

This had to be, at least partly, nonsense. Which meant ur-Carli had learned how to lie. A scary notion. Or else ur-Carli was into some major, intense, and complex processing effort that nobody knew about—equally scary. Syntellects weren't supposed to be *that* autonomous.

Something really weird was up with ur-Carli that needed to be investigated. Manda grimaced inwardly at the thought. *In my copious free time,* she amended. "Forget it."

"Do you intend to signal them?"

"I don't know yet." Manda glanced around at the others doing laundry. They were still ignoring her, but she didn't want them to overhear too much—even if only her side of this conversation. "Listen, this isn't a good time for me to talk. Perhaps later."

"Very well." Ur-Carli's projection vanished.

As she was folding her laundry, Derek stuck his head in. "Hi."

She attempted a casual nod, and kept folding. He came over, and looked at her swollen, bruised eye. "That must hurt."

Again, she didn't say anything, just kept folding clothes.

"I'm really sorry."

"Forget it."

Derek stood there for a minute. Finally he asked, "Can we talk?"

She shrugged.

He held up some rationing tokens. "Come on. I'll buy you breakfast. My treat."

Everybody knew about their fight at the funeral, of course. Everybody knew every-damn-thing. Manda could feel their furtive stares as she and Derek sat together, eating. At least they couldn't easily overhear.

"How's Paul?" she asked. Derek gave her a hooded look. "He's avoiding everyone. We're worried. Arlene has been checking in on him regularly." He got a vacant expression on his face, and added, "She says he's been in Hydroponics with the clone all this watch, trying to work, but he's totally shut down. Won't talk to anyone."

Manda sighed, and poked at her food. She never thought she'd feel sorry for Paul.

"Is it true," he asked abruptly, "what you said yesterday?"

Manda blinked in surprise. "Is what true?"

"What they did to you. When you were a kid."

She felt like laughing, then like screaming. *How could you not know?* "You think I'd lie about something like that?"

He fell quiet. She didn't say anything, just picked at the remains of her food, having lost her appetite.

"Why didn't you tell us?" he asked after a moment.

"Jesus Christ, Derek! Don't you remember all the times I asked you to let me go with you and be part of the team? Not to make me go back to the dormitories?"

He hesitated. "I thought you were just . . . I don't know . . . being a kid. Wanting to tag along. You never said anyone was hurting you, Manda. If I'd known . . ."

I did tell you. You were just too goddammed busy to pay attention. "It doesn't matter now."

He looked angry now. "Who did it? I want names."

Again, she was tempted to laugh. *What, you're going to go pick some fights on my behalf? Ride to my rescue? It's a little late for that.*

She toyed with the idea of naming names. It would shrink the influence of certain clones, make them look bad. Especially KaliMarshall. *It* may have forgotten some of the things its youngest twins did to Manda when they were young, but *she* hadn't.

But that would only hurt the colony, at a time when it needed all its people, all its resources, just to survive.

She shrugged. "Look, it's all ancient history. They did some mean things to me, but they were just kids. They're all grown up now and they've probably forgotten all about it. I've tried to forget too. There's no point in dragging it up again. I'm sorry now I even mentioned it."

He was quiet a moment longer.

"I'm sorry, Manda. I didn't realize how bad it was."

At this, an anguish came that she hadn't even known was there. She bowed her head. He took her hand.

"Those first several seasons," he said, "when we were trying to get the colony up and running, things were so tough—we were always so tired, trying to do too many things at once—I guess we didn't pay enough attention to what was happening to you."

"I guess not." She dashed away the tears and pulled her hand loose. This display of sympathy came cheap for him, and far too late. She didn't want to think about the past, anyhow. "Just forget about it. OK?" *I don't need your apologies.*

He shrugged. "Have it your way."

An awkward silence followed. He got that vacant look on his face, and she knew Arlene was talking to him.

"What does she say?" Manda asked.

"You can have more time on your project. But we *are* going to need you on the team. You have the right kind of basic skills to take over for Teresa. Without you we're sunk."

She sighed. "Derek, we don't even know how we're going to grow enough food to survive beyond the next four months! Can't we delay this discussion for a while?"

"OK. OK." He lifted his hands in surrender. "You can have three weeks—"

"Four."

He glowered at her.

"Four, then," he growled. "But after that, I'll be coming back to you on the terraforming project."

"I suppose. All right." Maybe she'd get lucky and find something in her searches to help keep her independence intact.

Dane didn't feel the explosion: she was too deeply buried in her work. Her first clue that something was wrong came when her sensory inputs began to act strangely—movement, sound, and sight all started to register at unrelated speeds—and her avatar's words turned to syrup in mid-sentence.

She shut down the ship syntellect, cancelled her virtu-*search, downloaded into her home proxy, and found herself in a ship gone mad. The ship's steady rotation had become erratic tumbling. People and machines were scrambling, flying every which way. Exodus shuddered and moaned like a frightened child. Dane was flung head over heels—banged into a bulkhead—grabbed a handhold. One of her crèche-mates reached out a hand and she caught him. "What's going on?"*

"Antimatter," he gasped. "One of the storage pods just went."

"Holy shit. Where?"

He tapped her into his interface and she saw: a quarter-hectare area containing one of their star-drive engines was now nothing but shrapnel. That section was rapidly depressurizing.

A large crew of clones had been working in there. Double-time, as she'd ordered.

It would take a good fifteen percent of their precious antimatter fuel to repair the ship. There was no way they were going to 70 Virginis now, not for a long time. Not ever.

Dane knew what had happened. Pablo had gotten the idea from the colonists' cave-in.

*   *   *

Once they were done with damage control and triage on the wounded clones (naturally, none of the crèche-born had been hurt), she confronted him.

"This was your doing!" she hissed. He merely smiled. She shoved him. "You sabotaged the ship, so you wouldn't have to keep your promise to Carli!" She shoved him again. "Murderer!"

They were both piloting proxy bodies right now: powerful humanoid machines. She so longed to give him a beating she could hardly stand it—but there wasn't much point. Even if they weren't evenly matched—even if she could tear his limbs off as she so longed to do—it would be pointless. All he'd do would be to turn off his pain receptors, plug into another proxy, or hare off into a virtual space.

"I have no idea what you're talking about," he said. "You're sounding paranoid. Maybe you should have a talk with ur-Carli."

"No way the blast was an antimatter pod. That much antimatter would have taken out the whole ship. You planted a charge. I can see it in your mind."

"So?" He leaned close. "I'm all over you, Dane. I know every thought in your puny little mind. You're nothing but a growth on my psyche. An abortive twitch I plan to dispose of someday, when I get around to it."

She ignored the threat. "What is it with you, Pablo? You've been undermining the clones from the beginning! Why do you hate them so much? We could have given the colonists a hell of a lot more technology—there was no reason to withhold it. Except pure vindictiveness. Do you have any idea how sick you are?" That's when it struck her. "My God—of course. You want them to fail, no matter who gets hurt. It's all about revenge, isn't it? Because Carli cared more about them, finally, than she did about you. You sick fuck."

With a roar, Pablo grabbed her proxy by the throat, and threw her against the wall. He stalked over.

"I don't give a damn about Carli anymore, get it?"

"Then why are you so angry?" she retorted, scrambling to a knee.

He leaned close. "You can't keep me away from Brimstone. It's going to be my world soon. Stay out of my way and maybe you'll live to enjoy it with me."

He left. Dane stood.

I'm going to stop you, she thought, and stood, unharmed in her metal body, while their shared flesh in its crèche deep in the protected heart of the ship shook with rage and fear. Somehow, someday, brother, I'm going to stop you.

anda got started very late on her first-watch shift—a chore shift in the machining caverns, inspecting reconditioned machinery—and finished almost at the end of the first-watch sleep period. The rooms and chambers were strangely empty, with almost everyone hard at work in Hydroponics. It made Manda feel a little lonely. Shut out.

Make up your mind, some voice inside said. *You wanted to be on your own. Manda the loner.*

Oh, shut up, she told it.

Her thoughts turned to ur-Carli and the secret chamber. With the cave-in and the funeral and her fight with Derek, she had managed to avoid thinking about *Exodus* and Carli's corpse and the existence of the secret room—but the idea that the crèche-born were still around and might be able to help was too compelling to ignore.

She tracked down the other members of her clone. Arlene was tied up in the machining caverns, though she promised to keep her link live and tune in as she was able; Paul and Janice were out of touch. Derek, Charles, Bart, and Farrah were working in Hydroponics. Manda joined them there.

When she arrived, they four were taking a break. Farrah looked miserable. Manda guessed that Janice was still busy with her exo-bond. From the glances she and Bart and Charles gave Manda, she knew they knew what had happened between Manda and Derek that morning.

But she wasn't here to talk about that.

"I need to show you something," she said to them. "Could you bring up your linkware?"

The others spent a few moments watching the simulation of the object circling Uma, while the rest of the planets and moons of the system followed their own paths. Their viewpoint was stationary with respect to the sun, at a distance just outside Fire's orbit, about thirty degrees above the ecliptic and looking sunward. Each actual observation made during the past two decades showed up as a flare of light as the object moved along the silver thread of its calculated orbit.

The conclusion was undeniable: something was out there. Something uncharted. Something that wasn't there before eighteen seasons ago.

Finally Farrah said, "Well, it's an object, all right. But how do we know it's *Exodus*? It could simply be an uncharted asteroid or something."

"In a perfectly circular orbit right in the plane of the ecliptic, in an optimal spot for using their arrays, appearing shortly after they dropped us here?" Manda asked. Then she noticed something in the simulation. "That's odd."

"What is?" they asked.

"I just noticed." She pointed. "Those flares you see along the orbit are the actual sightings by DMiTRI. I had the syntellect add those so you could see how clear the pattern is."

"Yeah; so?" Bart said.

"Well, it looks from here as if all the observations are showing up on the far side of the sun from Fire. Statistically, that shouldn't happen."

"Are you sure?"

"I can check. Astronomy syntellect, attend."

"OK," the syntellect replied.

"Leave us at thirty degrees above the ecliptic, but lock our radial position to Fire's."

"OK." With tones cuing the change, the perspective shifted. Suddenly Fire was stationary, and the other bodies surged in motion, in a crazy orrery of solar and planetary precessions and shifts.

"Ooops. Syntellect, make Uma's position stationary with respect to our perspective." "OK." "End sequence." "OK."

Motions stabilized: Fire and Uma appeared to be staying in one spot while all the other objects moved. Now the observations could clearly be seen to occur only when the object was on the far side of the sun from Fire.

Bart, Charles, and Farrah all stared at the simile. "You're right," Charles said, and Farrah and Bart nodded. "I see it too," Farrah said.

"Syntellect, attend."

"OK."

"Why are there only sightings of the object on the far side of the sun?" Manda asked. "Where is the rest of the data?"

"The data presented are all recorded observations of magnitude-ten-brightness objects that fall along the orbital path, as requested, plotted with respect to time," the syntellect answered. "There are no other applicable data."

"Phase changes!" Charles blurted. Everyone looked at him. "Like the phases of Fire and the moons. When the object is in front of the sun, its brightness drops off because it's mostly in shadow, with respect to us."

"Can't be," Farrah said. "You don't get that big a change in observed brightness from that effect."

"Why not?" Manda asked.

"Unknown," the syntellect said.

"Ooops. End sequence."

"OK."

Farrah shook her head. "All I know is that when I was a teenager, when we were approaching Uma and collecting observations to chart the system, Old Jeb let me help him with some of his astronomical computations. I remember very clearly that there was no significant change in brightness for the planet I was collecting data on."

While Farrah was talking, Manda remembered the statistical distribution she did before. "Wait," she said. "I forgot—there were *two* uncharted objects that showed up as anomalies: one at mag-ten and one at mag-fifteen. Syntellect, attend."

"OK."

"Call up the database of stars."

"OK."

"Collect all magnitude-fifteen stars whose observations would put them somewhere along the orbit."

A short pause. "OK."

"Rerun the orbit in a loop, starting at eighteen seasons ago and running at twelve seasons per minute, but add to the simulation all magnitude-fifteen objects whose observations fall along the orbit shown, as you've done with the magnitude-ten object." "OK." "End sequence." "OK."

To the others she added, "If the mag-fifteen object is a different one, the observed points won't correspond to the object's position in orbit; they'll merely be scattered at random points along the orbital path. If it's the same . . ."

She fell silent and they all watched the simile. The mag-fifteen points, nearly all of them, fell precisely on top of the object as it orbited the sun—on the near side.

"That can't be!" Farrah protested.

"Clearly, though, it is," Manda said.

"Look, I'm just telling you what Jeb told me."

They were all quiet for a moment.

"Maybe," Bart said with a frown, "that rule of thumb about brightness only applies to a spherical object, such as a planet. I mean, think about it. If *Exodus* is out there, it's got its solar arrays at full extension. That makes for a very high reflectivity on the far side of the sun. . . ."

"And very low reflectivity on this side," Farrah said slowly. She turned to Manda, her eyes wide. "I don't know what you've found, but it sure is suggestive."

Manda turned to Derek. His gaze was intense, his mouth a thin line. It struck her that he had been silent this whole time. Arlene's avatar had appeared beside him, looking aghast. Manda licked her lips, suddenly nervous.

"Well?" she asked. "Don't you think this merits action?"

Derek cleared his throat. "Would you all mind joining me in *virtu*-conference beta?"

Manda donned her plain-ol'-Manda-avatar (she sensed that copping an attitude right now would only get her into trouble), found Derek's *virtu*-conference room, and dove into the interface.

Beta was Derek's private conference room. He'd remodelled since she'd been here last. On the domed ceiling were murals painted by Italian artists who had been dead for a good eight hundred earth-years: mostly they were chubby, naked, white people floating among clouds; some had robes and wings. (Unlike in real paintings, these cherubs, seraphim, and whatnot were fully mobile, miming cocktail party chatter and chorus lines and whatnot.) Nearby were a set of marble seats and benches.

Beyond the conference space's marble pillars, moonlight splashed onto the stones of a desert landscape. Strange creatures roved the plains in the far distance. She didn't have time to view the creatures more closely, though, because her siblings' avatars started to arrive. They floated and bounded and drifted down all around her: all of them in slightly modified versions of themselves.

And once their avatars had all gathered, Derek-avatar said to Manda-avatar, "Please show me where you stored your analysis."

"Here." Manda-avatar extended a glittering diamond-sharp fingernail (her avatar's one irresistable affectation) and touched one of her commandballs. It opened like a geometric flower.

Contained inside it were numerous multihued datashapes, which hovered just above its unfurled surfaces; she batted at the simileball that contained her *Exodus* algorithms and data, and it bounced upward, growing in size, to hover in the room's center, a glowing orb. As she did so, Arlene-avatar lighted beside Derek-avatar.

"Syntellect, attend," Derek-avatar said.

"OK."

"This is Derek CarliPablo. Acknowledge my identity."

"Acknowledged."

Arlene-avatar came up beside him, looking grim. "This is Arlene CarliPablo. Acknowledge my identity."

"Acknowledged."

Together they touched the simileball and said, "Permanently destroy all copies of data and programs—" "—that pertain to the object whose orbit is simulated herein."

"Wait—!" Manda-avatar shrieked. "*No!* Syntellect, countermand!"

"Unable to countermand," the syntellect said. "All information destroyed." Manda-avatar slumped in dismay and stared at her eldest siblings.

"Why?" she whispered.

They sighed. Derek said to the syntellect, "End sequence." "OK," while Arlene-avatar shook her head. "I swear, Manda. You'll be the death of us."

"What's this about?" Farrah-avatar demanded.

"Yes—explain," Charles-avatar snarled.

Derek-avatar said, "Syntellect, attend." "OK." "Give us maximum privacy." "OK." "End sequence." "OK," as Arlene-avatar told the others, "What we're about to tell you, you mustn't repeat to anyone. On pain of ostracism."

Ostracism was the worst punishment the colony could dole out. Manda-avatar gaped, her heart pounding suddenly hard. "Why? What have we done to deserve this?"

"What the hell is going on here?" Bart-avatar demanded. At the same moment, Charles-avatar growled, "You threaten your own clone? *You dare?*"

"Warm it up, sibs," Farrah-avatar said, laying a hand on Charles-avatar's arm. "Of course we won't tell anyone," she told the eldest twins, "if you ask us not to. You needn't threaten us."

"You knew already, didn't you?" Manda-avatar accused. The flicker in Derek's and Arlene's expressions told her she had hit the mark. "The council is in contact with *Exodus*. You have been ever since we made landfall."

"No. We're not in contact with them," Derek-avatar said heavily. Arlene-avatar added, "But yes, we know they're there."

"Why hide it?" Bart-avatar asked. "I don't get this."

Arlene- and Derek-avatar shook their heads. "They can't help us," both replied. "When they dropped us off—" "—they gave us every last piece of equipment they could spare." "They need everything left for their flight to seventy Virginis." "They have no room for passengers."

"But—"

The eldest two talked over Manda's objection. "They grew us specifically for this mission, and they were pushing the tolerances to keep us on board—" "—as long as they did." "We are on our own," both said.

"But why—" "—didn't you tell us before?" "Why the big secret?" This was Bart-, Charles-, and Farrah-avatars.

Derek- and Arlene-avatar spread their hands in synchrony. "We didn't know—" "—till after they dropped us off." "After they left orbit, they sent us—" "—a message saying that they were through with us." "We were not to try to reach them." "Then they severed contact."

Silence fell, as Manda and the rest tried to absorb this.

"But—why?" Manda asked finally.

"You remember how rough it was back then!" "Can you imagine how everyone would have felt if they'd known we'd just been abandoned?" They both shrugged. "So the council decided—" "—it would be best, to keep morale up, if we created the—" A pause and a glance, and in unison, "—the fiction—" "that they were gone." "So that people wouldn't expect help from them—" "—or feel betrayed when they refused."

Silence pressed in around them once more.

"It's a cruel deception," Manda-avatar said. "Perhaps they're in a better position to help us now than they were. We should at least ask . . ."

Both said sharply, "No." "We have no way of reaching them," Arlene explained. "And Manda—" Derek took her hands. "—you were just a toddler when we made landfall, so you don't remember them. We do."

Arlene nodded. "They don't think about things the same way we do," she said. "They don't care about life or death." "Not unless it's one of their own," Derek amended. Arlene continued, "To them, the world is—" She broke off and looked at Derek helplessly. He struggled for words. "Not real," he said after a moment, and Arlene-avatar nodded. "That's it. Not the way it is to us. They're not human." "Not what *we* would call human, anyway," Derek-avatar said, and turned to the others. "Remember, Bart; Charles? Remember, Farrah? Tell her what they were like."

Bart-avatar turned away. It was impossible to tell what he was thinking. Charles-avatar wore a distant look. Farrah-avatar nodded, rueful. "It's true."

"They *were* strange," Charles-avatar acknowledged, grudgingly. "Rather horrible," Bart-avatar added. "If it weren't for Carli," Farrah-avatar said slowly, "I think we *all* would have gone mad."

"And even if they had a reason to rescue us," Derek-avatar went on, "they can't afford to. As I told you. They need every gram of food, fuel, water, equipment, and supplies they have on board to get them to seventy Virginis."

"So. Put them out of your mind." Arlene-avatar placed her hands over Derek- and Manda-avatars', and gave them a shake. "Please. Forget about the crèche-born," she told Manda. "They're a long-dead issue." Derek-avatar said, "Put that brilliant, unruly mind of yours to work on ways we can help ourselves."

Manda-avatar looked back at her oldest siblings through narrowed eyes. Beneath the flattery, their earlier threats hung in the air like a bad smell.

"You leave me little choice." She sighed and lowered her gaze. "All right. They're forgotten."

Derek- and Arlene-avatars extracted the same promise from the others, and then cancelled the *virtu*-conference.

For the moment, she amended silently, as the conference room's features melted to become the ruins of the Hydroponics cavern. Her siblings' avatars also dissolved, and the real versions materialized around her.

Janice came up, carrying food. She looked from one to the other of them. "What gives?" she asked.

No one answered right away. With a quick glance at Arlene, Derek replied, "Nothing."

And now we're hiding things from each other, Manda thought. Though she doubted Farrah would hold any of this back from Janice; Manda saw the flicker of unspoken communication that passed between them. Vat-mates didn't hold out on each other. And really, Arlene and Derek couldn't expect that. Word wouldn't leak outside the clone, though. They knew they could count on that.

Maybe *they can count on it,* she thought.

Later, as Manda was setting up her connection, the Luis-Michaels entered her workstation. They made an effort not to stare at her black eye, visible under the faint cover of her livemask, while she made an effort not to turn her back or put her hand to her face in embarrassment.

"Come in!"

Amy and Brian said, "Actually, we have to go." "Got a couple of quick things to take care of before we head out." "Appreciate the invitation, though."

"We'll be on your face," they told Jim, "if you need us," and he gave them hugs. As they departed, Brian and Amy gave her a penetrating look that made her face heat up. Her fingers went to her bruise, despite herself.

"'Bye!" "Come out and visit us, Manda!"

They warmed her with their smiles on their way out the door. She wondered if it was pity that motivated them. That, briefly, annoyed her.

Manda turned to Jim, but he seemed strangely distant, or distracted. Manda grew confused. Something was going on between him and his siblings. Or perhaps she'd angered him somehow. If so, though, why was he here?

Manda called up her linkware and ran the daily checks and calibrations. Jim came online, and she sensed him floating her facelink as she sorted and plotted the data from her four *Aculei* in the area.

"Look at that." He pointed at her plots. "The anomalous trends are continuing."

"Yes." She cupped her chin in her gloved hand, eyeing the virtual terrain all around them. "They're all getting some odd results. But no real pattern jumps out at me. Let's plot it all and factor in what we know about current flow, and see what we come up with."

She gave him an active face. The two of them worked together, linking faces, parting, laying out and manipulating the data. An hour later they took a break to study the results so far. Jim whistled.

"Brian, Amy, you there? Yeah, check this out. Do you see what I see?"

"What is it?" Manda demanded, but he held up a finger, and started sorting the data in apparent response to his siblings' requests. His face went through some changes and he made a series of grunts, affirmations, and negatives. Manda paced out her impatience. Finally he nodded.

"Ayup, we concur. Manda"—he turned back to her—"either you have widespread geothermal activity over a huge area here"— he gestured at an area about fifty kilometers to the south of *Aculeus Septimus*. It was the southeastern quadrant of the pie wedge he had made for her the day before; the deepest area of the trench, for which they had no data yet—"or you've got a big mama of a volcano. Or both."

She frowned. "Where do you get that? I don't see it."

"Look at the data over here, and here." He gestured at the southwestern and northern portions of the map, where *Aculei Duo*, *Quatuor*, and *Quinque* had provided new data, then at the northeast, where *Septimus* was. "I know the results are up and down, but look. In general, both temperature and sulfur content have an upward gradient in this direction. The fluctuations can be attributed to eddies and uneven diffusion. But if you smooth out the data enough . . ." He did so, and then drew a best-fit eclipse, ten kilometers wide and eighteen kilometers long, along the center of Rima Optabile. The ellipse's center was at the point where the upward trends, roughly, appeared to intersect. "This is where you should concentrate your search."

She looked at the data for a long moment, walking around it, chewing her lip. Then she expelled her breath and broke into a grin. "You're right. I wouldn't have seen it myself, but . . . you're absolutely right." Excited, she gripped his arm, and smiled at him across the shifting datascape. "Thanks, Jim. Thanks a whole lot. You've saved me a lot of time."

His face reddened, but he smiled in return. "Glad to help.

Listen, I'm heading out to the refinery in a bit. Keep me updated on your progress, will you?"

His smile lingered in her thoughts long after he left.

She spent some more time sifting through the data from her other waldos. *Aculeus Octo* was still out of touch. And interestingly—though it might be coincidental—*Octo*'s position now, if it continued on the trajectory she had originally ordered it to follow, put it wandering into the area they'd targeted as likely to have geothermal activity.

It could have gotten stuck en route, or even damaged or destroyed—perhaps by running headlong into geothermal activity. It'd be a shame to lose her first remote and ruin her perfect record. . . . Still, it might yet be functional. She tried all kinds of adjustments and attempts to reestablish contact, on numerous channels.

No luck. But if it had been sacrificed in the service of discovering the vents, well, it hadn't died in vain.

Tomorrow's a Long Way Away

That evening Manda visited her little, unnamed brother. Paul was with him—actually inside the intensive care unit, masked, holding the baby in his gloved hands under a bank of warming lights. The baby was hooked up to an IV and several monitoring wires; it looked so pitiful, all punctured and wired, that Manda winced. (Not *it*, she reminded herself sharply; *him*.) The look on Paul's face was so intensely sorrowful that Manda couldn't bear to look directly at him, either.

Manda had been avoiding thinking about Paul—trying not to think about what he must be going through. Now she scowled at her own cowardice. *That's not right. He needs his clone now more than ever.*

She grabbed a mask and entered the room—sauntered rather too casually over. "Hi." To her dismay, her voice quavered. He didn't even glance at her. She saw that Paul's right hand held the baby easily; he was that small.

"How is he doing?"

"I talked to the doctor. They say he's stable, he's gained a little weight, and his lungs are in better shape. He might make it." Paul stroked the baby's hair with a thumb. "Poor little guy."

Manda realized he meant, *poor little guy was going to* live. And that Paul was coming here to say good-bye to him.

"Being a single isn't *that* bad," Manda said mildly. He gave her a raw, shocky look; Manda guessed he hadn't slept at all in the three long days since Teresa's death. He opened his mouth; *you don't know what it's like.* But of course, she did—in her own fashion. He closed his mouth and looked at the baby again.

"It's different when you grow up together, I guess," Manda said.

Paul nodded, swallowed convulsively. "Perhaps you're right. He won't know this." His voice cracked and bled. "This pain."

Fear grabbed Manda—fear of saying the exact wrong thing; fear of what would happen if she remained silent. She took a deep breath. "Paul, we need you."

Anguish flicked across his face. He slipped his hands out from under the baby and turned away from her.

"I can't, Manda. I can't. Part of me is already dead." He paused. "I reach out," he said, lifting a hand to empty air, "and—where she was, I reach for her and—nothing's there. I'm hollowed out. I'm nothing." He closed his hand and brought it to his chest. "Teresa. Teresa." He doubled over. His voice became a growl of pain, a mantra. "I can't. Help me. Help me. I can't."

So Manda took hold of him, and they sank to the floor together, and his grief burst forth.

He howled his anguish. His fingers gouged into her and his tears poured out and soaked her sweater. Then he tried to silence himself against her, and bit her shoulder so hard it hurt even through the multiple layers she wore. She saw staff come running, and shooed them out.

Once his grief had abated, she took his face in her hands—his face so like lost Teresa's.

Teresa. Help me find the right words.

"Listen. Right now I know you don't care. Not about yourself, not about me, or our clone, or the colony. You don't have to promise me you won't ever do the recycler dive, or go walkabout without your gear. Just give me this one day. Just hang on till tomorrow."

He shook his head like a musk ox plagued by a shepherd dog's nippings. "Can't," he whispered. "I can't."

Manda gave his shoulders a shake, angry now. "You listen to me. You think I don't know the pain you're feeling because my own twin died before I was decanted and I don't remember him. Well, guess what. I live with that loss every fucking minute of every fucking day of my life, ever since I was old enough to understand why everybody thought I was a useless freak.

"Well, I'm going to prove to them how wrong they are. This colony needs me, Paul, whether they know it or not. And they need this little baby. And they need you too."

Paul had gone limp and unresponsive. After a moment Manda released him and draped her arms about her knees, sitting on the cold floor, eyeing the banks of equipment and the three other babies struggling for their lives.

"Teresa cared about this colony," she went on more quietly. "More than anything else. More than even her clone. If it had been you who'd died, she would have hung on through the pain. I know it."

Paul looked at her from the depths of his loss. He shook his head in denial but Manda knew he was wrong.

"She would rather you suffer every ounce of this pain you're feeling," Manda insisted, "than waste your own life by following her into death. She cared about the colony." *She cared about me.*

Anger coursed across his face. "What the *fuck* do you know about it? About her? You, with your selfish, loner attitude— you've always refused to have anything to do with me-us. With her. How can you possibly understand what it's like?"

Then he lowered his head and hunched his shoulders and sobbed again: this time a child's lost, heartbroken tears.

Manda felt abashed. She watched him for a moment, then stood up and took the infant in her own right hand. It terrified her, how tiny he was. It awed her, that a human could be this small, this unformed, yet live.

189

Paul gripped the edge of the incubator table and stood. Manda stroked the baby's skin. It was so very soft.

"His name will be Terence." She held out her hand to Paul. He gripped her hand in his own. His face, cadaver-white, went through several contortions.

"A good name," he said finally.

Manda set the baby down. "Give me till tomorrow," she said, and gave Paul's hand a last, hard squeeze. He didn't answer or even look at her when she left, but she sensed a softening in his resolve, and clung to that.

Exhaustion weighed heavily on her that night. She started toward her own private sleeping nook, but once more an impulse drove her to her clone's sleeping quarters.

The clone's cave was not much bigger than Manda's cubby— though better furnished and unlike hers, had a flat floor, overlaid with thick musk-oxen-hair bedding over thatch. Pillows were arrayed in a semicircle at the walls' base. The room smelled of people and of animal fur. It was a good smell.

Bart and Charles, already asleep, were nestled together to one side. Derek had stripped of everything but his long johns, yoke, livemask, and livegloves, and was presenting to someone elsewhere, speaking softly. Arlene was already under the covers, near Farrah. Janice wasn't there, and neither was Paul.

Manda walked across the middle of the bed, careful to avoid the tangle of feet. She pulled off her own outer layers and stacked them neatly on a nook dug into the stone wall. Ignoring the looks Derek, Arlene, and Farrah gave each other, Manda slid under the musk ox skins to curl up against Farrah's back. The warmth of her sister's body and the softness of her skin drew the tension out of Manda. She released a long, slow sigh.

"Roll over," Derek said, sitting down next to her. He'd removed his livehood, gloves, and yoke.

Manda tensed. She hadn't forgotten what he and Arlene had done when she'd told him and the others about *Exodus*. Beyond him, Arlene was watching her.

They read her defiance.

Please understand, their gazes said. *They can't help us. It was for the good of the colony.*

You're wrong, she returned silently. *You can't know the crèche-born wouldn't help; you can only guess.*

They only looked at each other and shook their heads.

I need my clone right now, she realized. *But I don't necessarily want them.*

With a reluctant sigh, Manda rolled onto her belly and let Derek massage the knots out of her shoulders and upper back. She hissed with pleasure-pain as his fingers found the knots and worked them, forcing them to release their hold on her; she only half-listened as the quiet voices of her siblings flowed over her like free-form poetry—voices like her own, voices she'd heard countless sleep shifts, till her self-imposed exile years before. Teresa's name came up, and they started trading stories about her that woke up Charles and Bart, and made everyone laugh. It was laughter that hovered near tears, and it felt good. Manda felt that Teresa was somewhere close by, sharing the moment with them.

How I miss you, Manda thought.

And they talked about the baby's progress.

Manda lifted up on her elbows. "His name is Terence," she said. The others looked thoughtful. Derek nodded. "A good choice."

"How is UrsaMeri doing?" Manda asked.

A brief silence. Arlene answered, "They're coping." Derek said, "They have each other, at least." And Farrah added, "The repairs are keeping them too busy to think about Rachel's death." She paused, and Manda realized she was waiting for Janice to pick up the thread. A painful pause spoke of unresolved trouble there. Finally, Arlene finished, "They care too much about the colony to go walkabout."

Derek slid under the covers between Arlene and Manda. Manda curled up into Farrah's S-curve again, and Derek rolled over with his back to Manda. He pressed his back to hers, and laid a foot against her calf.

"Lights down," he said. It went dark.

Manda lay quietly, listening to the breathing of her siblings, feeling Derek's foot pressing against her leg and Farrah's buttocks and back against her belly and chest.

It wasn't about sex. Vat-mates always shared their exo-bond lovers, and often shared them at the same time—but true sibling-on-sibling incest was rare. This sharing of the bed started in infancy, and it was about love. Sharing body warmth. Clone-bond. Trust.

It was that trust—that closeness—that had driven her away. At some point during Manda's adolescence, sharing a bed with her siblings had become a torment too great to bear. They spent the quiet moments before sleep talking about *their* work, *their* friends and enemies, *their* plans for the future. No one had seemed interested in what Manda had to say. In their eyes, all she'd been was a little copy of them. And a damaged one, at that: half of a person. Half-real.

"I told Paul to stay with us," she said softly into the darkness. "I told him we need him. I said he has to stay at least until tomorrow. He didn't promise but I think—I think maybe I reached him."

Derek groped for her hand and squeezed it. "Thank you." His voice was choked.

"He needs to hear it from all of us," she went on. "Often."

Arlene answered, "Good. You're right, of course." Derek sighed. "Yes. It's a good approach. Take it a step at a time." "Make it more manageable for him."

"I couldn't bear to lose Paul too," Farrah whispered, clutching Manda's hand.

A hushed pause followed. Nobody said it but they all thought it: *No single outlives a vat-mate. It's just a matter of time.*

Manda stiffened, pushing the thought away. *If we help him, he can make it. He can make it.*

They all sensed her denial. Farrah pulled Manda's arm across her waist and hugged it to her in silent gratitude.

"I'm glad you're here. Help us be strong." Then Farrah released her hold and crawled over them to hold Arlene, who was weeping softly.

Manda hugged her pillow, thinking again of Teresa. Wishing she had something of her lost sister to hold onto, to carry with her into the future, instead of this fathomless ache inside.

In the middle of the night, movement, or perhaps a soft sound, awakened her. She sat up and saw Farrah's shadowed form moving to the door. Manda carefully squirmed out from under the covers and crawled among her sleeping siblings to the doorway. She came out into the hall to find Farrah barring Janice's way. Her anger was so intense it made Manda's arm and neck hairs bristle.

"Where were you?"

Janice folded her arms and stared back at her twin. She had love, marks on her neck, her hair was tousled, and her lips were swollen. She'd been using them hard. She made no reply.

"I needed you!"

"And I needed *her.*"

"You should be with your family now."

"I did what you wanted. I shared her with you. Get off my case." She tried to pass, but Farrah grabbed her arm.

"If you see her again, I'll kill her. I swear it."

Janice jerked her arm free and slapped Farrah, hard. Manda

sensed her other siblings coming up behind her. Arlene brushed past. "Easy, Farrah. Easy."

Farrah burst into tears. Arlene steered her into the sleeping chamber, murmuring comforting words; Derek came to Janice and laid an arm across her shoulders.

"*Damn* her jealousy!" Janice burst out. "I covexed for her! What more does she want?"

"This is a difficult time for all of us," he said. "Maybe you should cool things off a bit with JennaMara. Just for a while, till I-we get my-our feet back under me-us."

Janice dashed away tears, frowning. "Derek, I'm not—do you realize how—" She drew a breath. "Christ. A beautiful young woman like Charlotte is in love with me. With *me*, Derek. Not Manda—not Teresa, even—but me. Do you know how long it's been since—" Then she saw Manda, and registered surprise.

Manda couldn't think of what to say, so she just went over and hugged Janice. Janice gripped her back, hard, with a small cry.

Manda had always thought her older siblings were beyond the sweet-painful allure of romance and desire. But Janice smelled of dust and live oil and sex.

"Come to bed," Manda said awkwardly. "Come on," and brought her older sister inside. "It'll be OK."

That ancient phrase: that most honorable, comforting of lies.

The next morning, Manda set *Aculei Duo, Quatuor, Quinque,* and *Septimus* to work mapping the topography and marine chemistry of Rima Optabile, starting in its northern quadrant. *Aculei Unus, Tres,* and *Sexis*—all thousands of kilometers away from the trench—she directed to stop what they were doing and come to the site. It would be a good week or more before they would arrive. Then she began in earnest to search for *Aculeus Octo*.

She needed to find out whether *Octo* was functional and receiving her signals. And there was a simple way to do that: she could route a signal through her other waldos telling *Octo* to generate a loud sonar pulse on all frequencies at once—and tell her other marine-waldos to listen for that pulse. If any of them heard it, she'd know that *Octo* was at least receiving her commands.

She brought up her other marine-waldos, commanded them to listen for a broad-band sonic pulse, and sent the *ping* command. Then she waited.

And there it was! They each heard *Octo*'s *ping*, well under a minute from when she'd transmitted the command. That meant *Octo* was operational and receiving her transmissions. And the lag in the other waldos' receipt of the signal gave her *Octo*'s exact location. It was about sixty-five kilometers due south of the other four units, at about five kilometers' depth. Promising too, this hint that *Octo* appeared to be operational so far below its design depth. And there was more good news: the return *ping* meant that the communication breakdown had to be somewhere along the path of the waldo's transmissions—not a problem with *Octo*'s navigational systems.

Manda's digital "conversations" with her waldos were transmitted via the colony's radio router to the satellite DMiTRI, which relayed the signal to the drill-site radio router, which in turn processed the signals and relayed them by wire to and from the sonar transponders at the bottom of the drill hole. Some device along that chain was losing track of or misinterpreting *Octo*'s signals.

She spent the next few hours pulling up the command interfaces of the different routers that carried her marine-waldos' signals, examining their routing instructions for errors. But she found none. Then she tried tricking the faulty phantom device by renaming *Octo*'s ID code—which resulted in *Octo* ceasing to respond to her *ping* commands at all.

Shit. She rubbed at her eyes and stared again the wraithlike, floating shapes of her liveface that hung before her—so tired and frustrated by now that she was losing track of which waldo was which. Time to call it a watch.

While standing in line in the mess to grab a quick bite, she checked her messages. One had just come in from Paul. She immediately pulled it up. It was a video recording, dated only a moment before. He looked calm and sad.

"I'm sorry for what I said to you the other night, Manda. But I just can't. I can't stay. Not without Teresa." A long pause, while he stared at emptiness. Then he gave her a look with a plea in it. "Forgive me."

Then he reached up and cut off the signal.

"*No!*" she shouted. Heads turned to look at her. She leapt to her feet, and stabbed at comm icons while dashing down the corridors, climbing down ladders, dogging waldos, robots, pedestrians.

He'd been at the recycling vats. She'd seen the catwalks behind him. Shit shit *shit!*

"Derek! Arlene!" She tried all of her siblings over the facelink, stabbing at the quick-icons in her commware, one after the other. No one was answering.

She entered the recycling cavern. The steamy heat and the overpowering smell of chemicals, of decomposition and reformation, made her stumble and gag as she ran out onto the metal catwalk.

She spotted the rest of her clone, converging on the catwalks, and hurried over, holding her gaiter over her nose. At their feet was a neatly piled stack of clothing and a livesuit and yoke. Paul's.

Farrah was holding onto Janice, who was sobbing. Arlene, Derek, Bart, and Charles crowded together, looking over the side of the catwalk, lost in shock.

Manda leaned over and looked into the huge, steaming vats

below. No sign of him in the syrupy-thick liquid. But the mixing blades would have pulled him under immediately, and nobody knew how to swim anyway. There was no need on a frozen world. And if he couldn't get out right away, the acids and enzymes would begin to liquify his tissues within moments. But maybe—maybe there was still time—

"Paul!" she yelled, leaning dangerously far over the top rail. "*Paul!*"

Charles dragged her back. "He's gone. He queued the messages to be sent after he'd taken his dive."

With a growl, Manda jerked free and climbed back onto the railing.

"Coward!" she screamed at the vats. "You fucking son of a bitch! I'll *never* forgive you! Never!"

"Stop it! Stop it! You'll fall. We don't want to lose you too." Her siblings were saying these and other things to her, but she wasn't listening. She took her anger at Paul out on them, hitting and shoving as they tried to pull her back. Bart, Charles, and Farrah finally managed to get her down, and Janice grabbed her in a hug till she stopped fighting them.

They tried to talk her into joining them in their sleeping quarters. But she refused. She was so angry she needed to climb right out of her skin. She needed to run till she stopped feeling the need to kill.

Eventually her run became a walk, and her walk became aimless wanderings, around and around through the main tunnels and up and down the stairs. Finally, exhausted but unable to imagine sleeping, she went to the infirmary and spent much of the first-watch sleep staring at her infant clone-brother Terence, her mind empty of anything but wordless pain.

A while later a RoxannaTomas pair, a young male and female, swam into view. Behind the twins were several other people. Manda looked up from where she had settled, hunched over her crossed legs on the cold, hard floor next to Terence's incubator, too tired to think or move.

"I'll handle this," the female told the rest, who left, except for her twin, who hovered nearby, looking worried. She helped Manda stand. "Where do you sleep?" she asked.

"Jeannelle?" Manda asked. "Vance?"

The others nodded. Manda muttered some response, and Jeannelle and Vance walked her there with a hand on each elbow. It was Manda's little cubby. Jeannelle stood by while Manda undressed. Then she climbed in and sat down beside her, and pulled the covers over her. Vance came to the door, pushing the plastic strips aside.

"You going to be OK?" Jeannelle asked. They both were looking at her with their four brown eyes.

Manda released a breath, glad to be horizontal under her down comforter. Behind her eyes and in her sinuses, a terrible pressure throbbed. She didn't figure she'd be sleeping soon. "Eventually."

Jeannelle seemed to be struggling with something. She gave Vance a glance. He nodded. Jeannelle turned back to Manda. "You remember when you asked us whether anybody could harm the vats?"

Manda nodded.

"Our older siblings told us," Vance said, "that rumors were circulating when we first made landfall that someone had poisoned you and your vat-mate, back on *Exodus*, while you were still in vitro." "They said that was why your twin died," Jeannelle went on. "No solid evidence was found so the matter was dropped."

Manda came up on her elbows, stunned.

"Why didn't you tell me before?"

Jeannelle and Vance looked embarrassed. "We didn't want to stir up trouble." "It was so long ago, and nothing like that has ever happened here, on Brimstone." "We're sorry we didn't tell you when you first asked." "Maybe we shouldn't be telling you now, but—""—under the circumstances—" "—we felt we owed you an answer."

Manda laid back down, trying to take it in. "It's all right. Thanks," she added, as the twins pushed the curtain of plastic strips aside.

They gave her identical smiles, standing under the craggy arch that made up the tiny cul-de-sac's entrance. "Get some rest." "We'll take good care of your little brother." "We promise."

Manda caught a glimpse of them walking away arm-in-arm, reminding her of how Teresa and Paul had been. It squeezed the breath from her chest. She gripped the covers under her chin.

I'll miss you, Paul. Believe it or not, you bastard—I'll miss you.

Finally, tears came. And afterward, sleep.

Paul had plunged into the recycling vats to escape his pain; Manda plunged into her work. She got up early—tired, but too wound up to sleep—and checked her messages.

ByronDalia had sent her an executable file: "In partial payment for your assistance the other day—" "—we thought you'd like to try out this app we've just developed." "It'll accelerate your liveface." "You'll no longer need a livepack to access the high-rez modes." "Alert us to any bugs." "Enjoy!" "—Oh, by the way. If you're ever interested in—" "—joining us down in the hot springs—" "—give us a buzz."

As if! she thought. Still, the corners of her mouth twitched upward as Manda opened and installed the app.

When she unplugged from her livepack and ran her liveface through its paces, she was delighted to find that it ran the highest-resolution mode of her marine-waldos' commandsphere beautifully. She noticed a few places where the icons took a little longer to render themselves or respond to her commands than she was used to, but that was a small price to pay for the freedom of movement she could now enjoy, no longer hindered by her livepack. It meant she'd be able to move throughout the caverns while keeping this high-rez mode! She was delighted.

Once she'd satisfied herself the accelerator wouldn't ruin her data, she called up her marine-waldo commandface. She messed around with a lot of different tricks, trying to isolate the problem area with *Aculeus Octo*. But every time she thought she was closing in on the programming bug causing the malfunction, it eluded her, popping up again outside the walls she'd erected to trap it.

Manda decided to do a different kind of diagnostic. First she set up her linkware to transmit an "attend!" command to *Octo* every second. If it was receiving her signal, it should make an automatic acknowledgment, regardless of whether she could detect it from here. Then she borrowed a spare radio transponder with a directional antenna.

The colony had plenty of radio I/O units; they and a parallel omni I/O port were a standard peripheral for all teleoperated waldos and robots, and were built into everyone's liveyokes as well. And the other day while preparing Crane, Mole, and Scaffold for the rescue work, Manda had come across some directional radio antennae—which would allow her to go outside and collect transmissions directly, instead of having to go through all the routers and servers that made up the wide area network. So she gathered her equipment, donned her radiation dosimeter and rad-alert link, and took the elevators (which, thankfully, were working this time) up to the surface.

The primary colony entrance was a cavern with black schist flagstones glazed with ice, and large metal doors that sealed out the elements. The doors were made from portions of *Exodus*'s titanium bulkheads, hammered and welded into shape. Set into the big doors were smaller, human- and animal-sized doors, likewise scrounged from the starship's castoff materials. Against the far wall, a huge, segmented, many-legged robotic fuel tanker clambered through a circular-shutter opening and across the flagstones, making a terrible echoing racket, to grab onto a lift cable and be lowered into a large hole in the floor.

Closer to Manda, a threeclone and its dogs were herding reindeer out; the skittish creatures didn't like all the noise the fueler made and tossed their antlered heads, prancing, trying to avoid being forced through the narrow door out into the brightness. But the shepherds with their canes and dogs kept them penned, and in ones and twos the animals darted out the door. Manda neared them. A breeze chilled her face. She pulled on her parka hood, put on her shells over her mittens, and followed the herders out, pulling her neck gaiter up over her mouth and nose.

Sun- , planet- , and moonshine burst on Manda, breaking her shadow into a cascade of pale colors as she exited and skated down the gentle slope. She ended up on her rump.

Manda blinked against the brightness and looked around. Along with Fire, all but full, and tiny, blazing Uma, several moons were scattered across the sky in phases varying from gibbous to crescent. It was a warm day, for Brimstone in early spring: approaching minus ten Celsius, according to her readout. She pulled her gaiter down and loosened the hood of her parka. Herds of animals and their tenders dotted the plain: dark flecks of life that moved across the snow, grazing on snow moss, algae, and lichens.

She had replaced her more fragile liveware with goggles, mic, and a wrist unit, all attached to her yoke. Despite her many layers, she still felt naked without her livesuit. Manda scrambled to her feet, adjusted her goggles, and took a deep breath, thankful that summer would be here in less than an earth-year. *If the colony lasts that long.*

Then she shaded her eyes and looked up for the window to Carli's hidden room. As she'd expected, she couldn't see it from here. She traced with her gaze the ridge's outline against the indigo sky, and trudged through the dirty snow to set up her equipment a short distance from the colony entrance, within line of sight of the radio tower.

Manda aimed her antenna at the tower and watched the digital readout of her unit. Plenty of radio traffic was going to and from the satellite. She reconfigured her unit to look for her repeating "attend!" signal to *Octo*, and received it right away. This merely confirmed what she already knew—or had thought she knew: that her transmissions were making it out of the colony network. But it was good to have direct confirmation.

Next, she pointed her antenna toward Fire, above the western horizon. Since DMiTRI was in Brimstone-stationary orbit between Brimstone and its parent world, she also should be able to pick up its transmissions with her directional antenna. And indeed, she picked up her signal: *attend . . . attend . . . attend . . .* was reflected back to her, a digital heartbeat broadcast across space. Since DMiTRI transmitted the same signals to Amaterasu as it did to the drill site, she now knew that the satellite DMiTRI was not merely receiving her transmissions, but was also relaying them to the drill site.

She then reconfigured her radio unit to look for *Aculeus Octo's* ID among the signals returning from DMiTRI.

Nothing.

A wave of discouragement overcame her at this, and Manda slumped over her knees. She was tired of fighting fate. She wanted to just leave the stupid malfunctioning piece of junk where it was. Serve it right.

Pull it together, Manda. This isn't like you. Giving up on Octo won't help Paul, Teresa, or anyone else.

She stood up to pace a bit, thinking.

OK. So. I know that DMiTRI isn't routing Octo's transmissions here to Amaterasu. What I still don't know is whether it's receiving them from the drill site.

As she watched a fuel tanker exit the waldo opening and scramble across the terrain like a gigantic millipede, heading toward the refinery, she realized that she had a way to find out. She called Jim.

"That's so weird," he said, a giant, disembodied face projected onto her goggles, and an equally huge arm that bracketed her on either side.

"What?"

"I was just about to call you."

"Oh?" She felt, absurdly, both nervous and pleased. "Why?"

"Well, I'm getting some odd interference with one of my sonar devices and I wondered whether—"

"Yes! Me too. That's why I was calling. Tell me more."

He frowned and shook his head. "I don't know much yet. The problem just started. I'm starting to get garbage from my underwater seismograph. As if it's gotten confused and started transmitting on multiple frequencies, all at once."

"Not all your seismographs?"

"No. And it's sporadic."

"Oh. That *is* odd." They stood there grinning at each other, awkward. Manda said, "My trouble is different. It seems that somewhere along the way, an intermediate I/O device has lost *Octo*'s ID."

"Maybe it's like you thought originally, that your waldo's been destroyed."

"No; I had it *ping* me yesterday and got a clear signal through from the other waldos. So I tried routing all its signals through them and lost contact altogether. I'm not getting any response from it at all now. I am pretty sure this is some bug in the signal-relay system."

"Just a minute." He talked for a couple of moments to someone Manda couldn't see, about refinery business. "Sorry. Where were we?—Oh, yes! The communication failure. I'm wondering whether your failure could be in some roundabout way related to my problem—perhaps some kind of sonic interference is scrambling your link with *Octo*."

She frowned. "I don't think so," she said slowly, "but I don't know enough to rule it out yet. And it does seem awfully coincidental that we're both having sonar problems at the same time. I was thinking—"

"What's that?" Jim lifted a finger, asking Manda to hold on, and looked at someone else, whose voice Manda could barely make out over his link. "More blockage?—Did you try reversing the flow and clearing it that way?—What about sealing off the line and steam-blasting it out?—All right. All right. I'll be there in a minute. Manda, we're having some difficulties with one of our reactor feed lines. I have to go. Maybe we can troubleshoot for each other tomorrow."

"Sure." Manda signed off, and collected her thoughts and equipment at the same time.

The fact was, she didn't feel like spending the rest of the day trying to hack around the bug via her livelink. Coding wasn't her specialty. And she didn't feel like being around her clone right now. Not so soon after she'd spent a sleep session with it. Not so soon after Paul's death.

Her glance wandered up to the fuel tanker robot, now a sinuous dark blotch creeping toward the edge of the horizon. Tankers left every hour or so. She could head back down to the caverns, pack a few things, and hitch a ride on the next fuel tanker out. It was still early in Brimstone's long day; the eight-hour ride and another hour or two to reach the drill site would still leave her a full watch's worth of sun- and planetshine to check out the radio relay and the sonar transponders. If Jim was too busy to go with her, there was no reason she couldn't go alone.

The tankers had originally been designed for liquid and pressurized gas, not passenger transport, but the leading segment of each tanker had been rigged to carry people and supplies for the refinery. At a signal from the controller in his station by the tanker hole, as the empty tanker leapt off the lift cable it paused, and Manda scrambled up the ladder set into its side and swung into the poorly-lit passenger and supplies bay. Belts, straps, and loops of knotted rope were set into the sides of the cylindrical tank, and a flat floor bisected the cylinder.

The tanker started to move. Manda slammed the door closed with all her might, then hurriedly secured her pack to the wall and grabbed a knot—and held on tight as the tanker lurched forward.

The terrain was rough. Anything not bolted to the floor or walls got quite a shaking. But the tanker soon settled into a rude rhythm, and Manda got the hang of staying upright. She found a pile of skins in the cold dimness and settled next to some crates. For a while she played *Commandos*, an early twenty-second-century action simile, to keep herself occupied. Then she curled up among the skins and dozed.

A particularly big jolt woke her up. She relieved herself in the small, makeshift lavatory aft of the cargo bay, and then returned to the main compartment and opened the sliding door. The wind stole her breath. Shivering, she tightened her hood till its fur lining tickled her cheeks and lips, and hung onto a knotted rope to watch the tanker's big mechanical legs flash underneath, flinging clots of snow and dirt high into the air.

Mountain cliffs—glassy-brown volcanic rock, ice-streaked, and marbled with veins of coarse, maroon-tinged stone—rose and fell past the door opening. The way the cliff face receded and returned reminded her of her datascapes. Dante crept across the heavens, waxing almost perceptibly as it neared the zenith from the east, passing God's Wrath on its way west. Uma shone down from overhead and Fire—now half-full, its upper curve lit and the lower reaches in shadow—was partway below the eastern horizon; they were nearing their destination.

Moments later the fuel tanker scrambled its way up the rise to the steel towers and tanks of the refinery. Manda heard voices outside the open door as the tanker skidded to a halt. She gathered her things, while the refinery lifter-waldos scrambled in and began unloading cargo onto a conveyor-waldo that had positioned itself outside the cargo door. Then she looked out.

Below, Amy was directing the waste oil unloading effort. Big pipes swung over and connected themselves to valved joints on top of the tank cars. All around were the makeshift towers, pipes, manifolds, and cylinders that made up the refinery— salvaged mostly from discarded pieces of the waldo space-pods that had delivered the colony's technological cargo and supplies, back before landfall.

Steam billowed and hissed among the pipes; fluids shrieked as they raced through feed and effluent lines; heat waves emanated from tanks and pipes, making the plant look like a poorly rendered virtual image set against the vast glacier Maia's banks. The main oil well stood a kilometer or more away, down on the ice floes: a blue flare and a stout, metal tower with a thick pipe down its throat. The pipe climbed the hill to a big valve manifold near the huge, ugly catalytic cracker. The well, like the cat-cracker, stood in a large stain of dirt, slush, and oil.

She caught a whiff of a sweetish organic smell, perhaps kerosene. In the early afternoon sun-, moon-, and planetshine, ice crystals billowed past the tanker opening like curtains of pale silver sparks.

A gust sliced right through Manda's parka as she slung her pack over her shoulder and scrambled down the ladder. Amy rode a gust over to her, arms outspread to keep her balance, and startled Manda by giving her a big hug.

"This is a surprise!" she said over the wind. "To what do we owe the pleasure?"

Flustered, Manda eyed Amy, who was beaming at her with features so like Jim's. "I have some work to do out at the original drill site. Is Jim around?"

"Sure." Amy hooked an arm through hers. "They're just serving lunch. He'll be there. Come on!"

Along with a small group of others, they hurried to a long, low, windowless building set into the hillside, and shut out the wind. They all stamped their feet, shaking the snow and dirt off their boots, and hung their parkas on hooks by the door. Jim and Brian sat at a long table nearby with perhaps another dozen people. Steaming pots of food lined the far wall. Manda's mouth watered.

Amy said, "Look what the wind blew us!" and heads turned. Manda looked from one to the other of the identical brothers, but Jim's friendly gaze made her able to distinguish him, even before he stood, looking pleased, to offer her a space next to his. "Just in time for lunch. Join us."

"We heard about Paul," Brian and Jim said in stereo, as Manda sat down between them. "We're very sorry," Jim added.

"Thanks." Manda tried not to choke on the word.

"When is the memorial service?" Brian asked.

"In three days."

"Did you hear?" Amy asked, returning from the buffet. She set a plate in front of Manda and another at her own spot, next to Brian. The refinery people didn't bother to ration their food so precisely as the main colony did; though food was doled out to the refinery according to how many people were here, the refinery crew was small enough, Manda supposed, not to require such a fuss about who ate how much. They were more like a big, rowdy, extended clone-family. She worried about depriving them of their share merely by being here, an unaccounted-for guest, and resolved to mail them some tokens when she got back to Amaterasu.

"Logan JennaByron was found outside this morning," Amy went on, "by the herders. Frozen to death."

Logan, the man Manda and the LuisMichael triplets had rescued, had been the last of his clone; the other four had been killed in the cave-in. Everyone greeted this news with silence, and they all ate their stew and *mana* without speaking.

She'd never liked Logan much. But it seemed such a waste, after he'd survived the quake and more than fifty hours of being buried alive.

"What's the latest on Hydroponics?" a female UrsulaTomas

asked Manda. Catching Jim's interested gaze, Manda stifled an urge to retort *how should I know?* and struggled to remember her siblings' words during yesterday's first-watch sleep.

"It'll be a while before there's much to report. They're still trying to clean up the debris and salvage all the scrap metal and usable equipment they can find."

This generated a heated argument having to do with the refinery. Manda failed to see the connection until Jim leaned over and explained, "We're trying to figure out whether we can retool one of our spare reactors to produce something from cat-cracker tars that's usable by the food recyclers."

"It's not that simple!" Amy was talking to an UrsulaTomas, a gaunt young man with green eyes and brown skin. "It just won't work."

He said, "What if up the acid content—"

"No, Amy is right," Brian said. "I-we've been looking over the recycler influx specs GeorgJean sent, and a one-step, two-phase process won't work." "Too many impurities crop up," Amy added, "regardless of temperature or acid-to-hydrocarbon ratio."

"But how can we be sure unless we try?"

"We did!" all three LuisMichaels replied. "I-we already did some bench tests," Amy said, and Jim added, "The product yield doesn't improve; the mix of impurities merely changes."

And the argument resurged, as others tossed in their opinions and ideas. Manda watched as all three LuisMichaels and the rest of their team argued fine points of organic chemistry. Apparently they were doing some bench-scale tests to see what reaction inputs, mixes, pressures, and temperatures might produce compounds the recyclers could use.

It's so hopeful, Manda thought, *LuisMichael. Determined. Always looking for solutions. We should clone more of it.* Then she laughed at herself. *Developing an interest in genetic politics, are we? I sound like Derek and Arlene.*

*   *   *

While they were cleaning the dishes, a radiation alarm went off both in-face and ex-face. A pair of UrsulaTomases called up the details on their faceware.

"Solar flare, looks like," they said. "A short one, they're telling us—" "—but a bad one." "No personnel outside for more than five minutes without protective gear."

Manda frowned at Jim. "I need to get out to the drill site."

"It'll be a while before it's safe," he replied. "Why don't you rest while I pack up some things? I'll escort you out there once the radiation storm subsides."

"You don't have to do that. I'll be fine alone."

"It's a safety rule," he said. "No one goes out without a partner."

Manda felt her face grow warm. For anyone else, it wouldn't be an issue; their vat-mate would be their partner. She had this urge to apologize, and an equally powerful urge to insult him—make him angry so he'd let her go alone. But Jim's friendly expression defused the latter impulse, and as for the former, she'd be damned if she'd apologize for being a single.

Her glance went to Amy and Brian, who were bundling up the trash. Jim saw where she was looking, and shook his head with a smile. "Don't worry. We're not as intro-bonded out here as you folks at the caverns are. Can't afford to be—don't have the bandwidth. I can handle a day away from them, if need be."

"OK." Manda smiled. "Thanks."

S he slept for a while, and was awakened by Amy. "Solar storm's past," she said. "Jim's ready to go."

Manda checked her watch. It was thirteen-ten: still a few hours left before occultation and sunset. She pulled on her parka and stepped outside after Amy. Though it was breezy, the gusts had ebbed. Temperatures had dropped to a joint-stiffening thirty below, but without the wind it didn't feel quite as bad. Jim was waiting for Manda nearby, making a last-minute check of his supplies. He gave Amy a hug.

"Back soon," he said.

"Be careful."

"Always."

Manda and Jim donned their canned air and respirators, and then skate-skied down past the refinery and the scrounge yard: a big pile of bamboo poles, castoff equipment, and scrap metal from *Exodus* and Amaterasu, kept for repairs and tooling. She paused to eye the metaglass submersible that JebMeri had used to explore the ocean floor, back when. It was a big sphere with a single hatch. Its sides were badly stained, pockmarked, and discolored, and she couldn't make out much detail.

"How did they ever recover that thing?" she asked. "I was so little I didn't really get what was going on." All she remembered hearing was that after several weeks of exploring, the crew had stopped sending its periodic info pods to the drill-site monitoring crew, and it was almost seven seasons after that that the pod was recovered and the remains of the crew brought home for recycling. They'd discovered a massive failure of the onboard computer systems.

Jim favored her with a wry look.

"Now *there's* a story. I-we found it my-ourself."

"Oh?"

"Uh-huh." He started moving again, and she followed. "I-we occasionally get satellite or weather-balloon information on Brimstone's topography and surface temperatures from the meteorology people. I-we use it for our geological surveys." He chuckled. "I was so full of myself, back then. No more than a kid. One day I was studying the surface data and happened to notice an odd thermal anomaly on the equatorial ice floes. Just a little pinprick, but I thought it might indicate volcanism under the ice. I pointed it out to my older sisters. They went out with a small team of waldos and did some drilling down there, and found the submersible jammed in the ice—ten or twenty meters below the surface. Apparently the crew had dropped their propulsion engines and did an emergency ascent in the sphere. But they couldn't get a signal out, and got stuck under the ice. They died waiting for rescue."

"What a horrible way to die."

Jim nodded sober agreement. "Yeah. Anyhow, the submersible's antimatter power source was still working and the unit was more buoyant than the surrounding ice, and it just slowly melted its way up through the ice and slush for ten seasons. In another few seasons it would probably have surfaced on its own."

"What's it doing out here?"

"The refinery got to keep it. Salvage rights, I guess you'd call it." He grinned at her. "We plan to use it as a replacement for our high-pressure hydrofluoric unit, eventually."

Manda gave it a last glance over her shoulder, and shuddered. Waldos were definitely the way to go, down in the depths.

The drill site was about five kilometers away, out on the ice floes. They followed the ice river Maia down the gently sloping valley it had carved through surrounding rock canyons, to the coast, where the ice floes lay that made up the surface of the Omi-Kami Sea.

In Brimstone's rarified air, pony bottles were needed if you did heavy physical labor. The trick to using them was to breathe through your nose as much as you could, but every fifth or sixth breath—more often if you grew winded or dizzy—pull some compressed air in. The air supply lasted longer that way, and you didn't have to carry a lot of spare bottles. It took Manda a while to get the hang of it again.

Omi-Kami sang a song more gutteral than the wind's soft waiting. Its groans, made by ice shelves rubbing and bumping against each other, were not as loud as Manda remembered, but still Manda heard the sea before she saw it, even over the hissing of air through the respirator she clenched in her teeth. Then they rounded the last curve and raced down a gully on their blades, and as they sliced to a stop on an outcropping, she saw it, spread out before them beneath the moon-spattered sky.

Uma was at their backs now, in mid-afternoon, with Fire peering over the horizon and waning to a crescent. The Host and Little Hellion had joined Dante and Archangel in the sky, just rising: all of them bright moons near full. Omi-Kami's surface was brilliantly reflective, even through Manda's polarized goggles.

The sea's surface sparkled, churned up in a frozen meringue with a billion peaks and slopes. Jim and Manda sat down on the rocks of the outcropping to remove their ski-skates. They slung the long blades onto their backs, then extended the cleats on their boots and helped each other stand.

Jim smiled at her and wiped ice from his mustache, and started down. Manda followed.

It was slower and rougher going out on the floes than their skate-ski down the hillside had been. Manda let Jim lead the way. He came out here often and was more familiar with the safest routes. They walked among jutting crests, hillocks, and tors of sparkling blue ice, and twice put their blades back on to cross mirror-smooth ice pools. In other places, cleated again, they waded carefully through neck-high brambles of frost daggers and spires that clattered and twinkled like bells.

They also encountered something in the midst of an ice bramble that Manda had only heard of: an ice-sprite, an airy, insubstantial ice-crystal structure as big as a house, suspended among Omi-Kami's rigid waves. Fractal, geometric, and spidery, it shivered and glimmered, breathtakingly beautiful. Manda gasped. Then a snowdevil swirled past them, and the structure exploded in a tinkling cloud of ice flecks that lighted on their cheeks and eyelashes.

"They're rare this time of year," Jim said. "Especially one that big. The spring winds usually knock them down before they have a chance to form."

Then he sat and dragged several breaths through his respirator. Time for a break. Manda gratefully joined him.

Though he was out of breath too, she guessed the stop was mostly for her sake; she was a lot more winded and shaky than he seemed. The cold had scoured her sinuses and lungs, and the sparks dancing across her vision had nothing to do with ice crystals. She was trembling with exhaustion and chronic hunger.

Her waldo piloting took no small physical effort, but long hikes out in the severe cold were a lot more demanding than even her typical sixteen hours' worth of pirouettes and arm motions every day. She hunched over her knees and drew several deep breaths through her respirator, then—when her lungs stopped demanding so much extra—took the piece out of her mouth and inhaled more slowly.

She checked the gauge. Almost empty. Going through air awfully fast. She dug through her pack and got one of her two spares out.

"Help me swap out bottles, would you?"

She turned around and let Jim disconnect her old bottle and put in a new one. Meanwhile she tightened the drawstring on the face of her parka and then tucked her gloved, mittened, and shelled hands under her armpits, wishing she had a way to warm up her feet, and the tip of her nose—and her eyes, which stung with cold-burn.

Don't think about it; you'll only make yourself miserable.

"I've been wondering," she said, after a moment or two. "When Amy and Brian left—" Then she broke off, frowning, not sure how to ask what she wanted to know.

"Go on," he urged, and Manda drew a deep breath and started over.

"At the cave-in—"

"Yes?"

"What made you stay?"

He just rubbed at the ice in his beard, with a thoughtful expression. Then he shrugged, with a smile. "It happens. They're used to it. They get the same way sometimes. Come on." He stood. "We're burning daylight."

They moved on. This early in spring the floes were still mostly solid, and the markers—high-visibility orange tape that fluttered in the breeze on tall poles of ice-encrusted bamboo—marked a safe passage for them. But Manda had had a close call on the floes with a waldo once, and was cautious. This close to the equator the floes were karst-like, even in this early in the spring. Air pockets and seawater-saturated caverns lay beneath the surface. People had been lost. Manda didn't care to be one of them.

By about fifteen-thirty, Manda spotted the radio antenna atop the drill scaffold. Ten minutes later they reached the drill site.

The hole itself was a good three meters in diameter, with a stout bamboo scaffold erected over it, supporting a stout bundle of wires and cables that hung down into the hole. The shelter stood nearby. It was made of half-meter-thick ice bricks over a domed, bamboo-and-mud structure, and looked like an enormous, dirty, lumpy ball of ice with a door in it, half sunk into the floes. Abutting the shelter was a metal toolshed, and beside that, a frozen-over trash pit and some large waldos and other equipment for maintaining the hole and the shelter.

Manda hooked herself to a safety line and walked over to look down. The drill hole receded into darkness. The lapping of water echoed up from far below.

"Let's have a bite to eat and take a short break before we get to work," Jim suggested. Together they chopped and hacked with their hand axes at a place near the hole, till they had several fist-sized chunks of ice. Then Jim led the way through the arch of ice-and-mud bricks into the shelter.

The musty, dark little room had a stove in its center. On one side were piles of musk-ox-hair blankets and reindeer skins, and on the other side were two bunks, a wash stand, and a chamberpot. Next to the stove stood a small bamboo table with two chairs of leather stretched across bamboo frames. Shelves with cooking utensils of aluminum or bamboo, nonperishable food, a battery-operated radio, and first-aid supplies were built into the wall by the door.

Manda dumped the ice chunks into a pot while Jim lit the stove and storm lantern. Then she sat down with a sigh, pulled off her shells, mittens, and gloves, and rubbed at her stiff fingers. Once the water had melted, Jim made them some tea, and Manda shared her rations with him. The rations barely satisfied her hunger.

"Can I share a secret with you?" she asked. "It's, um, kind of weird."

She didn't want to tell him about the secret room or Carli's corpse. And she didn't want to get him into trouble—nor was she ready to defy Derek so blatantly—by telling Jim outright about *Exodus* still being insystem. But she wanted someone else's perspective on it, and Jim had always struck her as both smart *and* sensible, not given to flights of fancy.

"Sure," he said, grinning, around a mouthful of sandwich. "Why not? Go ahead."

"Do you remember much about the crèche-born?"

He shrugged. "Sure. I was nine when we left the ship, old enough to remember some things. Why?"

"Suppose," she said after a pause—slowly, thinking through each phrase before she released it—"suppose we could contact *Exodus*. And suppose they had a way of helping us, if we could persuade them to. Perhaps send us more equipment to rebuild our Hydroponics, or at least some food supplies that would buy us more time. Everybody tells me how weird they are, but surely they don't want to see this colony fail. Why else would they go to all the trouble and expense of putting us here?"

His eyebrows shot up. "That's an odd question. What—"

"Please don't ask me to explain. Just play a mental game with me. Just *suppose*."

He leaned forward on his knees. "I shouldn't be dredging this up, but I'll tell you what I heard. The council doesn't *want* any further contact with *Exodus*."

The skin on the back of Manda's neck tingled. "Who told you that?"

"Bella and Dennie, shortly before they died." Isabella and Denise, Jim's older clone-siblings, had been killed in an accident at the refinery, back when Manda was an adolescent. *Another accident?* Manda thought, and then decided she was being paranoid. "They got totally junked one night at a covalence out here, and told us that just after landfall the council blocked all communications from the ship. But you probably know all this already, your clone being on the council."

Manda scowled. "No, actually. I didn't." But it made sense.

"Hmmph." Jim gave her a speculative look and sat back, twiddling with a lock of his beard. "Well, since then I-we've been cashing in coup on key questions here and there, and I-we've pieced some things together. I-we think something really bad happened, right before we made landfall—something none of the adult founders want to talk to us younger generation about. We kept hearing rumors of a big fight, mostly in-face, with the leaders of the colonizing effort and the crèche-born all involved.

"We don't know who was fighting who or anything. I mean, I was only a kid, but I was old enough to remember how worried everybody was. I didn't know why, but . . . Anyway, some even say a few of our kind disappeared, and a couple of the crèche-born turned up dead too."

Manda thought about the rumored poisoning of her vat. What possible motive could they have had? Other than to terrorize. But perhaps that was motive enough. "Wow."

"Yeah. Best I-we can tell, nobody but the councilmembers and maybe a few other old folks know it even happened—never mind what it was about or what the outcome was—but the next thing we knew, two of the colony's clones were being left behind, *Exodus* was out of contact, and the councilmembers were telling us they were gone for good. Which we—Brian and Amy and me, I mean—know had to be bullshit—they needed at least fifteen seasons to refuel their ship before they left. But I imagine they're long gone for real by now."

Manda thought, *what the fuck. If Derek and Arlene lie to me they can't expect me to protect their secret.*

"No," she said. "Actually, they're not. They're in a circular orbit about a third of an AU from Uma, and their solar collectors seem to be at full extension. They're still around."

Now it was Jim's turn to gape. "No shit."

"No shit."

They were both silent, watching the gas jets burn inside the stove, feeling its feeble heat on their bare faces and hands in the jarring cold of the shack.

"Do you ever feel like something is nibbling away at the fabric of the world," Manda asked after a moment, "and all kinds of seething, nasty stuff is hiding underneath, that you didn't even know was there?"

Jim looked at her, his eyes wide and glinting in the dimness. "I wish I knew what the hell was going on."

"Me too."

There seemed nothing left to say. Manda stood. "I guess we should get back to work."

His chair was closer to the exit than hers, so they both ended up at the door and reaching for the latch at the same instant. Manda panicked. She pulled her hand away and, as he turned his head to look at her, shrank back. Just a little—it was hardly a movement at all.

It was just too cliché, that they should exo-bond just because they were singling it together, out on the ice.

Jim gave her a look both gentle and a little sad, and merely pulled his mittens and shells on. "We've got a lot to do before nightfall," he said, pushing the door open. "Come on."

She followed him out, unsure whether to be disappointed or relieved.

Manda set up her radio equipment while Jim did some calibrating tests with one of his seismographs a short distance from the hole. Then she performed the same radio I/O tests she had done outside of Amaterasu. Jim came up just as she was finishing.

"What did you find?" he asked, as she rocked back on her heels. Manda pointed at the radio relay box and antenna on top of the scaffold.

"None of *Aculeus Octo*'s transmissions are making it past that relay," she said.

"Hmmph."

"And you?"

"Well, that one"—he jerked his thumb at the seismograph nearby that he'd been checking—"is fine, but I haven't been having any troubles with it, so it's no big surprise. It's the one underwater I'm concerned about. Let me borrow your radio transponder and I'll check my underwater unit's transmissions to and from the satellite."

"Sure. Meanwhile I'll head up onto the scaffold. I'm going to tap directly into the lines at the relay box from the sonar transponders, and see if *Octo*'s signals are making it up through the cables."

By the time she'd gotten her line-tap equipment and scaled the scaffold ladder, Fire and its ring were a slim, crisscrossed double-crescent of light, and Uma hovered less than a handspan from the gas giant's shoulder. Lightning storms crawled like fireflies across Fire's night side.

It was getting colder—perhaps thirty-five below or so. In less than half an hour, the eclipse that precluded nightfall would come. Archangel, gibbous now, had moved back up the eastern sky, after sinking downward for a while. Now it was in one of its rarer positions: inside the wobbly cluster of rocks that made up the Host. Fire's two innermost moons, Demon and Little Hellion, had raced past all the others in the last hour, and were now slim crescents setting beyond Fire in the west. Heaven's Gate, a big, bright, pale-aqua globe, was rising in the east as smaller, mottled, bronze-and-golden Dante, also full, set, almost directly in front of it.

Brimstone's skies never, ever looked the same, from one hour to the next. The other moons' phases and paths across the sky were always changing. Even Uma's path wasn't as constant as it would be from the surface of a planet. It was all a fabulous, impossible, carefully-choreographed dance. Only massive Fire remained unchanged, dominating the dance.

The skies reminded Manda of a cosmic game of billiards, in which the light source was constantly in motion, shadows shifted wildly, and somehow, miraculously, none of the balls ever seemed to collide. It was the one thing about this world that Manda loved without reservation or qualification. The skies.

At the edge of the scaffold, ready to climb, she eyed the clip and rope attached to her safety harness. She was exhausted, from her journey to the refinery and the hike out here, from her sleepless night yesterday, from being out in the stiletto-hard cold for so long. From grieving. Grieving took work. And she knew she had more of that left to do. A lot more.

At least it wasn't windy. But in the increasingly frigid air it hurt more than ever to inhale, and every muscle in her body ached.

Let's get this last check done, she thought, *and I'll know where the problem lies. I'm up for it. Come on.*

She took another hit of compressed air and then, carefully, she leaned over and clipped her harness's main safety line to the apex of the scaffold. Her destination, the relay box, was mounted just above it. Then she let go of the ladder and swung out over the hole—with a sharp inhalation of animal fear that she couldn't suppress—and carefully lowered herself alongside the signal transmission cables the short distance to the testing ports.

Dangling in her safety harness, trying to ignore the fact that she was hanging over a kilometer-and-a-half-deep hole, she found the right cable. She removed the ports' covers and connected several leads directly into them, and prayed that the bamboo poles supporting her wouldn't choose this moment to fail. The other ends of the leads fit into sockets at the breastplate of her liveyoke. She plugged them in, then turned on her linkware and called up *Aculeus Octo*'s command interface.

Contact! The controls responded. Manda laughed, all fatigue and cold forgotten. "It's the radio relay. Nailed you." She shouted down to Jim's crouched form, "I'm in!"

"Great!" he called, standing, and shaded his eyes to look up at her. "What have you got? Where is it?"

"Just a second." Manda put the respirator in her mouth for another breath of air, spat it out again, and called up the waldo's visuals. The false-color images were a jumble of confusing lines and shapes. "It seems to be trapped in a big rock pile or something," she said. "Hang on."

She issued *Octo* a command to turn on its floodlights. The waldo responded sluggishly, as though through syrup. Something was definitely wrong with *Octo*.

But at the moment, she couldn't have cared less. For what spread out before her was not at all what she'd expected to see.

"Holy freezing fire," she whispered.

"What?" Jim asked. "What do you see?"

But Manda didn't talk. She was too busy taking it all in.

She steered *Octo* slowly in a rising circle, looking and looking. It was like nothing she'd ever seen, and her eyes were having a hard time making sense of it. Whatever it was, it was huge. It was beautiful, multihued, multileveled, and very complex.

"This is amazing. You won't believe this, Jim! Hold on." Lag . . . lag . . . *come on, come on!* She-*Octo* fired three flares. And they shot up through the water in different directions, in arcing bursts of bubbles and light, and then hung suspended, casting light on the ocean floor.

It went on for kilometers and kilometers. She couldn't see the end of it. Glistening tunnels, loops, nodes, and spires, baroque cathedrals and towering skyscrapers, as elaborate and enormous and eye-bending as any Earthspace megalopolis she'd ever seen in any of her similes—but it had no sharp edges; everything was curved and round, and decorated with borders and arches and spikes all around.

It was a construct. An unmistakably alien one.

Some surfaces looked slick; others coarse. Many were ornamented with bulbs and spirals, giant spheres and teardrops and coils, with tangles of sinuous tubes connecting them all. Clear stretches spiralled around some of the surfaces and most of the

222

tunnels. They seemed to be windows—and she wasn't sure, but dim shapes seemed to be moving inside them. Light packets coursed along wires or lines strung between the structures, and in the clear patches between the structures lay vast forests of translucent, brilliant red *something*—it looked a lot like seaweed, though it seemed to have long tendrils, or fingers—flowing like mermaid locks high into the ocean's currents above. Rising alongside the structures, the craggy walls of the trench cradled the edifice, and she saw movement there too, through the fluttering curtains of weed-or-whatever-it-was.

All this happened in a quick set of glimpses. On an intuition, she-*Octo* turned on her-its auditory channels—and was immersed in sound: whistles, shrieks, and tappings. The noise came from everywhere; she-*Octo* couldn't pinpoint it. But she thought there must be creatures here, making those noises.

And beneath it, she heard something else.

"You found the vents!" Jim exclaimed. But Manda shook her head. "Shhh."

"What?"

"*Shh!*"

And she heard it again: a boom that made the blades of kilometer-high grasses quiver. This one was loud enough that it caused *Octo*'s visuals to tremble. Then another, and another, in quick succession. Then silence.

"I'm not sure what it is." She was quiet a moment, looking at it. It had to be the most awe-inspiring thing she'd ever seen. A fabulous edifice.

"A city," she said finally. "A magnificent city. Jim—I'm hearing your explosions. And a lot of other noise. Whistling, ticking, and so on. Let me see if I can triangulate—"

And then it was gone. All of it. As if someone had thrown a switch.

"No!" Manda stabbed at *Octo*'s now-dead controls. "Come back here! *Dammit.* It's gone! This can't be!"

"Unplug!" Jim yelled. *"Now!"*

She yanked the plug, and then stared down at him. *"What the blessed fuck is going on?"* she demanded. His answer was a troubled stare.

Intersticial: the crèche-born
Marine-Avatar Machinations

After Pablo's sabotage, Dane retreated. She couldn't bear to face him again.

She understood now why Carli had left. She'd always understood, more or less—but now her understanding went all the way to the marrow. Carli had tried and tried to make the crèche-born human, but finally she couldn't take it. She'd given up. Dane had a right to rest too. She was done with them.

If only I could have gone with you, Carli. At least I could have died in peace.

Eventually Buddy found his way through her many defenses, to the tiny dark mental haven where she'd cloistered herself. She felt him coming but was too weak to bar his way.

"Did you hear?" he asked.

She pretended he wasn't there. That had always worked before. It didn't, this time.

She found words. "Go away."

"One of the colonists has found life. Alien life."

He waited for her to react, but she wouldn't. He went on.

"Mara's team took over the avatar so the colonists wouldn't know till we could figure out what to do—"

Figure out what to do. *Dane knew what he meant. Now that Pablo had sabotaged their chance to leave, they had no choice but to go to Brimstone. A debate was raging over how to deal with the colonists.*

Perhaps a few had some vestige of conscience, but most felt the same way about the colonists as they did about the ship clones: they were property. Toys. But they were Carli's *toys, and even in death she retained some hold over them. (It helped that Carli had secretly programmed her syntellect, ur-Carli, to hack into their virtu-worlds before she'd left, appearing in times and places that they didn't expect her. It spooked them. They had a veritable catalog of stories about her ghost. Nobody knew what was really happening but Dane, and she wasn't about to tell anyone.)*

You'll have to figure it out without me, *Dane thought. What she said was, "I'm done."*

"We need you," he said.

"Do it yourself."

"Can't. You're the only check on Pablo. I'm not about to take up your mantle and buck him. No one else dares, either. He's ready to wipe out the alien life so the colonists will have no reason to halt their terraforming. I don't want that, but—" He opened his arms in a helpless shrug. "Everyone is going apeshit. They're losing themselves in power games . . . It's like a many-headed beast. We're tearing ourselves apart. We need you."

Dane sighed. Why are you making this my problem? I don't care anymore.

But alien life . . . ? Despite herself, a trace of curiosity penetrated her despair. Maybe it was enough. She struggled to emerge. Buddy helped her.

She shook her head after a while. Can't. Nothing left.

"I'm with you on this one. I promise."

She pondered Buddy's manifold betrayals.

"We-e-ll . . ." He caught a glimpse of the direction of her thoughts, and thought wryly, "If I decide to screw you, at least I'll give you a warning first."

It'd have to do.

"Let's go," she said, and somehow, managed to find the strength to emerge into full consciousness.

Once more, *she thought wearily.* Once more into the breach.

anda," Jim said, "someone is cracking you."

He had slammed the door behind her and was now pacing like a caged animal. Angry? Excited? Manda wasn't sure which. He was a big man already—the shelter was barely large enough to contain his agitation. Manda set her equipment down on the table and turned to face him. But she was having a hard time focusing on what he said; all her thoughts revolved around that marvelous thing she'd just seen—that underwater, alien metropolis.

"I can't believe it," she said. "All this time we've been up here and they've been down there, and we haven't even known. Here—" She pulled off her sweater and unlatched the top three hooks of her shirt to expose her yoke, with its row of sockets along the collarbone—deliberately *not* noticing him noticing her doing it. "Let's link up and I'll show you."

"No." He said it sharply. "If we go online we'll be exposed to whoever is cracking you. There's a chance you unplugged before they could delete the recording."

The idea that someone could be tampering with her interface gave her that falling-into-an-abyss feeling again. Really, the idea was preposterous. (But then—so were ancient murders no one talked about. So was a massive alien city below the ice.)

"All right, then. I can call up my liveware offline. My yoke should have enough processing power to display the images in a lower-resolution mode. Here."

She activated her liveware in offline mode, and called up *Octo*'s command interface.

"There's a new entry," she said excitedly, as the databalls surfaced from the waldo's storage bin. She touched the newest one and watched it unfold itself around her. A grainy panorama of the alien edifice played. She froze the image. "Yes! Here it is. Give me your octopus line."

He handed her a cord with a plug; Manda shoved it into her liveyoke's spare socket, and started the recording. Suddenly he saw what she saw. His eyes went round. They both gazed at the images for a long, long time.

I didn't dream it, she thought. *It was really there.*

"Let me copy it to my system," he said, and moved his hands across invisible controls. They sat there for several minutes till the copy was complete, and then Manda put her data away and handed him his octopus link.

"Are you sure it was inhabited?" he asked, tucking the cord back into a pocket of his yoke as she shut down her own liveface.

"No, I'm not sure. I didn't get a close enough look. But things were moving in there, Jim. Making sounds."

"Yeah. I heard."

"It might not have been intelligent inhabitants—it might have simply been lower-order creatures who've moved into the ruins. I just don't know. I wish I'd had more time before I got cut off." Then a thought occurred to her. "Why did you tell me to unplug? Because of this cracker you think I've picked up?"

He sat next to her on the bunk. "Manda, think about it. *Octo* fell out of contact immediately after it had come across your alien city, but before you saw any images of it. Other than the communication blackout, it was perfectly functional. All your efforts to box the bug in—to reestablish contact with *Octo*—failed to even identify the source of the problem. Finally you managed to hardwire in and make contact with *Octo*—and in less than a minute your connection was broken. Because the bug wasn't a coding error—*it was a person.* You had someone monkeybacking you—anticipating your every move—jumping outside every trap you set. He was always one step ahead of you."

"Or she," she said.

"Or she," he agreed. "At least, they *were* one step ahead of you, until you jumped outside of *their* box, by coming here without telegraphing what you were about to do."

"It's all circumstantial, though. We have no proof that—"

He lifted a finger. "Indulge me. You've been offline since before you left Amaterasu, haven't you?"

She thought it over. Shock spread through her. "You're right."

"I think you caught them by surprise." He sat back, slinging an arm over his chair. "If you'd called and told me you were coming out, they'd have picked up the transmission and guessed what you were going to do. You'd have never gotten through to *Octo* at all."

Manda shuddered. "This is really scary."

"Indeed. So—someone didn't want you to see what you saw. Who? And why?"

Manda hugged herself. Anyone could have been spying on her, sabotaging her work. For how long had they been watching her? For how long?

She thought of ByronDalia. Would they do something like this, out of vindictiveness—plant some kind of trojan in that accelerator app they'd sent her, one that would damage her liveface?

But no; *Octo* had fallen out of touch before she'd installed their accelerator.

The crèche-born, then . . . ? But they'd need an omnilink to crack her faceware, and the colony didn't have an omni.

She feared that the council was behind it. They seemed to have all these ancient, terrible secrets, these hidden agendas. "I wish I knew."

Manda relatched her shirt hooks and pulled her sweater and gaiter back on in an attempt to warm up. But her chill was due to more than the cold. Jim's gaze grew remote and the gas lantern's weak light etched deep worry lines in his face.

"We need to preserve this data until we can make a full report to the council," he said. "We have to stay offline till we get back to Amaterasu."

Manda remembered how Derek had destroyed her *Exodus* simile. "I don't know if we can trust the council, Jim. They seem to have all kinds of secrets. Maybe they're the ones behind this." She winced. "Derek and Arlene won't welcome this news, you know. Nobody expected me to find an alien city. A few snails or worms, maybe. But this—" She shook her head. "If it *is* a living city—if there are intelligent inhabitants there—it would screw up my clone's plans to terraform Brimstone."

"It's possible that *someone* on the council is playing deep games," Jim replied, "but I can't believe that they would all be in collusion. They can't even agree on what grade fuel they want us to make."

"You're right. I'm being paranoid."

He rubbed at his face, hard. "Let's have supper and get some rest. We're both exhausted and I for one am not thinking too clearly. We'll be in better shape in the morning to decide our next steps."

While he started dinner, Manda replayed the recording—in offline mode, of course. She watched the snippet numerous times and then shut off her liveware and sat back, thinking. Wind and floes played their counterpoint laments, and even the meter-thick walls of the shelter moved under the stormy gusts, changing the room's air pressure and making Manda's ears crackle. But she was barely conscious of this. She had lost herself in thought.

"Jim," she said after a moment, "do you suppose that seaweed, or whatever it was, might be made of amino acids?"

He looked up from the pot he was dumping dried vegetables

into, and gave her a puzzled look. Then he blinked. "You're thinking about the recyclers?" She nodded once. "It's certainly worth testing."

"*If* the weed isn't sentient," she amended, though she doubted it was. It was hard to imagine smart seaweed.

A flush of excitement chased away her anxieties. She came to her feet and started to pace, herself. "There are so many unknowns. We've discovered an intelligent alien race! At the very least we've found its ruins! Can you imagine it, Jim?"

She made a decision.

"Jim—we can't sit on this. It's too big. It's too important to *all* of us. We have to let people know as soon as possible. How can we get the word out tonight, and still guard against whoever might be sabotaging us?"

"Well, we certainly can't hike back now. Temperatures get down to forty-five or fifty below this time of year, with high winds. Even if we could withstand those extremes, I couldn't promise to get us safely across the floes in the dark. It'd be impossible to navigate." He stared into the fire in the stove and twiddled his beard and thought some more. "Whoever the cracker is—if they exist—they're obviously trying to suppress knowledge of the aliens. Maybe if just one of us went online, and released copies of your images to everyone all at once . . ."

She shook her head. "I don't think so. It's a huge file, coming from this site's network, and would take a long time to download. It'd choke the system—and make it all too easy for our mystery cracker to stop all transmissions from this location."

"True. But—" A gleam came into his eyes. "That gives me another idea. Suppose you go online alone and call Derek and Arlene. Tell them you have something to show them. If you get through without interference, and your copy of the recording isn't damaged, we can assume I'm just being paranoid, and they can set the necessary things in motion in town. If something interferes with your transmission, we'll have confirmed we have someone cracking us, and we might even get some clues as to who it might be."

"Derek and Arlene, *and* Jack and Amadeo," she amended. "PabloJeb would never collude with CarliPablo." And, conveniently, doing so would buy back some of the coup she'd lost to Amadeo.

Her thoughts turned back to the aliens. "Jim—I just realized. I may already have more data on the city."

"What—?"

"My other waldos will be closing in on it soon—if they haven't already."

He gave her a skeptical look. "Then I'll give you coup that they're *all* out of communication now."

Her lips skinned back from her teeth. "There's one way to find out, eh?"

She started to log on, then paused. "You don't think it could be the aliens themselves blocking us, do you?"

His stare was answer enough. In any event, they couldn't afford to sit around and wait to find out. Bracing herself for intrusion, she logged into the network.

Nothing happened. Everything seemed to be in order. She released the breath she was holding and—with a nervous stab at her soccer-shaped opsysball—called up a status report on all her waldos. It was almost anticlimactic, that—with the continued exception of *Octo*—they were all in contact and right where they should be.

"Well?" Jim demanded. Manda shook her head.

"Everything's normal. No interference whatsoever."

Jim looked surprised.

She did a thorough check of each of her marine-waldos. *Aculei Septimus* and *Duo* were about a day away: eighty kilometers north and around a hundred kilometers northeast, respectively, of *Octo*'s last position, and more than a kilometer above it. *Tres* and *Quinque* would be closing in a couple days after that; *Unus*, *Quatuor*, and *Sexis* were still several days away. Temperature and current anomalies were continuing to increase, as well as sulfates and nitrites, as they headed south and west.

But they were swimming into the current; it'd be at least six hours before *Septimus* would reach the artifact, and eight or so before *Duo* did. The rest were out of the picture, for the time being.

"OK." Jim looked a little less worried. "Maybe my cracker idea was off. But do me a favor and be alert for other tampering, OK? Just in case."

"Naturally," she said. "I'm going to go ahead and try calling the colony now. If anyone *is* interfering, this should be where they strike."

She made contact with Amaterasu's network, and put an urgent call through, both to her oldest clone-siblings and to PabloJeb. Derek-avatar dissolved into focus in one of the colony *virtu*-spaces, conference room upsilon: seated in midair in mimicry of his physical body. He broke off a conversation in midsentence when he spotted her-avatar.

"Manda! How is your search for the vents going?" Then he got a look at her face, and came half to his feet. "What is it? Are you all right?"

Just then, Arlene's face came into focus over Derek-avatar's shoulder. "I'm dealing with an urgent matter in the liveware shop. Can it wait?"

"I'll cover you," he said. "Tell me what's going on," he told Manda.

"Hold on just a second," Manda said, as Jack's avatar sank down into the conference room through its reflective ceiling.

"What's the meaning of this?" Jack-avatar demanded. Amadeo didn't even bother to respond to her summons.

"We've found something down there," Manda said. "Under the ice."

Jack-avatar looked baffled, but Derek-avatar's eyes went wide. "Something? The vents? Or—good God—*you found living organisms?*"

He knew her very well.

"Well—here. Just take a look at it. It'll explain better than I could." And she started transmitting.

The images were projected onto the surfaces of a vertical, triangular prism. There was no interference. "No trouble transmitting," she whispered offline to Jim. Meanwhile Derek- and Jack-avatars watched the transmission. After it ended they turned to Manda-avatar. Both looked visibly rattled.

"Is that what I think it is?" he asked.

"Um, what do you think it is?"

"I don't know how big your marine-waldos are—"

"About three times as big around as a human and ten times as long."

"—but that looks like the biggest underwater city I could ever have imagined," Derek-avatar said. "I wouldn't have believed it."

"Is this some practical joke?" Jack-avatar demanded.

"Careful, councillor." Derek-avatar spoke in a dangerous tone. "Manda's no liar."

Jack-avatar gave Derek-avatar a calculating gaze.

Coup in play. But what are the equations? Manda wasn't privy enough to the council's doings to know.

She interjected, flatly, "It's real. LuisMichael was with me and can confirm. We just picked up those transmissions less than half an hour ago."

At the mention of Jim's clone-name, the deadlock between the two councilmembers broke. It took her a moment to realize that she'd stumbled into a good coup move; after Amadeo's gratuitous insult to LuisMichael the other day at Derek's party, Jack couldn't afford to show hostility toward LuisMichael. His clone owed Jim's too much coup. Derek gave her an appreciative glance.

Manda told Jack- and Derek-avatars exactly what had happened, including the interference they'd had, and Jim's suspicion that someone might be cracking Manda's liveface.

Derek-avatar said to PabloJeb, "We should call an emergency session of the council right away."

"Agreed. Finish up with your sister. I'll gather the others. Meet us in *virtu*-conference delta right away."

Once Jack-avatar had gone, Derek-avatar turned back to Manda.

"That was an excellent idea, including PabloJeb in the same report you gave me."

"I thought you might be annoyed."

"No. He'd need to be informed anyway, and this way he can't accuse us of hoarding coup or trying to manipulate the council." He gave her an approving nod. "Now, how soon will you have more information? Is there any way you can get more recordings of the artifact, and perhaps some samples of it? And of that grassy stuff?" She grinned at him; she hadn't had a chance to mention her idea about the seaweedy substance and the recyclers.

"Two of my other waldos are nearing the location now. But the one that took this image has fallen out of contact with me yet again, and it'll be at least another six hours before I have much to report. And I do need to sleep. I've been going all day. I'll call you as soon as I have new information."

"Very well. Good work. I'll fill the council in. Meanwhile," he said, "learn as much as you can about these aliens."

"Of course."

"But Manda—be careful. If you find aliens that appear intelligent, avoid direct contact."

Manda gave him a sardonic look. Derek scowled. "Don't start. We don't know what they might be capable of. You could be putting the whole colony in jeopardy, simply by letting them know we're up here."

"I may be a bitch, Derek, but I'm not stupid. Of course I'll be careful. But for all we know, they may know about us already. And even if they don't, there's a lot of open water down there with no place to hide, and it's their territory. I have no idea what they're capable of—if they're even still around. Which we haven't confirmed yet." She shrugged. "I'll do my best. But I can't make any promises."

"Then perhaps you'd better hold off on any further exploration until I can confer with the others on the council."

Manda sighed in exasperation. "Derek, one of my waldos is sitting right in the middle of their city, waiting to be discovered—if it hasn't been already. The other waldos could stumble across the aliens before I even know what's happening. Jim and I have both been having sonar troubles since yesterday, and it's possible that the aliens are responsible for it. They might even have been reading our transmissions for some time now."

He stared at her, alarmed.

"We need to find out as much as we can," she said, "as quickly as we can—and naturally, also as carefully as we can. We've seen no evidence of hostility, but all kinds of odd things are starting to happen all around us, and we can't just sit here and let things happen without finding out why."

"I know that," Derek-avatar growled. "That doesn't mean we can afford to be reckless!"

Her temper flared. "I wish you'd to trust me to use good judgment! I'm not an idiot!" *Easy, Manda; easy.* She took a calming breath. "Jim's right here with me, and I'll confer with him every step of the way. You're going to have to trust us."

Derek's avatar gazed at her for a long moment. Then he sighed. "All right. But report to me on a regular basis—*before* you make any major decisions."

Thanks for the vote of confidence, she thought.

"Call me when you have news," he said, "no matter what time

it is. I'll keep my yoke by my pillow tonight and wear my live-mask to sleep."

He signed off.

"I should call my siblings," Jim said then, and did so. He borrowed Manda's yoke—"Just to be on the safe side," he told her. She undid the leads and stays, stripped it off, and handed it to him.

It was about three sizes too small, and rested around his chin and neck, rather than on his shoulders. Consequently his beard had to go under instead of over it, and it moved up and down when he talked. The sight made her want to giggle.

She only heard his side of the conversation, but like her, he had no difficulty transmitting the images, and from his comments, Brian's and Amy's reactions seemed to be very similar to Derek's and Jack's: flabbergasted.

He told Manda, after he'd signed off, "They said they'll study the recording tonight and see if they have anything to report in the morning."

By the time Jim had wrapped up his call, Manda had the food on the table. They ate and then washed and put away the dishes in silence.

Jim collected more ice and snow from outside and heated a big pot of water. Once it was boiling he filled the washbasin with it, which he carried to the wash stand. There he stripped and, with his back to her, urinated in the chamberpot. Then he soaped up with the by-then-already-tepid water, doing the feet-are-freezing hop. She knew the water was tepid since she'd experienced it countless times herself. At sea level on Brimstone, water boiled at seventy-five degrees C, and in no time, at what Brimstonians called "room temperature"—anything above zero C—boiling water dropped below forty degrees, not warm enough for tea or a good, hot bath.

Manda couldn't resist glancing over at Jim while he washed.

The lantern's flickering light fell across his back and shoulders, showing the movement of his muscles as he poured water over his head and rubbed suds in. He had a fine ass and legs too. He squeezed a sponge over his head, and sudsy water ran down him in rivulets. Oh, she did like a muscular ass. Then she averted her eyes, made miserable by the onslaught of unwelcome arousal.

It's your own fault, Manda. He's not some simile you can ogle to your heart's content. People's feelings are involved, and you don't need to complicate your life like this. Get over it.

After he'd toweled off and donned a clean set of long johns and socks, he came over, rubbing his hair. He smelled of soap.

"Shall I heat some water for you?" he asked, and when she hesitated, added with a deadpan expression, "I promise not to peek."

You're a stronger man than I, then. She shook her head, cheeks burning, heart knocking about in her chest. "Thanks. I just bathed yesterday."

"Suit yourself. Good night."

"Good night," she said.

He carried bedding over to the bunks, threw it onto one of the top ones, jumped up, and climbed under the covers.

What's the big deal? she asked herself. *You've had plenty of experience in-face, and you're no virgin, ex-face, either.*

But the nervousness didn't fade.

She waited until she could hear him snoring lightly, then went over and relieved herself in the chamberpot. His wash water she poured into the chamberpot, to subdue any odors during the night, and then stripped down to her underwear. Gooseflesh spread over her. Manda inspected her fingers and toes. They were little more than blunt sticks—made nearly useless by long exposure to hard cold. A couple spots on her toes were whitish and hard, portending frostbite. She wished now she'd accepted

Jim's offer of a bowl of warm water. Too late—she wasn't about to go out and gather snow in this weather.

Her thoughts turned again to her discovery. *Aliens. All this time.* The cold and dark—as always, on Brimstone's surface, at night—waited like a patient predator beyond the feeble circle of lantern's light. But always before the night had been a threat empty of volition. Not anymore.

They may be peaceful, though. And they're deep-sea dwellers. They may not even be able to come to the surface.

But any civilization that could build a city like that couldn't be without means to explore outside their own realm. Could they?

What will they think of us? Will they be curious? Afraid? Do they even have feelings like ours? Will they see us as invaders? Will there be a war, or will we find a way to understand each other?

Go to bed, girl, she thought finally. *Jim was right. You need to be alert tomorrow.*

First she'd better deal with her frostbite, though, or she could lose a few toes.

After she'd put on clean long johns and tucked her dirty ones back into her pack, she moved a chair beside the stove, threw a large skin over it, fur side up, and sat down, wrapping herself in the skin. Then she tucked her left leg carefully under her (so as not to damage the frostbitten areas on her left foot) and gingerly held her right foot, which had suffered more cold damage, between her hands. She breathed on the foot. The numb, hard, cold patches on her toes soon began to soften, and to tingle and burn, as warmth returned; it looked like it wasn't serious. She repeated the treatment with her left foot, and then pulled on two pairs of clean socks and grabbed more bedding from the pile by the door.

Manda went over to the bunks. Three empty ones remained. The other top bunk would probably be the warmest.

No, Manda, a little voice said, *the warmest bunk would be* his. *Oh, sure,* she thought. *Trade sex for warmth: how's that for contemptible?*

She walked over and looked at him. He slept deeply, unmoving, with his eyes open just a crack and his mouth slightly open too. It was endearing. He wasn't a thrasher, it appeared, the way she and her siblings were.

His bunk was right at eye level. She liked his cheekbones. They were about the only facial feature of his she could make out through his beard. (Well, not the *only* feature. He also had friendly, hazel eyes, a Roman nose, and a broad, toothy smile that always made her want to smile back.) She had an urge to stroke his cheek.

LuisMichael didn't have that sinuous, wickedly seductive manner that ByronDalia cultivated. (She admitted it; she'd been tempted to take the quadruplets up on their offer of a hot-springs date.) But LuisMichael was handsome, in its own idiosyncratic way. And playful. Steadier too; less volatile. More trustworthy. ByronDalia surged and ebbed like Omi-Kami's chaotic and powerful tides. LuisMichael's feet were firmly planted on the rocks. She liked that.

She wanted to run her fingers through his clean, still-damp beard and hair, that splayed out on the pillow. He smelled good, like soap and skin. She could smell him from here. Unlike Brian, while at Amaterasu he usually wore his long, black, curly hair in a loose braid that stuck out beneath his livemask, while Brian wore his in a tight knot at his neck. For the longest time that had been the only way she could tell them apart. Funny how now, even though they still looked exactly alike, she could tell them apart. She'd known him instantly when she'd seen him at the refinery. Funny.

She thought, *he probably laughs at me behind my back just like all the others. He's got vat-mates to keep him warm and make him feel safe. Just like all the rest, even if he doesn't admit it.*

She threw her bedding onto the other top bunk, then went over to the table and turned down the lantern wick till its flame went out. In the faint light cast by the gas flames inside the stove, she groped her way to the empty bunk.

Oh, what the hell, she decided suddenly, and stripped off her long johns and wool socks as fast as she could. Shivering, she scrambled up onto Jim's bunk.

"Wha . . . ?" he muttered, half asleep.

"Scoot over," she said, nudging him. Like all the colonists, he was used to sharing a bed with his siblings; without really waking, he squirmed until his back was to her, and she slipped under the skins next to him.

Jim was a big man and the bed was tiny; her buttocks hung half off the edge. But his warmth soaked into her front side, better than any sauna, and another kind of warmth started low in her belly. Manda pressed herself against his back and wrapped her arms around his torso as best she could. His long john top had bunched up, and the glaze of hair on his belly tickled her fingers. By the way his muscle tone changed she could tell she'd awakened him.

"Um," he said. "Manda . . . I don't think I will be able to sleep next to you all night like this, and keep my hands off you."

"Who asked you to?"

He was quiet for a second. "Are you sure about this? I mean—"

She gave his shoulder blade a little shove. "Oh, don't be an idiot. Roll over and kiss me."

And he wrapped himself around her like a big, warm bear, and kissed her, and he tasted so good Manda wanted to lap him all up.

The bed was too small. They nearly toppled off it.

"Here." Jim leaped down and dragged two of the mattresses onto the floor, then piled a heap of skins on top of them. Grinning, he stripped off his long johns and got under the covers.

Manda jumped down off the bunk and burrowed underneath the skins. In the faint blue light of the gas jets they explored each other. All their pent-up fear and excitement over what had happened that day and what tomorrow might hold, they expended on each other. And the panicky little voice inside her, for these few hours, she somehow managed to ignore.

Finally, late in the night, they collapsed with exhaustion. Manda fell asleep lying next Jim with her legs tangled up in his and her buttocks against his pelvis, still connected to him crotch to crotch.

Emotive Temperature Fluctuations

It was dark when Manda awoke. Sometime while they'd slept, Jim had rolled over onto his back and she had ended up in the crook of his arm.

Still groggy with sleep, she stretched and yawned, luxuriously warm everywhere but the tip of her nose and her cheeks. She pulled the covers up and pressed her face into Jim's chest and soon her cheeks and nose were warm too. He smelled so good. She breathed him in. The room was quiet. Outside, Omi-Kami still moaned, but the wind had died down.

Her crotch ached, and her inner thighs were still wet and sticky. The feel of him remained, in her own body's memory: she felt him still moving inside her; she felt his lips sliding like kitten fur over hers; felt his teeth and palate, hard ridges against her tongue. Her hands remembered the movement of muscle in his buttocks and back; her breasts and abdomen remembered the press of his torso and his work- and weather-roughened hands; her legs remembered wrapping around his hips and pulling him close; her fingers remembered snarling themselves in his hair. His soapy, musky smell lingered in her nostrils.

Manda had felt a little awkward during their lovemaking. Elbows and knees had gone awry; they'd had difficulty finding a good position. His touch had been a little too vigorous at first. But it had all come together, once they'd found each other's rhythms. He'd been passionate, gentle, responsive.

Manda propped herself on an elbow and looked at him. His

eyes flicked back and forth under his eyelids. Dreaming. She stroked his cheek.

She had lost her virginity halfway through her adolescence, but that had merely been a deflowering. (It had been Abraham and Robert, during a covalence. They had gone afterwards to the others in the nursery and said insulting things about her. Especially Abraham. The shit.) The few other sexual experiences she'd had when she was an adolescent and young adult had merely been flesh bumping up against flesh, her mind so hazed out with ceremonial drugs (or desire-filled fear) she hadn't cared who she was with. She barely remembered now who her partners had been. This was different.

Her face and shoulders were getting cold. Manda pulled the skins back up and laid down on Jim's chest. His heart beat strong and steady against her ear, as deep as the booms she'd heard coming from the underwater city.

People said similes were better. She didn't see it. Tidier, certainly. More poetical: they lacked the bumps, nicks, gropes, and misses that marked real sex. But she liked the evidence that lingered on her body—however messy, achy, and clumsy it felt. Sex had its own smell too, and the similes failed to reproduce it with any accuracy.

I could get used to this, Manda thought. *I could get used to Jim.*

But the thought sparked panic in her belly. A band tightened across her chest and she sat up, trying to catch her breath. Suddenly she wanted to get as far away from this man as she possibly could.

Shit. What have I done?

Careful, Manda. Careful.

She scrambled out from under the covers and pulled on her long johns and socks. Then she piled extra bedding on one of the bunks that still had a mattress, and curled up under the cold furs.

Cold and alone, she reminded herself sternly, shivering, *is better than letting people get close enough to hurt you.*

He was fixing breakfast when she awoke again. She dashed over to her pack, and put on her liveyoke and clumsily hooked up the leads to her gloves and specs and earpieces. Then she hurriedly pulled on her outer layers. Only then did she turn to face him.

He made no comment about the fact that she'd gotten up in the night and slept apart from him, but simply put a bowl down for her.

She looked at the hot cereal, arms crossed protectively over her chest. Her stomach rumbled, but she felt too nervous to eat. And she didn't want to sit down across from him. She didn't know what to say to him. *Thanks for the experience; now, let's forget it ever happened?*

"Thanks. I'm not hungry."

He shrugged. "Up to you. But it's going to be a long, cold day, and you have a lot of hard work to do."

He sat down and started shovelling barleymeal porridge and *mana*-honey cakes into his mouth. Manda stood there watching him.

He's right. If you don't eat you'll get light-headed and careless with your waldos at a critical time. Stop being childish.

With a sigh, she sat down and dug into her own barleymeal and *mana*. While eating, she glanced at him several times, and he met her gaze each time, with smile lines beside his eyes and his lips quirked up, but said nothing.

Fine, she thought irritably. *I can out-casual you anytime.*

"Do we stay here," he asked, "or return?"

Manda thought it over. "I'd like to stay. I don't want to waste any time. Even if I haven't picked up a cracker, there seem to be enough bugs in the network to mess up communications. I'd like to operate with the fewest intermediate devices and lags getting in the way."

He pursed his lips, then nodded. "Sounds wise."

"I'll need to arrange to have a full livesuit brought out, if it can be transported safely."

"We have some heated transport waldos at the refinery. I'll make sure it's packed carefully, and I'll also have them send us out some more supplies."

Us? She frowned.

"I work best alone," she said, stiffly. *It's my discovery. I don't need your help.*

Jim blinked at her. "Oh, come on, Manda. I'm not leaving you out here by yourself. The floes aren't safe."

"I'm perfectly capable of taking care of myself."

"I told you, it's a safety rule. No singles."

"I *am* a single." *Last night doesn't change that.*

He sighed. "You're not making sense. We don't know what you're up against yet. We're still not sure you haven't got a cracker monkeybacking your signals. And you told Derek you'd confer with me-us every step of the way. I heard you."

"So? I lied."

He glared. Suddenly she was frightened. He was a lot bigger than she was. She stiffened, defiant.

"Maybe you could blacken the other eye," she suggested, touching the bruise Derek had given her, now an orange-and-green stain across her cheekbone and temple. "Give me a matched set."

Jim slumped back in his seat with a frown.

"Manda," he said, "I'd never hurt you. Never." He paused, searching her face. She didn't know what he was trying to find there. "I'm not trying to take anything away from you."

The hell you aren't.

But the sorrow in his gaze and tone tugged at Manda. She leaned forward, clasping her hands together.

"It's not you," she said. "It's me. I can't—I'm no good as part of a team. I'm sorry. I'm just not. It's how I am." She spread her hands. "I'm a single. I don't do 'us.'"

He looked at her for a long moment. Then he rubbed thumb and forefinger across his eyelids and pinched his nose.

"Excuse me," he said, and stepped outside. She caught a glimpse out the door as a blast of icy air entered around him. It was still predawn; the sky was mauve and orange and the floes reflected moon- and planetlight.

A few moments later he came back in, slinging their pony bottles, which had been hooked up to a compressor in the tool shed all night. He set them down near the stove, and they steamed as the glaze of frost coating them evaporated.

"I've asked Brian and Amy to bring us more supplies," he said. "I'm going to head out and do some maintenance on my seismographic equipment for a while.

"But I'm not leaving you here alone, Manda. No matter what you say or how hard you try to drive me away. Because I don't give a damn how much you cherish your privacy or are suddenly afraid of me because you made love to me—"

She said, stung, "Believe me, it was a mistake I don't intend to repeat."

She scored a hit with that one. She could tell by his flinch. Her satisfaction wilted into chagrin almost instantly, though. "I'm sorry, Jim. I'm sorry. Last night was wonderful. *You* were wonderful." *I guess we're going to talk about it after all.* She found herself reaching out to touch his hand. Oh, she remembered his touch. And his smell. She hadn't forgotten. "But it *was* a mistake. I'm no good around other people. Not even someone as gentle and wonderful and—and tasty—as you."

A tear slipped down her cheek despite her best efforts. Jim cocked his head at her, and wiped the tear away with his rough, weathered finger. "How do you know till you try? You're giving up before we even get started."

247

She released his hand angrily. "Stop trying to make me into something I'm not."

"You came to me! I didn't put any pressure on you."

"I know. I know." Her shoulders hunched and she gave him a desperate look. "I don't know what came over me."

"Maybe I'm just irresistible," he said with a smile, but the pain was still there behind his eyes. He sobered. "Manda, this is not about us; it's about the colony. Exploring the city is not a one-person job. It could be dangerous. You need me. Whether you like it or not."

With that, he went out again, buckling his toolbelt outside his parka.

"Bullshit!" she responded, as the door shut. She knew she was being an idiot, but she couldn't help herself. "I don't need you." Her voice trailed away at the end, and she wiped away a few more tears, before finishing her breakfast and cleaning up.

I won't let him get to me, she thought, dipping her bowl, spoon, and mug into the pan of soapy water he'd heated. But he already had. If he asked her again, she'd go to him.

It was that knowledge, more than anything else, that angered her. She'd worked hard and long over the years to build up that pride, that barrier against pain. All those years. And he'd taken it from her. At a touch of his hand it'd crumbled like eggshell.

After checking her equipment Manda went online, and sighed in relief as her command- and datashapes bloomed around her, as shining and geometric as ice-sprites. She sighed. On familiar ground again. Well, sort of.

Aculeus Octo was still out of touch. All the others were in contact. Though anxious to check *Aculeus Septimus* and see if it had had a second sighting of the city yet, she forced herself to go through her standard startup. Her waldos and linkware needed to be at peak form. This was no time to take shortcuts. So she spent a few moments going over the summary data. The dodecahedral commandball for each marine-waldo displayed its summary info in glowing, iconic format on each face. She noticed right away that signal efficiency, a number that told her how clear and fast the connection was between her linkware and her waldos, was down by almost half from its usual. No big deal—terrain, eddies, ice-floe noises, and a dozen other factors all affected transmissions—but it wasn't usually this pronounced, and didn't usually happen to all of them at once.

Getting kind of noisy down there, eh? she thought. It could just be the spring warming, which caused Omi-Kami's groaning to increase in pitch and volume. That could affect the sonar transponder array down in the drill hole, which would interfere with all her waldos equally.

Or it could be something else. *We'll find out soon enough.*

Next she ran down her startup checklist, checking each waldo's power usage, remaining antimatter stores, hull integrity, depth, velocity, position, and response to a menu of basic commands. All of them seemed in order—though *Duo* and *Septimus*, both below four-and-a-half kilometers in depth, were showing early signs of hull stress. Last, Manda did her standard triangulation, placing all the marine-waldos on her incomplete map of the ocean floor.

Septimus was only a few kilometers north-northwest of *Octo's* last position. Manda felt a rush of exultation. *Perfect!* It should be nearing the city—if not already on top of it.

"All right," she muttered to *Septimus*. She rubbed her livegloved hands together and flexed her fingers to warm them. "Let's see what you've been up to." Fingers trembling with excitement, she touched its command interface. The other shapes receded to the periphery of her vision as *Septimus's* controls and translucent contours unfolded around Manda, fitting themselves to her form.

First, the visuals. She-*Septimus* was speeding southward through darkness, about 4.62 kilometers beneath the surface, forty-one meters above the ocean floor. She shut off false-color imaging and turned on her-*Septimus*'s floodlights. *Septimus* took a long time to respond, and she fidgeted till it did so.

The lights showed her nothing but yellowish gloom in all directions. High particulates, she noted; visibility was low: less than ten meters. Interesting—and unusual for Brimstone, which had no phytoplankton to interfere with light transmission. A strong indicator of thermal venting. She-*Septimus* rotated her-its camera platform to check above and to the sides—again, with long delays between Manda's command and *Septimus*'s response. Nothing visible. She augmented with sonar. About fifty meters to the east she-*Septimus* detected the trench wall. It appeared to be very sheer; the sonar echoes were crisp. And water temperatures were spiking to five or six degrees Celsius. In Brimstone's subzero waters, that was downright balmy. There *had* to be some kind of geothermal activity nearby.

She-*Septimus* cut back her speed, reduced buoyancy, and descended slowly. Thirty meters . . . twenty meters . . . fifteen . . . twelve . . . nine. Then she-*Septimus* got a visual on the ocean floor. It was rocky, and heavily silted in the low areas. No sign of the city. A rise that *Septimus*'s sonar detected to the south might be obscuring it. She-*Septimus* stopped her-its descent.

Then she realized something was glowing down there, and her mouth went dry. She-waldo continued to drop, heading toward the dim, orangy-red light. Gradually she realized she was looking into a fissure in the moon's crust. At the fissure's mouth, water gouted and frothed in a boiling frenzy. Then water temperatures shot up above two hundred fifty degrees and her chemical and light-scattering sensors went berserk—everything turned topsy-turvy as she-*Septimus* passed into a column of hydrothermal fluid gushing from beneath the sea floor.

Easy, Manda; easy. She took slow, deep breaths to calm her racing heart.

Septimus recovered its bearings on its own. She-waldo had to veer sharply to avoid plowing into fresh, dark, still steaming lava rock. With only livegloves and voice to control the waldo, it was more difficult than usual. Manda wished she had a full suit on.

She reversed course and brought *Septimus* around, rising again. It was as if she-*Septimus* were swimming in syrup—then *Septimus* raced ahead—and she overcorrected, and re-overcorrected again, swearing. The pockets of boiling steam tossed her-*Septimus* around like a toy. As she-waldo passed through this overheated mess, black gouts of smoke billowed up all around her-it and below, lava poured out onto the sea floor, spreading like paste over rocks and silt, darkening as it cooled.

"Come on, *come on!*"

The boiling sent *Septimus* spinning out of control. She flinched as *Septimus* headed for a collision with the young cone's edge, and forced herself not to react—any command she sent would come far too late and create more problems. After knocking a few rocks loose with *Septimus*'s rudder she-waldo was past the boiling mass, and she-*Septimus* slowed, to hover only a few meters above and to the side of the volcanic activity, with cameras and chemical scanners all running.

The inner mouth of the fissure wavered, mirage-like, barely visible amid the bubbles and hot water. From here, she-waldo could see that the small cone was growing faster on the northern side.

She watched for some time in fascination.

How close can I get? she wondered, and ordered *Septimus* to move slowly in. But its response time was getting more sluggish by the moment. Manda frowned. Any worse and she'd lose real-time control of the unit. This was no time for cutting things close. So she halted the marine-waldo about three meters from the edge of the gash. Temperatures rose to about a hundred eighty degrees C at *Septimus*'s front end, and about one fifty at the tail.

Time for audio. "Let's see what racket is interfering with the transmissions." She turned the sound on. Noise assaulted her ears. Beneath Omi-Kami's groaning came a deep roar—perhaps emissions from the volcano—and beneath that, the slow *boom-booming* she had heard in the city.

All this she'd expected—but it didn't entirely account for the signal interference. There seemed to be something else to it than usual.

She dampened the deep registers, and a chorus of clicks and discordant tones stood out, in about the same range of frequencies as she used to communicate with her waldos, or perhaps just slightly above it. Manda tried to triangulate on the source of the sound—and as she did so a flurry of blurred shapes burst past her, flashing in her-*Septimus*'s floodlights. She stifled a startled shriek. Tense with excitement, Manda-*Septimus* tried to pursue the—whatever they were. But they moved too fast for her-it to even begin to keep up with.

"Holy fuck!" she gasped. A tingly, numb feeling spread over her and her breath came short.

Alien life. She'd found it. Or rather, it had found her. With trembling hands she triple-checked that the recorders were on.

Hundreds of the creatures—maybe more—spilled past her-*Septimus*, heading to the lava flow. There they slowed, and milled about the crooked volcanic cone in a shifting shoal—first glinting like mirrors—then nearly vanishing as their angles changed. They spread into a star-like pattern directly below Manda-*Septimus*, and staying in that pattern, hovered over the lava flow.

While they schooled, Manda was able to study them a little more closely. They were semi-transparent, with mottled areas inside that ranged from pink to dark grey to nearly white. They moved by opening and closing themselves—like parasols in a Japanese dance—incredibly quickly—and were vaguely reminiscent of jellyfish or squids, though they were flat—disc-like—instead of bulbous.

She estimated they spanned half a meter to a little over a meter-and-a-half, and were perhaps twenty to thirty centimeters thick near their apex, tapering to a few centimeters thick at the edges. They had a hole in their apex with an odd cluster of organs of some kind around it. Like parasols, their outer edges were ruffled. These edges flapped like a canopy's edge in a breeze. And like a parasol's spokes, about half a dozen ridges ran from the hole in their apex to the edges. At the end of each ridge was a thing that looked remarkably like a human hand, though Manda couldn't count the fingers or tentacles, or whatever they were.

After a few moments the creatures began to circumnavigate the base of the cone, remaining in their star pattern. Once they'd finished, they burst into motion and swarmed over the area, darting here and there in smaller clusters while clicking and humming. Several swooped past Manda-*Septimus*, but didn't linger to investigate her-it for very long. Most of them seemed quite interested in the volcanic fissure, though others spread out over the ocean floor nearby. The creatures got alarmingly close to the lava flows. It looked almost as if they were touching it, defining its boundaries, tasting its hellishly hot secretions.

Manda watched for a while. Some of them had to be in waters above a hundred degrees C. Maybe even above two hundred. Manda whistled. "Tough little buggers, aren't you?"

Then she got an idea.

"Let's try feeding you some of your own noises." She quickly stripped the deep registers—Omi-Kami's groans, the volcano's noises, and the deep booms—from the recordings *Septimus* had made, filtered out her own waldo communication frequencies, and fed what remained through her-*Septimus*'s speakers.

The parasol-creatures all froze. *I've confused them,* she thought. Then they blasted upward from the lava flow and swarmed over her-*Septimus*. The clicks and tones they emitted swelled to a cacophony, her views disappeared in clumps and layers of translucent alien flesh, and her connection with *Septimus* dissolved in a sea of sparkles and static.

"Oh, shit." She switched over to her communications liveface. "Jim, are you there?"

"Here." Her view showed a sickening swirl of sky, moons, clouds, and ice as Jim lifted his arm to point his wrist video unit at his face. He was out of breath. Icicles hung from his beard and eyebrows and his expression was odd.

"I found something," she told him.

"I did too. Just now. You won't believe it."

"What is it?"

He hesitated. "I'll be right there."

He came in, face and parka crusted with ice, and held up a sonar transponder with insulated wire sticking out both sides, severed on the ends. The wires and signaller had something hanging from them. It looked like a big glob of gelatin, maybe about six or eight kilos—the size of a large cat or a small dog: a semitransparent glob with pinkish, dark, and white areas in its midst. Seven tiny, handlike tentacles, each with seven little greyish fingers, gripped the wire. The signal box was buried inside the folds of clearish flesh. Manda stared.

"I just pulled this up from below. It was attached to my seismograph. The one that has been giving me trouble," he said.

"About a thousand of them just knocked *Aculeus Septimus* out of commission," she replied, "down on the ocean floor."

They looked at each other for a long moment. Then they broke into silly grins. They hooted and thumped each other and jumped up and down till sparks danced before Manda's eyes and she had to sit down to catch her breath.

They laid the creature on the table and used a screwdriver and a fork to try to get it to release the wire and box. It wouldn't let go. She noticed it had clusters of shiny tubes around the apex, which were tipped in black.

"Do you think we should put it back?" she said. "It may still be alive, and intelligent."

He shook his head, thoughtfully. "It was twitching a little when I first pulled it up, and some of the organs inside *and* out were doing things, but it stopped almost right away. I'm afraid— I'm pretty sure it's dead now."

"Oh." She eyed it, just a bit sad and worried.

"I didn't know what it was," he said. "It took a long time to haul it up from below before I realized what I had."

Manda shook her head. "It wasn't your fault. You couldn't have known." She hesitated. "And we don't *know* that it was intelligent."

"Let's hope not." With a deep frown, Jim poked at the creature with the blunt end of the screwdriver. Its flesh was surprisingly taut. He looked up at her.

"They're all over down there," she told him, "at the vents. And they communicate, or navigate—or both—using sonar. They're interfering with my link to my marine-waldos. I don't dare take a waldo fleet into the city, with things as they are now. I could end up doing serious damage."

"What do you want to do, then?"

Manda thought for a moment.

"We have to get back and report this. Right away. Have this"— she gestured at the creature—"autopsied. Study what we know. Come up with a plan. We need a way to investigate what's going on down there that gets around the sonar problem."

Jim nodded. Air streamed from his nose and mouth, billowing frosty white, as he regarded the thing on the table.

"I do wish I hadn't killed it."

Manda didn't know what to say so she simply patted him awkwardly on the arm.

They gave a report of their findings to the council, who listened gravely and asked questions, and then ordered Manda to return to Amaterasu for a fuller debriefing. She redirected *Aculeus*

Duo, which was coming into range, toward *Septimus*'s last location. Then they packed up and left, travelling as swiftly as they could across the floes. Within an hour of their discovery they had reached the tow line up to the refinery.

The tow line wasn't fancy, but it was functional. Inverted, T-shaped metal bars hung suspended from a cable loop whose other end was attached to a promontory overlooking the refinery. The damn things made Manda nervous, but climbing the icy hillside was out of the question. She didn't have the strength or the equipment for it.

Jim opened the switchbox on the bottommost pole of the loop and started up the cable. It made a horrible screeching noise. Then the T-bars began to move, marching up the hill at an alarmingly fast rate.

Jim gestured for her to go first. Manda skate-skied over to the line, skated alongside for a moment, and then grabbed at the midriff-height handlebar as it moved past her arm. She felt quite pleased with herself when she managed to avoid falling on her butt, and gave Jim a wave over her shoulder. She saw he'd grabbed the one immediately behind her. The wind stung her face and snow sluiced under her blades.

She looked up the hill. She had perhaps ten or fifteen minutes to kill before they reached the refinery.

Using voice only, she brought her liveface up. She didn't dare relax too much or she'd have quite a fall—possibly right into Jim's blades—but she intended to try to reestablish contact with *Aculeus Septimus*. Its controls had come on for an instant or two, then blinked out again, when she'd checked it during a rest stop on the floes. From the glimpse she'd caught, she was pretty sure it had sunk to the sea floor and gotten stuck in fresh lava. Lava that was now rapidly cooling.

First she checked on *Duo*. It was about three or four kilometers away from *Septimus* now, and one-hundred-eighty meters above it, midway down beside the western wall of the trench. She sent it down into the depths toward its trapped counterpart. Then she concentrated on *Septimus*.

Almost immediately on bringing up the interface, she caught another grainy glimpse. Yes, *Septimus* was definitely stuck in the lava. The creatures were still around. Manda considered. *Septimus* was recording the aliens, anyway, and the longer she waited to try to get *Septimus* free, the more difficult it would be.

Saving *Septimus* wasn't as important as getting back to Amaterasu with the alien corpse—but she hated to ruin her nearly perfect record with her waldos. And they couldn't afford to lose more equipment, if it could be avoided.

It had been bad enough trying to maneuver *Septimus*, though, with only livegloves and voice. With voice alone . . . she sighed. *Let's get started.*

The moments of contact were too brief for her to make much headway. She kept trying, though—*come on, you fucker; come on!*—and got *Septimus* rocking sporadically. Not enough. Not enough.

I need to send a routine, she thought, *that will keep it rocking even after I'm cut off. And I'll need a routine to cancel the rocking once it breaks free, and another to fill its buoyancy tanks and get out of there fast.* She gnawed her lip. This was going to take a while. She got to work.

"Heads up!" Jim shouted suddenly—only an instant later, it seemed—and Manda saw the end of the line just ahead. She released the line barely in time and flailed her arms as she skidded downhill. Somehow, she managed to stay on her feet.

"Thanks," she said, as Jim came up beside her.

"Any progress with your waldo?"

She shook her head. "Not yet."

Word had apparently spread like a flash-freeze throughout the colony. As they sluiced down into the waves of warmer air and the muddy slush of the refinery, someone spotted them and shouted. They were mobbed. Faces intruded among the icons of her liveface—asking questions, jabbering excitedly, slapping her and Jim on the back. Jim and Manda pulled off their blades, and then the others began ushering them toward the cafeteria.

Jim moved between her and the others and raised his arms. "Back, people! Get back! Manda's trying to maintain a link with her waldos! Quiet!"

By dint of his imposing size and booming voice, he managed to clear a path for her. And now Manda had use of her livegloves too. While struggling to build a set of commands and shoot them through during the connected instants, she felt his hand on her arm, guiding her away from the big cafeteria building and toward a smaller one. His office.

"Work in here," he said. "I'll handle the rest."

She breathed a sigh. "Thanks."

He nodded, but his face didn't respond to her smile. "I'll pack you some provisions," he said, "and arrange a ride back for you to town."

Shocked, Manda stared at him through her thicket of active data- and commandshapes. "You're staying here?"

He shrugged. "Yeah. They need me here, and I'm no biologist." He held up his pack, in which the alien creature was wrapped. "Not much I could do with this. You take it back and see it gets into the right hands." He set it down next to her feet.

Come with me. Please. Please.

Of course pride wouldn't allow her to ask, not after she'd rejected him. She bent down and picked up the pack with the alien in it. He gave her a brief smile. "You're a hero now. You'll do fine."

Manda hunched her shoulders and shoved her hands between her knees. He looked at her wordlessly from the door, as if he wanted to say something more, then closed the door and left her alone.

*   *   *

She spent almost an hour trying to break *Aculeus Septimus* free. At first her attempts were thwarted by poor transmissions. Eventually the creatures left and she could get a clear signal, but by now it was clear that *Septimus* was irrevocably one with the lava flow. She-*Septimus* couldn't see back there too well, but her-its tail end seemed to be completely buried.

She switched over to *Aculeus Duo*, which was closing in on *Septimus*. She-*Duo* steered down to inspect the stuck waldo from several angles: the lower tail fin and a portion of its hindsection were buried in the rock. *Septimus*'s hull had taken some heat damage at the rock's boundary, but otherwise the unit seemed intact.

She-*Duo* used a pincer claw and cable to try to yank *Septimus* free. But it was no use. After straining and pulling and pounding for a while, she realized she was going to have to give it up and let *Septimus* go.

My second waldo loss, in two days. Regretfully, she-*Duo* left *Septimus* behind, and headed off in the direction the creatures had taken.

In a valley beyond some low hills, she-*Duo* discovered more of the seaweed-like stuff she-*Octo* had seen in the city. Here it wasn't so tall or tangled; she-*Duo* snipped some samples loose— about a kilo or two—and deposited them in her-*Duo*'s sampling receptacles.

A knock at the door made her start. UrsulaTomas stuck his head in.

"The tanker is about to leave."

"I'll be right there."

She ordered *Duo* to head back to the drill site for pickup, and then corrected *Quinque*'s and *Unus*'s trajectories, to have them rendezvous and await instructions at the fringe of the seaweed forest.

*   *   *

Jim wasn't among the crowd of well-wishers who sent her off. That hurt. Manda stood at the door of the fuel tanker, looking down at the refinery people, and felt depressed.

What do you expect, after the way you treated him?

She couldn't leave it like this. Manda jumped down all the way to the ground: a four-meter drop. Brimstone's gravity was only about half a gee, but she still felt the shock in her feet and knees.

"Where is Jim?" she demanded.

"The chem lab," two UrsulaTomases said together. She ran to the building they pointed at. "You don't have time!" they shouted after her.

Inside was a big room with lab benches and glass pipes and containers and cabinets and analytical machines. Jim was talking to Amy and Brian at one of the benches. They all turned to look at Manda when she burst in on them.

He'd told them what happened. She was certain of it. They must hate her. *He* must hate her.

She stood there, trying to catch her breath. Jim was watching her, the eyes of his vat-mates like cool mirrors on either side of him. Terror kept her rooted to the spot. *What do I do? What do I say?*

UrsulaTomas burst in, all four of it.

"The tanker's about to leave," they panted. "Hurry—" "it's timing out—" "—we can't hold it any longer."

Manda came forward and held out her hands to Jim. "I messed up. This isn't what I wanted."

He hesitated, not reaching for her hands. "What do you want?"

She stopped in front of him and lowered her arms. She struggled for words, then gave up and just said it. "You. I want you."

He closed his eyes with a sigh and opened his arms. She walked into them. They kissed, and it was as sweet as the first time.

"Now go!" he said, with a quick brushing away of her tears, which had started to fall again—and a stroke on her hair, and a look on his face that told her he didn't want her to go any more than she wanted to. "We'll talk later. I'll call you tonight." She kissed him again at the door to the labs, in front of everybody—

"Come, on!" urged UrsulaTomas.

Shit—what are they all going to say?

Who cares?

—and then rushed down the slope, with the UrsulaTomas fiveclone running ahead of her and flanking her, toward the tanker that was already starting to move.

More joined the parade. With an escort of refinery staff running alongside, shouting good-byes and encouragement, she put on a burst of speed down a small hill and caught the bottommost rung of the ladder. Manda climbed up into the compartment.

From the open door, still crying, but smiling now too, she waved good-bye. This time Jim was waving back. His vat-mates, standing on either side of him, were not.

Though she was very tired and sore from unaccustomed exertions—and from the emotional and mental impact of all the recent events—Manda didn't get much rest during the eight-hour ride back. The cold and the bouncing around jostled her body, and thoughts about aliens and Jim jostled her thoughts. She had also exhausted her supply of rations, and by the end of the trip hunger pangs were jerking her stomach into painful knots.

The tanker reached Amaterasu at fourteen o'clock, smack in the middle of first-watch break, and scrambled to a stop in the main entryway cavern near the tanker descent cables. On opening the door Manda found that many Amaterasans had either foregone their midday sleep or had gotten up extremely early: a sea of curious eyes was staring up at her.

Derek waved and called a greeting; he and the rest of the council stood at the crowd's front. A few others waved too, but the low hum of the colonists' murmurs were all that carried to her ears. With all those eyes on her, Manda felt a bit like an alien herself.

The rest of her clone stood just behind Derek. But they were too few. Who—? Then she remembered, and the pain reared up, fresh and raw, and sank its claws in. She had forgotten.

Get a grip. Manda descended the ladder—breathing deeply with each step till she had regained control—carrying her gear over one shoulder and the smaller pack in which Jim had packed the alien corpse over her other. It was a lot of weight and bulk, and her steps were slow. She alighted. The tanker scuttled noisily over to squat in a corner, out of the way.

Meanwhile, Jack and Amadeo, Derek and Arlene, Lawrence and Donald, and the others of the council approached—rather cautiously, Manda thought—followed by their younger siblings. RoxannaTomas was there too. Jeannelle and Vance and two of their siblings were dressed in containment suits; two had a collapsible specimen box.

Oh, shit. Manda gaped, suddenly terrified. She recalled how she and Jim had poked at the thing. She'd never considered the possibility of contamination. *Jim.*

The rest of the crowd hung back. Manda slung Jim's pack off her shoulder.

"Go ahead and set it down on the plastic sheet there," one said in a muffled voice, gesturing, and she did so. While the two with the box unfolded it and maneuvered the specimen out of the pack and into the box, Jeannelle and Vance had Manda step over to a heated portable stall lined with curtains. The stall was up on a big metal stand with a rim that, when she stepped up onto it, thudded hollowly. She realized it must be a catchment basin.

"We're going to have you take off your clothes and livesuit," Jeannelle said, "and toss them over here." She pointed with her suited hand at a plastic-lined bin next to the stall. "And put your pack in too."

Manda dropped the pack into the bin, then stripped off her parka and dropped it in too. She sat down on the scalloped edge of the catchment basin and took off her boots and socks. Her feet instantly turned white; the heat radiating from the glowing orange coils over the stall wasn't nearly enough to warm the metal floor.

Jeannelle showed Manda the handles and nozzles while Vance fiddled with something Manda couldn't see on the other side of the curtain. "This one," he said, "is warm soapy water. We want you to thoroughly spray yourself with this until we tell you to stop. Then you'll rinse with this." She gestured at a second one.

"What is it?" Manda asked.

"It's an isopropyl alcohol solution. You'll do the same thing— keep spraying till we tell you to stop. Then you'll spray yourself all over with this." She gestured at the third nozzle and knob. "It's acetic acid solution. Don't worry—it's a weak solution and won't harm you. Last we want you to do the soapy water wash again. Be sure to get in all the cracks and crannies with each wash. OK?"

"Is all this really necessary?" she asked, but she was already removing her tam and sweater.

"It's going to be OK," Vance said. "This is just a precaution."

"Yeah, sure," Manda muttered. She closed the curtains, stripped and tossed her clothes into the bin Jeannelle had indicated, then washed herself in the prescribed way.

It took a while. The isopropyl bath was the worst. Once she'd finished, her skin tingled all over. It felt good. Jeannelle handed her some towels and clean clothes to dress in and took out her old stuff. Cold and hot air drafts swirled against her skin as she dried her hair, and she shivered.

"I don't think I've ever been quite this clean," she remarked as she exited. But no one was paying attention to Manda anymore. Everyone was staring into space, while the eldest RoxannaTomas twins stood in a small clear space, going through motions and gyrations. The box rested near their feet. The rest of RoxannaTomas and the other councilmembers' clones— including the rest of CarliPablo—had formed a protective phalanx around all of them to keep people from pressing too close.

The eldest RoxannaTomas twins must be piloting waldos around or even into the alien creature, exploring its surfaces and orifices, broadcasting their signals to the colony at large. Manda felt a spasm of frustration that they'd taken her yoke and goggles. She'd like to have seen and heard their initial impressions. She'd have to check the recordings.

Then everyone tuned back into reality, as if waking from a mass dream. The eldest two RoxannaTomases removed their suits and dropped them in the same bin that held Manda's old clothes and pack, and their younger, suited siblings began packing everything up. Jack gave a signal, and the whole group—councilmembers, biologists, decontamination team, and Manda—moved forward, with the protective barrier of their siblings ahead of them, nudging people out of the way.

The eldest RoxannaTomases bracketed Manda as they followed the councilmembers. They fired question after question at her: "Did you see any other mobile species, besides this?—Did they all look like this?—How big a variation in size did you see?—Any signs of sexual dimorphism?—Did you see any thermal vent chimneys?—Any sense of how big the city is?—Are they the only occupants?—We need samples of the grassy substance as soon as you can get it to us . . . —and perhaps some scrapings of the walls . . . —Did you detect any sign of aggression, when they approached you?" and so on, while they boarded the lifts and rode them down to the main caverns and tunnels of the colony.

They shot the questions almost too fast for her to answer (most of which boiled down to some variant of "I don't know")—tripping over each other in their eagerness to learn all she knew. Finally they started talking excitedly to each other about the creature, in a stream of bio-babble Manda could make little sense of. She tuned them out. The first rush of excitement she'd felt at all the hubbub had faded, and she was too numbed by exhaustion and hunger to pay attention.

Then the doors opened, and the RoxannaTomas twins carted

the containment box housing the alien corpse away down the tunnel without so much as a farewell to Manda. Their youngest siblings who had come down with them hurried along after; Jeannelle gave Manda a quick wave over her shoulder as she departed.

Derek stepped out of the neighboring lift as the doors opened, and laid a hand on her shoulder. "You're exhausted. Come on."

More people were waiting in the corridor. They greeted her with big smiles and pats on the back. She knew she should be glad—it was what she'd always wanted: to make a big contribution. To prove to them she mattered. But all this attention made her want to run screaming upside, where all she had to worry about was deadly cold, radiation, and alien lifeforms.

Her other siblings—Arlene, Bart, Charles, Farrah, and Janice—*is that* really *all I have left?* she thought, once more—were there too. They read her distress and fatigue, and surrounded her protectively. "Enough questions.—You can talk to her later.—Please, not right now."

She found her eyes tearing up again. *Why am I always pretending it doesn't matter what they think of me?*

"Why don't you come to our quarters?" Farrah suggested, and the others agreed. "We'll bring you lunch and then you can sleep."

Her stomach growled noisily. "Yes. All right. That would be good."

In her clone's chamber, her siblings brought her food, and Manda ate—at first slowly, as her too-empty stomach unknotted—and then more greedily, as she realized how famished she was. Manda suspected they were sharing their own rations with her, and felt guilty for taking more than her share, but the severe cold and long hours of hard going had made her so hungry she couldn't force herself to refuse it.

They let her eat in silence. Almost in mid-swallow, she laid down and slept. She barely remembered them pulling covers over her. She drifted off with their whispers fluttering overhead.

Manda woke alone. Her brain felt stuffed with ox-hair batting. She lay with her arms under her head while consciousness returned. The ache of hunger and fatigue that had dogged her throughout her trip to the floes had faded. It felt so good.

She'd slept fully clothed. She saw that they'd left her a livesuit and yoke in her size—either a new one or, more likely, her old one, decontaminated—on the foot of the bed. Her parka and utility belt were also there, still damp from their cleaning. Manda stripped and donned her livesuit, mask, gloves, and yoke, and hooked up the leads. Then she activated her liveface with the touch of a livegloved finger and it bloomed once more around her.

It was past twenty-three o'clock—well into the day's final work-shift. She'd slept eight and a half hours. An alert blinked across the top of her vision, announcing the impending autopsy of the alien, telling what channels people could tune into and/or what room they could come to, to observe. All but the most critical tasks had been suspended, for this watch.

Guess I know where everyone is.

Manda pulled her long johns and outer layers of clothing back on, and then checked in on her marine waldos. *Aculeus Duo* had reached the drill hole with its sampling of "seaweed," and was hovering in the chilly water beneath the ice ceiling, awaiting further instructions. The rest had arrived at the underwater city, and had arranged themselves in different locations in the sea-weed forest, along the city's periphery. They had begun record-ing information: chemical, thermal, radar, and sonic. She browsed back through the data and found numerous static-filled gaps, as the parasol creatures had approached the waldos.

Well, they certainly know we're here now. But they seemed to be leaving the waldos alone, by and large. *Thank God for that.*

The clearest signals were *Aculeus Quinque*'s. Manda stepped into *Quinque*'s systems and as its interface sprang up around her, she-waldo looked down on the strange alien city, using night-vision technology with false-color imaging. The views and textures wavered, due both to thermal gradients rising from the many geothermal chimneys scattered through the city, and to the poor quality of the signal. The constant fading in and out made her seasick as she-*Quinque* tried to maneuver. Finally she gave up and remained still. On a hunch, she turned off the visual enhancements, tuned in audio, and let her eyes adjust to the dark.

As before, the city resonated with sound. The high-pitched clicks, tones, and whistles of the parasol creatures mingled with the deeper tones of other creatures, and the deep booming she'd heard before underscored it all like the percussion changes in a post-rad-progression chorale. Slowly, she-*Quinque* could see that the enormous edifice had its own, very faint lighting. Strands and globes of multihued phosphorescences traced the forms of the towers and arches and tubes and strands. Schools of swimming creatures moved here and there, shadows and luminous globs silhouetted against the glowing strands and structures. Giant shapes lumbered through the gaps: moaning and clicking.

She-*Quinque* did a sounding, and shortly detected the sonar signatures of her other nearby marine-waldos: dark, still shapes in the frigid waters surrounding the city, slick-hard and complex against the impingement of her-*Quinque*'s sonar, where the creatures were softer, and always moving, and the city structures were huge, imposing, and coarse.

Manda didn't dare move any of her small fleet. She should probably wait for the council's clearance—but more importantly, she needed to figure out a way past the havoc she and the inhabitants of this city caused to each other's sonic communications.

As she was wrapping up—intending to leave her five waldos

at the city's edge to continue collecting data; giving them some last-minute instructions on what to monitor for—she-*Unus* detected a large dark shape moving past her-it that didn't register like one of the big creature-objects. Puzzled, she turned on her-its flood lights—just in time to see maybe four or five dozen parasol creatures swim past. They were towing inert *Octo*, which was bound in some kind of web.

"Aw, shit," she muttered. Particulates and signal lapses made it difficult for her-*Unus* to track the towing team very well, but she tuned and magnified and focused as much as she knew how to, and "saw" them drag the machine into a tunnel opening. She marked the location on the map she was making of the city.

Two marine-waldos lost, and five others now vulnerable at the city's perimeter. If she lost them, there wouldn't be any more. She suddenly felt very vulnerable and exposed. She wasn't about to wait for the aliens to decide to capture them too.

She blasted a broad-band emergency ascent command. One-by-one, as they received the signal, her waldos responded—their fans geared up, creating a machine chorus in her many machine-ears. Water stirred across Manda-waldos' skin in a flurry of tactile feedback as all her waldos surged upward, dropping ballast in a rain of boulders from their underbellies. The five machines—and Manda, riding them—shot up past cliff walls defined by blurs of glowing flecks, and up further into the black, briny currents of Omi-Kami's pelagic zone. Her communications links rapidly improved with the ascent.

It took a while for Manda's panic to ebb. But her-waldos' sonar detected little reaction from the parasols. A few followed for a bit, then fell back. Then her-waldos' scans registered only silence.

Manda relaxed a bit. She commanded her *Aculeus* fleet to return to the drill hole, where she would have them wait above the ice for further instructions. Then she switched over to *Aculeus Duo*, the marine-waldo that had earlier sampled the weed-like substance. It was still at the drill hole, waiting for instructions. Manda slipped into its controls. The ice crust's craggy underside hung overhead, visible in her-*Duo's* sonar sight. Manda succumbed to a surge of claustrophobia. *Get me out of here.*

She-*Duo* ejected her-its several arms. Like a centipede, she-waldo grabbed hold of the submerged section of drill cable—near the strings of sonar transponders—and scrambled up past the circulatory fans that kept the drill hole open, using a good deal more power than was strictly necessary. A bit later, perhaps two-thirds of the way up or so, she-*Duo* reached the surface and broke through. A film of ice crystallized instantly on *Duo's* surfaces. She switched the waldo over to radio control, brushed the crystals from her-its cameras with her-its forward arms, and continued her-its long climb. It seemed to take forever. But the tiny circle of light above grew bigger. At the top of the scaffold, she-*Duo* swung over and slid down one leg of the scaffold, and landed in a crouch on the ice with a loud *whump!*

Manda quickly reconfigured *Duo* for land travel while it homed in on the refinery's beacon. She pointedly did *not* look in the direction of the hut.

The waldo could move much faster than she and Jim had; within a handful of minutes she-*Duo* had skated over the marbled and pitted surface of Omi-Kami, past the array of cracks and holes that spring thaws and tidal surges were forcing onto the ice at Arcas's shores.

She-*Duo* skated up the hillside toward the refinery, using jets to propel it. Its automatic programming—the same programming the tankers used to navigate up Maia to the plains near Amaterasu—kicked in then. Manda released the controls to the transport syntellects and disconnected. *Aculeus Duo's* icons folded up and put themselves away.

Manda rubbed her face, still shaken. First she'd better update

Derek and Arlene. She put in a call, but their comm syntellects answered for them. Manda left an urgent message.

"The aliens have *Octo* now. Check out the attached video and call me. I'll give you an update." And she attached the footage she-*Quinque* had just recorded of *Octo*'s capture.

She took a few seconds to calm herself, breathing deeply and slowly with her eyes closed and her legs crossed, till her heart slowed and her stomach stopped churning. Then she lifted her head. During her waldo work she'd forgotten where her body was. She looked around this sleeping space of her clone's. This was the first time she'd been here alone in seasons and seasons.

So little had changed. She found that oddly comforting. The belongings of her siblings hung on the walls and lay on the shelves. She crawled over to Paul and Teresa's corner of the bed and buried her face in the pillows that had still had indentations from where their heads had rested, and smelled the scents that still lingered there. She touched their shelves, eyed their few belongings.

It still seemed unimaginable that she'd never see either of them again. It just didn't seem possible that they weren't in the world anymore. They were nothing more than a collection of molecules, now. Nutrients. Incipient dust.

She felt another flush of anger at Paul, for leaving. She felt anger at the universe for taking Teresa away, and forcing him into that pain-filled oubliette. She shed more tears over them: over the cold, smooth, unrumpled space where they'd used to sleep.

It had been six days since the cave-in had killed Teresa, and two since Paul had taken a dive into the recyclers. It seemed like so much longer. Eons. Yet any minute she expected Teresa to stick her head through the entryway and scold Manda for lying around when there was work to do, or to tease her about muttering to herself.

She decided to visit Terence first thing.

*   *   *

Traffic was fairly light, but as Manda made her way toward the medical areas along the wandering curves and bamboo staircases and ladders, people passing by exchanged greetings with her, asked her questions about the alien, or just looked at her out of the edges of their eyes. Others stuck their heads out of doorways as she walked by, as if word were being passed via liveface. It gave Manda the crawlies.

A tremor shook dust from the ceiling as she walked, and once again her mouth went dry and her heart rate leapt as dust motes settled around her.

We have to get out of these caves, she thought. *We need to get out into the open air and build cities and towns—till the soil—surround ourselves with a thriving ecosystem, like our ancestors on Earth have. We* need *Project IceFlame.*

But what will we do, now that this world turns out to be inhabited? Brimstone isn't ours for the taking.

In the infirmary, several people who normally wouldn't have spared a glance for Manda greeted her and congratulated her on her discovery. Someone mentioned that the autopsy had just started, and everyone was either attending, or telepresenting into the operating chamber, or both.

"Thanks," she said.

But not just yet. First Manda visited the Neonatal ICU. She waved at the nurse on duty and went over to the window. Beyond it lay Terence, alone in the small room now that the triplet premies were gone. She wanted to go inside, but given that she might be infected with some alien microbe, decided against it.

He still looked so tiny. Tiny as a newborn kitten; his head no bigger than a plum; his body no longer than the span of her outstretched fingers. On his little abdomen was an orange-stained area with a puckered incision squatting on it like a flesh-colored caterpillar.

But maybe . . . maybe he'd grown a little. He didn't seem as bony as before, and his skin looked healthier, somehow. Not so greyish.

He slept, utterly motionless, eyes closed. If it weren't for all the instruments reporting his heart rate, blood pressure, core temperature, and respiration, she might fear he was dead. But she talked to him anyway, as he lay there under the thicket of life support equipment. She told him she was here and he needn't be afraid, and to her annoyance she started crying again. *Damn these tears. When will they cease?*

Jeannelle and Vance rounded the corner. "Manda!" they both said. "Somebody said you were here." "I-we am starting the autopsy." "You should be there." "Your clone saved you a seat up front."

Manda dashed the tears away. *I'll be back,* she promised Terence. She wanted to hold him close—nuzzle him—whisper loving words to him. She knew how much he needed her. Even if *he* didn't really understand yet. Even if later he wouldn't remember.

"How is he doing?" she asked, as they wended their way through the tunnels to the operating chambers. Vance and Jeannelle gave her a considering glance.

"He's improved a lot." "He's breathing on his own now—" "—and he's put on quite a bit of weight." "At this point the NICU"—the Neonatal Intensive Care Unit; they pronounced it *NICK-you*—"team is confident he'll live."

Their expressions said there was more to it than that.

"But?"

The RoxannaTomases didn't answer.

"I want to know," Manda said.

"All right." Some sign passed between the twins. Vance pressed fingertips to his lips. "You should be prepared for the possibility that he'll suffer some health complications, going forward."

"What kind of complications?"

"Neurological damage," Jeannelle replied. "He's suffered some intraventricular hemorraging in his brain that might have caused some damage." "He's had a few seizures," Vance said.

The hair bristled along her neck and forearms. They sounded so matter-of-fact about it. They might have been describing what he'd had for lunch.

"There's some other stuff that might be a problem." "He has no suckling reflex, so feeding him will be tricky, once he's on his own." "He's had to have a section of necrotized bowel removed." Jeannelle squinted at Manda. "But his condition is stabilizing." Vance nodded concurrence. "I-we expect we'll be turning him over to the nursery in a few weeks." "But he'll need close watching for a several months, so we can identify any problems early."

"How—" the word came out a croak. Manda cleared her throat. "How certain are you? About the neurological damage, I mean."

They said in unison, "We're not." "It's hard to be sure quite what to expect." "Babies have amazing powers of regeneration." "He was barely two weeks into his third trimester of gestation—" "—we didn't expect him to survive at all—" "—so he's made remarkable progress." "Under the circumstances." "He may continue to."

"Surely there must be statistics to give you an idea—" Manda started, but they both shook their heads before she'd even finished.

"A baby isn't a statistic." "Occasionally they make amazing recoveries and suffer no long-term side effects." "Other times, not." "You just never know."

"Oh."

Seizures. Neurological damage. Manda had been assuming—pretending?—that if they could get him off the respirator, he'd be fine. It didn't seem fair.

"I've been studying up on neonatal medical interventions back on Earth," Jeannelle went on, "and passing them on to my older sister Tania" "She's the NICU team leader," Vance added at Manda's blank look, "but our records are all several Earth-decades out-of-date." "I-we am sure by now Earth has all kinds of medical magic that could help us help him, if we could only access it." "But we're stuck with what we've got."

Manda gritted her teeth. *The crèche-born are only a few hours away, by radio. They could get us whatever information we needed.* She felt helpless.

Vance left Jeannelle to escort Manda to the alien autopsy, while he remained to help the NICU staff. The audience seating up in the mezzanine above the operating room was jammed full. People had also lined up along the walls of the theater itself. A team of livepack-bedecked physicians, nurses, and scientists pantomimed and cavorted in an open area. Near them, in a portable, glass-enclosed cubicle in the middle of the theater, their miniature waldos climbed all over and inside the dead alien creature. It reminded Manda, vaguely, of similes she had seen of life on the African savannahs back on Earth: a mob of metal, plastic, and metaceramic scavengers picking at a carcass.

Frost traceries had condensed on the glass windows; the cubicle must be refrigerated. Perhaps even depressurized. Cameras and lights and other equipment whose uses Manda didn't know surrounded the forensic waldo team.

"Do you really think they might be able to infect us?" she asked Jeannelle.

"Oh, it's certainly possible! The creatures could have all sorts of bacteria or viruses inside them, or molds or fungi—or some other orders of species we can't even imagine—microorganisms the creatures have adapted to over billions of years, that they've developed immunity to and we've haven't. If there is enough compatibility between their biology and ours, they could wipe us out before we even knew what was happening, if we had to rely on our own, unaugmented immune systems to protect us."

"Jim was exposed too," said Manda.

Jeannelle nodded. "Yes. I-we've sent teams out to decontaminate him. And the tanker, and everything else the alien creature came in contact with."

"That reminds me." Manda told Jeannelle about *Aculeus Duo*, which was bringing the seaweed sample in. "I'll notify you-you once it reaches the colony."

"Great. Thanks for letting me-us know."

Manda eyed her. "How can you be so calm about all this?"

The other woman smiled. "I'm just not that worried. We already knew a bit about Brimstonian biology from the traces we found when we first arrived. We know their biochemistry will be different from ours—different enough to make it unlikely any microorganisms will be able to leap the gap easily. We know that the bacteria—or at least the traces we'd found—uses something like RNA, though we don't know yet whether they have DNA. We've identified that their tissues are cellular organic matter, but at the molecular level it could all be based on some other replication system we don't know anything about."

Manda frowned. "How could that be possible? I thought DNA was universal."

"Anything is possible, Manda. We don't know yet what the constraints are on the formation of life. We have some good guesses based on biophysical principles we've gleaned from Earth life and a smattering of extraterrestrial hints, but . . ." Jeannelle shrugged. "The fossilized stuff they found on Mars in the 2020s didn't leave a whole lot of clues, and they weren't done analyzing the Europa organisms when we fell out of contact. We do have a few ideas based on analyses we'd already made on the native bugs, early on, but we weren't able to isolate them well enough to get complete results.

"This alien is a whole new game. Everything we think we know about Brimstone life could change in the next few days. It's very exciting."

Manda looked down at the operating cubicle, hugging herself. Jeannelle's gaze followed hers. "I suppose I'm counting on the fact that the creatures will be highly attuned to this world's ecosystem," she said, "and not ours. Back in Earthspace, after billions of years of coevolution, most viruses and bacteria can infect only a limited number of species."

"Oh." Manda wished that made her feel better than it did. "Why did you go to all that trouble of decontaminating me, then?"

"Like I told you at the time, it was just a precaution. Oh, that reminds me. We will be monitoring your vitals for a while, via your livesuit. We'll be keeping a close watch on everyone who's been exposed, for a while."

"Sure." Manda attempted to sound casual, but the word came out strained. Jeannelle smiled.

"Look, even if you did pick up something from the alien— which I seriously doubt—we have a full complement of analytical and treatment tools for dealing with this kind of thing. Earth made huge advances in fighting infection while we were en route here. The crèche-born collected loads of infection-fighting and immune-bolstering nanotech programs over the years, all of which we have access to. And when we first made landfall, *Exodus* gave us a suite of smartware and nanobug templates to help us protect ourselves against xeno-organisms, and we still have all of that."

"So why can't you-you use all that fancy medical equipment and those special techniques to help Terence?"

"Terence's problem isn't infection by alien microorganisms. We don't have the facilities to manufacture new forms of nanoware here, even if we had the blueprints for them. All we have are what we can regrow from the samples the crèche-born left us with."

"Defenders, Suit-Makers, and Recyclers," Manda said.

"Exactly. Reformatting them to take on different orders of functions is a huge leap. It takes highly specialized knowledge and equipment, which—"

"Which the crèche-born have and we don't," Manda finished. Jeannelle gave her a sharp look at her tone.

"I'm afraid so," Jeannelle said. "Manda, I promise you we're doing our best for your little brother. And we'll continue to."

"All right." Manda sighed. "I know."

While they talked, Jeannelle had led Manda across the theater and up the carved-stone steps to the mezzanine. Now she showed Manda where the rest of CarliPablo was, and then excused herself to return to NICU. Manda worked her way past the others and sat with her brothers and sisters. All four (Derek and Arlene weren't there) were intent on what was going on below. She turned on her liveface and tuned in, to get the different views being broadcast to the colony.

At first she was so worked up over Terence that she had a hard time concentrating on the events below, but the small team's work, and their running commentary, soon drew her attention. And, as she had every time she'd brought up her liveware, she silently blessed ByronDalia for its gift of a liveface upgrade. The autopsy came through in vivid, highest-resolution, full-surround mode.

Five of the colony's forty communications channels bore the "alien autopsy" label. Channel four showed a magnified view of what was going on down in the chamber. Seven, eight, and twelve focused on teams elsewhere that were using the data already gathered to analyze different aspects of the creature's makeup, and channel ten showed some of the interpretive and predictive similes ur-Carli was running. Manda switched to channel four and watched them perform the autopsy.

"... OK, I'm cutting through the seventh discrete subcutaneous layer now," a voice was saying. "It looks like we're finally into the central organ cavity."

On Manda's live display, a magnified image of a four-pronged medical-waldo—a med-hand—was cutting through some greyish stuff with its scalpel attachment, revealing, gradually, an assortment of lumps, sinews, and tubes of many translucent colors, while a second med-hand took tissue samples and a third adjusted the lighting. Manda knew the med-hand waldos were a lot smaller than human hands—not much larger than insects— and each bristled with an assortment of retractable, reconfigurable attachments. The surgeon would be operating up to four of them at once, and directing his vat-mates in the support tasks.

"Careful," someone said; "William's micro-waldo is in a vein less than a centimeter away from your incision."

The display informed viewers that William was piloting a waldo doing ultrasound on some of the interior tissues. He'd wandered a little too close to the incision site.

"In which direction?"

"Toward the cephalad annulus. Here's a visual."

"Got it," said the first voice. "I'll continue on an oblique angle." Three of the four med-hands reconfigured themselves and inserted their array of tiny lamps and tongs and retractors, holding the upper tissues out of the way as the fourth wormed and sliced its way further in. Purplish liquid leaked out around the med-hand doing the cutting. Other med-hands with sponges slithered in to soak it up, while the fourth med-hand tipped with sensors felt around. "I'm looking at some translucent, orange and pink globular clusters, which communicate with the dark grey, soft ovoid organ I described before. . . . Feel this, Mary."

Two more med-hands crawled into the incision, and the sensory attachments "sniffed" and fingered the tissues the first med-hand was gesturing at. Sinewy tubes emerged from some gloppy stuff as the new med-hands felt them. "Interesting! Look. More structure than we guessed at the beginning."

"Get a couple samples here, Val," the first voice said, and one of the med-hands in the incision gestured. A med-hand with syringe attachments crawled in from the periphery and took a sample from the opaque white fleshy tubes the first set of med-hands were holding up. The fluid that filled the syringe was purple-tinged. "I'm beginning to suspect that this is a manganese-based circulatory fluid. Do we have the analytical results back yet? . . . No?"

Several med-hands scuttled up out of the incision. Meanwhile, one of the original four med-hands maneuvered yet deeper into the tissues, and drew out an enormous, bright yellow bulb, shot with grey and purple streaks. "I'm holding a . . . oh . . . I don't know, maybe five-by-six-centimeter, firm, globular shape. Its interior feels friable with partially calcified excrescences. Sort of like grit in a balloon. Is this a deposit of sulfur?"

"Here?" One of the second set of med-hands returned. "Maybe."

"Let's get a sample. This could be further evidence that these creatures metabolize sulfides instead of oxygen. . . ."

"Well, but if that's the case, they wouldn't have a need for a manganese-based oxygen-transfer circulatory system."

"It might be a hybrid system." "True." "Here, get a sample, then we can rinse this out and let's see what it communicates with." Another triad of med-hands went in after the first four, inserted a needle into the yellow bulb, and took a sample. The object was drawn out. "Hmmm. Here we have more linear structures underneath the yellow object; they appear to be near the cephalad aperture. An analog of cartilage maybe?"

It went on like this for a while. They opened, studied, and then cut samples from all the organs and tissues, a tiny segment at a time. Manda found it fascinating, but it also made her queasy. She wondered whether the parasol creatures were doing the same thing to *Octo*, dissecting it and looking for its brain and other organs. A vivid image intruded, of herself as a corpse somewhere in the labyrinth of their city's buildings and tunnels—of being gutted, fileted, and picked over by their physicians. With a shudder, she switched over to see what other analyses were being done.

On channel seven she browsed through a series of scans showing the creature's physical structures and the scientists' guesses as to what its biological systems were. So far these were pretty sketchy. They had identified what they thought was the brain, or at least an important component of the central processing system. But it was quite small proportionate to the creature's size, compared to the human brain, and one of the scientists suspected that these creatures' nervous systems were wired quite differently than ours, with perhaps more than one brain, each handling different kinds of sensory and nerve-processing tasks. They'd also found what they thought was the mouth (or mouths: a series of small holes—hundreds of them—around the parasol's outer edge, between its seven, seven-"fingered" "hands"). But they weren't totally sure; besides, these holes didn't seem to be hooked up to a digestive system, best they could tell. They might have been reproductive, instead.

Channel eight showed the different electron micrographs of the creature's cellular and molecular structures. They had just confirmed that the creatures had DNA, constructed of six base pairs, as compared to Earth life's four. Three of their base pairs matched ours. Early indicators were that they metabolized sulfides instead of oxygen—or possibly in addition to, since physical examinations had found some slits that might be gills—though perhaps vestigial—and their circulatory fluids contained manganese-based proteins that seemed to serve a similar function to our hemoglobin: oxygen and carbon dioxide exchange.

Channel twelve was dedicated to the scientists doing micro-scopic analyses of the creature's tissues, looking for any para-sites or other organisms they might house that could harm Earth species. So far they'd found several kinds of microscopic cells and clusters, but were still trying to sort out the foreign organisms from the things that belonged there.

Meanwhile, the similes on channel ten used all this other data to start building a model of their biology and ecology. There was a sensory/nervous system model, a consumption/excretion model, a reproductive model, and a motor model. All of them, so far, were sparse on specifics.

Watching ur-Carli's similes, Manda thought about *Exodus* once more.

Just how had ur-Carli known it was there? Why had it told Manda about the ship? Why had it shown her the secret place? And for that matter, why *hadn't* the crèche-born left the colony the knowledge they needed to make full use of their technology?

Something really strange was going on.

Manda tucked away her icons and shut off her liveface, then left the operating room and wandered down to the bamboo cav-erns. On the way she looked in on Hydroponics. It was still a mess, but a lot of the dirt and debris and been moved and packed down, and some structures were starting to take shape here and there. The heavy construction machines stood about, frozen mechanical giants. She wondered how the two remaining UrsaMeri triplets were faring. (She wondered whether she should start thinking of them as twins, now. She didn't like that idea, much.) Then she entered the bamboo and walked for a while, till she found a quiet, grassy place to sit.

First she reactivated her liveface to check on her waldos. But she noticed at the periphery of her vision a row of three faceless little balls: ByronDalia had neglected to remove some of their hacking features from the accelerator software they'd provided her. They were so unobtrusive she hadn't noticed till now.

She poked at them. Two didn't do much; when she finally figured out how to open them, they merely showed arcane strings of coding and debugging information. The third, however, blossomed open to reveal an alphanumeric input ball and a short phrase that spiraled lazily in midair.

ReadDisk by E(mptySector)/T(imeStamp)=__?

It must be a search routine for scanning the colony computer systems' unused sectors, a hacker's undeleting tool. She tried typing in **E-<enter>**.

It came back with:

Enter#-# (range) / A(ll)=__?

What the hell, Manda thought, and typed **A-<enter>**.

The column opened out into a display. Inside appeared a marching sequence of fragments of junk data: a requisition for kitchen supplies; a snatch of poetry; extra copies of a few popular songs erased from the archives; facemail; spreadsheets; fuel and food inventories; programming code. Each snippet had its own identifying string of numbers at the top. The significance of the numbers escaped her, until a piece of video appeared, a report from the Fertility labs, just after the cave-in. The eldest RoxannaTomases were reporting to the council on the damage. It started in mid-sentence and cut off abruptly after several seconds, switching to an analysis of orbital mapping data for the four moons of Boddhisatva, the next planet in from Fire.

Manda realized then that the strings of numbers displayed at the top of the segment had matched the date and time the cave-in had happened. All these junk sectors had their own time stamp. And that gave her an idea.

Something ugly had happened back on *Exodus*. Something that had been buried—deliberately forgotten by the older colonists. And her instincts told her that this held the key, somehow, to ur-Carli's odd behavior, as well as the secret room and the mystery of Carli's corpse.

She'd noticed, before, the scarcity of archived files as *Exodus* had approached Uma. With this disk-scan software, it was possible she could recover pieces of some of those files.

The data blackout period would have been between twenty-two and twenty-five seasons ago. She returned to the "scan by" command line, and typed in **T-<enter>**, and then entered a range that covered the time about one fire-year—three earth-years—before they'd made landfall, around the time she had been decanted.

As before, most of it was garbage: requisitions; readouts from assorted monitoring equipment; facemail; boring journal entries; half corrupted scientific tables and charts. There were tantalizing tidbits, though—she found part of a text file that made veiled reference to a "hidden war," snatches of distressed voices in an audio file, and so on—amid all the mountains of trivia. But she wasn't coming up with anything tangible, and was about to give up, when suddenly a thrideo recording came up of some repair work being done on the exterior of the ship by a pair of suited figures.

She could hear two sets of voices. One set was the astronauts, talking to each other about the repairs. The other set was a pair of observers, whose voices the astronauts didn't respond to—apparently because they couldn't hear them. From the information imprinted at the bottom of the video, she recognized the video as an official recording from one of *Exodus*'s exterior cameras. Amaterasu had these official recordings as well; the food fight had been recorded on one.

The suited figures were attempting to detach a segment of pole from the hull of the ship that was connected to a large solar panel. They appeared to be having some difficulty. They were joking about it, not overly concerned.

Then one of the observers said, "Mara's ready to blow the charges." Mara was one of the crèche-born.

When the words' meaning reached her, Manda gasped. *The charges?* Explosives?

The other observer said, "Wait. They're not in position yet."

"Roger."

Then the recording flickered away, replaced by a copy of an entertainment simile.

"Shit." Manda called up the sector-reading software again, and put in a much narrower range for the time stamp, starting the instant the first segment had ended and extending for about ten minutes. After sifting through dozens more trivial segments, she found more.

The same two astronauts she'd seen earlier were further out onto the pole. It was about two minutes after the other fragment. Two sparks of light flashed: one at the base of the extension the astronauts were climbing, and another at the hook further down the spine of the ship to which their lifelines were attached. The pole came dislodged and the astronauts tumbled flailing off into space, snarling themselves in the extension and their lifelines. This segment had no audio attached, so Manda couldn't hear their voices, but she caught glimpses of their terrified expressions. They were KaliMarshalls: a male and a female, a young pair—younger than Manda. The sequence was abruptly replaced by a sector containing audiochromatic strains of code from some deleted program or other.

The KaliMarshalls don't have a male and female set of twins, she thought, then corrected herself: *not anymore.*

Manda had just witnessed a murder that must have happened long ago. Twenty-three seasons ago, according to the time stamp.

The crèche-born had killed the eldest siblings of her childhood foes, Abraham KaliMarshall and his vat-twin Robert. She wondered if they knew. Or did they believe it was an accident—as her own brother's death had supposedly been?

Rumors were one thing, but this was proof.

What could anyone do about it now? And in the grander scheme of things, what did it matter? Surely they had nothing to fear from the colonists. Not after so long.

But she wasn't so sure of that anymore. She began to understand her older siblings' reluctance to contact them.

Manda thought of Derek and Arlene, how they'd reacted to her revelation that the crèche-born were still around. The crèche-born had been, in a very real sense, the colonists' parents. How could they have perpetrated such horrors? And so casually. The observers' voices hadn't even sounded strained.

Sick at heart, not sure what she should do with this archaic revelation (she knew Arlene and Derek wouldn't want to discuss it, and she had no one outside the clone she could talk about this with), she saved the snippet, then put the software away and pulled up her waldo commandface. She'd give the matter further thought. In the meantime she had work to do.

Aculeus Duo had just reached the highland plateau rimmed by the Scimitars, the mountains atop Amaterasu. It was a huge plateau; the waldo would not arrive for another two hours. Presumably the waldo would require decontamination. She put into *Duo*'s queue a command for the waldo to wait outside the main entry cavern, once it reached Amaterasu, and to call Jeannelle and Vance RoxannaTomas for further instructions.

Aculeus Septimus, still stuck in the hardened lava, was continuing to collect and transmit data on the eruption there. The lava was solidifying much further up the slopes now, and *Septimus* seemed to be in no further danger. She had it start work on disassembling and reconfiguring some of its chemical samplers and monitors to improve its data collection. Might as well get some use out of it; it was going to be there a good long while.

The other five waldos were speeding toward the drill hole, which was several hundred kilometers away from their current position. She-they did radar and sonar soundings and detected no sign of pursuit.

Manda reconsidered her earlier decision. Really, she shouldn't have panicked. If the parasol creatures hadn't tracked her marine-waldos here, they were not in immediate danger, and it made sense to leave them within reach of the city. So she had them halt their flight and descend to pick up more ballast from the ocean floor. This was outside the trench, where the sea floor was only two kilometers or so below the ice layer, presenting no threat of implosion.

While they were gathering rocks, she created the series of commands that would have them return to the city, spread out in an arc about ten to fifteen kilometers away from it, reduce their sonar output so as not to draw attention to themselves, and make frequent radar scans. She'd keep them at about three kilometers below sea level, well above the aliens' domain. That gave them plenty of time to see something coming. Then she put the instructions in her waldos' work queues.

As she was logging off, out of habit, she glanced at her waldos' readouts for power and so on. That's when she realized: *Aculeus Octo* had an antimatter power source. If the parasols tampered with it, a big section of their city would be blown to bits.

Shit. Stomach a-churn, she tried calling her eldest siblings again, marking the call *urgent.* Arlene—seated now in the operating mezzanine—answered immediately. "A moment. I'm on a call."

Manda waited. Finally Arlene came back. "Derek is tied up in council. Let's meet in *virtu*-conference tau."

Manda donned her cat avatar and bounded into the colony's virtual data corridors.

Arlene's avatar was already there, below the glassy surface of the conference room's interface, waiting for Manda-cat. Arlene-avatar paced, frown lines on her virtual face—then turned as Manda-cat alighted on the wood floor of the conference space.

A cool wind blew through. Bright sunlight—not Uma's; the color was wrong—trickled down between the slats of the wood ramada's roof. Flowered vines crept up the posts. The ramada sat in a clearing by a stream beyond whose banks a path wound away among the fir trees. A squirrel darted up a tree.

"I just saw your recording of the city," Arlene-avatar said. "Is this what you wanted to discuss?"

"Yes."

"How big a problem is this capture? Will they view the waldos' presence as a serious threat?"

"We know so little about them. They haven't shown any real aggression so far, but . . . who's to say what they might do?" Manda-cat turned a paw over in a shrug. "Our real problem is worse, though. It just dawned on me that they now have in their possession a machine containing enough antimatter to wipe out a large portion of their city, if they manage to break through *Aculeus Octo*'s containment field."

Arlene-avatar's eyes went wide. "I hadn't thought of that. What a mess! How big an explosion?"

Manda considered. "We have some data—remember that overland expedition we lost a few seasons back, when one of the waldos' batteries went? It was the same size battery—the same basic unit with different fittings and configurations. That created a crater about two to three kilometers in diameter."

"How big is their city?"

"I don't know. Just a minute." Manda pulled up her simile programball and did a quick calculation. "Water is essentially an incompressible fluid, so the explosion would be a lot worse down there than it would be if it happened up here." She filled out a few more parameters on the programming sphere and made some assumptions. It gave her a simulation of the explosion in miniature. She uploaded the simile to the conference space, and she and Arlene watched it play out. Then she-cat took a quick set of measurements of the post-blast configuration. "According to this, the antimatter blast alone would create more like a ten-kilometer crater, and do heavy damage beyond that. That would level their city. And if they have anything explosive in storage—which they may; we've detected periodic explosions down there—it could be even worse." She gave her sister a significant look. "Their ecosystem is tiny—localized around the vents. It might well wipe out Brimstone-based life altogether."

"Shit. What a way to make first contact with an alien race." Arlene-avatar sat down in midair and cradled her head in her hands with a sigh. She-avatar looked up at Manda-cat. "What do you recommend?"

Manda pondered this. "Ideally we'd get *Aculeus Octo* out before they could break into its containment. It's a sturdy piece of equipment—those antimatter batteries are triple-guarded—so we have a little time. And if I can get a waldo close enough to *Octo*, I may be able to pick up its signal and track it."

Arlene-avatar shook her head slowly. "We don't know yet what they're capable of. They may have methods of disassembly we can't predict."

"True. And I can't control my waldos with sonar; there's too much interference in the city and its immediate surroundings. We'd simply end up with two—or more—waldos in their possession, and that much bigger a boom."

"Wait here." Arlene-avatar's expression went blank, and Manda realized she had disengaged. Manda-cat paced and waited. A few moments later Arlene's avatar stirred and blinked. "I've alerted Derek and the rest of the clone. I want me-us to have a crack at solving it before Derek takes it to the council."

Manda nodded. She could feel her pulse pounding in her

neck. *Major coup has just gone into play.* "What do you want me to do?"

"I can't get everybody together for a few hours. They're all really busy, and we've also got Paul's service." Manda nodded, sober. "Just let the problem simmer and let's see what I-we can come up with." Arlene-avatar paused, tuning out once more. "I've just reserved this conference room for twenty-eight o'clock. Try to get some rest before the funeral." And she-avatar dissolved away, waterpaint in rain.

Paul's funeral was much smaller than Teresa's had been: a family affair. Other than the servers, only his clone attended.

Manda attended too—but only out of love for Teresa. She found herself more angry than ever that he'd chosen to end his life. She sat through the memorial with her hands wringing a handkerchief and the muscles in her jaw working, and when they passed *mana* around in remembrance of his contributions, she refused to take a bite. A grave insult to his memory—her siblings glared—but she didn't care. The minute the ceremony was over, she left.

It was twenty till twenty-five by the time she got back to her own cubby. She undressed, tossed her clothes in a pile at the edge of the bed, and laid her livelink outfit carefully on top.

"Lights down," she said, and as they dimmed she ducked under the covers. As the fur slid across her skin, her body remembered Jim's touch on her, and memories of his taste and his skin's smell returned to linger in her nostrils and on her tongue.

Oh, I miss you, she thought. Desire pierced her with a sweet suddenness. Why were sex and death so closely bound? It troubled her that her body wouldn't let her go numb, retreat from the pain.

She wondered why Jim hadn't yet called. He might still be angry or hurt.

I should call him.

Just wait, Manda. Wait. He said he'd call. He might feel pressured if you call.

But if he is mad . . .

But calling might alienate him. . . .

But he might be afraid to call. . . .

Round and round, round and round.

She wanted to talk to him about the funeral. She needed help. She wanted touch. She needed to remind herself that she was still alive. That she mattered. She felt somehow as if Paul's death had tarnished her, poisoned her. As if she herself were now only a breath, a heartbeat from death too. Jim's voice and the memories of his touch would prove that she was still alive.

Let it go, Manda, she admonished herself. *You're going to be up very late with your clone trying to figure out what to do about Octo. You can call Jim tomorrow, if need be.*

With this compromise worked out—after bringing herself to climax with her faceware to relieve the ache of need in her belly—she released thoughts of Jim and rolled over.

But now other thoughts intruded. Thoughts about Terence. She couldn't get his tiny, helpless figure out of her mind.

The crèche-born might have information we could use, she thought. *We don't need to ask for their help. If only someone had the nerve to hack into their systems, we could take what we needed.*

Manda pondered this. Without an omni, the only means were radio or optical. She recalled that DMiTRI had a communications maser. But hacking into DMiTRI's communications system—even if she could, which was extremely doubtful—would immediately be detected, and get her into a lot of trouble. Besides, all she could do with the maser was to broadcast an emergency beacon—and clearly, in light of what she'd been learning about the crèche-born, just phoning them up and asking for help seemed like a bad idea.

Ur-Carli seems to have access to a lot of secrets. Maybe it could help. Though most of ur-Carli's resources would be tied up right now with the alien-data analysis. She wondered if ur-Carli knew what happened between the crèche-born and the colonists, back when.

For that matter, she thought with a shock of fear, *whose side was it on?*

Ur-Carli had almost certainly been programmed by the crèche-born. If there *had* been some sort of power struggle between the colonists and the crèche-born—or among assorted factions between the two groups—ur-Carli might have been instructed to spy on the colonists and report back to its designers in secret at some point. Which might explain its odd, elusive behavior.

But did it really? If the syntellect were a crèche-born spy, showing Manda Carli's secret room and telling her *Exodus* was still insystem made less sense than ever. It seemed more as if ur-Carli were working at its own purposes.

I just don't know enough to make any guesses about what ur-Carli is up to, she decided—*if anything.*

Manda knew little about syntellect coding and design, but she *did* know that even the most clever and adaptive programs were based on some very simple and basic drives tied to their original programming. No matter how autonomous it was, no matter how clever about learning and adapting to its environment, by human standards ur-Carli had to be quite narrow in its ability to reason and learn, simply by virtue of its hardware and software limitations.

The means of creating self-aware syntellects had been discovered, back in the mid-2000s in Earthspace, but self-awareness in artificial systems had been found not to be a desirable characteristic. Setting aside the moral issue of using sapient creatures as slaves (not to mention the legal liability—a major dis-motivator for the transnational corporations that had developed the first prototypes), sapient syntellects had been found to use up way too many processing cycles for what they were intended to do. And they all-too-quickly developed their own ideas about how things should be done—and *what* should be done—that might not agree with their makers'. The risk was also there that they might eventually figure out ways around their basic programming constraints. All in all, consciousness was not a desirable design feature. Thus, the more autonomous a syntellect was, the more hard-wired its behavioral and cognitive constraints were. The UN Conference on Artificial Intelligence in the twenty-teens had adopted a set of stringent required protocols in an international treaty back in the early part of the twenty-first century.

So strict behavioral constraints were buried deep in every syntellect's code, along with other analytical constraints to keep it from developing too far along certain cognitive lines. Ur-Carli would remain ordered and digital—straightforward—in its coherence to its original, fundamental goals. Those goals were built into the very heart of each syntellect's core design, and couldn't be eliminated no matter how much other aspects of their coding changed. So she'd been told.

So why not just ask? It was worth a try. She had a little time to kill, and sleep was a long way off.

Manda donned the minimum needed liveware and, feeling really paranoid, turned on her recorder. Then she put out a call to ur-Carli. To her surprise, it responded very quickly.

"How may I assist you?" it asked: the old, white-haired, parka-wearing faux-lady of a syntellect Manda expected, floating a hairbreadth from the top of Manda's bed furs, glowing with its own light.

Manda wrapped the covers around herself. *Let's get basic,* she thought. *It won't deceive or evade me if my questions don't trigger any of its defense mechanisms.*

"Ur-Carli, who programmed you?" she asked.

"Carli D'Auber was the lead designer," it replied after the

slightest of pauses. (Why a pause? It was a simple question.) Carli was one of the few non–crèche-born of the original *Exodus* crew—and rumor had it she hadn't liked the crèche-born much.

"The primary coders were Mara Rubikov, Pablo Taylor, and Tomas Esquivel C de Baca," the syntellect continued, "with assistance from a few others." The crèche-born, in other words.

"And what is your primary function?"

This time it answered promptly: "To explore this world and analyze its physical, geological, and biological systems, if any. To determine whether any threat to human life exists as part of my analysis, and if there are threats, to protect the colonists from harm."

"And what are your other important functions?"

"To report to the colony on my findings, and to serve the colonists in whatever other capacities they might require, whose priorities are set by Amaterasu's governing council."

All pretty much as she'd expected.

"Where are your core hardware and software housed?" Manda asked. This question had been on her mind in a low-grade way for a while, amid the chaos of recent days.

A longer pause. (Again, why the delay?) "Carli built my hardware matrix into the satellite DMiTRI," it replied. "Once beta testing on my basic software systems was completed, the initializing, operating, and application systems were downloaded into the satellite hardware and engaged. I am allowed to expand and reconfigure some of my subroutines and calls, within certain constraints, to increase efficiency and improve my learning capabilities. So my functional profile has changed somewhat since then."

Manda tapped her chin thoughtfully. She had assumed that ur-Carli's systems were housed somewhere in Amaterasu. "Just how far have you deviated from your original profile?"

Its affect went blank for a second. "Approximately forty-two percent of my systems have been reconfigured since I was brought online. Most of these changes have been to improve efficiency and to support the changing nature of my tasks. However, my basic functions remain unchanged."

"That's a relief." Manda hesitated. *I'm being truly paranoid.* "And is one of your basic functions to monitor and secretly provide information on the colonists' activities to the crèche-born?"

Another, extremely long pause. "Yes," it said.

anda couldn't get through to Arlene, nor to Derek, with her liveware. So she tracked Derek down in person, by asking people if they'd seen him or Arlene until someone said yes. She managed to bully her way past those who told her the council wasn't to be disturbed, and found him with the rest of the council in the main Bio-Sciences conference room, getting an update on the alien physiology analysis. The Bio-Sciences team had them riveted, providing livelinked images and three-dimensional renderings of the parasol creature and a running commentary.

"We just don't see how these creatures can be all that intelligent, based on their physiology," one elder RoxannaTomas was saying as labelled organs appeared and rotated in midair, and his twin went on, "Their brains—or what we believe to be the functional equivalent—just don't appear large and complex enough to house linguistic, logical, and other higher-order cognitive functions." "If we were to guess based on analogies with Earth species, these creatures might be as intelligent as, say, gengineered dogs or herd animals of some kind. Not as bright as primates."

"But behaviorally," Jeannelle and Vance said, as tapes of Manda's explorations appeared in front of them, "we see in the tapes CarliPablo"—with a gesture toward Manda standing at the door—"has made of their activities some clear indications that they are a good deal more intelligent than that." "They show purpose and coordinate their activities, far more precisely and complexly than you would expect based on their apparent brain size." "In addition to the city they've built and maintain, they appear to use some sort of vehicles, or perhaps other creatures, for transportation purposes. LuisMichael"—Manda started at the mention of Jim's clone-name—"has begun an analysis of their sonics and believes it may have detected some indications of language patterning."

"In the meanwhile, we are stuck with this paradox," one of the senior RoxannaTomases continued, "of a discrepancy between their apparent cognitive capacity and their abilities." "Also," his vat-mate said, "strangely, the level and kind of abilities they have appear to change." The third vat-mate finished, "We are analyzing Earth social-insect colonies, avian and reptilian nervous-system analogs, and applying self-organizing-systems mathematics to their behavior, to see if we can find any parallels. Here are our results so far."

Manda walked quietly over to Derek and whispered, "May I have a word with you?"

"Arlene told me about our meeting later tonight," he responded. "Can't it wait till then?"

Manda shook her head gravely. His look of annoyance melted into puzzlement at her expression.

"Very well." He excused himself to the other councilmembers and RoxannaTomas, and followed Manda out into the corridor.

"Where are you taking me?" he asked. But she didn't answer, just gave him a *look*. (Camera monitors were all over. The crèche-born might be listening.) To his credit, he trusted her, and followed her without any more questions. And she took him up the rock stairs, through the tunnel, to the secret place.

From within the room, Manda watched him climb out of the ice tunnel. *Will he forgive me?*

"Lights up," she said, in a quavery voice, and watched as he wandered throughout the large, knife-cold chamber.

He didn't say anything at first, merely walked around staring at things. From his reactions, she could tell he recognized some of the materials and equipment here, if not the room itself. Manda went and looked out the window at the night landscape. The cold, as before, already began to burn her cheeks, to seep in through her many layers, and she began hopping from foot to foot to warm herself.

He'll be angry.

It was twilight. Fire was only visible in the royal blue of the evening sky as a darker-blue curtain against which a tapestry of lightning glittered. Beyond the darkened plateau below them, Brimstone's own lightning played across the banks of clouds that capped the distant mountains in sheets of lavender.

"We can't stay here long," she said. "But I wanted you to know—" She broke off at Derek's sharp look.

"We can use all this," he said, examining the antique waldos, other machinery, and tools in the workshop. Manda turned. He was looking at her now, arms folded. *How long have you known?*

"I found this place," she replied, "just before the cave-in. I started to tell you a couple of times, but you were so busy with Project IceFlame, and then the cave-in happened, and things got so crazy . . ."

She tapered off, embarrassed at her excuses.

He sat down at Carli's desk and looked at the knickknacks and other paraphernalia there. He said something, softly.

"What?"

"I said, I always wondered where she went off to. I thought it was outside somewhere."

Manda sat in the small chair beside the desk. "How well did you know her?"

"She was like a mother to me." And he bent his head.

After a few seconds he wiped his eyes.

"I miss her," he said, "still."

"She's in there," Manda said, gesturing, and at his look of

298

shock, she amended, "Her body, I mean. I'll show you."

And she did.

Looking at him looking at Carli's frozen corpse, Manda regretted her earlier attempt to burn it.

He touched the old woman's hair, then lovingly pulled a blanket over the corpse's head and turned back to Manda.

"I don't understand why you waited," he said after a period of long, silent regard. She sensed he was—not angry—but severely disappointed that she'd kept this secret for so long. Then he took a slow, deep breath and let it go. "But I'm glad you told me now. I'll take care of it."

"Derek—wait." She took his arm as he started to go. He folded his arms, waiting, marble-still. She drew a breath.

"Look. I'm not saying this to make you feel bad, but I want you to understand."

She hesitated, seeking the words.

"Go on," he said. His expression remained guarded.

"It's been hard for me to care about anybody else, when nobody has ever really cared about me. Don't—" she told him, when he started to object. "Hear me out. You all just expected me to be another little carbon copy and fall right in line. But things have been different for me than they were for you. Really nasty things happened to me growing up, and I guess . . . I guess I wanted to get back at the ones who did it. And you-us, for letting it happen."

"I know that," he said.

"Please. This is hard." She paused, and eyed Carli's body. The raggedness of her breathing surprised her. "I know I've done some vindictive things. Some angry things. Things maybe I shouldn't have done. But I do care about this colony. And sometimes—sometimes, Derek, behaving yourself and doing what others expect of you *isn't* the right thing. I'm not always just being an asshole. I've got that reputation, but . . ." She shook her head, violently. "Everybody's always so afraid of losing coup, or being ostracized, they don't speak out when bad decisions are made. It's not right. We can't sacrifice our conscience for the sake of getting along. It happens too often."

Derek was shaking his head. "Come on, Manda. Your motives are rarely that pure. Hey—I gave you your chance," he said, when she started to protest. "Now give me mine."

"All right," she said, and held onto her patience.

"I know you care. And I know things were different for you. But you're not the only who pays the price, when you rip into someone. We all suffer. And you do it a lot. All the goddam time, in fact."

She faced him—*You'll never understand, will you?*—and saw the same thought blazing in his eyes. With twin sighs they shook their heads, and he clapped a hand on her shoulder. "Come on. Let's report this. *Damn*, but it's cold in here."

He'd made it well into the big room before Manda said, "There's something more."

Derek turned, wearing a quizzical look.

"I'm not sure we should tell anyone about this room, just yet," she said.

His face knotted with irritation. "Don't start."

"I mean it. This is important. I had a conversation with ur-Carli. It told me it's spying on us and reporting on our actions to the crèche-born."

He gaped. "*What?*"

"Watch." Manda brought up her liveware, and played back her conversation with ur-Carli. When the recording had finished, she said, "Check your own liveface. It's in offline mode, isn't it?"

His gaze unfocused and he moved his hands, muttering. Then he nodded at Manda, frowning.

"I think this is the only place in the colony that's fully shielded from their scrutiny," she said. "We're not on the LAN. Even ur-Carli can't come here." She paused, thinking. "I think maybe that's why Carli built this place. For privacy.

"I believe there might be important clues hidden here, things Carli hid from the crèche-born that should be protected till we have a chance to explore her files and notes. If we tell others about this room, the secret will spread. The crèche-born will notice and infiltrate."

"That's a lot of conjecture."

"It is." She hunched her shoulders. "I guess what I'm trying to say is, if the crèche-born are all that sneaky and dangerous, as you say, and if they *are* watching us as ur-Carli says, and if here we have a place they apparently don't know about . . ." She shrugged. "I just want to make sure we're not giving up something important, before we know what it is we'd be giving up."

"Hmmm."

"And I'm not sure," she went on slowly, "but I *think* ur-Carli is somehow on our side—at least partly—despite its programming. I think that's why it showed me this place—"

"*Ur-Carli* showed you this place?"

She nodded. "And it also told me about the crèche-born being insystem. That's how I knew to look for them."

"Ah." His eyes had gone round. "I-we'd wondered."

"I think it may be trying to obey its primary function, to protect us from a threat it perceives to our safety—the crèche-born—without violating whatever commands or constraints the crèche-born have built in."

Derek released a long, slow breath, eyeing her, and the fog from his exhalation briefly obscured his expression. Then he crossed over to the window. Looking out, as she had earlier, he said softly, "Manda, I have something to tell you too." He sighed deeply.

"There was an ugly fight," he said. Manda remembered what Jim had told her, out on Omi-Kami. "It started as we were preparing to make landfall and ended just after we'd touched down, when the colony was first being built." His gaze unfocused and emotions played across his face. Then he shook his head, and anger gelled in every facial line and wrinkle. "They treated us like pawns. Manipulated us, turned us against each other. They killed your twin brother, almost killed you—spaced Kali-Marshall's oldest sibling pair—all to force us to do what they wanted." His hands clenched, stretched, clenched again. "They're evil. Utterly alien. We want them far, far away from us. The other end of the universe, if possible."

Manda remembered a few of them: remembered their plastic-mechanical bodies, ex-face, and their panoply of bizarre avatars, in-face. To the very young child she'd been, they'd seemed almost . . . well . . . magical. Mysterious and ancient.

"What made them that way?"

Derek's brow furrowed. He took a long time to respond. "They grew up completely in-face. Their bodies have always been sealed in crèches for as long as they can remember. Uncle Marshall's treatments, back when he was still alive, made them all but immortal from infancy. They've never been vulnerable. To anything." Derek managed a bitter smile. "To them, reality is just a highly persistent illusion."

Manda processed this.

He continued. "They made us, raised us. I guess a few of them even cared for us in their own way. But I think in the end they just couldn't see us as anything more than another fabrication. Another clever construct put there for their amusement. That's all they do, spend their time creating miniature universes and running them together, fighting, maneuvering—infiltrating each others' fantasies and competing for mindshare. Nothing matters to them but their face games." He fell silent again, and Manda saw old memories flickering behind his eyes.

"I still don't understand what happened, though," she said after a moment. "I mean, what was the fight about? Why were they killing our people?"

He hesitated. "We're not entirely sure. It was complicated." *He's hiding something*, she thought. "The final blow, though, was that they couldn't agree on whether to commit all their resources to this colony and settle here with us, or to move on. We got pulled into their struggle." He leaned back against the wall and regarded Manda. "Luckily for us, the faction that wanted to move on won. So a truce was negotiated. They dropped us and our supplies, and within a few weeks they left."

"Christ," Manda breathed.

"Yes. Carli extracted a vow from them that they would leave us alone. I didn't understand at the time, but—somehow she bound them. She had some kind of hold on them." He shrugged.

"Anyway, they've left us alone since then, and we don't want that to change. If they decided to mess with us, it would only take them a few days to get here from their current orbit, at which point they could take over the whole colony—even wipe us out—if they wanted to. They designed all our original systems and could infiltrate them easily—and they have a lot of resources at their disposal that we don't. Things that can be used as weapons. We'd be helpless against them."

Manda had guessed much of this, but hearing Derek say it made it that much more real. Here was that good, hard look beneath the terrain of Manda's life, that hidden nastiness that she had sensed. She wished it had remained hidden forever.

"We've been quietly keeping an eye on them through DMiTRI," he said, "ever since landfall. They've been showing signs of getting ready to leave—they finished furling their solar arrays just a few days ago—so it won't be long before they head for parts unknown.

"They're well out of omni range already, and a few months after they launch they'll be out of effective radio range. At which point they'll be committed to their next interstellar jump and no longer any threat at all. . . . As long as we don't give them a reason to stay." He eyed her. "So you see now why I urged you not to try to contact them, before?"

"Yes," she concurred with a sigh. "But what are we going to do about ur-Carli?"

"There's a bigger issue," he said. "They would have heard ur-Carli tell you. They must know we know now."

"Do they?" Manda asked. "Ur-Carli may be able to shield certain things from them."

"It's a big risk, to assume that."

"They would have to screen tons of information if they were watching us themselves, every minute," Manda pointed out. "They must rely on ur-Carli to filter and prioritize."

"True." He thought for a moment. "And the syntellect does seem to be acting in our interests, when it can. It's giving us good information on your parasol creatures."

"So what do we do about this?"

"We don't know enough to act, yet," Derek said slowly. "Perhaps . . . I'll see if I can arrange a stroll outside the caverns with Arlene, and then a couple of the other councilmembers—without our liveface equipment—and let them know what's going on. We may quietly begin looking for ways to shut the crèche-born out of key systems. Create a few secure tunnels—in-face and ex- ."

He gave Manda a thump on the back and a smile. "Good work, little sister."

They headed back down to the colony proper. To Manda's surprise, it wasn't even twenty-six-thirty yet—it seemed as if a whole season had passed since morning. So she went back to her own sleep cubby to try again to get some rest. Sleep eluded her once more. She thought again about Teresa and Paul, but found no solace in her memories, only pain.

Then the room syntellect notified her that she had an incoming call from LuisMichael.

Jim. Manda sat up, wide awake and nervous, and put her yoke, hood, and throat mic back on with shaking hands. But at his crinkly-eyed smile, memories of his loving words and face and his gentle touches flooded her, and the nervousness transformed itself to something more complicated.

"Hi," he said. He cleared his throat. "You OK?"

She nodded. "You?" Her own voice came out a bit shaky.

"I couldn't sleep." And he held up a face-sex attachment: a live-condom. "You interested?"

Manda put her full liveware on and, repressing a giggle, got out her own face-sex attachment—a condom-like fitting identical to his, only her attachment received instructions from his body, and his attachment from hers. And they made love.

It wasn't as good as if he'd been there himself—live-sex was an excretion-less experience, which removed an important element of the experience. And the stinklink processors worked hard but the smells were just not quite right. But it was far better than lying alone missing him. Afterward they lay together, livesuits transmitting their touches, and whispered in the dark. She talked to him about Paul's death, and Teresa's, and he held her. He asked about the project and she told him about *Octo*'s capture and the antimatter risk.

He said, "That's a problem, all right."

"My clone is going to hash it out later," she told him. "Maybe we'll come up with some ideas."

He told her about his own clone's efforts to analyze and decode the parasols' sonic communications. "I-we'm not sure yet, but there do seem to be some linguistic features to it."

"That's exciting!"

"That's not the only exciting thing," he muttered, giving her a leer. She laughed and nestled her head against the crook of his arm, and through the liveface, stroked his chest. It felt too smooth. She frowned. "I wish I could play with your chest hairs."

"Soon," he said. "Soon." And one thing led to another.

Once they finished their second round of lovemaking, Manda felt well and truly reamed. Replete. She kissed him again, languidly. (Virtual kisses just weren't the same.) After removing the live-condom and dropping it in a bowl of alcohol for cleaning, she pressed against him through the liveface.

"Ah, Manda," he whispered as she started to drift off. "I love you too much. Too damn much."

She giggled again. "Good," said she, and fell asleep with a crooked smile on her face, an arm flung across space and time and up over the curve of his chest, his faraway fingers a soft, soothing pressure against her shoulder and hair.

Manda dreamed she was encased in a bubble of thick glass. Her fellow colonists outside the glass were going about their business, ignoring her. Their lips moved but she heard no sound. She saw a huge blaze approaching—a wall of fire—and pounded and shouted, trying warn them of the danger. They ignored her. Then they began to bursting into flames: *phhhwoosh! pop!* As incendiary as pitch-wood.

She saw her brothers and sisters go up. Teresa and Paul. Jim started to burn.

No! she screamed, and pounded her fists against the icy-cold glass. But there was nothing she could do. Finally, she sank back against the curved, clear floor and watched them all smoke and char, and only awoke as the flames began licking at the glass of the bubble itself, and she realized abruptly that the fire was on the inside with her, not outside at all. She was burning.

Manda sat up. She was breathing heavily, sweating. Her alarm was summoning her to her clone's late-night meeting. Sometime while she'd slept, the communications software had disconnected her from the virtual space she'd shared with Jim, and she was once more alone in the dark of her own cubby. Her skin crawled from having slept in her livesuit.

She laid her hand on her chest, to feel her heart beating hard against her palm. "What the hell was *that?*"

But once she'd calmed down enough to think it over, it actually gave her an idea.

Manda donned her bitch-goddess avatar. Once everyone had arrived—floating down through the slats of the *virtu*-ramada: a rain of avatars—Derek-avatar said, "Fill us in."

So Manda-goddess did. And when she-avatar finished summarizing their problem with *Octo*, her sibling-avatars eyed her without speaking. Manda-goddess fell silent and waited, while *virtu*-birds swooped overhead among the posts and vines of conference room tau's rough-wood roof, twittering, and sunlight played off the surfaces of the running stream. Its babbling seemed abnormally loud.

Manda thought about the crèche-born eavesdropping on them right now, and shuddered at the notion. Then she thought about her earlier live-sex session with Jim, and felt angry and disgusted. *What right do they have to intrude like that? What right?*

"Manda proposes I-we find a way to get *Octo* out before they break the antimatter containment barriers," Arlene-avatar said. Manda-cat started at the use of the double pronoun. *I-we?* She couldn't quite decide how she felt about it. She sighed. *Partnerships. First Jim, now my clone.*

"How?" Charles-avatar asked. Bart-avatar pointed out, "Their sonics interfere with Manda's marine-waldos."

The moment had come. Her heart was pounding as hard as her dream fists had on the walls of that metaglass bubble. She drew a breath. "We don't send a waldo. We send me."

They all gaped.

"JebMeri's deep-sea submersible is still around," she-avatar went on, into their stunned silence, "out at the refinery. I propose we retool it, hook up one of my marine-waldos to power it, and take it down to the city. I'll pilot it using a direct link of some kind, and meanwhile see what I can see. See if I can find a way to communicate. Tell them they're in danger."

They raised an uproar. She hadn't anticipated such resistance. She'd assumed that, as she had, they'd immediately see why it was necessary. But it was their only real option, and Manda answered their arguments again and again.

It touched her, though, that the reason they didn't agree—she could read it in all their faces and gestures—was that they didn't want to risk losing her.

They didn't give up without a struggle. But their curiosity about the alien city and the creatures who lived there—and their feeling that it would be wrong to stand by and do nothing, in the face of such massive devastation—gradually overcame their fears. Finally Janice- and Farrah-avatars, the last holdouts, held up their hands in mirrored submission.

"All right," said Farrah-avatar. "All right. It looks like our only choice. Just—" She-avatar broke off and Janice-avatar finished, "—be careful, Manda, OK? I-we've lost too many of me-us."

A hot excitement, spiced with fear, spread through Manda as she looked around at all her siblings. She'd done it. She'd won them over.

"I will," she promised.

But they still had to persuade the rest of the colony. And that meant the council. Given the ragtag state of her coup with them, Manda was apprehensive.

Early the next day, after a too-brief night's sleep, Derek, Arlene, and Manda took their proposal to the council.

Derek and Arlene had prepped Manda. *Let us do the talking. You describe the situation and we'll carry things forward from there.*

"Trust me," Derek said, holding onto her arms, as they stood outside the council chamber. "Follow my cues."

Manda looked deep into his eyes. *Are you really with me on this, brother? Can I trust you with something this important?*

He gave her a little shake. "Trust me. Or we're finished."

She took a steadying breath. "All right. Let's do it."

The door opened. They three looked at each other. *We're on.* Arlene gestured for Derek to lead the way.

They laid it all out for the council, and the four other councillors listened. Then, chin cradled in his hand, PabloJeb asked the others, "Comments? Questions?"

"Is this a serious proposal?" one of the PatriciaJoes asked in an incredulous tone. And so the discussion began.

Manda tried to be patient; really she did. But the "discussion" was such a travesty. She'd known beforehand exactly what would happen, and now it was all unfolding before her eyes.

To a clone, the other councilmembers' early comments and questions to Derek made it clear they thought it would be best to just wait and see. Apparently they didn't see the parasols as

a serious threat and didn't approve of wasting colony resources—not even marine equipment that was already in use
down there, a scrap submersible, and Manda, whom they had
never had much use for anyway—to try to help the creatures.
Derek's coup, as formidable as it was, just wasn't enough to overcome their objections. ˙ Especially since Jack and Amadeo
PabloJeb seemed cool on the idea.

Manda sat there, listening to them outgas over the loss of
resources, the risk, and so on, hearing their excuses for why it
couldn't possibly work, and that it wasn't *our* fault the waldo got
trapped down there (the implication being it was Manda's, of
course), getting angrier and angrier. Even JennaMara—whom
she'd have expected to be an ally, based on their exo-bonds and
coup-sharing—showed reluctance, and Lawrence's glances at
Manda were not especially friendly.

Guess I shouldn't have run out on the covalence.

But she didn't regret her choice. Not for the sake of this. *I'm
not going to buy coup with sex.*

Arlene kept calming her down with glances and touches while
Derek worked the council, but when PatriciaJoe said, "I was
against the ocean-mapping effort from the start," Manda
couldn't take it anymore. She threw off Arlene's touch and
sprang to her feet.

"This is an outrage. Listen to you! All of you!"

Arlene hissed, "Stop it!" but Manda ignored her.

"We've discovered *an alien civilization*, people—if folks back
in Earthspace knew, *billions* would be going apeshit right now!
And you're pissing in your livesuits over the idea we might lose
a marine-waldo."

Even as the words were tumbling out of her mouth she knew
she was being stupid again. But goddammit it, it was true. She
flung an accusing hand at them. "This council is nothing but a
small-spirited, coup-slinging gang of cowards! No wonder we're

310

BURNING THE ICE

stuck in this hellhole, dying by microns, with people like you in charge."

Derek gave her a look that would have shriveled her if not for the explosive force of her own anger holding her up. But even as she glared defiantly at her older siblings and the councilmembers, some small part of Manda felt dismay as her sister and brother shook their heads in disgust, and the expressions on the others' faces went hard and their gazes slid away from hers.

You screwed up, she told herself. Again. You just pissed away whatever chance you had. Good going.

Jack and Amadeo cleared their throats. The look they gave Manda was flat and angry. "We should take a vote and be done with this." "We have a lot of other critical issues to deal with right now."

This should be about issues, not about personality. They should rise above their anger at me and make the right decision. I shouldn't have to manipulate them or stroke their egos to get the right response.

But it was that or lose it all.

"Wait." She said it sharply. Everyone looked at her. *Just say it.*

"Those insults were uncalled-for," she said. "I'm sorry."

And the councilmembers registered shock. *Manda, apologizing for being rude? Impossible!*

Manda leaned on the rock table. "I know my mouth runs away with me," she admitted, with a swift glance at Derek. "But let me try again, and I ask you to look past the messenger and hear the message. We've discovered alien life. We should be thinking about more than just what's in it for us."

"Oh, please!"

". . . how dare you lecture us?"

". . . self-righteous . . ."

"Think about it!" she urged, ignoring their muttered insults

311

and rolling eyes. This part wasn't manipulation, wasn't coup-slinging. She believed this. "Imagine what knowledge they might have. Imagine what we might learn! We've discovered the first solid evidence that something more than viruses and traces of bacteria have developed on other worlds than Earth! We could learn so much more, to the benefit of both species. Who knows what marvels we might find?

"But if *Octo* goes, it could wipe out not just their city, but their entire ecosystem. And we'll have nothing left—nothing but a huge tragedy—to show for it. Unless we act, and act now."

More disparaging mutters passed between the councilmembers. She gave Derek and Arlene an appealing glance.

Derek spoke. "Isn't it worth a single machine, of our many machines? Isn't it worth risking a few odds and ends that we can spare, and a single, willing human life"—he gestured at Manda—"if the result is that we preserve perhaps millions of beings—what may be another intelligent species—and even, perhaps, make contact with them?"

Manda nodded emphatically. *Exactly.* She and her oldest siblings stared across the silence at the councilmembers.

"We don't *know* they're intelligent," PatriciaJoe pointed out. "Bio-Sciences is still divided on the question. And if they aren't, they won't be able to break into the waldo's antimatter containment field. We would be risking a life and irreplaceable equipment for no reason."

"But we do know there is an alien civilization down there," Jack said, as Manda opened her mouth to retort. "Regardless of who built it," his twin added, "and whether it is still an active society."

She turned to stare at them. *Are you on our side, now? Or are you simply waiting to deliver the coup de grâce?*

Jack and Amadeo continued, thoughtfully. "So. The questions we must ask ourselves are these." "First, are we willing to risk one of our own, and one of our waldos, to learn those secrets and possibly save an alien civilization from destruction?" "And, if we are, is Manda CarliPablo the right person to send?"

Manda twitched, and glowered. She hadn't anticipated that—that they might go with her idea, but give the project to someone else.

You don't dare! she started to say; *I won't let you*, but Derek gave her a warning glance, and with great reluctance she subsided, and hung there silently, in the crux between hope and despair.

"We'll do this in two votes," Amadeo said, and Jack PabloJeb cleared his throat. "The first question before the council is, shall we send a peopled mission under the ice, to attempt contact with the alien species and salvage of our confiscated waldo? Log your votes."

Derek said, firmly, "An alien civilization is worth trying to preserve, even at substantial risk. And Manda is the best pilot this colony has. Absolutely yes, to both questions."

The PabloJebs rapped their knuckle on the table. "Point of order." "We are restricting the vote first to the question of whether to do the mission at all."

"Very well. Yes, we do the mission."

Victoria PatriciaJoe wore a deep scowl. Her twin wasn't there. "This proposal is a fool's errand and a waste of precious resources at a dangerous time. We've already tried sending people down, and failed. I vote no."

Anne, Ron, and Jenna RoxannaLuis shook their heads. "The colony is in serious trouble." "All resources are needed." "And the likelihood is too great that whomever we send will die." "No," they all said.

After a pause, JennaMara nodded once. "We stand to gain a lot. The risks are worth it. I vote yes."

Everyone looked at Jack and Amadeo. "In cases where the council vote is split—" "—as head of council, we're required to break the tie." They spent a long moment mulling the question over, exchanging mutters, while Jack fiddled with some unseen icon that floated between his hands: a nervous habit. Amadeo meanwhile gave Manda a smug look. *I'm doomed,* she thought.

"We must concur with JennaMara and CarliPablo—" "—that this risk is worth taking. The possible benefits are enormous—" "—and the notion that an alien civilization might be wiped out if we don't act seems an equally compelling reason to act now." "We vote yes."

Manda released her breath. *And PabloJeb does the right thing.* She wouldn't have believed it if she hadn't seen it for herself.

They were probably up to something.

"The motion to go forward with the mission," Jack announced, "carries, three to two." "As to who should be on the mission," Amadeo said. "Does the council want to discuss this first—" "—or are you all ready to vote?"

Arlene added, "I move we vote."

"Seconded," said PatriciaJoe.

"The question before the council is—" —"shall Manda be the pilot for this mission—" "—or do we choose someone else?" "Let's start with CarliPablo."

Derek pressed his hands on the table and looked around. Despite his confident demeanour, Manda could tell he was worried that the question had been raised, and his unease rattled her. And she could see that something was also going on between JennaMara and PabloJeb—some kind of power struggle or calling of coup.

Derek lifted an eyebrow at Manda, and then she understood— or thought she did. *PabloJeb wants Lawrence JennaMara to deny me. They guess that RoxannaLuis will vote yes since she owes me-us major coup right now. PatriciaJoe will vote no—her earlier comments made that clear. PabloJeb wants to control the outcome with a tiebreaker.*

Meaning they will either deny me the mission—or if they grant it to me, it will be at great cost to my-our coup.

Derek's eyes narrowed as he pinned the other councillors in his gaze; he too was calling in coup. From Arlene's nod at Manda's querying look, and from the considering glances the others were giving Derek, she was certain of it.

"Manda is the best pilot we have," Derek said. Arlene added, "We needn't remind any of you that the aliens are her discovery." "We also owe her great coup over the fact that she rescued two of Ursula-Meriwether." "We vote to send her."

PatriciaJoe made a rude noise. "Manda is reckless and unreliable. Her discovery of the aliens has brought us only trouble—"

"That's absurd!" Arlene protested, but PatriciaJoe bulled on, "—and she was only one of many on the rescue effort. With her abrasiveness and inability to work with others, she has depleted any reserves of coup she's accumulated. We shouldn't reward that sort of behavior." She paused, glaring at Manda. "If we must go forward with this, we should find someone more mature to lead it. That's my vote."

Manda and her siblings exchanged glances, and Arlene rolled her eyes.

Meanwhile, the RoxannaLuis triplets studied Manda. Then their gazes flicked in unison to Derek. The wizened old women sat back. "CarliPablo—" "—we know my-our coup with you-you will take a big hit for this, and my-our life would go easier if we could do otherwise." They shook their heads. "But we must abstain." "The proposal is a suicide mission—" "—and we don't want Manda's death—" "—or anyone else's—" "—on our conscience."

Manda tried not to flinch. Derek too, visibly reacted. Pablo-Jeb's expressions were sour as well. Manda realized that she'd read him right. *It's one-to-one. JennaMara's vote will decide, not PabloJeb's.* As leader, PabloJeb only voted to break a tie.

Everyone was watching old JennaMara now, who was picking at his fingernails, all gnarled and split. A worker's hands. His

face was devoid of expression, but she was certain he was en-
joying hoarding coup for this moment.

Which didn't make sense. Either he would have to give up
coup to all of PabloJeb *and* to Manda, who had insulted his
clone through her behavior at their covalence, to maintain coup
with the rest of CarliPablo and grant Manda the mission; or he'd
have to relinquish coup to all of CarliPablo and—far worse—
the rest of his own clone, by denying CarliPablo the project
when the two clones were in exo-bond. He should be sweating,
not gloating.

But when he looked up, Lawrence JennaMara's glare raked
Manda, and she caught reflections in his eyes of the pain she'd
caused, not only to her sister Janice, but to Farrah, Charlotte
JennaMara, and to the two young JennaMaras she'd walked
away from without so much as a good night, that night before
the cave-in.

He wouldn't dare refuse to support me-us, Manda thought,
heart pumping. *He'd be sacrificing the exo-bond—causing grief
for his own clone as well as my-ours.*

But his eyes, the same eyes that had held so much warmth
and friendliness the other night as he'd held the smoke bulb for
Manda, held so much hostility now. . . .

Arlene shrugged microscopically at Manda's nervous glance.
See what flaunting custom will get you?

"Manda's coup isn't worth much with me-us right now,"
JennaMara said in his liquor-and-smoke growl. "PatriciaJoe is
right: she is difficult, disruptive, and often impulsive. If we were
voting whether to publicly censure her, I would support it." He
exhaled. "But as CarliPablo points out, her skills as a pilot are
impeccable. She has demonstrated ingenuity, determination,
and great courage in dangerous situations.

"Will she be able to control her worst impulses in a crisis? If
so, we gain much. If not, well . . ." He smiled. "That's why they

316

call it *evolution in action*." He paused, letting Manda take the hit, and then finished, "I vote we send her."

Manda marvelled, even as she fumed. He'd found a way to do it: slap Manda down before the council—taking coup back from her—while still preserving coup with CarliPablo. And even PabloJeb was smiling a trifle, his gaze hard on Derek. Whatever coup Manda had lost to JennaMara, Derek had apparently also lost to PabloJeb by having to stand by silently while Manda was insulted. So PabloJeb's coup balance had shifted, but hadn't diminished.

Coup games. Pah.

They gave her permission to select up to five clones to help her prepare, and then invited her to leave. As Manda exited, she happened to glance back at JennaMara. He gave her a tight little smirk.

You're good, she thought. *You crafty old prick.* Yes, he'd manipulated and insulted Manda. He'd gained coup on her. He'd gotten exactly what he wanted. Manda didn't care. So had she.

She called Jim and told him the news. To her surprise, he looked appalled. *"What—?"*

Nervous, she repeated herself: "I'm taking JebMeri's submersible down after *Aculeus Octo*."

He said nothing for a long moment, merely floated in livespace before her and stared.

"The council has approved it," she went on. "I'd like you-you on my team. I'll need you-your help to retool the submersible—"

"You didn't tell me anything about this!" he burst out. "You just went and did it."

"It's not—I didn't—" She broke off, and forced calm on herself. "I didn't know any of this was going to happen till early this morning. You're the first person I've called."

Anger and betrayal blazed in his gaze. Her mind filled with a barrage of objections, apologies, anger, guilt, confusion. "I thought you'd be happy for me."

"Happy? That you're throwing away your life chasing one of your stupid machines down under the ice? It's a suicide mission! And you didn't even talk to me about it first, just went and arranged it with the council."

She stiffened. "I'm not a child. I don't have to ask your permission."

"Oxshit. We both know exactly what you're doing."

"What are you talking about?"

"You'll go to any lengths to avoid getting close to someone, won't you? Even throw your own life away."

"What an ego! Listen to yourself. As if this has anything to do with you."

"Stop it. Just stop." They gazed at each other wordlessly through livespace.

"I'm going," Manda said. Her lips felt numb.

His face went blank. "I need time to think. Please don't call." He said it carefully and formally. Then he cut the connection.

Fortunately Manda had enough to do, getting ready, that she could avoid thinking about Jim. Her clone—all except Derek and Arlene, who couldn't be spared from colony management and Hydroponics repair efforts—signed on to help develop the retooling and testing plans for the submersible. She also got the ByronDalia quadruplets to start modifying the waldo command systems to suit her special requirements. Jeannelle, Vance, and their siblings fed Manda a constant stream of information about the aliens. Other clones kept showing up or telepresenting to her work space with offers of materials and information for the mission.

Manda's planned trip under the ice seemed to somehow be transcending all coup debts, petty grudges, and cynicism. An excitement was building: a commitment to action that coursed through the colony, energizing it—transforming it.

Suddenly they had a purpose larger than themselves. A purpose long forgotten, but so integral to who they were and why they were here—seeded back in Earthspace by the *Exodus*'s original makers, long before the colonists were born, when Brimstone was first discovered—that it might as well have been coded into their very genes.

And Manda wouldn't have believed it if she weren't seeing it for herself, but for the first time in her life, people were treating her with respect. They deferred to her requests, hurried to carry out her instructions, asked for her advice.

It was rather nerve-racking.

And when GeorgJean announced in a colony-wide broadcast that the Bio-Sciences team had found the seaweedy stuff was made of huge globs and strands of Brimstonian bacteria—which the Recycling team had found could be used to produce edible *mana*—the uproar could be heard throughout the entire cave-colony. If the bactoweed (as it had been dubbed) wasn't atomized by an antimatter blast first, the colony's food problem was solved.

(Naturally, it wasn't that simple—the *mana* produced wasn't nutritionally complete and would have to be heavily supplemented with other substances to be a viable food source for any length of time. And it looked and tasted funny. But hey, it beat starvation all to hell.)

So the race to get Manda under the ice was on.

She worked hard and furious all day, developing specs and outlining plans with her teams. Vance tracked her down and gave her an injection to ward off any xeno-infections. As Vance had warned, it left her feverish and restless.

Several times she started to call Jim, despite his warning. But each time she stopped herself.

Some part of her wanted to rage at him. To make him pay for his selfishness. But some other part of her didn't feel that way. Not about Jim. On some level she just felt sad.

She didn't trust herself to be able to keep her temper leashed. So she didn't call.

She knew how capable she was of shredding the tenuous thread she and Jim had begun to spin between them. But she was tired of being angry and lonely. It was time for a change.

To what, though? To what?

Late that evening, after supper, Manda decided to head down to the hot springs. Though exhausted, she was too keyed up to relax, and wasn't looking forward to returning to her own, lonely cubby. Nor were her siblings' quarters where she wanted to be. Being there only brought back memories of Teresa and Paul.

Beyond the bamboo caverns, the Honeycomb—a network of small caves and passageways riddled with holes and gaps— wound through Brimstone's crust. While the rest of Amaterasu was melted out of a massive calcite structure, the Honeycomb had large amounts of other rock, so the caverns were smaller, with fewer speleothems and a higher variability in mineral content.

The upper portion, along one wall of the bamboo caverns, was accessible from above via a separate set of lifts from the main entrance, as well as via a secondary entrance a few kilometers to the northwest. They were used mostly for the herd animals, when radiation, cold, or storms made it impossible to take them out. The Honeycomb's lower section led down through fissures and rifts into the hot springs: an interconnected series of heated lakes and pools that had been discovered several seasons ago, after an earlier big cave-in exposed the entrance to them. Manda hadn't been down there for nearly a season.

She reached the Honeycomb's lower entrance, in back of the bamboo caverns near some animal stalls. There she lingered, drawing in air thickened with the smells of animal fur, urine, and herbivore feces, all overlain by the fresh, sweet smell of cut bamboo. It was a powerful odor, and not an altogether unpleasant one.

A small herd of musk-oxen—squat bovines with brown curved horns streaked with white, and thick glossy hair that rippled down all the way to their hooves—grazed on cut bamboo shoots in the fenced-off cul-de-sac. A cow looked at Manda and lowed, as her calf butted his head against her belly, nuzzling into the fur, seeking teats. Further along, a young buck reindeer with a fine new crown of antlers pawed through the cut bamboo stalks scattered in his stall, looking for the tenderest shoots.

Manda picked up some stalks that had spilled out on this side of the fence. She fed them to him, stroking his narrow, velvet-soft nose with her fingertips as he nipped at the grass, eyeing her warily with eyes the dark, rich brown of liquid *mana*.

Two children, a pair of twins, were cleaning reindeer stalls. One of them saw Manda and excitedly grabbed the sleeve of her companion, pointing. Manda felt her face grow warm. She gave them a wave and then—not quite sure why she was embarrassed; they were just kids, after all—ducked into the nearest lower-Honeycomb entrance before they could decide to come over and start asking questions.

The lights didn't come on. The cave-in must have knocked out power in this area, or perhaps some other equipment failure had occurred. Manda pulled out her flashlight, strapped it to her head, and turned it on. The yellow beam played across the tunnel's broken surfaces, as she waded through dust that choked her nostrils, as she scrambled down inclines and over boulders and squeezed between jutting promontories encrusted with raw jewels—garnets and amethysts—that grabbed at her clothes, scrapped exposed skin, and robbed the heat from her palms. Finally she reached the cavern that held the holes down to the springs.

This chamber was bigger than it seemed, segmented as it was by so many protuberances and outcroppings. As she turned her head, looking around, veins of gold threading across the walls glinted in the beam of her flashlight, woven in with smaller strands of black silver ore, shadowy-green copper oxides, intense-blue cobalt oxides, and thick clots of purple-and-brown manganates.

Someday they would mine this chamber. Already others were being mined. She was glad they were preserving, for now, the way to the baths. They were one of the colony's few luxuries.

Throughout this series of small chambers—the heart of the

Honeycomb—a small forest of sturdy, knotted ropes hung down. Their heads were secured to steel hooks buried in the cavern's ceiling and their tails disappeared into depths from which warm heat curled up. Manda donned and turned on her headlamp, then removed her sweater and stuffed it into her daypack—here the air was warm enough that she didn't need it, and it would hinder her ability to climb. She grabbed a rope and swung down into a nearby fissure.

Tremors rumbled through the dark catacombs while she was descending, making her rope swing like a bell cord. Pebbles pelted Manda and rained on the floor below with a clatter. She clung to the rope, terrified. Here, where the fissures barely allowed passage, it was so easy to imagine being crushed, as Teresa had been. It was all too easy, now, to picture herself a lifeless corpse.

Well, at least I don't have to worry about my brother ending his own life in response.

A moment later she lowered herself to the slick-wet rocks of a bath chamber. A light came on. Power had been restored in the baths themselves, at least, since the cave-in. Or perhaps the baths had their own generator.

Manda perched on an outcropping to take her boots and socks off, stuffed the socks into the boots, and tied the laces together. Then she swung her boots around her neck and rolled up her pants legs. Skirting the pool—this one was too shallow for her tastes—she scrambled along the warm, slippery ledge to a passage. The short corridor was filled with a few centimeters of water. Hot water burbling up from numerous natural jets flooded her feet with warmth.

A sigh hissed through her teeth. As always, the first touch of wet heat made her ask herself why she didn't come down here more often. (Of course, the eighteen-meter rope climb and the dusty scramble through undeveloped tunnels afterward with filth settling into every clean, moist pore—not to mention the chill that quickly set in if you didn't keep your clothes completely dry—were not trivial deterrents. But every time she stepped into water hot enough to sting, she remembered that it was worth it anyway.)

The hot-spring baths were lit by motion-sensitive lights, which came on as she moved through the caves and cul-de-sacs, and went off behind her shortly after she moved away. Other bathers' voices—laughter and whispers—coiled around corners, faded, and swelled—wobbled through the hollows and across the dripping, shivering, steaming pools. The air was wet and hot and smelled of sulfur. Dust wasn't a problem down here. Her skin and sinuses were saturated. Inhaling felt like breathing water.

None of the pools were very deep. (The deep pools were a separate aquifer system, reached via a different route. They were used for heating and drinking water, not swimming or bathing.) Usually Manda made a point of finding a remote spot, but this time she wasn't feeling so intensely the need to be alone. Still, she respected others' privacy, and avoided the lighted chambers and voices, wandering for a bit till she came to an unoccupied pool she liked.

It appeared to be fairly deep in the center. Its waters lapped against the far wall, languidly sending light patterns quivering back and forth. Water dripped musically down the walls from another chamber, and sizzled up through a set of small fissures in the floor.

Perfect.

Manda stripped and stuffed her clothes in her pack. She doffed her live-equipment and laid the resulting package on top. Then she waded into the pool, hip-deep, and squatted. Stinging-hot water swallowed her, relaxing away the chill, removing the ache of sore muscles, scrapes, and fatigue.

With a happy sigh, she submerged herself, warming herself even to the cheekbones, the nose, the scalp. She got out her soap—a special soap their engineers had designed to degrade swiftly on exposure to water, to protect the hot springs—and washed. Then she moved over to lie on the warm, gentle incline at the pool's edge, letting hot water sluice across her belly and legs as she propped her head on her palms. She lay still enough that eventually the chamber lights went off. Soft, rippling ribbons of light filtered in from other chambers, steam rose from the water and formed warm beads that rolled down her skin, and the water's whispering music continued.

Despite her intentions, she thought about Jim, and once more, felt anger. But remembering the ragged fear and hurt behind his eyes, once again her feelings mutated to something more complicated.

Should I have done differently?

No. She was doing her job, and it was important. If she herself doubted that, the colony's reaction proved it. And despite what he said, she didn't believe she was throwing her life away. She couldn't regret her decision. He was being unreasonable.

On the other hand, going down under a kilometer of ice and four kilometers of water in a metaglass bubble to an alien city, to try to salvage a waldo, *was* dangerous. She supposed she might feel the same way if Jim were going down there without her.

But she believed in her own competence and resourcefulness. And she might actually be the first human to communicate with intelligent extraterrestrials—! Wasn't it worth the risk?

She wished she could comfort Jim with her hands, with her body. It was hard to find the right words.

But he wasn't going to let her near him, now. Not even inface.

How did I let him get to me? she wondered. *How did he come to matter so much, so soon?*

Loneliness was infinitely easier, it seemed, than dealing with this. Easy, and utterly sterile.

Then she heard Janice's voice—she could tell by the cadences.

It didn't surprise her in the least—though ordinarily it would annoy her—that her siblings would serendipitously find the same spot as her, at the same time. She'd lived with this all her life: Gene expression played out in weird ways. Bound as it was by physical laws—there was nothing supernatural about it, she supposed; it was all about preferences and unconscious desires guided by basic drives—still, gene play seemed to her to be possessed of some uncanny magic.

Manda had never liked the idea that she was so thoroughly programmed by her DNA. She'd never been comfortable with the notion that her choices weren't her own, that her body—her very life—was simply a vehicle for her genes to express and replicate themselves. But fighting all her life to avoid being a carbon copy hadn't worked very well either.

How do you escape your genes? How do you escape your programming either by biology or *environment?* It seemed so unfair.

She sat up and the light came on as Janice stepped over a promontory into the cave and extended a hand for Farrah. Manda had half-expected to see her with Charlotte JennaMara. She wondered whether they were still together.

"Hi," Manda said.

Her elder twins greeted her with smiles.

"Care to join me?" Manda asked.

They stripped and lowered themselves into the water.

Janice and Farrah were in their mid-forties. Their hair was silvering and their faces and lanky, small-breasted bodies were beginning to show wrinkles.

Janice and Farrah washed, helping each other do their backs and hair. Then they did Manda's back for her. Once clean, they three floated and bobbed in the pool, languorously picking up the threads of the conversation the elder two had been involved in on entering the grotto: the findings on the alien so far, and Manda's mission under the ice.

"What's the latest?" Janice asked Manda.

"I've been poring over the videos," answered Manda. "I also plan to take some expert systems with me, with whatever results we've got from the biology studies." She shrugged. "I'll try to use whatever means I can to let the creatures know that *Octo* is a threat to them—that they shouldn't tamper with it. I also know where *Octo* entered the city, so I may be able to use chemical and sonic tracers to find *Octo* and salvage it." She broke into a grin. "As for the rest, I guess I'll find out when I get down there."

"We're frightened for you, Manda." Farrah extended her hand and Janice took it, locking fingers with her. "We couldn't bear to lose you."

They read Manda's sudden distress. *What?* they asked with their eyes and brows. Manda sighed. Her nose stung.

"LuisMichael." She swallowed the lump in her throat, and drew a deep breath. "Jim. He's angry. He doesn't want me to go."

There. It was out in the open. But the clone must have already heard the rumors about her and Jim sharing an exo-bond. Little stayed secret for long. Especially if it had to do with sex.

"I don't know what to do," Manda went on. "He's afraid for me, I guess, and angry that he has no say. But I have to do this. It's been my one ambition, to find living creatures under the ice. And . . ." She chewed her lip. "I can't cower up here and let an alien civilization be obliterated, simply because it's risky. It's my doing that *Aculeus Octo* is down there. I have to do what I can. Jim doesn't understand that." She shook her head. "He basically accused me of using the mission as an excuse to avoid him."

"Now that's what I call paranoid," Janice remarked. But Farrah gave Manda a sharp glance. "Not *that* paranoid."

"What do you mean by that?" Manda asked stiffly. Farrah only laughed. "Come on, Manda, you know exactly what I mean."

Janice gave her twin a stern look, but Manda sighed. "No— she's right. I can be defensive. I know that. But that's not what this is about."

"Are you so sure?" Farrah asked. "Are you sure there's none of that?"

Manda met Farrah's gaze, and found herself unable to reply.

"Look," Janice said, "give him a chance to calm down, and then talk to him."

Farrah agreed. "LuisMichael is friendly and easygoing. On the surface. But from what I hear, it's been a long time since any of them has exo-bonded." Janice gave Farrah a nervous glance, and Manda realized that her own exo-bond with JennaMara was still a sore point between them. "It's never had an exo-bond of any note since the older twins were killed, you know. Jim may be struggling with his own fear of getting too close to *you*."

"Or his siblings'," Janice interjected, and Manda remembered how cool Amy and Brian had been toward her, on their return to the refinery. "I hadn't considered that.

"Well—" Manda stood. "Thanks." She grabbed her towel and rubbed herself down, then dressed and shouldered her pack. Then she told Janice, "I'm sorry I ran out on the covalence the other night. It was rude." She hesitated, surprised at herself. She hadn't known she was going to say that. "I panicked," she added.

She couldn't read the look the twins gave each other.

"Apology accepted," they replied.

Are you still with JennaMara? she asked silently, but Janice only squeezed water out of a sponge onto her twin's head. *Not now*, clearly, was her answer. But Manda didn't know what that meant. Part of her hoped it was over, for the sake of tranquility within the clone; part of her hoped not.

With so many people helping, things moved swiftly. A mere two and a half weeks after the council approved Manda's mission below the ice—very early on the fourteenth day after she'd discovered *Aculeus Octo*'s seizure by the parasols—she was set to go.

The gear and equipment she would take with her was all packed—the units and coding for a blue-green laser link to *Aculeus Duo*, which would tow her submersible; a stripped-down, no-frills version of ur-Carli's expert systems, highly compressed so they would fit on her on-board computer; the assorted analytical and communications tools Jeannelle's group had put together for attempted contact with the parasols; a wide array of new, fancy detection and sampling fittings for *Aculeus Duo*; spare air tanks; oxygen recycling equipment; heaters; spare batteries; a spare livesuit; two changes of clothing; blankets; water; food. The supplies were neatly arranged on the icy flagstones of the entrance cavern, awaiting a jet-waldo to fly them out to the drill site.

She still hadn't heard from Jim.

Manda waited with the supplies. A small crowd—the team members who had helped her get to this place and others—waited with her. Derek and Arlene were there, as were all of PabloJeb, JennaMara, and RoxannaTomas. The PatriciaJoe twins were pointedly absent, but Manda noted with satisfaction that the youngest triplet of their clone had shown up anyway to see Manda off. Everyone was cold and tired—they'd all been working hard to make this mission happen, on top of working hard to repair Hydroponics, on top of working hard, period. But no one complained. They passed jokes and a flask of mead around.

After moistening her lips with a sip of mead, for luck, Manda abstained. She planned to start down below the ice as soon as her things were loaded and the last-minute tests were completed, and she didn't want alcohol interfering with her thinking or reflexes.

She'd spent a long evening with her baby brother Terence the night before. When she'd entered NICU, the team was taking him off monitoring and life support. The nurse at the station informed Manda that he had "graduated," and was about to be moved to the nursery.

Manda had watched through the observation window, trying not to grimace while they removed needles and probes. Her own ankles, chest, and head twinged in sympathetic reaction.

Seizures, she thought anxiously. *Possible neurological damage. Poor little guy.*

Still, she was reassured that he had visibly improved. He was bigger, plumper, and his coloring was natural, no longer ashen. Still, he was so very small—smaller yet than a full-term decantling.

They gave her the signal to come in. The chief neonatal specialist, Vance and Jeannelle's older sister Tania, was inspecting him: checking his ears and nose with an otoscope, listening to his chest, pressing on his abdomen, moving his legs around, and such. He squalled—an outraged scream that made Manda want to shove them all aside and snatch him up. Then Tania set aside her instruments, diapered the still-fussing baby, wrapped him in a thermal blanket with practiced ease, and handed him to Manda.

Manda fended off a wave of terror—*I might drop him!*—and

took the bundled infant into her arms. She tickled his chin with a finger and hummed softly, and he quieted.

His head nestled in the crook of her elbow. His hazel-blue gaze soaked trustingly into hers, warming her. She wondered when his eyes would turn green and his hair tawny-blond.

Manda touched the chesnut-dark fuzz on his crown and found it soft as musk-ox fur, and when she touched his ruddy little cheek, he turned his head and mouthed her finger with velvet-wet lips and tongue. His little arm had wormed its way loose of the blanket and was waving in the air. She put her finger in his palm. He gripped it so tightly that she had a hard time working the finger free. She laughed.

"Quite a grip you've got there," she said. She gave Tania a querying gaze. "His head has an unusual shape." It was narrower in the face and chin and longer from front to back than the rest of the clone's. "Is that normal?"

Tania nodded. "For premies."

"Does it mean—"

"It doesn't mean anything, necessarily." She smiled. "Though he won't appear quite identical to the rest of you. His head and face shape will always be different."

You'll be even more a singleton than I, then. She stroked his head again, unable to decide whether that was good or bad.

While Manda spoke with Tania, Terence began to act tense. Restless. He started fussing. She tried arranging his blanket, tried jollying him with words or a song, but it didn't work this time.

"What is it, Ter? What's wrong?"

"Here," someone told her, and handed her a bottle. She managed to work it between his cherub lips, and once he got hold of the nipple (it took a few tries; his tongue kept pushing it away), he began sucking. Manda looked up in delight to see Tania standing there, smiling.

"You're having better luck getting him to take a bottle than any of us have had," she remarked. "Maybe we'll have a job for you in NICU, when you get back."

Manda had volunteered to drop him off at the nursery. She'd entered there with him, and watched as toddlers and older infants, multiple copies of each, played or climbed the play structure at the back or fought over toys. She observed the caregivers making sure vat-mates always stayed together and didn't fight. One boy tried to wander off, and was steered gently but insistently over to his twin brother, who was at the sandbox.

Small wonder I felt so isolated, she realized. *They didn't know what to do with me. I didn't fit their schematics.*

"Treat him carefully," she'd told them, as she handed him over. "He's still weak." And, "He'll need plenty of attention. Be sure you check him often."

They assured her repeatedly, and a bit condescendingly, that the doctors had given them complete instructions—they would make sure he got excellent care. She wondered if her caregivers had given her older siblings the same assurances about her.

Once they'd gotten him into his warmed crib in the small cave at the back, with the other infants—the only one in a crib by himself—she came in to check him over one last time and say good-bye. It reminded her disturbingly of Paul's farewell to Terence the other day.

Seizures. Neurological damage.

The idea that he might be impaired wormed through her thoughts, distracting her. What if he grew up retarded? They didn't have the means to repair that sort of damage, here. Livesuit technology enabled the physically impaired to function normally—but they didn't have the resources to care for severe mental impairment.

She thought again how much easier it was to not have connections. To not have reasons to care. Especially about babies. So much could go wrong.

"I'll be back soon," she whispered. He was already asleep, a trickle of formula and drool drying on his chin. Small clumps of adhesive still clung to his neck. She picked off the adhesive and then dabbed at the fluid on his chin with a corner of his blanket. Tears flowed like snow melt down her face. "I'll come back and make sure they treat you right."

She'd heard in her own words a touch of bravado, and prayed that she would live through this. Not only for her sake, but for Terence's.

Now, the next morning, as Manda waited in the entry cavern, she wondered once more how he was faring in the nursery. She again admonished Derek and Arlene to be sure to check on him often, and not to let the caregivers neglect or scold him simply because he had no partner they could play him off of. And once again they assured her they would.

Standing there, waiting for the jet-waldo, Manda also thought about Carli, whose body lay overhead in the secret chamber, and wondered what the grande dame would think about this venture. *What secrets could you tell me, that might help me,* Manda thought, *if you were still alive?*

Probably nothing. Oracles were badly overrated. Despite all the similes, no Secret Masters hid out in the desert waiting for you to discover your True Destiny; no Great Truths lay locked away in a chest somewhere, awaiting your discovery.

Life didn't come with an operations manual. You prepared as best you could—studied the information, gauged your feelings, made your best decision—and then took your courage in hand and flung yourself into action.

They all heard a big machine bumping and clanking against the tunnel walls as it ascended the loop. It sounded different than a fuel tanker did, coming up. Manda's heart leaped high like a startled reindeer, and her breath quickened. She stood and straightened her clothes. *This is it.*

The jet-waldo dropped off the cable and rolled over on its

auxiliary wheels, and squatted onto its skis in a hiss of hydraulics. People formed a brigade and began loading the last of Manda's supplies and equipment into the cargo compartment in its underbelly. It didn't take long before they had everything loaded. Then everyone crowded around and slapped her on the back, wishing her well.

Faces smiled at her, faces of people she'd lived with all her life but had never really known. The ByronDalia hacker quadruplets: Yvonne, Sherry, Samuel, and Anthony (she'd made a point of learning their names)—hornet-sting-smart, and *funny!* She'd enjoyed working with them. They'd made her sides ache with their slippery, alkaline wit. And they were wicked flirts.

And RoxannaTomas: Jeannelle and Vance, the youngest; the eldest pair, Jan and Robert; and the middle set, Sean, Malcolm, and Tania. Deep thinkers. Never quick to jump to a conclusion—sometimes maddeningly slow to make decisions—but ferocious in pursuit of solutions. Quiet, deadpan—slow to warm to her, but steady as a heartbeat once they had.

And others, so many others.

These people had supported her, were counting on her. And she was only now coming to truly know and care about them. Now, when she was about to leave them all behind.

Most of her time over the past fourteen days had been spent walking through similes and drills with the different teams, testing equipment, studying Earth species as well as the biological and behavioral clues they had so far on the parasols' communications and cognition patterns. To communicate with the creatures, she would have to imagine how they thought, how they perceived their world, how they communicated. Manda had run numerous sweeps with her five waldos that were still near the city, trying to gather additional information. But nothing appeared to have changed down there—not in any recognizable way. She'd heard LuisMichael was exploring some means of interpreting their sonics, but she hadn't gotten word on its progress since her fight with Jim—and hadn't tried very hard, not especially wanting another fight.

So all she had to go on were Bio-Sciences's best guesses made from her earlier data, and ur-Carli's wild-ass analyses. And at this point no one could even agree whether the creatures were sapient, much less how well they saw light (and in what ranges), what sonar ranges they could "hear/see/speak" in, how their apparent chemical sensory systems worked, or to what purpose. She had all the information about them she was going to have, until she actually got down there among them.

She climbed up the ladder and waved good-bye from the cockpit. They all sent up a cheer, waving their scarves, gaiters, and tams. *Good-bye! Good luck!*

Manda plugged her livesuit leads directly into the console and then sat back, moving the waldo's icons into her preferred configuration with livegloved hands as the commandface bloomed around her. The hatch closed and the cockpit began to pressurize. (They kept the cabins at below-sea-level pressures; otherwise pilots tended to pass out during takeoff and high-acceleration or -deceleration maneuvers.) Her ears popped, and she yawned and wiggled her jaw. Then she ran down the checklist for the waldo. All go.

She activated the auxiliary engines. The buckles snaked over her chest and lap. Manda started with a gasp—she had piloted jet-waldos plenty of times; she'd just never *ridden* in one. A rush of excitement spread through her. This was only the beginning.

The freighter doors opened as she-waldo sledded forward. Using body and voice, she piloted the small, wide-winged aircraft out into the ice-crystal winds. As she-waldo spread her-its wings to their full extension, she-jet built up speed across the frozen plain on her-waldo's skis. Her-jet's jets spewed flame, and she-jet blasted up into the slow, rosy sunrise and glorious planet-shine of Brimstone's spring morning.

*   *   *

Once aloft, the jet-waldo's automated controls did everything—giving Manda all too much time to reflect.

Bart, Charles, Farrah, and Janice had headed out to the refinery last week, to take charge of the submersible's retooling. They'd been working round the clock, and Janice had reported late last night that the submersible had just been delivered to the drill site. Everything looked good to go. They would start getting *Aculeus Duo* hooked up to the bubble in the morning, while Manda was en route.

As Janice had started to sign off, Manda had asked if she had talked to Jim. Janice shook her head. "Brian and Amy have been around. They've been helpful. We couldn't have done the retooling without them. They know from pressure vessels. But Jim, no. I don't know where he's been."

"Oh."

She tried to keep her expression neutral, but Janice gave her a sympathetic look. "Do you want me to ask around?"

"No!" Then, more quietly, "No. I'm sure he's planning to meet me in person, when I arrive."

But after signing off she had curled up and sobbed for a long time, muffling her anguish with a pillow.

And staring out the cockpit window, now, at the moon-studded indigo sky, with the white-capped peaks and the river of pale blue ice below, Manda had to ask herself once again if all this pain was worth it.

It's a moot question, though, isn't it?

Because she no longer had a choice. She was quite thoroughly ensnared.

You lower your guard for an instant, she mused, *and wham! That's it. You're in it for the ride. Wherever it takes you.*

It seemed unfair, somehow, that a simple, animal act like climbing into a man's bed on a cold night in a moment of need could result in all this worry and pain.

*   *   *

anda followed the snaking glacier down to the refinery, and then homed in on the drill site's radio beacon.

Omi-Kami dazzled her with its crystalline brightness. From up here, it looked less like tossed meringue and more like the coarse shell of an egg: white mottled by pale aquamarine and shot through with dark, reddish-purple lines and sprays, as though about to hatch. From this high up, she could even make out a slight curve at the horizon. The violet lines and sprays were embedded dirt and snow-moss, which better absorbed Uma's rays than the high-albedo ice and snow. Along the shore line, and in the purplish areas, well out over the continental shelf to the south, fingers of surface slush and slate-colored, under-ice pockets of brine wandered across the ocean's hard shell.

Spring thaws were underway. For the next two seasons, equatorial Omi-Kami would become an increasingly dangerous place to be.

They had marked a landing strip for her just beyond the drill site. She waggled her-jet's wings at the tiny figures below her-jet, before lining her-waldo-self up between the coils of scarlet smoke and starting her-its descent. As she-jet touched down— skis squealing as they barked the ice—a terrified certainty grabbed her that she-jet would hit a weak pocket in the ice. The idea was nonsense, of course—they would have checked for karst pits the very first thing. A new pit wouldn't have formed so quickly. And of course, the landing went fine. *Christ, but I'm jittery.*

She-jet coasted to a stop. As she disengaged from the jet's liveface, UrsulaTomas, all five of it, approached in a small fleet of snow tugs. She climbed down the hand holds on the aircraft's side. Two, an older man and woman with broad faces, high cheekbones, and big black eyes, sped Manda back to the drill site, while the rest offloaded the supplies she had brought. They chatted excitedly about the mission with Manda as they sped her toward the drill site.

Manda resisted asking UrsulaTomas about Jim. She wasn't sure she wanted to know—yet she also desperately wanted him there. She would almost certainly run across one or both of his siblings. Facing their hostility, emanating from their faces so like his, would be almost as hard as facing him. The question of how to handle a meeting had become moot. All the colliding waves of anticipation, desire, anger, and fear had battered her down. She'd be lucky to get a coherent sentence out. The most she could hope for—a tepid and mournful hope at best—was that she wouldn't see him at all.

They arrived at the site. As she debarked the snow tug, Manda avoided looking at the shack. No point in stirring up unwelcome memories. She needed to keep her mind on the mission.

She clenched a fist, and the packed snow crunched in the folds of the shell. *Fuck him, for causing me such grief at a time like this!* With that, she thrust him and his siblings from her mind.

She approached the work area at the drill hole. A crane-waldo held the submersible aloft while two spider-waldos and several human helpers attached it to *Aculeus Duo's* back. Manda saw that the spider waldos were piloted by her sisters. She could tell by the waldos' body language. Vehicles, work-waldos, and other equipment clustered around, as well as two large thermal tents and three smaller ones: black, puffy affairs with inflated walls, all lashed down with tarps, cables, and pitons that rippled and billowed in the wind.

Manda gasped as she got close to the submersible. It had been washed and buffed to a high gloss, and glistened like a soap bubble in the many-shadowed sun-planet-moonshine of early morning. It hung in a mesh net suspended between two massive cranes. Its name, *Trieste*—after the first bathysphere to descend into the deepest reaches of Earth's oceans, almost three hundred earth-years before—was painted across its lower forward quadrant in big block letters. Lumpy sacks of rock ballast were strapped below it. *Aculeus Duo* lay atop it, the rear three of *Duo's* four segments curving clumsily around the sphere. To Manda it looked like a mechanical caterpillar attempting to free some larger creature's egg from its sac and make off with it.

She noted with approval that they had been careful not to restrict the waldo's attachments with the cords that lashed the two units together. But the rigging and unit-to-unit contact used up a good quarter of *Duo's* exterior surface along its belly—and hence rendered useless almost a third of its unused attachment ports.

This created a serious problem. The communications equipment that Vance and Jeannelle's team had jury-rigged to aid Manda in communicating with the aliens needed to be attached to *Duo's* ports—not to mention all the high-powered new sampling and detection tools the other teams had requested ports for. She'd have to sacrifice some important attachments, in order to preserve the critical ones.

She was going to take heat from some of the clones back at Amaterasu, who had worked hard to get equipment and experimental protocols ready for this trip. But time was of the essence. She couldn't afford a long debate over what should go and what should stay behind—communicating with the aliens came first, and for the parts left over, she'd just have to make a command decision and let her clone deal with the fallout.

At least, she thought ruefully, *I have a history of annoying people. So it won't come as too much of a shock.*

But this additional complication meant they wouldn't launch till this evening, or possibly even tomorrow morning. (She'd be damned before she'd let it go later than that—experiments or no.)

She walked toward the bubble, and saw that the two figures inside installing and testing equipment—moving in easy tandem among the boxes, racks, and coils of wire in the small space;

two bodies and a single mind—were Bart and Charles. As Manda handed off the hall-external components of the laser link to Farrah-spider, Bart stuck his head out through the open hatch, removing a length of wire from his mouth. "Want to come check it out?"

She did. On the stepladder, she stamped and kicked to dislodge the snow from her boots. Then she removed them, hung them on the rail next to her brothers' and, pushing aside the strands of mesh, crawled in through the hatch. The sound of her own movements and breathing closed in around her—echoing like a host of whispering phantoms—as she moved into the bubble. Her motions set the bubble swinging, slightly, in its cradle. She pulled the clear hatch to, using a handle and lock magnetically attached to the hatch's outer surface, and crouched in her socks on the curved floor.

The air in here was warm, several degrees above freezing, and fog and condensation beaded on the walls. She frowned. That would be from Charles's and Bart's breathing. The dehumidifiers must need tuning. Or maybe they weren't up and running yet.

Manda crept down the slow curve among the containers and equipment to where Bart and Charles were working.

"Here's the laser," she said, and handed Charles the bag with the blue-green laser and the transponder and translator that would port the laser signals between her commandface, housed in *Trieste*, and *Duo*. While her elder brothers slid the equipment into its rack and fiddled with wires and settings, she looked around.

They had used large suction cups and vacuum pumps to secure the biggest pieces of equipment to the walls and floor, and lashed smaller ones to the larger. Bundles of wire and cable ran between the machines, taped to the bubble's inner surface.

Trieste seemed bigger inside than she had imagined: once she'd gotten past the thicket of equipment in the back and was standing in the middle, even standing on tiptoe she couldn't reach much more than halfway toward the top. Even with Charles and Bart inside with her, it didn't seem so crowded. (Though it might after a couple hours.) *Aculeus Duo* loomed overhead, its metal and metaceramic surfaces pressed against the outer surface of *Trieste*'s smooth metaglass curve. Stout steel coils secured them together. Underfoot and to the sides of the bubble, Manda could make out the waldo crew taking strain measurements on the cables.

She sat down cross-legged on the small thatch rug and looked out. Even with *Duo* lashed on top of *Trieste*, she had a terrific view. From here, she could see forward, below, and to the sides quite well, and had a none-too-shabby view out the lower back quadrant of the bubble too.

Bart and Charles finished with the laser link and came up on either side of her. "*Duo* needs to be on top," Bart told her. "Because otherwise the attachment ports can't be used. But it's created some buoyancy problems." Charles added, "The equipment has had to be distributed carefully to keep the sphere from flipping *Duo* over. "We've provided ballast below, and that will help—" "—but you'll have to take care if you need to move any of the heavier instruments."

"Notice we mounted as much of the equipment as we could behind you," said Bart, "to free up more space and viewing forward." "We put the thatching in for comfort." "We have some cushions on order too." "We're not sure they'll get here in time."

Manda shrugged. "I can just toss some furs in, if necessary."

"I doubt you'll want furs." "It's going to be quite comfortable in here."

Manda couldn't imagine ever being warm enough not to want furs.

"We'll want to run down the emergency systems in detail with you, at some point," Bart said. "We've decided," Charles continued, "to make sure you're prepared for an emergency ascent, so the chances you could get trapped under the ice are minimized."

Minimized, she thought. *Great.* "*Duo* has been equipped with pressurized ascent balloons." "Your sounding equipment will be far better than JebMeri's—you'll need that to communicate with the aliens anyway—" "—and it could be used to find gaps in the ice cover, if you needed to make an ascent." "We've included climbing and hiking gear as well—" "—and an emergency beacon," they finished.

"That seems a bit paranoid," she said. "Don't you think?"

Her older brothers frowned. "No! We don't."

She looked from one to the other of them, and the corners of her lips turned up. "I submit to your good intentions."

They went on, "The heaters will keep the submersible at a balmy twenty Cee, and the carbon dioxide Recyclers—" "—have been repeatedly tested." "We see no way that they can fail as they did for JebMeri."

"Good," Manda replied. "Um, what *did* cause the Recyclers to fail for them?"

"We think," they said, "that the CO_2 Recyclers got contaminated, somehow, with a minute amount of a food Recycler template—" "—perhaps even a single molecule." A single template molecule could completely transform a batch of nanobugs. Template bugs were a sort of nanomechanical "reverse transcriptase," an inside-out version of the machine-molecule they were supposed to trigger production of, trapped inside a spore-like buckyball casing. A jolt of electricity disassembled their casing and they immediately started stripping down and converting other nanobugs, which began stripping down other nanobugs, till the full batch had been converted.

"We figure it had to be a small enough amount of contaminant that it took a long time for the error to result in transformation of the rest of the nanobugs." "When it was recovered from the ice floes, the submersible's recycling unit was filled with basic food Recyclers instead of CO_2 Recyclers."

"About the time the CO_2 levels were starting to be a problem, the submersible apparently experienced a temporary systems failure that disrupted the life-support systems. We don't know what caused that." "It could have been anything." "Faulty wiring, hardware failure in one of their computers . . ." Bart and Charles spread their hands in identical shrugs.

Equipment failure. Amaterasu's bane. She almost wished her brothers hadn't raised these issues. It was easier to keep her courage when she ignored them.

"They had a more jury-rigged system than yours, though," they assured Manda. "We're using much higher quality hardware and software, and we're confident your systems are much more stable."

And older. How comforting.

"We've installed four Recycler cylinders, and a smart system to monitor them," they went on. "A single Recycler canister can handle one person's carbon dioxide load indefinitely." "So you have plenty of backup, even if more than one cylinder gets contaminated."

Manda's brothers read her worried expression, and Charles gave her shoulder a squeeze.

They said, "We wouldn't send you out in anything we didn't consider completely safe." "And besides—if you're not satisfied with any of the safety aspects—" "—you'll be able to kill the project—" "—when we do the final systems test this evening."

Five different teams were working on the submersible: Farrah and Janice headed the team that lashed the two units together and then installed and tested *Duo*'s new attachments; Bart and Charles worked on the experimental instruments and life support and operating equipment inside the bubble; ByronDalia, back in Amaterasu, provided computer technical support, troubleshooting software and hardware problems throughout the integrated systems; LuisMichael (or at least, Brian and Amy) kept communications, maintenance, and transport systems running and made sure that the submersible was airtight and seaworthy; and UrsulaTomas hammered away on a series of emergency similes that would reveal (theoretically) any weaknesses in the systems and provide workarounds. Manda moved from group to group, getting updates and giving instructions. She caught only brief glimpses of Brian and Amy, who UrsulaTomas told her were resting up after their frenetic effort getting the submersible retooled. Jim still hadn't made an appearance.

They must hate her, and they had been the ones to prep *Trieste*. She was trusting her enemies with her life.

Everyone else took a meal and rest break at thirteen o'clock. Manda worked longer, seated inside the bubble, getting used to the new controls (and avoiding Amy and Brian). Later, once everyone else had gone into the dormitory tent, Manda headed over to the mess. As she opened the flap, her icons folded themselves away, and the dim, stark interior of the tent greeted her. She got herself a cup of tea and some meal rations from the stand at the back of the tent, and sat in one of the low folding chairs along the table, and ate her rations. Then Amy came in, stamping her feet and brushing snow from herself. She and Manda saw each other at the same moment, and both froze.

Manda's mouth went so dry she had a hard time swallowing her last bite. She took a sip of tea, supporting the cup with both hands to keep from spilling it with her sudden trembling. Amy gave Manda a long, hard look. Then she went over to the thermoses and snack station and got some food and drink.

After a long, awkward silence, Manda asked, "How are the supply runs doing?"

It was a pointless question; she'd already received a briefing from Brian. But she wanted to say something.

"Fine," Amy replied.

"And the vacuum tests?"

"They look good. But the critical test will be the pressure test. We'll want you to take it as deep as you can."

"Of course."

More silence. Manda ached to ask about Jim, but Amy's demeanor forbade it. After a few moments Amy got up and picked up some more rations and tea—presumably for Brian—and went out.

This is ridiculous. Just ask!

Manda ran out of the tent after Amy, and stopped her.

"Yes?" Amy's tone was cool, polite.

"Look—where is Jim?" Manda asked, panting. "What is he doing? I've been waiting to hear from him."

Amy's tone was cool. "He's at the refinery, just now. You can ask him yourself what he's doing, when he arrives. I'm sure he'd rather tell you himself."

Manda recalled Amy's effusiveness, her kindness, when Manda had first arrived at the refinery the other day.

"Amy—" She reached out a hand. "Wait. Please." The other woman shook off her touch.

"Let him go," Amy snapped.

And she stalked off.

Manda didn't respond to Amy's words, because the only response that came to mind was, "Fuck you, bitch!" And tempting though it was, it would only make matters worse.

All Brimstone's interminable afternoon, Manda sat in the bubble or paced in the command tent, running through what seemed like zillions of tests and simulations, arguing with people about what should go where, while a flurry of effort whirled around her. But always part of her mind was on Jim. Finally, as Uma neared Fire, Farrah stuck her head in.

"We're ready."

To be cleared for the trip, the submersible had to pass an exhaustive systems test as well as a submersion test. They would be done in combination. The submersion test involved lowering the submersible into the sea, where Manda, operating it via her liveface, would take it into deep waters. There it would undergo a series of pressure tests, perform some basic maneuvers, and run through some emergency-response similes.

Any problems found would mean more delays. And every minute she spent up here, waiting while tests were run, increased the risk that the aliens would breach *Octo*'s containment. The only thing that kept Manda from cancelling this last test out of sheer, wild impatience to *get down there right now* was the realization that nobody at all would be served if she died on launch.

Brian and Amy emerged from one of the black tents and walked together to the crane. She caught brief glimpses of them watching her. Heart pounding, Manda stayed on the far side of the drill hole, where Farrah and Janice orchestrated the lowering of the submersible with the two big crane-waldos. The physical distance made no difference; Brian's and Amy's faces, instructions, and commands, carried through livespace, brought them all too near.

She paced, watching *Duo*'s displays, as they slowly and carefully lowered *Duo-Trieste* down the drill hole into the water. It took almost half an hour to get it into the water and below the ice. She thought she'd go mad from the waiting. Finally it sank below the fans at the hole's bottom.

"You're on!" her siblings informed her. She retreated to the black tent that had been set up as a command station, and gratefully escaped into the shallow waters under the ice, via her liveface.

She sent more kind thoughts in ByronDalia's direction as her-

Duo's control face sprang up, unfolded itself, and fitted itself to her form. It was less cluttered than it had been, and the controls responded more quickly and cleanly than her own inexpert, patch-and-paste job had done. ByronDalia had cut minimum lag by almost a third. Since *Trieste*'s presence greatly increased her-*Duo*'s drag profile and threw off her-its navigational responses, she'd need all the compensatory time she could get.

She-*Duo-Trieste* released her-its grip on the cable and kicked in the motor at one-tenth power. Unwieldy, the submersible wobbled and only slowly began to move away from the drill hole.

"Pressure holding steady at ten-point-two bars," reported LuisMichael's voice in her ear. Manda jumped. *It's Brian, Manda. Just Brian. Calm down.*

She cleared her throat. "Navigational controls are sluggish as hell."

"As we expected," Janice's voice said in her ear. "From here everything looks good."

"Taking her out toward the shelf edge at twelve knots," Manda said, and set course. Manda listened to the murmur of her siblings' voices, of ByronDalia's droll comments back in Amaterasu, and LuisMichael's quiet, businesslike reports on the different systems. She contributed her own inputs on navigations. Twice, she-*Duo-Trieste* scraped and bumped against the ice cap's underside. The height of free water here was only a meter or two greater than her-*Duo-Trieste*'s own height. The balance and maneuverability were very different from what she was used to.

A short while later, the precipice neared.

"Sonar indicates drop-off in two seconds," she reported. ". . . and here we go!"

Darkness loomed in her-*Duo*'s floodlights. Manda-*Duo-Trieste* dropped down, down, down. She exhaled her relief as the ice cap's slushy sonar profile faded away above.

"Depth one hundred meters below the ice cap . . . two hundred . . . five hundred . . . eight hundred . . . one kilometer," she reported.

"CarliPablo," said UrsulaTomas, "why don't you level off here and let us run through a couple emergency similes?"

"Acknowledged. Turning over controls," Manda said, and waited, watching their readouts. A short while later, they reported, "Emergency response similes report eighty-seven-point-three percent conformance to design specs."

Eighty-five percent was the cutoff point. A cheer broke out in the command tent and online; lots of people in Amaterasu must be tuned in.

"We have one hundred percent hull integrity at one kilometer depth," Amy reported. "Go ahead and take it down as deep as you can, CarliPablo."

Manda did. *Trieste* passed muster—one hundred percent hull integrity—at 2.67 kilometers depth. Like glass, a metalglass sphere increased in strength, structurally, with depth. Odds were excellent that the submersible would do fine even at twice that depth.

"At five kilometers down, you could even survive an antimatter blast," UrsulaTomas had remarked, "as long as you weren't right at ground zero."

Filled with growing elation, Manda-*Duo*-*Trieste* breezed through the navigational exercises her siblings ran her through, and then brought the conjoined waldos back up—this time with nary a bump or scrape against the overhead ice shelf or the ocean floor. She heard mutters of admiration as she brought the submersible in, and smiled to herself.

At the bottom of the drill hole, she-*Duo* hooked her-itself up to the tow line, disengaged from her liveface and, as Luis-Michael's team began bringing the submersible up, exchanged excited hugs with her siblings and the rest of the team. *This is it.* Nothing more stood between her and the dive.

Well, almost nothing.

*   *   *

They tried to talk her into resting overnight and leaving in the morning. Manda refused. She knew she wouldn't sleep. Her siblings insisted she eat a big meal and take a nap, while the drill site crew finished loading supplies and tinkered with a few last-minute items. They would launch her expedition at twenty-seven o'clock, an hour and a half from now. Manda reluctantly agreed.

The only place that wasn't being used was the shack where she and Jim had spent the night. She went inside, lit the lamp, turned on the heater, and set her meal down on the table. It took her about two minutes of staring around the place to decide, the hell with it. She was going to call him.

She brought up her communications face—and found a message there from him, time-stamped early this morning, shortly after she'd reached the drill site. It had been sent as a normal-priority message, and her filters—which she'd activated so as not to be distracted by anything that wasn't urgent—hadn't alerted her.

Why hadn't he sent it as high-priority? Damn him.

She opened it, and his face appeared in front of her. He tugged at his beard and didn't speak for a second.

"I was an idiot," he said finally. ("You got that right," Manda growled.) "I was angry. Then I got tied up with something." A pause. He stared at her, intense. "I'm onto something with the language patterning, Manda. I need a few more hours to beat it into presentable shape. I'll be out to the site sometime this afternoon to show you what I've got. Wait for me." He started to disconnect, then paused. "Please—don't launch before I get out there. I'll try to get there by mid-afternoon."

Manda wiped away angry tears. She glanced at her displays: by now it was almost twenty-six-thirty, well past mid-afternoon. Manda contemplated walking out and ordering them to have the submersible ready in ten minutes.

She didn't. She sat there waiting for a few minutes—unable to eat—sick to her stomach with anticipation. Then she paced. *What do I do if he doesn't come soon?*

Just launch. Forget him. If he cared that much, he'd have called sooner—left a higher-priority message.

She went outside into the freezing winds and scanned the shoreward horizon with binocs. No sign of him. Her siblings queried her, and after a hesitation, she told them Jim was coming with new information. UrsulaTomas, Amy, Brian, and others joined the Jim-watch, as *Duo-Trieste* reached final readiness. The last brilliant sliver of Uma was sliding behind Fire and the sky had emptied, briefly, of moons. Temperatures had plunged to forty below.

They took to watching for him in ten-minute shifts, with breaks inside the command tents—otherwise they got too cold.

Manda took another turn at watch. The floodlights came on as she strode out to the camp's edge, and the world beyond the pool of light that defined the camp boundaries grew that much darker. Daggers of cold seeped in through her parka, boots, and gloves. Manda exhaled sharply. She went up to Brian and Amy, who were huddled by the cranes, watching the southwestern horizon.

"Where is he?"

"He's coming," they both said. Brian added, "He left the refinery about thirty minutes ago."

Gee, volunteering information unprompted. But she saw the worry in their eyes, as they stared out at the horizon.

More minutes ticked past. Moons crept back into the heavens and the stars began to appear; the winds grew fiercer. *Duo-Trieste* swung in its mesh cradle. Much more wind and they wouldn't be able to safely get the submersible into the hole. But in these temperatures Jim wouldn't last long. If he hadn't fallen into a karst pit somewhere and already drowned or frozen to death.

What'll it be, then? Leave Jim's fate to others? Or delay the

*launch till he's found, when further delays may mean disaster for
the parasol creatures and us?*

Sending the snow tugs out at this hour would be dangerous.
Manda was the best qualified to fly one of the jet-waldos, which
were the only alternative to the tugs. Delaying the launch any
longer was chancy—but even if she decided to disregard her
own feelings about him, Jim had information that could be critical to the success of the mission.

Make a decision.

"The launch is on hold," she told the others. "I need Jim's
information." *I need to know he's OK.*

"What about the wind?" Janice asked.

"We'll risk it. Take me out to the jet," she told the nearest
UrsulaTomas. "I'm going to see if I can find him. Brian, you
come with me."

He looked startled; Amy looked truculent. But someone
shouted and they all saw a speck of light flare, way out across
the floes. It disappeared, and they all strained, looking for it—
but no—there it was again.

A dim silhouette appeared over a rise. It was Jim. Brian and
Amy started running. Manda and the others came close behind,
crowding him as Brian and Amy helped him into camp.

All annoyance fled her at the sight of him. His parka, snow
pants, boots, gloves, and face were so encrusted he might have
been a snowman. His lips were cracked and blue, and he was
shaking so hard he could barely speak—teetering on the edge of
collapse.

"Thanks for waiting," he stuttered to Manda, as the others
hauled him in.

"Oh, shut up," she said. "Use the shed," she told Amy and
Brian. "It's warmest."

She'd left the heat on, so it was warm inside. The camp medics, a pair of TomasJebs, examined Jim and then had him sit

351

next to the stove swathed in heated blankets, and gave him something warm and medicinal to sip.

"Mild hypothermia," they reported. "He's improving quickly, though." "Some rest and warmth and he'll be fine."

While the medics and Amy and Brian attended to Jim, Janice and Farrah signalled Manda from the doorway. "We've rescheduled the launch for twenty-eight-oh," they said.

"OK." Manda checked her displays. That gave her about twenty minutes. She glanced back at Jim, who was watching her over the heads of his siblings.

The feelings were all there, right where she'd left them.

Jim said something to his siblings, and they left with Farrah and Janice. Amy shot Manda a disapproving look as she left. Once they were alone, Manda came up and took Jim's hands, still frigid and white. "Pushed it a little close, I'd say."

"I'm fine," he replied in a gruff tone, through chattering teeth. "Just chilled, that's all. Making a big fuss over n—n—nothing."

She breathed into his hands to warm them, and he took her face in those frigid hands and they kissed. She climbed onto his lap and wormed her arms under his blankets and layers of clothing, touching bare skin. Even his torso's skin temperature was low. His cold, rough hands worked their own way inside her parka and under her clothing, and she shrieked.

"Jesus! You're a block of ice. Wait right here."

She jumped up, grabbed the biggest fur, threw it over him, and began rubbing and breathing on his hands.

She wanted to climb all over him, right here and now—she wanted the feel of him against her. She wanted something of him to hold onto when she was down there, alone, below the ice.

But there really wasn't time. And she was pretty sure orgasm was bad for hypothermia.

"Listen," he said. "There's something you need to know and not much time—"

"Yes?"

"I've had a major breakthrough on the parasols' language."

"Yes! You hinted at something like that in your message." She pulled another chair over. "Fill me in."

"Well—I wasn't getting anywhere at first—I didn't have a frame of reference, and only a few recordings to go on. There just wasn't enough information. And then—" He broke off. "Do you remember those explosions I mentioned to you, before we ever found the city?"

She nodded once, slowly.

"On a hunch," he said, "I compressed them—increased the pitch and sped them way up." He gave her a grin. "And guess what it sounded like?"

She gaped. "No."

"Yes. Same as the parasol sonar-talk, only much deeper, slower—and a whole lot more elaborate."

"Holy shit!"

"And I had several seasons' worth of that data. Plenty to be able to pick out patterns. So . . ." He shrugged, but his expression was pleased. "Using the parasol-talk as a kind of primer, cross-referenced against the boomspeak, I've managed to identify several basic phrases, and I'm making headway with others. I don't know what they mean yet, but I have some guesses based on the parasols' responses to each other—"

Manda whooped and threw her arms around him, dislodging his thermal blankets. "Jim, that's fantastic!"

With an answering smile, he drew her close and nuzzled her neck.

"Yeah, I guess it is," he said. Manda muffled his words with her lips, and they kissed long and urgently. She wanted him so much she could hardly contain herself. It didn't help that she could feel his erection pressing against her buttocks, even through all their layers of clothing.

Easy, there. Keep your mind on business.

353

With a deep breath, she forced herself to return to her own chair. She slipped her hands between his knees. *Such self-discipline. They should give me a medal.*

He gave her an appreciative smile, then twirled a finger in his beard and stared into the gas flames inside the stove. "I have no doubt there's an intelligence at work down there—one at least an equal to our own. . . ."

"But?" she prompted, when his voice tapered off.

He scowled. "I just find it odd that the parasol-talk is so much simpler and less complex than their boomspeak. I'm estimating the parasol creatures only use a vocabulary of a few dozen phrases—a hundred at most. The boomspeak is much more highly ornamented, and I've barely begun analyzing. The count could go into the thousands. Maybe higher. I can't think of a reason for such a dichotomy.

"And guess what else?"

She lifted her eyebrows.

"There are two boomers down there," he said. "Not just one."

Manda gasped as the implications hit her. "Are you sure?"

Jim nodded. "Positive. At first I thought it had to be echoes, but the echo patterns aren't simply distortions of the first—they're a different set."

"Um—what are you saying, exactly?"

"I'm saying that on the far side of Brimstone—exactly opposite our city—I'm pretty sure there's a second underwater source of explosions, ranging at a slightly different pitch and cadence."

Manda stared. "There are *two* cities?"

"I think so. The boomspeak seems to be some sort of long-distance communication method between them."

She was silent a moment, thinking. Then, suddenly annoyed, she slapped him on the arm. "Why didn't you tell me any of this earlier? Do you know what you've put me through over the past several days?"

He just looked at her for a moment, then rubbed at his mouth and chin. "I know. I'm sorry. Look—Manda." He released an explosive breath. "When you told me you were going under the ice, I felt like you'd slugged me in the face. The idea of you going down there alone—" He fell silent, with a frown. Then he shrugged. "It just got to me. It really made me mad. Like you didn't care enough about me to talk about it before you made up your mind." He sighed, deeply. "*You* got to me."

"You got to me too," she said.

He rubbed her thumbnail. "And Amy and Brian aren't handling this real well. You and me, I mean. It made things complicated. So I—" He shrugged, helplessly, and looked at her. "I guess I was mad at you for meaning too much to me, too fast."

She laughed. "I was feeling the same way." A painful lump formed in her throat. "What a sorry pair, eh?"

He chuckled, though his eyes were a little sad. "Yeah." Then he took her face in his hands, again, and kissed her once more, hungrily: deep and long.

She scooted onto his lap, twined her fingers in his, and laid her head on his shoulder. In a few minutes it would be time to launch. She didn't want to leave, just yet. She wanted to soak up every minute, every centimeter of him.

"I'm in love with you," she said, and stroked his bristly cheek. She felt him tense, and drew back.

"What is it?"

Jim sighed. "You're not going to be happy about this, but . . . well, I sent a report to the council this morning and . . ." He cleared his throat. "The council has requested a meeting with you and me to discuss a change in plans."

"What? Everything's all set!"

He cleared his throat again, looking embarrassed. "I've asked permission to go along with you. To help you attempt to communicate with the aliens."

She pushed away from him and stood, shocked. "Why wasn't I told? Why didn't you tell me first, before you went to them?"

355

He didn't answer right away. "I was afraid you'd fight my request. I wanted a chance to plead my case to them. Without any complications."

Complications. Manda turned away, silent.

"I asked them to let me talk to you," he said.

She remembered the looks she'd been getting all day. "How many knew?"

"Brian and Amy. Probably the rest of the refinery crew."

She turned back to him, furious. "First you shut me out, keep me in the dark for two weeks. Then you go behind my back to the council."

"*You* didn't consult with *me*, either."

"What—turnabout is fair play?"

"I didn't intend it that way." He sighed. "Or maybe I did. I don't know. It seemed like a good idea at the time." He shrugged. "I didn't want you to go without me."

Disgusted, Manda said, "Well, let's get it over with." She started to head out for her livegear, which was already packed in the submersible.

"Wait. I have to know something."

She turned, hands planted on hips.

"Would you have said yes, if I'd asked?" he demanded. "Would you have even considered it? You've been playing push-and-pull with me all along. You're not an easy woman to be in love with, you know."

She registered that. *He used the L-word.*

Then she thought, *At least you have vat-mates to go home to, who'll comfort you, who'll take away your hurt. When you're not there, all I have is a cold bed and silence.*

And whose choice, asked a tiny voice in her head, *is that?*

Jim shook his head. "Look, this is going all wrong. I suppose it's my own fault. I stood on my pride instead of—"

Then he broke off and pulled an info cube out of his pocket. "Here. This is everything I've got on the aliens' language. If you

356

tell me not to come, I'll formally withdraw my request. You can go down there on your own and I'll give you whatever support I can from up here. This can be all your show." He dropped the cube into her hand. "But you need me on this mission, Manda. I think you know it too." He turned away. "So, it's your call. I'll be outside."

"Wait," Manda said sharply. "Just a minute."

He paused with his hand on the door latch.

Manda eyed the tiny, sparkling info cube, rolled it between her fingers. She shook her head with a frustrated sigh. "I love you, Jim. So much I can hardly bear it. But you haven't given me much reason to trust you, pulling this coup trick on me."

Jim nodded, looking bleak. "All right, then. Fair enough. Just . . . just come back alive, OK?" His voice cracked on the words.

"Oh, don't be an idiot," she said, exasperated, grabbing his wrist. "Of course you're coming with me." She grabbed his parka hood and pulled him to her. "But never do anything like that again."

His teeth flashed white, and his laughter filled the room to bursting as he wrapped her in a hug.

Part III
A Meeting of Minds

The question then becomes: how did this expansion of awareness from radial to circumferential relationships occur?

The quickest and most efficient means would be to substitute
the constant, the *I* in their preexisting mental equations, for a
variable. In other words, [*I*] became instead an unassigned slot
into which any appropriate [*role*] might be plugged. Thus, "if a
strange male beats his chest, [his rival] feels intimidated." "If a
baby cries, [the mother] picks it up and suckles it." They already
had a large collection of rules for interpersonal dynamics based
on their own interactions. This single change, from a constant *I*
to a variable *role*, vastly expanded their ability to apply those rules
to a broader range of situations with one simple change of the
rules.

The self, the *I*, now became only one of numerous roles that
might fit a particular behavioral rule. And this brought about an
awareness that the others in one's social network were other
selves as well. We could now see ourselves as others saw us. Humans opened a larger window onto the world of social interaction,
and accidently caught our own reflection in the glass.

The *I* was no longer implicit. The ego was born.

—ibid.

With Manda's consent to the change, the meeting with the council was a non-event. They gave their blessing for Jim to accompany her, and after a brief good-bye to Arlene and Derek, Manda signed off.

Another delay ensued while they loaded the additional supplies for Jim. And yet another delay, because the winds had gotten too strong. Manda and Jim waited with other members of the launch team in one of the big tents, drowsing but too keyed up to sleep, until finally, at thirty-thirty—the middle of the night—Brian entered and announced that the winds had died down and it was safe to launch.

By now, it was nearly fifty below. They all went out into the life-robbing cold—muscles cramping through all their layers—hurrying with mincing steps, gasping in pain—over to the drill hole. Manda and Jim had donned their livegear earlier and in this cold, Manda feared as much for it as for herself. Good-byes, shouts of encouragement, and scattered applause surrounded Manda and Jim as they went up to the now ice-coated stepladder in the freezing winds.

As she gazed up toward *Trieste*'s hatch, Manda's courage failed her. She could barely communicate with her fellow colonists. How could she possibly find a way to talk to aliens? What the hell had she been thinking? She twisted around, panicky. But her siblings were right behind her. Bart squeezed her shoulder. Farrah, beside him, gave her a calm smile. Janice and Charles were nodding encouragement. *You can do this, Manda. We know you can.*

They wouldn't lie to her. They'd never pulled their punches. Their confidence in her was a hard-won gift—a stout piton set deep in the ice, one she could lash herself to and weather the fiercest of storms.

She could do this.

With a deep breath, Manda climbed up the ladder and squirmed through the hatch. She noticed the cushions had made it here in time. They'd been lashed to handholds set with suction cups in the front bottom quadrant of the bubble. The submersible's air had dried out some: all the frost and dew was gone from the bubble's inner surfaces.

Jim crawled in behind her and shut out the cold, while she got her boots off. She stripped all the way down to long johns and liveware, and then rubbed and slapped herself, shivering. The outer layers' bulk would make handling piloting difficult, and it was plenty warm in here—but it would be a while before the night's chill would melt from her bones.

She showed Jim where things were, and then stuffed their outer layers of clothing into a locker secured between the machines. They moved forward into the central cradle of the submersible then, and Manda sat down on one of the new cushions and brought up her liveface.

He whistled sharply, and ran a hand over the glass. "Cozy setup."

Manda spared him a quick grin. He had stripped down to his long johns too. She was abruptly conscious of all the eyes on them, the circle of watchers preparing to launch the submersible. "It's going to get cozier. We'll be sick of each other before this is through."

He grinned back. "I'll take my chances."

Manda gave the OK. They waved to those standing outside, and listened to their good-byes over the liveface, as the cranes lifted them up and over to the drill hole. Manda's pulse had quickened again. The support for the cables running down through the hole had been moved to the side to accommodate *Duo-Trieste*'s size, which was rather a tight fit through the hole. Manda and Jim now hung over several hundred meters of empty space.

"Ready?" she asked.

Jim hesitated the briefest fraction of a second, then nodded. "Let's do it."

Manda gave Amy and Brian, who stood over near the cranes, the thumbs-down: *descend*. Rocking only slightly, they sank below the lip of the hole. Manda-*Duo* strained for and caught the main drillhole cable with her-its foremost claw attachments. She drank in the view of the moon-filled night sky beyond the lip of the hole; it'd be their last glimpse for a while. She caught Jim doing the same thing.

She might as well admit it; she wasn't entirely sure they were going to come back alive. But what a way to go.

"Hang on," she warned. He tried to grip the edges of the cabinet beside him, looking a bit alarmed.

"To what?"

She pointed. "The handholds on the floor. Here, and here. You may as well have a seat—it'll lower your center of gravity. We're going to tip forward ninety degrees." She grinned again. "You and I will go for a little slide."

They braced themselves. Manda-*Duo* took hold of the cable with all four pairs of her-its grasping attachments. Manda felt her own body nearly go forward into a somersault as the submersible swung down. Jim grabbed her shoulder to keep her from going over, and a moment later they released their grips on the handholds to drop onto the front window, which was now pointing straight down. All the equipment hung in a crude ring on the front, sides, and back of the bubble; the cushions clung halfway up the curve behind them.

"Sure hope all that stuff is well secured," Jim remarked, eyeing the equipment.

Laura J. Mixon

"They used power-assisted vacuum cups. It'll hold." Manda-waldo detached her-itself from the tow line, and they started down.

They descended. The rough-hewn ice glistened in their flood-lights, baring the scars of ancient drill teeth. It reminded her a bit of her climb into that secret room. She-waldo took them down a good deal faster than the cranes had lowered the unit last time—though not as fast as she-*Duo* would have gone, unencumbered by *Trieste* and its human cargo. Jim was looking pale, she-*Duo* noticed, and she-*Duo* slowed down a little.

Manda had seen this sight numerous times through her waldos' cameras, so it held little excitement for her. But once he'd gotten over his initial nervousness, Jim seemed fascinated; he pressed his palms against the metaglass, staring. She gave him a distracted smile while monitoring and correcting *Duo*'s progress. Finally she-*Duo* spotted waves below. She-waldo slowed, and eased her-itself into the frothing, seething water. Further below they heard the whir of the immense drillhole fans, which kept the water circulating and prevented refreezing.

Here, at the ocean's interface, the seawater seemed restless: a living thing.

Be kind to us, Omi-Kami.

They continued to sink as Manda-*Duo* climbed down the cable. Finally they reached the fans. Manda-*Duo* navigated them past—nicking a corner or two, but with no serious harm. She-waldo righted the submersible with *Duo*'s propellers, and Jim guided her back onto the cushions. He was looking at the strands of sonar transponders and the sandy ocean floor that stretched out on all sides. The whites of his eyes were visible all around the dark irises.

"This is so incredible," he murmured.

"Roger that, *Trieste*." It was Brian and Amy via the liveface.

"We're down, Topside," Manda reported. "As you can see for

364

yourselves." She listened and looked with her own inputs and with *Duo*'s. "No sign of any parasol creatures," she reported.

"Sonar communications have been minimal," Janice and Farrah said via the face, "since you laid off exploring their city." "Maybe they got bored of hanging around the transponders."

"Jim, I'm going to have to tune out for just a bit," Manda said.

"Let me be your armchair, then." He scooted behind her, and Manda leaned back against his chest and rested her arms against his legs. "This is going to be distracting."

"I'll move, then."

She gripped his arm as he made to get up. "No, no. I'll manage."

Cushioned by his body and warmth, she turned her concentration to her liveface controls. She-waldo carried her-its passengers carefully under the ice rocks and spears toward the edge of the continental shelf. Once more, she-waldo managed it with nary a scrape or knock.

Nice work, girl.

"There it is!" Bart and Charles said a while later, and Manda saw it approaching too: a ragged chunk broken off infinity.

"Here we go," she said, and took them down over the edge into the dense, cold black.

Jim's body tensed against her back as all bearings outside the bubble disappeared. Her own heart pounded against her ribs. *Duo*'s floodlights stabbed forward and down, creating a path that stretched perhaps ten meters before them into the watery void, and the sound of the waldo's engines and propellers carried through *Trieste*'s hull, thrumming hypnotically.

They were sinking into a void so dark it seemed palpable: some gelatinous ink. Pressure gauges on her commandface registered an increasing weight outside the bubble. But inside, other than the thrumming of *Duo*'s engines and the hum of their equipment, all was quiet. And warm. Especially with Jim's arms encircling her. Blessedly warm.

Once she'd gotten *Duo*'s settings where she wanted them, Manda said, "Looks like our top speed isn't going to be much more than twenty-five kilometers an hour. I estimate we'll reach the city in about twenty-eight to thirty hours."

"Roger," Farrah's voice replied. Fatigue slurred her words. Janice said, "We're going to turn in, then."

"We're going to turn in too."

Bart and Charles said, "We're on the first watch. Call if you need us."

"*Duo-Trieste* signing off."

"Pleasant dreams." "Safe journey." "Holler if you need us." "We'll be right here." That was Bart and Charles, trading off.

"Good night, Jim," said Brian. Manda could hear the strain in his voice. "Be careful," Amy added.

"You know we will," Jim replied, using *we* even though Manda was certain they didn't intend to include her. "We'll call you in about eight hours or so. Sooner if we have anything to report."

Manda cut the voice communications link.

Jim was staring out at the darkness, his brow puckered.

"Scary to think of all that water overhead, eh?" Manda said.

"Yeah. And all the ice above that. We couldn't surface if we needed to."

"Well . . . the geothermal area is right on the equator, and there've been some thaws. There may be cracks and slushy areas in the ice crust we could break through, if we had to," she said. "It's all the nothing below that gets me. Fear of falling. Totally irrational, but I can't help it."

He gave her a wry look. "I noticed you staying away from the cushions' edges."

"Yeah."

"It really digs up something primal, doesn't it?" he remarked.

"It does."

They were silent another moment.

"You know, Jim . . ."

366

He gave her a querying look. She sighed. *I'm glad you're here.* Pride wouldn't let her say it. She shook her head. "Nothing."

Sidelong, she caught Jim giving her a fond look, as if he'd heard it anyway. She turned in his arms to give him a kiss that ended up with both of them on the cushions.

They were so worn out that even their desire for each other wouldn't keep them awake long. They stripped each other, clumsily—trying not to lose contact as they removed their long johns and liveware. And they kissed and touched and tasted each other, till finally they coiled naked across each other: searching mouths and fingers, breasts and tongues and crevices, all convex and concave surfaces, sliding across each other—finally he penetrated her—and they moved in a slow, focused rhythm punctuated by their breaths.

Despite her hunger for him, Manda was so tired she didn't think she'd be able to come at all. But an orgasm burst upon her, nearly blinding her with its intensity—she clutched his buttocks, grinding her hips against his pelvis and groaning. And Jim climaxed as she was coming down: his back arched and his face contorted as though he were in pain. She could feel him pulsing.

She hugged him to her and stroked his dark hair, now damp with sweat. She liked that feeling. She liked being able to make him come.

I'll take this over live-sex anyday.

He gave her a languid smile. Then he withdrew and pulled Manda into the crook between his shoulder and arm. Within seconds his breathing changed. He was asleep.

Manda touched his cheekbone. Happiness suffused her: a happiness so deep it was almost an ache. *I love how you smell,* she thought.

Would he be able to resist the contempt and jealousy his siblings felt over her? Or would she lose him to them, as Janice had lost her JennaMara lover to Farrah's jealousy and need?

She didn't want to allow herself to care too much, if she was just going to lose him again. She'd been alone a long, long time. She knew—to the microgram—exactly how much she had to lose.

But she didn't have the patience to fret over a catalog of imagined horrors, and the fear slowly bled away, leaving her leaden-limbed. Her feet and hands were so warm. And her face. She stretched. Sleeping nude in the warm air of their bubble, skin-to-skin with Jim, with only a single blanket thrown over them—no frigid air stinging the sinuses or scouring her cheeks—seemed such a luxury. She coiled an arm across Jim, who muttered in his sleep, and then closed her eyes, drifting away.

Manda spent a while worrying about being cooped up in a tiny space with Jim. Anything could happen. What if they fought? What if they ended up hating each other? She wasn't exactly renowned for her people skills. And once you got past the more graceful social facade, Jim seemed unsure of himself too. But she needn't have worried. They seemed to get along better now, in this tiny, cramped space, than they had when they were hundreds of kilometers apart.

It didn't make sense. Manda could only wonder at it. It was almost as if they were vat-mates.

But no—that wasn't right. Vat-mates fit because they were the same. Manda and Jim fit because of their differences. His sense of humor—his mild ribbing, his even-temperedness in the face of her volatility—helped Manda relax. She found she didn't need to bristle at every teasing remark. She didn't have to defend herself all the time. And her own drive to achieve, her intensity and independence, gave him something he seemed to need, in some way she didn't fully understand.

They filled each others' spaces—in more ways than just the physical. Like pieces of a puzzle, they fit.

It helped too, that the next twenty-eight hours slipped by almost too fast. They had all sorts of tests to run on their equipment—which uncovered a string of mostly minor equipment disasters—which they sweated and swore and tried not to panic over and eventually managed to patch or work around, with the tele-help of ByronDalia, CarliPablo, LuisMichael, and Ursula-Tomas.

Jim spent a lot of time in-face, working with Amy and Brian to crack the language of the parasols. Jealousy burst over Manda, nearly choking her with its intensity, each time he submersed himself in his liveface, gesturing and muttering and laughing casually with his vat-mates. The urge to interrupt him, to remind herself constantly that he was hers, was powerful—even when she was preoccupied, or should be, with her own work. For the most part she managed to restrain herself—partly out of pride, and partly because she knew it would only create more tension between her and his siblings.

They could hear Jim's booms long before they reached Rima Optabile. The first time she heard it came after a fairly long silence. It had grown in loudness so slowly—*boom, boom-boom ba-bump, whummp, boom*—that when Manda first heard it, she also realized she'd been hearing it for some time and simply hadn't been conscious of it.

Jim dutifully recorded the boomspeak, as he called it, and he and his vat-mates sweated over its many beats and filips and spaces, trying to find meaning. But as he ruefully confessed at one point, its complexity made translating the parasols' still-incomprehensible songpidgin look easy.

The void beyond the bubble's surface became a fixture as they drifted downward. Every time she glanced up from her work, or took a break to sleep or eat or pee or chat, there it was, an impenetrable wall of nothing, with no stream of bubbles or cloud of particles to hint that they were moving. To Manda it seemed they were in a tiny cul-de-sac somehow outside of time and space, with only each other and the humming and throbbing of the engines, and their rather banal sonar communications with Topside, for company.

So it was a shock when they finally neared the ocean floor and the blackness dissolved into visible shapes: rock and silt dunes that flowed past below *Duo-Trieste's* glassy, turgid belly.

Manda was faced in when it happened, with *Duo's* commandface surrounding her, a faintly-felt pressure against her skin and a barely-visible glaze over the yellow-stained rocks that lay outside the metaglass curve. She heard Jim's breathing change, and her reflection in the bubble smiled. A babble of excited voices from Topside sounded in their ears a moment later.

She-*Duo* got a reading from Manda's other marine-waldos, positioned well above the city in different quadrants. She commanded them to move in toward the city's fringes.

"We're about twenty-point-three kilometers from the city's northern perimeter," she reported. Jim laid his hand on her shoulder. In the metaglass reflection his eyes were wide.

"OK, Topside," she said, "we're almost within sonar range of the city. I'm changing us over to packet mode."

To keep from interfering with their communication attempts with the parasols, they were switching over from continuous-stream communications to a series of compressed, phased-array sonar bursts outside the parasols' communication range. Topside would get an update on their progress every five minutes, but wouldn't respond except on request or in an emergency. Jim looked nervous; she knew without him saying so that losing continuous contact with his siblings would be hard for him.

Manda hoped the creatures weren't harmed by the packeted sonar bursts. Just because they didn't communicate at that low a pitch didn't mean they couldn't be affected by it. It might be like a deep roar in their ears. (One presumed they had ears. . . .)

"Roger, *Trieste*," Topside replied. "Good luck."

Manda switched over. The steady, low-pitched thrums and growls that had surrounded them for days cut off, and it suddenly seemed way too quiet.

"The drop first, right?" Jim asked. They had a package for *Aculeus Septimus*, new tools and attachments that she might later be able to use to break the marine-waldo free of the lava entrapping it. Jim had faced in with her: he would handle the drop while she navigated their craft.

"Right," Manda said. She-*Duo* steered toward the volcanic cone, which loomed out of the murk. It was a good deal taller now than it had been the other day. Around the cone, like a crowd of gargoyles gathered around a monument, stood a field of lumpy geothermal chimneys of varying heights, many spewing smoke or geothermal fluid, sending fields of wavering water upward. Here and there, bubbles trickled up in slow streams.

They rounded the cone. Outside temperatures spiked and a mass of boiling water erupted from the volcano's mouth. Within it they caught glimpses of bright, mottled lumps of lava that glopped out of the fissure in the cone's side, like a family of orange worms humping out of their burrow—only to turn to stone before getting very far down the slopes. At the boiling water's fringes, smoke and curtains of murky, high-temperature fluid billowed up. The volcano's wavering glow lit the surroundings for several dozen meters.

"It's gotten huge," she breathed.

"Look!" Jim pointed as they came around. A large number of parasols—perhaps a few hundred or so—were doing—something—among the chimneys on the volcano's far side. Manda couldn't make out much detail from here. But numerous parasols were clustered around some of the chimneys, while others moved back and forth from over the nearby rise.

Manda-waldo hovered and they watched for a while through

371

Duo's telescopic lens, their view enhanced with false-color imaging. Jim gestured, and a red mark appeared in Manda's field of vision.

"They're extruding something—those two over there. See?"

Manda focused in with *Duo*'s telescopic lenses. Two parasols had joined all their seven "hands," forming a sort of bowed-out double torus with their bodies. The annular opening of one of the partners seemed to be attached to a shiny tube that coiled around the base of a chimney. Though she couldn't see the tube growing it did appear to be coming from between the two parasols, somehow.

"Over there too," she said, marking another location in-face. Jim nodded. "And there," he added.

She-*Duo* swung her-its cameras and floodlights slowly across the scene. Around several of the chimneys, pairs of parasols appeared to somehow be slowly building spiral tubes. Other parasols were bringing nets full of bactoweed up to the forward partner of each pair, and stuffing it into the outward-facing partner's aperture. Still others brought nets full of new bactoweed from over the rise to the south.

"Are they making tubes out of bactoweed?"

"I don't know. Sure looks like it. But how? What are they using to convert it?"

Manda simply shook her head. She and Jim watched, robbed of words by the strange, slow intricacy of the parasols' creation.

At that moment, a signal-packet blasted from *Duo*'s transmitters, and the parasols scattered, shrieking, leaving only the paired creatures, who were quivering and acting distressed.

"That answers that question," Manda said. "Topside, I'm afraid we're going to have to shut down communications altogether. It's too disruptive."

Jim was eyeing her, sourly.

"Do you disagree?" she asked.

"No. I see no other option."

"All right. This will be our last transmission for a while, Topside. *Duo-Trieste* out." She sent this as a signal-packet, then they waited. A brief acknowledgment came from Topside a moment or two later. Manda switched *Duo*'s sonar transceiver off.

Gradually the parasols returned, the water filled once more with their cries, clicks, and calls, as their work on the spiral tubes continued.

Manda shook her head. "I just don't get them, Jim. If alien creatures came to us when we were out doing something, we'd stop what we were doing and go have a look."

Jim nodded thoughtfully. "I'd noticed that in some of your tapes. They seem to take a long time to react to things. It took them days to decide to capture *Octo*."

Manda frowned, considering. "Maybe curiosity isn't selected for with these creatures the way it was for our species."

He mulled it over. "Maybe they don't have to be so curious, because not much changes in this ecosystem—not much threatens them. But . . ." he paused, frowning. "Isn't curiosity necessary for the level of intelligence it takes to design and build a city?"

"Is it?" Manda asked, lifting her shoulders. "I don't know."

"Perhaps they're waiting for us to make the first move," he said. "Or perhaps they're 'blind' to us in some way, till we engage them sonically."

Manda eyed them for a moment longer. Then she covered her mouth. "Oh, my God—I just realized."

"What?"

She pointed at the tubes. "They're biomineralizing!" Jim gave her a confused look. "They're making seashells," she explained. They both knew what seashells were; among *Exodus*'s extensive libraries from Earth were many nature similes. For those who'd grown up on a ship between stars, or on this barren world where life struggled so hard to survive, the behavior of Earth's lush and elaborate biosphere was bizarre and fascinating to behold.

"It's a biological process," she said. "Not an artificial one."

Jim looked back at the creatures and nodded slowly. "I think— I do believe you're right."

"Let's go ahead and make the drop, and then try to make contact."

Manda-waldo maneuvered her-itself over to where *Aculeus Septimus* was trapped in the hardened lava. From above, they could see that the lower segment of the tail rudder was buried in about twenty centimeters of lava.

"That doesn't look so bad," Manda said, after studying it from several angles. "I'm sure I can get it loose. If worse comes to worst I can cut off the bottom section of the rudder."

Jim-*Duo* extracted the package of attachments and tools from where it was strapped to *Duo*'s back and made the drop; the packet floated down to rest next to *Septimus*. Then they-waldo headed over nearer to the parasols.

"It's your show," Manda said. Jim pulled up his commandface. She had faced in with him, in observer mode, and watched now as his liveware's distinctive features—a glaze of controlshapes and defining surfaces—surrounded him.

"Deploying sonar dishes," he said, as *Duo* extended a set of underwater speakers. "I have what I think is a greeting. I'm going to try that first."

He moved, and a *click-click-whistle-click* filled the water around them. After a pause, the message repeated.

The parasols stopped what they were doing after the first transmission. At the second one, all darted over. Manda watched their little, rubbery finger-tentacles rub and squeak across the metaglass. She noticed that the tips of their fingers seemed to have some sort of bumps or growths on them. They grabbed at, bumped against, and tugged on every feature or protuberance of *Duo-Trieste*'s that they could. Their clicking, crying, whistling song rang all around the bubble in a cacophonous chorus.

"That got an effect!" she said. But Jim was frowning.

"Yeah, but . . . they're not really responding. Not as if they recognize us as something other than a monstrosity." He gave Manda a wry grin. "I guess my pronunciation was off."

"Maybe you just propositioned their younger sibling. They look pissed off or something."

Jim laughed, then sobered. "I hope they don't damage the equipment."

Manda gnawed a nail, worrying, as the parasols pulled on different attachments and tugged at the knots and lines lashing the two units together.

They did no real damage, though, and gradually the crowd of parasols thinned till only a few remained. These continued swimming around the submersible, singing and clickety-clacking to each other as they explored the vessel with their tiny fingers and a set of black shiny spots around their annuli. Manda saw that the orifices in their centers contracted tightly and pulsed when they were communicating, and she guessed that that somehow helped them make the sonar noises. The rest had returned to whatever it was they were doing at the chimneys.

Manda looked at Jim, who shrugged.

He tried a different combination of sounds this time, one he said he thought might be a simple declaration to help others with echo-location. This time the four parasols still remaining at the submersible made a series of sharp, loud noises. Some of the others responded. Then they four swam off, toward the city.

"What do you make of it?" Manda asked after a moment of silent regard. Jim was running a series of similes that Manda caught only a glimpse of: colorful patterns shimmered around him and he studied them.

"That seemed purposeful enough, I suppose," he replied. "If frustrating. Hang on." He watched his similes for a while, tweaking things. Finally he shut off the similes with a heavy sigh. "Nothing. I mean, I'm picking up some similar patterns to what

I already had, but it doesn't tell me anything. Well, no one said it would be easy. We'll start with the basics."

A series of ticks started emanating from the speakers: *tick, tick-tick, tick-tick-tick, tick-tick-tick-tick,* and so on, up to seven ticks in succession. Then the speakers paused, then started over with *tick, tick-tick,* and so on. None of the remaining parasols seemed interested.

"What are you doing?" she asked. Jim rubbed at his face.

"We just don't have enough information on their language to begin decoding it. I thought I'd identified a greeting, but it appears I was wrong—or somehow I misapplied it, or something, like you thought. Maybe it means, 'Howdy, Cousin Bob!' or something that would be equally ridiculous in this context." He hesitated. "Those two phrases were my best guesses. I have some other patterns I could repeat, but using them without knowing their meaning isn't really communicating. And after seeing their reaction to the first two phrases, I don't want to try any more wild guesses. We have to come up with a common basis of understanding. So I'm switching over to the old SETI approach."

Manda blinked, confused. "The what?"

He flashed her a smile. "You're not up on your history, girl. S-E-T-I. The Search for Extraterrestrial Intelligence. It was a project run by astrophysicists and other scientists back on Earth, a couple hundred seasons ago. They scoured the skies, looking for interstellar signals that could only have been produced by intelligent beings. The theory was that if another intelligent species was out there, that species would use something universal as a starting place for communication. Physics, mathematics, chemistry. The value of pi, for instance, or a series of prime numbers. Physical constants—physical laws—would all be the same for both species however the alien intelligence might differ from our own, however far away they might be.

"So if our fishy friends out there are intelligent enough to count to seven, they should be able to pick out the simple pattern I'm sending now," he said, gesturing up at his speakers, which were still transmitting their monotonous set of ticks, "and—theoretically—respond."

An hour later they had still gotten no response to Jim's counting routine. The parasols were still busy creating spirals around the bases of the chimneys, and by now Manda and Jim could confirm that the spirals were slowly growing in length. One of the pairs appeared to be turning aside from its chimney, starting a curved tube over toward one of the other pairs. At the rate they were going, it would be months before they got there.

"Are they too stupid to realize what it is we're trying to do," Manda asked, "or do they just not care?"

Jim shrugged. "Maybe there's some kind of rigid social structure, and these guys aren't the Official Talkers-to-Aliens."

They watched for a while longer. Manda couldn't avoid a nagging suspicion that these creatures were just not all that intelligent. Not on the same level as humans. But how could she be sure? How could she prove it, when they didn't even know how the creatures perceived their environment—much less what their communications meant?

"Maybe we should head on into the city," Jim suggested, "and see if we have better luck there."

"At least we could start looking for *Octo*."

Jim-waldo shut off the counting sequence, and Manda-waldo rose in the dark water and headed over the rise. Once well away from the chimneys, they and Topside exchanged a few rounds of signals, to get agreement on the plan. Then they headed toward the city.

Soon they reached the forest of blood-colored bactoweed

Manda had discovered before. The enormously long strands separated from their bases as *Duo-Trieste* brushed against them, and either floated off to reattach themselves to other blade-clusters, or reattached themselves to their own bases. Manda thought she saw small, hard-shelled creatures crawling along their stalks, as the lights played across the weed, but she wasn't sure.

Booms now dominated the sonar landscape. Like a mountain so tall it drags the horizon up around it, the slow, irregular beats drew the world in and pushed it out again. It made the bacto-grasses shift and pushed the swimming creatures to and fro. It was a sound both powerful and—for some reason—calming. Like listening to the world's heartbeat.

Finally they emerged among the tubes and towers on the city's outskirts. Manda pulled up the 3-D map her waldos had made of the huge, labyrinthine structures, and overlaid its gridwork on her own vision. She had already selected their entry point: it was the one into which the creatures had taken *Octo*. The entry was well in toward the edifice's center, so they wove among gaudily-appointed arches and pinnacles, tubes and bridges for some time.

Manda turned off her floodlights, and turned the interior lights off too. She and Jim intertwined fingers, and waited for their eyes to grow accustomed to the dark. Soon they were surrounded by soft colors. The tubular, curving structures were laced with gentle light. Parasols puffed and billowed past, identifiable as seven-spoked, pearlescent strands. Other creatures in different glowing colors and shapes darted before them, and still other phosphorescent blobs moved along the invisible ocean floor, defining its contours.

Manda turned on the imaging software, which enhanced their surroundings with an in-face rendering program that converted sonar to visuals. The shapes around them now appeared in dull grey and silver tones. None of the other creatures seemed to pay much attention to *Duo-Trieste*.

"RoxannaTomas would have a field day down here," Manda remarked, eyeing the glowing sprays, beads, and lines around them and thinking of Jeannelle and Vance, "with all these creatures to catalog."

As they'd agreed, while Manda navigated, Jim used *Duo*'s cameras to capture as many images of the different species as possible. They had decided not to take samples just yet, for fear such an act might not be perceived as friendly by another intelligent race.

"I don't see that many different species, actually," Jim replied after a while, squinting into his commandface. "Less than a dozen, so far, judging from the phosphorescent patterns. Possibly even less, if they go through different life stages. . . ."

"There may be more that don't phosphoresce," Manda pointed out.

"True."

Mostly they just saw the parasol creatures. Manda also spotted one of the hulking mammoths she'd seen before. She focused sonar on the creature: it looked spiky and dangerous, a bit like a seven-pointed, monster starfish, bloated up, with a fleshy central section. Thin membranes stretched between the outer segments of its seven points and a huge, many-toothed opening gaped in its middle. A series of paddled antennae or tentacles were set around its orifice as well as at its seven outer points. It paused, reacting briefly to their sonar's touch—or so it seemed—and Manda and Jim tensed. Then it turned and continued toward a tunnel opening, pulsing its outer tentacles to propel itself.

"Um, let's stay well away from that, shall we?" Jim said.

"I don't think it could actually swallow us; we're too big. But it could take a nasty bite if it wanted."

Manda gave the creature a wide berth. It was puffed up to a great volume, she noted as they passed—until it disgorged a host of parasols at the opening of a tunnel. Then, a good deal slacker about the midsection, it swam away, darting after and scooping up other parasols as it went.

"There it is." Manda pointed at their entrance. The tunnel's dark mouth—just beyond the one the big creature had spat parasols into—gaped at them, its edges strung with pale, glowing, blue-and-green beads. The booming was louder here, and Manda-*Duo* could feel the currents pulse as the booms carried the sound out of the tunnel.

"By the way, what do we do if this tunnel gets too small for us?" Jim asked, as Manda-*Duo* slowed and positioned her-itself to drift into the entrance. Her pulse thudded in her throat; she dabbed at the sweat beaded on her lip. She thought of Teresa and Paul once again, and of Terence, and again prayed that she live through this.

"Let's deal with that question if and when we have to."

They moved inside.

The glow in this enclosed space was enough to faintly light up their faces. Manda looked over at Jim, who sat beside her on his cushion, his interface a soft glaze of lines around him.

"You look good in aquamarine," he told her. She slipped her hand out of her interface and twined her fingers in his, once again thankful she wasn't doing this alone.

They floated amid parasols and smaller creatures through a winding, up-and-down tunnel. They moved along it for some time. It wasn't till Manda scrapped *Duo*'s back against the roof, slightly deforming one of its attachments, that she realized just how much the tunnel had shrunk around them. According to her sonar, it continued to shrink ahead. She couldn't tell by how much.

She-waldo halted. Jim asked, "What now?"

Duo-Trieste was about twenty percent taller than it was wide. And *Duo*'s main propeller had full range of motion; the unit could propel itself sideways if it had to.

We know they got Octo *in here,* she thought. Trouble was, *Octo* was a lot narrower around the midsection than it was long. And with *Trieste, Duo* wasn't.

"Get ready to move backward," she said; "I'm rotating us," and she-waldo tipped her-itself back ninety degrees, so that *Aculeus Duo* was stretched across *Trieste*'s backside rather than its top. All the cabinets that had been on the floor just behind them now stuck off the front, and the equipment that had hung overhead was now behind. Jim helped her step back among the paraphernalia as she-waldo tilted, till they squatted on the hatch. A cabinet door fell open and dumped its contents—several sealed packages of food and drink—all over them. Jim gathered them together and packed them out of the way. Their seating cushions now clung to the front in a diamond pattern, partially blocking their view.

Manda-waldo crept slowly and carefully through the tunnel, scooting and bumping along on her-its back. It took a bit to get the hang of it; she scraped the walls several times. The propulsion torqued them as well as pushing them forward, so Manda-*Duo* had to use her-its correctional jets and push off with the arm attachments against the tunnel roof to keep them from flipping over.

At first they had plenty of room, at this angle, but after a bit *Duo*'s propeller started scraping against the tunnel floor, with little clearance on top. She-waldo halted again, and retracted the propeller so it lay flat against her-*Duo*'s hindmost segment. The submersible could still continue through the tunnel, in this configuration—but retracted, the propeller was useless. And the unit had no other means of propulsion.

Parasols squeezed past them on either side and continued down the dark tunnel. Glowing blue-and-green swirls continued on the walls.

Manda crawled around the craft, looking at things from several angles. *There's got to be a way.* She sensed Jim's tension, and was grateful that he remained silent.

A stiff current pushed them forward—except when the booming pushed them briefly back. But the current by itself wasn't enough to carry them where they need to go. And even if it were, how would they get back out?

"We've got the correctional jets," she mused after a moment. "But they're not in the right position to give us any forward momentum, and even if they were, it would take forever to get anywhere."

We need a push. Could we lasso some parasols?

A look of alarm sprang onto Jim's face. "Trouble's coming."

She turned and saw what he saw: coming up behind him was one of those big seven-pointed-starfish monsters. Teeth first.

It was the starmonster's method of squeezing through the tunnel that gave her the idea. The creature was pushing off against the knobbly walls with its paddle-tentacles, contracting them against its sides and then stretching them forward as it wriggled along.

Duo had twelve arm attachments along its flank. She-waldo extended them down and forward—awkwardly; they didn't all bend in exactly the right places to fit past the submersible—grasped at the bumps in the walls, and pushed and pulled and wiggled—and the submersible began to creep forward, rocking and bumping. But the knobs in the walls were slippery, and she-waldo had trouble coordinating her-its motions.

The eyeless starmonster slowed as it neared them, grating its circular row of teeth and ticking its sonar in apparent confusion over this strange obstacle in its path. From here it looked all mouth.

Manda partially deployed the propeller and started it up, full-force. The sudden wake it created shoved the monster back and slammed the submersible into the tunnel floor, sending Manda and Jim flying. Manda barked her shin on a cabinet corner, and knocked her shoulder and head against the curved metaglass. But the push enabled her-waldo to gain better purchase and co-ordination. She righted herself with Jim's help, and then she-waldo retracted the propeller again and built up speed with her-its arms, shoving her-itself through the tunnel.

They went down an incline and scraped through a bottleneck into a larger chamber. The starmonster darted out behind and— before they could even react—passed them, pulsing and waving its tentacles, stroking away with its paddle-hands.

Manda righted the submersible, shaking with relief. Jim was looking in wonderment all around as she seated herself on the cushions again and readjusted the settings. Then, rubbing her throbbing shoulder and shin, she followed his gaze.

They hovered in a chamber of colored lightnings. All around them, multihued sparks and flashes shot about in a flickering array of patterns. These sparks and flickerings weren't enough to light up the chamber, so Manda turned on all the floodlights. She and Jim gasped.

The chamber was enormous, filled with columnar walls of glistening crystal. Within the crystalline columns were opaque, thinner columns that looked like—in fact, they were! Manda was sure of it—geothermal chimneys. On top of and partly embed-ded in the crystals lay spiralling, opaque, shiny tubes that looked like those they'd seen the parasols making earlier, and other stout, seashell-like tubes wove a pattern through the space be-tween the columns. The chamber was also crisscrossed with thousands of long, clear strands and tubes that carried electric flashes back and forth. The parasols and a few starmonsters moved back and forth among the strands. Bulbous sacs of var-ious sizes hung in clusters from the ceilings and tube mouths.

"What do you make of it?" she asked.

Jim shook his head slowly. He pointed. "Let's have a look at those crystal columns."

Manda-waldo took them slowly and very carefully over, avoiding the interlaced network of strands and tubes, using *Duo*'s mechanical arm attachments to gingerly push them aside when things got tight. The strands were elastic, to Manda's surprise. Like silicone rubber.

She gripped Jim's forearm with a gasp. "Jim, they biomineralize silicon *and* calcium. This is all biological. Like a giant seashell, or a coral reef." But her excitement at the realization soured to dismay as the full implications hit her: no alien intelligence was at work, here. This was no city. Manda had made a huge blunder.

"It's beautiful," Jim whispered. "Like a fairyland." Then he gave Manda a startled look. "Biological? . . . My God, I think you're right." He scrutinized the crystals closely. "Silicon-based crystals, biomineralized? There's nothing like that back on Earth. Is there?"

Jim's musings pulled Manda out of her own unhappy reflections. She shrugged. "I don't know. I don't think so."

"Surely not just silicates, though. Amy's the chemist in my clone, but I'm pretty sure you wouldn't get the elastic strands they're suspended in from a straight silicate/glass structure."

"Well . . . hmmm. Seashells back on Earth are layers of calcium interspersed with protein layers. Perhaps something similar is at work here."

Jim frowned. "Maybe."

"Should we sample it?"

"Not until we know more, I think. If there *are* intelligent creatures about, we don't want to annoy them by messing with their stuff."

Manda said, "I don't think there are intelligent creatures. Or not as intelligent as we'd hoped for. They've extruded this place. Not constructed it. That much I'm sure of."

What was it, this feeling of letdown she had? They'd discovered a truly alien ecosystem, and creatures that—while they might lack that generalized sapience, that finally honed sense of *I* and *other* that humans alone among Earth species seemed to possess—still had a rudimentary language, which suggested a substantial degree of animal intelligence, and perhaps even limited self-awareness.

Why did it matter so much?

And even as she wondered, Manda knew: she wanted a meeting of minds. She sought contact with an alien sensibility. Not simply an oh-that's-interesting study of some intellectually less-complex creature.

She knew her attitude was shortsighted, and resolved to set it aside, if she must. *But the boomspeak has yet to be explained. I'm not quite ready to give up on my hope yet.*

Jim said, "But what are all these power conduits for?" He gestured all around them. "This is a big consumer of energy. It has to have a purpose."

"Let's look around some more," she said. She took them up to the ceiling, a good fifty meters above the chamber's floor, and they approached the sacs. Inside the translucent bags hung some sort of creature. They couldn't make out much detail. Most of the sacs seemed to hold creatures bigger than the largest of the parasols, but a lot smaller than the starmonsters.

Jim grabbed Manda's arm and pointed. "Quick! Over there!" Something was happening at one of the other sacs, all the way across the chamber. Manda-*Duo* trained her-its lights and telescopic cameras on it and fed the sight into their shared link. They both watched as the sac burst open. Hundreds of tiny creatures swam out and darted away. Manda-*Duo* focused in further.

"They're parasols," she said. "Baby parasols."

"Look at the sac," Jim pointed out. "Two adults are in there."

Manda could see that he was right. Two parasols hung in their now-collapsed sac: one still attached to the mouth of the tube, the other now detaching itself from the first. After a moment they started doing something to their sac—eating it, perhaps.

386

Manda and Jim turned back to look again the intact sac near them. Now that Manda knew it had a parasol couple in it, she could see some of their features. "So those ones back at the new chimneys," she said. "They're building something like this, aren't they? Somehow it's tied to their reproduction."

Jim nodded slowly. "The geothermal heat must give them enough energy to reproduce," he said. "They're sexually dimorphic." He gave her a leer, and she laughed.

Manda-waldo guided them away from the pouches and moved through the vast, catacomb-like space, navigating her-its way through the webwork of strands and columns, for a long time. The landscape of this electric-pulsing-crystalline space changed as they went: in several chambers they found starmonsters instead of parasols bound up in pairs inside the sacs. They found others attached to large tubes like the one through which they'd entered the chamber and others not; in yet other chambers they found tiny pouches containing one of the other species they'd seen—a tiny, shelled creature with three eyestalks Manda mentally dubbed *rotoshells*, because of their shells' resemblance to a rotary blade—attached to the mouths of a series of miniscule tubes. Plenty of other chambers held parasol pairs. Some areas were not as well-lit as others, and they couldn't always tell what was going on.

The further in they went, the more oddities they saw. They saw a starmonster attack and kill a different kind of creature— one they hadn't seen before, a large one with long pincers— which had been chewing on the silicon cabling inside a chamber. They also saw starmonsters herding other creatures here and there. Thousands of rotoshells crawled along some of the walls. Manda guessed they might be either building or breaking down walls, or repairing damage or something. But mostly they saw parasols, moving about, carrying objects, doing incomprehensible things in numerous places.

At one point a pair of large, snake-like creatures fell upon a parasol. The parasol released a complex burst of sound and sur-prisingly, a starmonster came to its aid. Among them, they killed and ate the snakes.

"Some kind of symbiosis," Manda said. Jim was pleased. "We've got their distress call now."

They debated how much time to spend recording these activ-ities. Jim felt this trip was a rare opportunity to collect data and that they should take some time to observe the numerous activ-ities they encountered. Manda disagreed.

"Our overriding priority right now is to find *Octo*," she said. The booms rumbled, thunder-like, while they spoke: loud enough that they both had to raise their voices or pause till a boom finished, to be heard.

"I just don't think they're smart enough to break into a com-plex technological system like *Octo*," he countered, "and figure out how to get past all the bars and locks on its antimatter stor-age container. *We* would have a hard time doing it, and we have the specs for it."

Manda pondered this. He did have a point.

"I'll make you a deal," she said. "Let's find *Octo* first. If you're right, and it's just sitting abandoned somewhere, we'll leave it for a bit and do some more exploring before we salvage it. OK?"

"Fair enough," he replied.

They wandered for quite some time before they emerged into a large room Manda instantly dubbed the chamber of bladders. This room belled out like a gigantic horn with multiple tubes leading into its narrower end. At the far end was an enormous, dark wall. On all sides leading up to it, clusters of quivering pinkish bladders bulged out of cul-de-sacs. Rubbery tubes thicker than those in other chambers ran from the bladders to the large wall at the end. That wall had more rubbery strips stretched across it. It flexed with each boom, like the head of a drum.

The booming played all around them, now. The sounds reverberated in Manda's feet and made her breath tremble in her lungs. Each boom pushed the submersible insistently outward, and the unpredictability of the rhythm made it hard for Manda-*Duo-Trieste* to hold her-its station without bumping into the crystalline and pearlescent structures.

She emphatically did *not* want to start smashing into things, after seeing what the starmonsters did to creatures who messed with the furniture.

Long strips of some pliant, clearish substance bloomed in the great room's central section in a series of circles, like long strips of vine. Each vine ended in several smaller vines.

Bound by them, near the room's bottom, was *Octo*. Some of the strips lay across *Octo*'s housing and others intruded into its innards, most of which were exposed. Parts and attachments had been removed from inside the housing and were tangled in various strips. The whole thing moved back and forth as the booms sounded—as did *Duo-Trieste*.

Using *Duo*'s telescopic lenses, they were able to make out strips and vines coiled around the antimatter containment pod. The outermost shell of the containment was already opened. And on a section of the floor beneath *Octo*, on a bank of crystals encircled by the strips, images shone in an array of soft colors: a series of three-dimensional sketches of *Octo* and its many components.

et's—" Jim's voice came out a squawk. He cleared his throat. "Let's not jump to conclusions."

Manda whooped. She pointed at the sketches. "Jim, don't you see? This *is* the alien intelligence. All around us! We're inside it. The parasols, and the starmonsters, and those other little things, they're just the helpers. All these banks of crystals are biomineralized semiconductors. Doped silicon! They're its neurons!"

About this time, Manda noticed an odd shifting of the light patterns. On a hunch she-*Duo* turned off all her-its floodlights— and saw that the chamber had its own lights, less bright than their own. The alien's beams originated in five brightly-glowing, translucent bladders set around the chamber. These were set on stout stalks between the big bladders. The lights appeared fluorescent, rather than incandescent. They had been focused on *Aculeus Octo*, she realized—and were now creeping away from *Octo*'s position, toward them. Manda grabbed Jim's arm with a gasp.

"I think it knows we're here," Jim said.

Manda had a wild urge to laugh. "Good guess."

They watched the beams track across the floor and walls, heading for a convergence on their position.

"Try your counting sequence," Manda said.

"Right." Jim brought up his communications face and fiddled with it. *Duo*'s speakers emitted their pattern: *tick, tick-tick, tick-tick-tick*, and so on. He ran the pattern through about four times, with pauses between.

There was no response.

"Did you notice?" he asked. Manda had noticed one thing: they were both whispering now. But that, she was pretty sure, wasn't what Jim meant.

"Notice what?"

"The booming's stopped."

So it had.

"Jim . . . try slowing your pattern down. Make it deeper and louder. Given its size, I bet it operates on a slower time scale."

"Ah. Yes!" He fiddled some more. The pattern emerged from the speakers again, this time at a much louder and lower pitch, and a good deal slower. He ran it through once and waited. Nothing. He ran through it again, and again, waited. Nothing. He started it again—and then cut it off when the booming started up again. *Boom.* Pause. *Boom, boom.* Pause. *Boom, boom, boom.* Pause. *Boom, boom, boom, boom.*

Jim grabbed Manda and lifted her up with a shout. They both babbled excitedly as the booms continued to mount. By now the oddly colored beams were shining on them. They floated in a pool of soft light.

"It must have some optic capabilities," Manda said. "Or it wouldn't need the lights."

Manda-*Duo* turned her-its own lights back on—not being able to see beyond the spotlights made her uncomfortable. She looked around the walls. Some of the cell banks looked different than the rest: curved, smoother, bigger. They might be optical instead of neural. It occurred to her that *Duo*'s floodlights were almost certainly much too bright for the creature, so she dimmed them to roughly match in intensity the creature's light stalks—and aimed them away from what she thought of as the eye-cells.

She noticed that the creature's counting booms were noticeably faster than the other booms they'd been hearing for so long. And a lot less loud, as well as higher-pitched. It had deduced that it didn't have to use as big a boom for them to hear—and that they operated at a faster pace.

"Manda . . ." Jim interrupted her reverie. "It just finished counting to ten."

"So?"

"So, I used base seven! It's counted our fingers and guessed that we use base ten—"

"Oh, my God." Manda eyed the crystal eye-cells set around the chamber. This was one very smart creature. An incredibly *big* smart creature, with lots and lots of minions. *I sure hope it's friendly.*

"Come on, friend," Jim said, "let's build us a mathematical grammar." He pivoted back and forth, elbows pumping, arms and fingers flying. He-*Duo* and the alien boomer started talking mathematics, defining sounds that signified different mathematical concepts: true, false, addition, subtraction, multiplication, division, equals, and so on. She knew what he was doing; he'd told her about it beforehand. She brought up her own interface to listen in, but some syntellectual function in her faceware was trying to get her attention.

"Emergency: attend. Emergency: attend. Emergency: attend," it was saying.

"All right. All right, already!" replied Manda, irritably. "I'm attending. What's going on?"

The syntellect said, "Listen very carefully. You are in immediate danger."

"What are you talking about?" she demanded. "I didn't program you. Who made you?"

The syntellect replied, "When the colony first made landfall twenty-one earth-standard-years ago, the crèche-born hid an omni field generator inside the satellite DMiTRI—a twin of the one they have aboard *Exodus*. They have had instantaneous access to all of your computer systems ever since. They have cracked all your communications software and have been observing the colonists via omni transmission. They've been monitoring your progress up until a few moments ago, shortly before you entered the alien's exam-chamber. I've got them on a false loop but we only have a few minutes before they figure out what I've done."

It took a moment for the syntellect's words to make sense to Manda. Then she remembered Jim's earlier certainty that she was being cracked—recalled the difficulty she'd had pinpointing the difficulty with *Octo*. Dread settled at the base of her spine.

"Jim!" She grabbed him. "Jim, listen—"

He shook her off, looking exasperated. "Can't you see I—"

Manda gave his arm a shake. "Listen. It's important."

He did, and she replayed the syntellect's message. His eyes grew wide as its words registered.

"The crèche-born already know about the alien intelligence you've found," it was saying now. "We've known about it"—*We?* thought Manda. This being wasn't a syntellect at all; it must be one of the crèche-born!—"since the JebediahMeriwether twins discovered it twelve Earth-standard-years ago. Some of our number killed the JebediahMeriwethers to prevent them from telling the rest of the colony, and have now decided to destroy the alien, if it doesn't destroy itself by exposing your marinewaldo's antimatter core."

"*But why?*" Manda cried. "Why now? How can you do this to an intelligent being that has done you no harm?"

The other said, "We're not all in agreement about—the way things should be handled. Last time around, the extremists managed to kill the JebediahMeriwether brothers before we could stop them, but we managed to keep the—worst elements—away from the alien. Now, I fear we've lost. My people are growing desperate."

Manda eyed Jim. She wished she could read him the way she could read her siblings. She wished they were with her, right now. Derek and Arlene would know what to do. She was numb with terror and couldn't think. Jim put an arm across her shoulders, his expression grim.

"Now listen," the other continued. "It appears to them right now that you are simply doing further explorations of the interior of this structure. But they know you are close to this chamber. If they figure out that you've reached this place and received a warning from me, they will kill you. They can't afford for you to know the truth."

Jim spoke, his voice harsh. "What truth? Who are you?"

"I am a hidden friend of yours among the crèche-born." A hesitation. "My name is Dane. Right now I've hijacked your expert systems and am funneling my message through it."

It fell silent. Manda burst out, "*Why?* Why are you people doing this to us? We've never done you any harm!"

"We desire the colonists to continue Project IceFlame—to accelerate it, in fact. Our antimatter manufacturing plant has been damaged, and we have insufficient fuel and supplies to make another interstellar journey. Our crèche technology will begin to fail us in the next hundred years. Our bodies are completely dependent on technology to survive and we need a habitable world with a manufacturing base to sustain us. Therefore we mean to return to Brimstone.

"Some of us don't want to see the alien creature harmed—nor do we believe that we should impose our will on the colonists, but would reveal our intentions and negotiate with you. You are our children, our responsibility.

"But the most extreme and desperate faction has gained the upper hand. They fear that if the colony learns there is an intelligent species under the ocean, you will change your plans to terraform this world. They are going to destroy the alien in a supposed 'accident' so that the colonists will have no reason not to terraform Brimstone."

"And if we refuse?"

"Then they intend to force you to do their will. They will make you their slaves, or kill you."

Manda stared. "*What?*"

"This is an outrage!" Jim exclaimed. "You have no right!"

"How can you do this?"

"I'm sorry. I've tried to stop them, but—you don't understand all the parameters. It's—complicated."

Manda exchanged a look with Jim. "Is ur-Carli on our side?" she asked. "Or yours?"

"When a schism first began to appear among us, Carli secretly programmed ur-Carli to protect your people against our worst elements, as best it is able. But ur-Carli is highly constrained, and its conflicting priorities render it a dangerous ally. You can only trust it to a limited degree. Be careful.

"Carli has hidden other weapons and information for your use. I don't know where. As far as I know, her cache remains undiscovered by my kind." The other shrugged helplessly. "You'll have to find it for yourselves. If it exists.

"But for now, you must get back to Amaterasu and warn your people that the colony is in danger. You must prepare for an invasion. I'm afraid I can't save the alien, but I've done what I could to help you.

"We're running out of time," the other said abruptly. "You will need to return to this place"— an image appeared in their live-faces of one of the chambers they'd explored before reaching this place —"within five minutes and twenty-seven seconds. Orient yourselves so." A timer, and a rendering of *Duo-Trieste* in the destination chamber, appeared. "I calculate that it will take you three minutes and ten seconds to get there, so there's little time to waste—"

"Whoa, slow down!" Jim said, and Manda added, "You could have warned us before we ever even got here! The alien would never have been put in jeopardy!"

"Well, no, actually, the alien has been making steady progress in defeating your marine-waldo's failsafes. It's only a matter of time before the alien succeeds in blowing itself up, even without our help."

Manda made a disgusted noise. "We were en route for almost a day. You could have hacked in and warned us at any point, and kept us from danger—and maybe even bought yourself time to save the alien. Why didn't you tell us before?"

"I—I didn't," the other said; "I couldn't . . ." There was a pause. "Till I saw you approaching this chamber, I told myself I couldn't interfere. But I . . . I just couldn't live with another set of murders of our children." The voice caught. "I'm taking a big risk, doing this. This is—you don't know what we've been through."

Jim and Manda looked at each other.

"There's no more time for argument," the other said. "I must disengage before I'm detected. You must get to that chamber and be in the orientation I've shown you when the timer goes off. Then you must get as far from this place as you can, as quickly as you can. The alien is not far from breaching the inner barrier to the antimatter container."

The syntellect's signal ended. The clock said they had four minutes left before the protective hack ended and they were monitored again.

Manda stared at Jim. "What do we do?"

Meanwhile, the alien's booming continued. Some part of Manda's mind noted that it had reverted to the counting scheme. What must it make of their sudden silence?

Manda sighed, heavily. *The chance that we can save the alien is minuscule, and trying will probably get us killed. We should save ourselves—get back and warn the others. It's the prudent thing to do.*

But she didn't feel like being prudent. She felt like bashing the crèche-borns' arrogant faces in. Anger—welcome ally!— reared up, dispelling the fear. She had worked hard and long to come to this place, and she didn't intend to leave the alien in the hands of crèche-born psychopaths. Not without a fight.

Besides, she'd brought them back here. The alien wouldn't be threatened if not for her. And the colony wasn't in immediate danger. They knew about the crèche-born threat, if not that they were taking such an aggressive role.

She had to try.

Think, Manda. Think.

"If we're going to get to that chamber in time," Jim said, "we need to leave now—"

Manda glanced at *Aculeus Octo.* Not long before it breached the antimatter container, their secret friend had said. She hoped that with their arrival the alien had suspended its explorations of *Octo*'s antimatter battery. She didn't fancy being vaporized while plotting to save its life.

"Jim—we can't leave here without trying to warn the alien."

He gave her a troubled glance. "But what can we do? The crèche-born have the advantage of us. They killed JebMeri. We don't know what booby traps they may have installed in our equipment. If we even give a hint we know, they'll kill us too."

She reflected back on what her brothers had told her.

"I think I know how they killed JebMeri," she said. "They must have poisoned the submersible's air Recyclers. All they'd have to do was contaminate the tubes with a dormant Template bug. And once they decided JebMeri was a threat, they'd simply tickle the template to start it converting air Recyclers to food Recyclers—and then crack the warning systems so the carbon dioxide alerts wouldn't sound. And why mess with a system that worked? I bet anything you like that—"

"—they used the same trick for us," Jim finished.

"Yup."

"How do we know we can trust our hidden 'friend'? It could have been anyone. For all we know, whoever-it-was lying to us."

Manda shook her head. "Whoever it was, they said some

things that fit in with things I already know. I just learned the other day that ur-Carli has been spying on us for the crèche-born—and I was pretty sure that it was also secretly trying to protect us.

"And remember how you guessed before that someone was cracking me? It wasn't the aliens' sonar that messed *Octo* up. I think the crèche-born hijacked *Aculeus Octo* when it came across this city—or rather, this alien—to keep us from finding it. When I plugged in at a location they didn't anticipate, we got the images *Octo* was sending. Remember?" Jim's eyes narrowed, and he nodded thoughtfully. "Our visitor was telling the truth."

Jim hesitated. "Manda . . . if the colony is truly in danger, shouldn't our first responsibility be to them?"

"They've lived with this danger for years, Jim. They're watching *Exodus*—the council knows the crèche-born are no friends of ours—and they know now too, that we're being spied on." She gripped his shoulders and looked straight into his eyes. "I can't leave without trying to do *something* to keep them from destroying the alien. It would haunt me for the rest of my life."

Jim returned her gaze. Then he sighed. They both watched as the timer ticked down below three minutes.

We're committed, Manda thought. In a way, it was a relief.

"I take your point," he replied. "So, what now?"

Manda thought for a moment. "The only way they can stop us is via the omni. No matter how they do it. Maybe I can shut off their link before they know what's happening. Then we can resume trying to warn the alien. If I disable all my waldos' omni links at once, they'll have no way to stop us."

Jim grimaced. "I don't like it. They've surely embedded all sorts of back doors in your code that you don't know about. How can you hack all your different marine-waldos' systems without them getting suspicious? They'll be watching every move you make. We have to assume they'll have teams on this—you can't fight them all at once. Besides—it will be years before we'll be able to communicate well enough with the alien to let it know what's going on. We don't have that kind of time."

Manda sighed. "Look. We either fight them, or we let them destroy the first sapient alien humanity has ever made contact with, without a fight. If you have a better idea, I'm all for it."

"All right, then. Let's take the direct approach. We can't sneak up on them, so let's not even try. Let's just grab *Octo* and run. You keep them out of our systems while I get us the hell out of here. It's simple, it's quick; if we make haste we can easily outrun the other waldos."

"I should do the piloting. I've logged thousands of hours piloting these marine-waldos and you have no experience with them."

"True, but you can't do both jobs. I've piloted other waldos, and I'm at least reasonably familiar with the commandface. Meanwhile you had a hand in designing *Duo*'s and *Trieste*'s communications code, whereas I haven't got a clue what's where."

"True." Fear clutched at her. She took a deep breath. "So let's do it!"

"Goddamm them." He said it harshly. "Let's do it."

They strapped themselves into lap-harnesses and clipped these to handholds in the floor. The time was ticking down toward the end of the hack loop as Manda called up the communication programfaces for *Trieste* and *Duo*. Meanwhile Jim took over the controls of *Duo*'s commandface. The submersible dipped down toward the center of the chamber, with *Duo*'s mechanical arms preparing to grapple *Octo*. Manda cut all auditory inputs. And then they were live.

"We're online," she said. "They're watching again." Her heart beat like fists against her rib age. She felt as if some part of her sat in a control room in her head, away from the tumult, observing coolly, without feeling. "I cut our audiolink. They can't hear us, but they'll figure out any second now what we're up to."

Jim-*Duo* was taking them down toward the captive marine-waldo with his-*Duo*'s two forward grappling arms, extended while Manda brought up the I/O systems. *Duo*'s and *Trieste*'s both sprang up: two large, transparent globes with white letters etched into panels on their fronts. Contained in *Duo*'s I/O commandglobe were four gleaming balls in blood-orange, pale yellow, blue-green, and silver: radio, sonar, laser, and omni, their faces stamped with summary info. From the large globe—the I/O commandball—a rope of sparking threads coiled upward, umbilical-like, to the main system level, whose datashapes and icons had shrunk and moved up above Manda's head.

They lurched as Jim-*Duo* grabbed *Octo* by its extensions and tried to tug it out of the vines' grasp.

Manda reached through the transparent commandglobe's boundary—which gave like rubber and then sprang back, sealing itself around her wrist—and grabbed the silver omnilink-ball. She wadded it up and flicked it toward the virtual trash can in the corner of her vision.

That should have disabled the omnilink altogether. It didn't; instead, the silver ball promptly reappeared. Simultaneously, the first strike came.

"The controls are dead!" Jim shouted, as *Duo*'s arms released *Octo*. The submersible veered and caromed toward the far wall. "They have us!"

"*Shit.*" Manda barely had time to flinch before the submersible smashed into a bank of crystals. Her head and upper torso whipped forward and back. She and Jim clung to their handholds. Debris scattered outward around the submersible in a spray of twinkling shards as they bounced away from the crushed crystals of the wall.

Duo's nose had left a puncture; *Trieste*'s belly a wide, shallow indentation. Trickles of smoky fluid bled from the site. A wound. Manda hoped the alien could heal itself. She caught a glimpse of rotoshells crawling from various crevices that scurried toward the damaged area.

I wasn't fast enough. Goddammit.

Hold it together, Manda. Hold it together. Swiftly, hands trembling, she grabbed the silver omnilink-ball with both hands and tried to rotate it; at its base was a dodecagonal panel that should have detached itself when she touched it and become a discrete dodecahedron: the program that ran omni communications. Instead, the linkball slipped out of her grasp and returned to its original position.

She glowered at the icons spinning before her. *They can lock me out of the program, but they can't lock me out of the data flow it generates.* She opened the linkball itself. Its sides peeled down. Raw data—the enemy's commands to *Duo* and *Duo*'s responses— fountained between the concave base of the opened ball and the top of the clear I/O globe, in a shower of spidery data strands that streamed past far too quickly for her to process.

Manda began plucking bits from the stream, flicking them over her shoulder toward the trash, and the stream pinged and twanged in complaint. The datastream's touch stung as though her livesuit had sprouted needles: the feed had been programmed to use pain to repel interference. That wasn't supposed to be possible, that a livesuit could actually hurt you.

Duo-Trieste listed as Manda yanked data out of the stream and began flailing, jerking back and forth, spasming between Jim's laser-link control and the omni control of their unseen, distant enemy. Stray glowing numbers and symbols swirled around Manda's head. She whisked them impatiently away. The submersible's jerking around made it hard for her to keep her grip on the datastream.

"Trouble," Jim said. "Antibodies."

Her glance followed his gesture. Three starmonsters surged into the chamber from different entrances. The massive creatures came at them with mouths wide and spiky tentacles fully extended.

Time for desperate measures. "Be ready for full control."

She plunged both hands into the omni datastream. Pain spread up her arms. She ground her teeth—growling, eyes tearing—grabbed hands full of data—yanked hard. The stream begin to shred and give way in her hands. The harder she pulled the more it hurt. It took all she had to keep her grip.

Jim-*Duo* sent them catapulting drunkenly away from the attacking monsters—barely in time to avoid their grasping, whipping tentacles—across and down toward *Octo*. The starmonsters followed. When the submersible fell in range of the alien's vinelike appendages, the vines whipped up and ensnared *Duo-Trieste* like a spiderweb catching a fly.

Well, we're not going anywhere now, no matter who's in control. Manda released the datastream and withdrew her hands, and hunched over her throbbing arms and hands. The pain slowly faded.

With a thankful sigh, she wiped at her eyes and nose. Then she bunched up the sleeves, peeled back the gloves, and surveyed her hands and arms. The skin of her hands and forearms was mottled—red, and raw, smeared with dabs of blood.

The injury wasn't serious, but it troubled her, that a livesuit could be used to harm. She shook her head ruefully. Jim glanced over and his eyes went wide. "Holy shit."

"Nasty, eh?" Manda smoothed the livesuit back down and glanced back at *Duo*'s I/O display. The omni datastream was intact again: the crèche-born once more had charge of *Duo*.

She needed to attack the problem at its source, either by destroying the hardware that transmitted the omni signal, or by wiping out the commands in the rest of her software that assigned priority to the omnilink.

If only she could get at *Duo*'s hardware. It was only centimeters away—but it was on the outside of the bubble. And she couldn't use *Duo*'s attachments to get at it either; the crèche-born controlled the marine-waldo now. But all *Duo*'s command software was housed in *Trieste*'s systems, which she had full access to.

At a sharp, slap-moan-clicking signal from the bladders clustered at the edges of the dark wall, the starmonsters had stopped where they were, and now floated about a meter or so beyond the walls of the submersible: teeth and spikes still extended, quivering with what looked like—what must be—suppressed aggression. Meanwhile, *Aculeus Duo*, at the bidding of their unseen crèche-born enemy, thrashed, strained, and tugged to pull free of the vines.

Jim said, "If the submersible does more damage, our alien friend is going to lose patience and loose its monsters on us."

"I know. Give me a minute."

Fear-sweat trickled down her torso across the mesh of her livesuit as Manda ripped open the programball that held the coding for *Duo*'s motor controls. She scanned the program index.

Manda herself had patched the original coding together, with numerous modifications, from some standard program modules, but that had been years ago. ByronDalia had just updated the software; this time around she didn't know the code. And even if she did, she didn't have the crèche-borns' many decades of experience. To her, program code was something she pieced together—often from preexisting modules—when she needed something done. It was a means to an end. To the crèche-born, she'd been told, it was life—language—being. They bathed in the stuff. Slept in it. Ate it for breakfast.

But she had designed her programs' basic structures—its overall architecture—and knew precisely what all the modules were supposed to do. And she'd done enough jury-rigging and debugging over the years to know how to track down the communications protocols.

The submersible was still lurching back and forth. Beyond her liveface, Jim swore. She didn't like seeing him look so scared. "The starmonsters are coming at us again. Hurry, Manda."

She found something: a useful little program floating almost hidden among the larger programballs that she'd written long ago. It temporarily disabled a waldo's I/O bus. It was programmed to put the affected unit to sleep for an hour. She'd used it to take her waldos' systems offline and run a series of tests of her software, back when she had first designed the marine-waldos' commandface. It had been such a useful, clever little hack that she'd hung onto it.

"Got an idea," she grunted. "Hold tight."

The submersible lurched once more—she caught a glimpse of attacking starmonster flesh. Tuning out the distraction of the attack, and of Jim struggling beside her to regain control of his own commandface, Manda pulled the program out of the cache. She turned the small red globe over in her hands, studying its summary information. The bus disabler should work. The crèche-born appeared to merely be overriding the standard communications protocols. She couldn't think of any way they could force a disabled I/O bus to work from a remote location.

Theoretically.

"Jim, *Duo* is about to go down. Get ready."

"Ready."

Manda lobbed the dodecahedral icon for the disabler into the I/O commandglobe, which she'd left open. Abruptly *Duo*'s array of icons vanished in a silent blaze, as did the little icon at the periphery of her vision that told her *Duo*'s commandface was active. A little chronometer appeared in its place, which started counting down from 00:60:00.

She sat back with a sigh and rubbed at her cheeks, eyes, and brow, trying to dispel the tension there. The sour scent of her own fear, and Jim's, filled her nostrils. Overhead, *Duo*'s propeller had sputtered and died, and its mechanical arms—which had been slashing at the vines that held them—now froze in place. "They're locked out of *Duo*," she said. "For the moment. But so are we."

Jim eyed the starmonsters, which had ceased their attack at some instruction from the alien when Duo had stopped flailing, and then looked around the chamber. "We don't have much time. They'll send the other waldos. And I think we've pissed the alien off."

Manda looked around too, and saw what he meant: beyond the net of vines that held them (some of which were now moving slowly across all their surfaces—and, she noted with mild alarm, fingering the catches to *Duo*'s housing and *Trieste*'s hatchway), a small army of starmonsters had gathered. The chamber was filled with a chorus of alien moans, whistles, and clicks. Manda began to think that if the crèche-born didn't kill them, the alien would.

"At least the other marine-waldos won't be able to get at us easily."

"Not with this lot in the way," Jim agreed. "But we've got to find a way to communicate with the alien. Or we'll never get out of here."

"OK. You deal with that; I'll worry about shutting the crèche-born out."

She needed to clean up the link protocol files: find all the crèche-borns' back doors and eliminate them, before *Duo* came back online.

But first things first. *Trieste* too, had an omni I/O port the crèche-born could hijack—and probably already had. She turned to *Trieste*'s I/O commandglobe, which had three linkballs inside: orange for radio, yellow for sonar, and silver for omni.

"Jim, get ready. *Trieste* is going to sleep."

"Just a second. I want to download the latest copy of my language programs into my own liveware." His hands did a dance, then he sat back. "Do it."

She dropped the disabler dodecahedron into *Trieste*'s I/O commandsphere, and *Trieste*'s control icons vanished from Manda's liveface, which reconfigured itself to offline mode. A second chronometer appeared below the *Duo* reactivation clock, and started counting down from sixty minutes for *Trieste*.

Jim unbuckled. "I'll get us hardwired to *Trieste*'s systems."

"I'll check the Recyclers." Manda unbuckled too, and grabbed a flashlight from the supply locker on her way over to the equipment. She climbed up and through and, squatting on top of a shelf, reached down through a crevice to slide open the door of the cabinet containing the Recyclers.

The cabinet was vented. Inside were four transparent cylinders linked by clear tubes, in a weighted gimbal that kept them all upright irrespective of the submersible's orientation. Air entered at the bottom of the first, bubbled up through each in succession, and exited through an opening at the top of the fourth. The cylinders each had a CO_2 readout gauge at their inlets and outlets, and each was about three-quarters full of a roiling liquid. Though not a lot of liquid was being exchanged, the containers were not isolated from each other. She had to assume they'd sabotaged the smart systems, so all it would take was a single bad molecule passing from one to the next.

Manda studied the CO_2 readouts. She couldn't tell much, though: in all four canisters the air Recyclers were still eating CO_2, spitting out tiny carbon pellets into their traps and emitting air with less CO_2 out their tops. Without a detailed analysis over several minutes, she wouldn't know whether or not they were contaminated. They didn't have time for that. Still, she set up her liveface to record their data.

Then she did a quick color check. In the first, third, and fourth cans, the liquid's color was a rosy pink. In the second—Manda wasn't absolutely certain, and flicked the light back and forth several times to try to tell—but it seemed to her the liquid's color was a shade off. A tad deeper, more red.

She wondered if she was imagining things. It might be a trick of the light, caused by the shadows that fell across it from the cylinders in front.

I have to assume not. I have to assume the crèche-born have poisoned the Recyclers and disabled the monitoring system.

She reached around and shut off the airflow valves at the cabinet entrance. The liquid in each cylinder settled down to about half full. Then she sealed off all the valves at the cylinders' tops and bottoms. The tubes connecting the cans were filled with little ruby-pink droplets of Recycler liquid.

Jim was rummaging around in the supply cabinet below. The space was too small for both of them to access supplies.

"Jim, could you please get me some supplies while you're in there? Once you've got your stuff."

"Sure. What do you need?"

"At least two meters of one-centimeter plastic tubing, and a knife. And an airtight storage bag too. And, um, some needle-nose pliers and ten or twelve choke-ties. Let's see—I'll also want some tubing tees, a can of lightweight lubricating oil, if we have any. Alcohol, if we don't have oil. And a catch basin of some kind. An empty meal container would do."

From below, he craned through the cracks to see. "What is it?"

"I *think* they've poisoned one of the Recycler cans. But I've caught it early—there's a good chance that the contamination hasn't spread to all four yet. Right now the units are all hooked up in series. I'm going to remove the contaminated one and isolate the rest by hooking them up in parallel."

He straightened, frowning. "I thought that wasn't as effective a combination."

"It's not. But it's the only way to keep the contamination from spreading to all the cans, if it hasn't already."

Jim laid the supplies beside her on the shelf. By this time the second canister's liquid was visibly different from the rest.

She eyed the arrangement of tubing, canisters, and the gimbal posts. *Not much elbow room,* she thought, worried. She didn't want to risk spreading the contamination. All it would take to ruin a whole canister would be a single bad molecule, smeared on the new tubes she intended to cut.

"Do we have any surgical gloves, or disposable bags, or anything?" she asked.

"Nope," he said.

Manda bit her lip. "I'll just have to be extra careful."

She called up her local reference library on a heads-up panel, and searched for quick tips on containing and cleaning up contamination. The only thing useful she found was a suggestion to start with the least contaminated area and work her way in to the more heavily contaminated areas, to avoid spreading toxins to previously clean spots.

The absolute cleanest, obviously, was the new materials. She stripped off her livegloves and then cut new tubing from the roll Jim had given her, and attached three new tubing *T*'s in a row with three short pieces of tube. Then she attached four long strands to the open ends of each *T*. This serially-branching manifold she swapped for the existing connections: first the fourth cylinder entry tube, then the first, then the third, and finally, with shaking fingers, the second. As the rosy droplets ran down her fingers from the last and most contaminated tube, she had to remind herself that even if there were food Recyclers in this liquid, as long as she washed her hands in the next minute or two she would suffer no damage other than mild irritation. Thoughts of Paul intruded—Paul sinking into a vat full of the stuff, turning slowly from man to *mana*.

She bagged up the old tubing and tossed it on the floor, made sure all the existing connections were sound and that the tube tops were properly vented and the carbon collectors in good shape, and then turned on the airflow. Then she climbed back down, and as quickly as she could, poured the oil into the empty food bowl. It wasn't livevat oil, but it would do. She cleaned first her hands, then the equipment—twice with oil and twice with soap and water.

When she checked the air Recyclers again, number two had gone dark red and number three's color seemed to be going off. She shut off number two—it was useless now—but left three on. It couldn't contaminate the other cylinders, now; might as well let it do as much work as it could before it died. Then she slipped her livegloves back on and set an alarm on her commandface, to remind her to manually check the other Recyclers every five minutes.

"Number two Recycler is down," she said, "And I think three is contaminated as well. Maybe one and four will be OK."

Two Recyclers could handle the carbon dioxide load for two people indefinitely. One couldn't.

"OK. This should do it." Jim dragged cords over and plugged one into an empty port on her yoke. As he did so, *Trieste's* command icons flowered open around her, in the same configuration she'd left them in when she'd shut down all remote communications. From the top-level commandshapes she drew out and brought up the series of globes, dodecahedrons, pentahedrons, and other shapes that represented *Trieste's* various operating systems, and called forth a search-elf.

"This will take a while," she told Jim.

"Can I be of any help?"

"Not really."

"Then I'm going to see if I can come up with some way to communicate with our alien," Jim replied. "Let it know we're in trouble."

"Um, while you're at it, tell our friend to leave the hatch alone, would you?"

Jim glanced up at the tentacles that had entwined themselves in *Trieste*'s hatch. Unless the vines were much stronger than they looked, that hatch door wouldn't be opening, not with several kilometers' worth of water pressure on it. Still, one never knew.

They got to work.

Finding the crèche-born bugs in *Duo*'s and *Trieste*'s systems was not so difficult, it turned out. It was removing them that got tricky.

First, using the search-elf, she scanned every program file *Trieste* and *Duo* used and found seventeen different instances where the omni link was given permission to hijack the connection from other communication links. She stripped each hijack command out and patched up what remained, but didn't have time to run even hastily thrown-together similes to make sure everything functioned properly.

This was a big risk. The danger was not so much that the crèche-born would be able to take advantage of holes she'd left in the code. Rather, pointers from other areas might now be directing the process flow toward code that Manda had deleted. *Trieste*'s systems were governed by smartware, which could supposedly correct for the worst of these problems. But she'd had system crashes often enough just during normal operations that she didn't entirely trust it.

The other thing that scared her, as the minutes ticked down toward *Duo*'s reboot, was that she *knew* her programming skills were no match for the crèche-borns'. It was entirely possible they had installed other back doors using techniques she was unfamiliar with. All it took was one missed line of code, out of billions, and they'd be screwed.

But she'd done what she could. There was no point in brooding about it.

Manda climbed up into the equipment that hung like stalactites from the ceiling, and checked the Recyclers. Canister three was dead now: a dark, blood red. So was canister four. With a sick feeling in her stomach, she shut both of them down. All they had left to give them air was canister one.

Bart had told her that one canister would support one person indefinitely. How long would it support two people?

She searched her own files, and then Trieste's, and found the air Recycler process data. She did the calculation, factoring in the reservoir of air and the backup compressed air bottles they had. Then she rechecked her numbers, praying she'd made a mistake. She hadn't. They had maybe eighteen hours.

No way we can get back to the drill hole in time.

Manda climbed back down. She checked the clocks: they had just over fourteen minutes for *Duo's* remote I/O bus to reboot; almost sixteen for *Trieste's*. In front, Jim uncoiled cables, working fast, talking to himself as he got a hardwire link set up. Manda pondered whether to interrupt his work to tell him about their air-supply problem, and finally decided not to: if they managed to escape the crèche-born, there would be time enough then to look for alternatives. The omnilinks would go live again soon, and he needed all that time to establish contact with the alien.

She rubbed at her face. *One disaster at a time, Manda. One disaster at a time.*

She shuffled her liveshapes around and then disengaged and moved toward the back to do a few quick stretches, drink some water, and fix herself some *mana* and dried fruit. Her wits were dulled by all that had happened, and by the continuous threat of attack.

She squatted among the equipment to eat her snack. She wanted desperately to talk to Jim. Right now he was only a meter and a half away—so close she could reach him in a single step; she could even feel the air currents of his movements—but mentally he was far away: preoccupied with his own work.

"Can I help?" she asked.

"What?—oh—no; I'm almost done here. Thanks."

Manda found her mind wandering as she cleaned and put things away—perhaps retreating from the sustained terror of their situation. She did notice that the alien's finger-vines had released them. *Duo-Trieste* had settled to the floor of the chamber near *Octo*. On the black wall panels beside them, a rough sketch in flecks of color was slowly taking shape near the sketches of *Octo*. The alien was making a sketch of *Duo-Trieste*, with oddly formed caricatures of themselves inside.

She shuddered, awed. She looked up and around at the big, bell-like chamber, and wondered what thoughts were flowing through that vast mind. What it thought of them. How it perceived its surroundings. How it spent its time. Its mind must be so very different than a human's.

She'd recently found in the *Exodus* archives a copy of Erasmus's formative book on the origin of consciousness, *THE VARIABLE I*. The book had confirmed her sense that self-awareness *felt* like looking in a mirror. There was a recursive feel to consciousness: that dizzying sense of looking at oneself from the outside-in and the inside-out at the same time. She wondered if the alien's sense of self was the same, or if it had come about in a different way than humans'—a path that made its self-awareness very different from our own.

What sort of mirror would an alien sensibility hold up to the human mind? What might we learn about ourselves? What light might be cast into hidden corners of our minds and hearts? She ached to know, with an intensity that surprised her.

Is it our differences that make us more whole, more human? Was that why the colony, with its tiny, stagnant pockets of exactly-like beings, who avoided intimacy outside their own clones, felt so incomplete, so unformed? Amaterasu, it seemed to Manda, was in some ways like a child that had refused to grow up. Afraid and cold and alone in the dark. A group of people each huddling with their mirror-selves, threatened by anyone too different—sure that monsters lurked in the shadows. If so, the alien with its vast differences from humans might—somehow—be the colony's salvation. A meeting of minds could turn on the light, chase away the monsters. That process had already started. The mirror the alien would hold up to the colonists, simply by being who and what it was—the promise of new knowledge, new understanding it held out—these were a treasure beyond price.

The alien must live. No other outcome was conceivable.

Which reminded her of something Jim had said just before they'd left on this journey: that another alien lived on the opposite side of the world. A counterpart to this one.

Companion? Rival? Unrequited lover? Humans surely didn't even *have* a word to describe their relationship.

She wondered what it must be like to live truly alone in the cold dark, with one's only contact an unseen other, tens of thousands of kilometers away. She imagined the kind of intelligence that must pound on the crust of the world, releasing a slow trickle of speech, and then strain, patiently listening for a thread of sound that told it the other was still there. She tried to imagine what it would be like to spend an eternity waiting and listening in the dark.

And then shuddered again—this time in shock. If his liveface had been active, the crèche-born would have been listening when Jim told her about the other one. Which meant it would be in danger too.

One disaster at a time, she thought once more, but she felt queasy.

She handed Jim his food and drink. He thanked her, and took a deep draught of water and a bite to eat while she looked over the set-up he'd jury-rigged.

He'd strung equipment and cabling across the floor around the cushions, and had mounted a big speaker up against the

414

metaglass on his side, which would transmit sound through the submersible wall into the water. He'd also set up a projector on the cushions to cast images on the metaglass in front of them. He moved invisible controls around, then paused to take quick bites of food while the speaker transmitted sound and the projected images shifted. After a few seconds, the alien responded.

"How's it going?"

"Making progress," he replied. "You?"

She shrugged. "I've done everything I can. We'll see. What are you telling it?"

"I've abandoned the mathematical approach. Since it has sight and hearing, I'm trying to use images and sonar together to deliver some basic information. Like, we're friendly and the other marine-waldos aren't.

"We'd already agreed—I think—on terms for *True, False,* and *I don't understand.* So it can confirm whether it gets what I'm trying to tell it or not."

He gestured at the projection on the curved front of the submersible, which showed a crude sketch of a starmonster and a parasol side-by-side with parallel vertical bars between them:

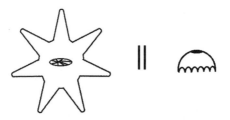

Meanwhile three discrete bursts of sound came from the speakers, and Jim played a video of the starmonsters transporting the parasols beneath it.

"I'm using sketches and short clips with some made-up sonar sounds," he told Manda, while the sequence played out. "We've agreed on visual and sonic symbols for us, the alien, the parasols, the starmonsters, the eels, and your marine-waldos. At least, I'm pretty sure we have. Now I'm trying to define relationships between them."

He pointed at the projection—a reverse of what the alien saw from the other side. It had the starmonsters on the right, the parallel bars in the middle, and parasols on the left. "Right now both the sonar and the picture are trying to say that the starmonsters and parasols are friends," he said. "I'm assuming it has the capacity to understand grammar in the same way that we do. May be a false assumption, but—" He shrugged.

The alien didn't respond right away. After a minute a *click-click-whistle* issued from the bladders. "That means *I don't understand*. So I'll try again with a different 'sentence.'"

The image and sound from Jim's speakers changed again. "The little shells and the alien are friends," he said. The pictograms showed a rotoshell and the alien, with two parallel vertical bars between them:

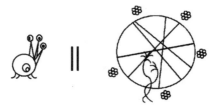

Meanwhile, three bursts of sound played, and a video showed the tiny shells repairing a damaged area on the alien's wall. This time no response came from the alien.

"That's interesting," said Manda. "Maybe it's starting to get it."

Jim's eyes glinted and he sat forward, moving hands, feet, and arms. "Maybe. Now I'm declaring us as friends of the alien." The pictogram looked like this:

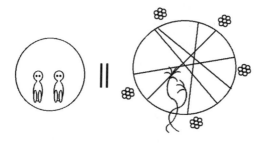

—as three sounds played.

They waited. A bit later, the alien repeated the sounds Jim's speakers had made, added numerous others, and added a coda: *rising moan-whistling shriek.*

Jim sat bolt upright, gripping Manda's arm so hard she winced. "It understands! . . . Or so it says." He scanned data Manda couldn't see. "Yes. Yes, it repeated back all the 'friend' sequences, and confirms that they're true. Good!"

He fiddled with his controls some more. "Now let's broaden the concept."

The screen changed to include an eel, teeth, and a parasol:

—as a new series of sounds left the speakers.

"I'm declaring that the parasols and eels are enemies. And see how I show our video of the eels attacking the parasols," he said. "I know I'm rushing things. But we're running short on time."

They waited. *Click-click-whistle,* the alien replied.

Manda raised an eyebrow at Jim, who was scowling. "No? All

right, try this one. The starmonsters and eels are enemies." First Jim displayed the symbolic meanings, and below them the clip of a starmonsters devouring an eel:

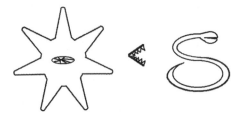

No response came from the alien.

Jim shrugged at Manda.

"We have no choice—I'm going to have to push it. Now I'm saying the other marine-waldos and we are enemies. I only have the symbolic sounds and pictograms for that."

The projection showed this:

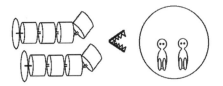

A long pause, as the sounds and pictograms played, played again, played a third time. Manda and Jim looked at each other.

Click-click-whistle came from the alien's bladders.

Jim slumped, discouraged. "Dammit." Manda laid a hand on his arm.

"Jim, I don't think it's used to getting so much information so quickly, the way we are. Its nervous system is huge. It must be used to only very basic communications with the parasols and starmonsters, and a very slow—albeit complex—conversation with its counterpart on the other side of the world. It may just need more time to process what we're saying. We must seem to it like sentient mice jabbering away at a zillion kilometers an hour. We're probably giving it a terrible migraine."

"I know. I know." Jim pushed hair away from his face, frustrated. "There are so many unknowns! I don't know how its brain works. It obviously uses language, but . . . it may construct meaning from symbols in a totally different way than we do. A way that makes what I'm doing seem like gibberish. I don't know what else to try. Damn it, I need more *time!*"

"Which is exactly what we don't have." Manda glanced at her chronometers. "Look. We have less than a minute before *Duo* comes back up. This communication business just isn't going fast enough. When *Duo* comes back on we're going to try the grab-*Octo*-and-run scenario again. OK?"

Jim sighed. "You're right. So, what? We'll do it like before? You're on intrusions while I pilot?"

"Right." Then Manda gripped his arm. Her heart rate leapt. "I hear their engines." The other marine-waldos were coming.

Thirty seconds to reboot. Twenty. They buckled in. Ten.

"There they are!" Jim pointed. Five seconds.

Lights shifted, then blazed into the chamber as beyond the fleet of starmonsters still keeping watch, two marine-waldos entered and came at *Duo-Trieste* with their attachments ready to grapple and attack.

And Manda's liveface bloomed with *Duo's* control- and commandshapes. "Go!" she shouted. Jim-*Duo* was already moving.

She navigated through the system, commandballs and other shapes tumbling past her, alert for signs of intrusion. Miraculously, there were none. She began to believe maybe she'd succeeded in shutting them out, after all.

Meanwhile Jim had grappled *Octo*—the alien vine-hands had released it during their communications—and lifted it up. He-*Duo* was trying to dodge past the starmonsters toward an exit.

The two other marine-waldos were moving to block *Duo-Trieste*. Manda saw from their call letters that they were *Aculei Quinque* and *Unus*. Rage filled her at seeing her units, her waldo-selves, under the power of their enemies.

Jim-*Duo* had a severe disadvantage, burdened not only with the bubble submersible but a partially disassembled *Aculeus Octo*, which was littering the chamber's water with parts as they climbed upward amid churning teeth and tentacles. The creatures did not try to stop them, apparently awaiting instructions from the alien. But already the other marine-waldos had almost reached them.

Trieste's remote links came back up. As Manda had done with *Duo* a moment earlier, she swam up and down through *Trieste's* many levels, looking for intrusion. And she got lucky: even as she touched a small utility function, the dataflow spouting from its interior shifted in tone and color. Which it shouldn't do. Unless someone was in the act of changing the program that generated the stream.

Intrusion!

She tore open the programball beneath the datastream. It was unlocked; seconds later it would not have been. She displayed the code, which was mutating in real-time as the crèche-born were altering it, turning the utility into a vehicle for infesting the rest of *Trieste's* systems.

But she'd caught them very early. And it was easier to destroy code than to write it, no matter how obscenely fast and clever a hacker was.

She searched, found the call she'd missed earlier that gave them access to this utility, and tore it out. Then she sat back and watched as the dataflow streaming from the opened sphere above the program shifted back to its original color and tone.

Manda slumped, released the breath she'd been holding. The intruder was gone.

Meanwhile, Jim-*Duo* was lurching back and forth, trying to

dodge *Quinque* and *Unus*. *Quinque* had surged through the star-monster blockade and now whipped grappling cables around *Duo-Trieste*'s lashings and reeled *Trieste* in, climbing onto it like a predator mounting prey. As she finished her check of the system, Manda saw *Quinque*'s drill-saw attachment come at them. The drill-saw bounced off the metaglass surface. At the same time *Unus* came up behind them and attacked *Duo*'s propeller housing with drill-saw and grapplers.

Manda heard the alien blast a command, and suddenly they were all buried in a mass of starmonster flesh. Maws opened; teeth gnashed; spiked tentacles whipped about, squealing and scrapping across the bubble's curves. The mass of struggling marine-waldos, submersible, and starmonsters lurched and listed sharply sideways.

The starmonsters were trying to pry the other marine-waldos off them! The alien had commanded its fleet to save them.

But the waldos were very strong, impervious to pain, and *Quinque*'s drill-saw had already begun carving tiny scratches in *Trieste*'s outer surface. Metaglass was very hard, but the surface had to be near-perfect to resist four kilometers' worth of water pressure. It wouldn't be long before the scratches became grooves. Then implosion, and the deluge. Manda shared a terrified look with Jim. "Shit."

"I'm on it." Jim-*Duo* released one grappler cable's hold on *Octo*—which dangled now precariously from three of *Duo*'s arms—and used it to reach back and grab *Quinque*'s drill-saw arm.

A series of hard yanks bent the other waldo's arm enough that *Quinque* couldn't reach *Trieste* without letting go and turning on its side. Which *Quinque* tried to do—and was yanked away by a starmonster. The renegade waldo sank under a mass of star-monster flesh.

Meanwhile, the screeing sound of *Unus*'s attack became a growl, as *Duo*'s propeller broke off and floated free. *Unus*'s grip on *Duo* slipped when the propeller came free, and it too was yanked away by starmonsters.

Duo-Trieste settled to the floor. They could only watch helplessly as the battle between the starmonsters and the two marine-waldos raged overhead. Soon the chamber's currents were stained with purple fluid from the starmonsters' injuries. The starmonsters far outnumbered the marine-waldos, but the machines seemed unstoppable. More and more starmonsters drifted away, gouged and mauled, while the two waldos showed little damage so far.

It was only a matter of time before they broke free and attacked *Duo-Trieste* again. Manda gripped her cushions, rocking back and forth in frustration. "It's a massacre! We can't help them!"

Jim laid a hand on her arm. "Easy. We need to stay clearheaded. Is there any way to hack into their systems?"

Manda drew a calming breath. "Right." She thought it over, and slapped her forehead. "Idiot! Of course!" Jim gave her a querying look. "There may be something . . . hang on."

She pulled up her disabler program, the one she'd used to disconnect their omnilink earlier. Everything hinged on two things.

First, had the crèche-born bothered to turn off *Quinque*'s and *Unus*'s sonar links? Manda was willing to bet they hadn't. Before they'd reached the alien, the crèche-born wouldn't have wanted Manda to realize they had the means to take over her marine-waldos, and would have left the sonar links on so that they would appear normal. Afterward, they had been preoccupied with breaking into *Duo-Trieste*'s systems, and she doubted they'd had time to think about it.

Second, could she get a sonar signal through the barrage of grunts, whistles, clicks, and groans coming from the starmonsters and the alien? She thought perhaps she could—the parasols communicated in similar ranges as her sonar interface with her waldos but the starmonsters' communications were pitched a good deal deeper. And in this small chamber, the source and receiver were much closer together than they'd been when she was communicating from Amaterasu.

She made a minor modification to the disabler program so that it would self-execute once the other waldos downloaded it—briefly explaining her plan to Jim as she did so. Then she shut down *Duo's* sonar-link and broadcast the program.

The disabler was a small program, but sonar was slow. It took over a minute for the program to be transmitted. Manda prayed the crèche-born pilots would be too busy fighting starmonsters and too confused by the other sounds filling the chamber to notice what she was doing. She and Jim clung to each others' hands and waited.

Seconds after the deep warbling and moans ceased issuing from *Duo's* speakers, *Unus* and *Quinque* went still and sank to the chamber floor.

After a disbelieving pause, Manda and Jim whooped and hugged each other. The starmonsters carried their injured and dead away; four of them lugged the renegade waldos over to the forest of vine-hands, which bound them tightly to the floor.

After a few minutes, the alien issued another command. Three starmonsters descended to lift *Duo-Trieste* up, still clinging precariously to *Octo*, and carry them over to the eyecells. The light-stalks shone into the submersible's interior, and Manda and Jim looked into the globes of the alien's many optic sensors. From this close, the field of eyes looked like thousands of tiny pearls, or a cache of gleaming fish eggs.

"Thank you," Jim told the eye field.

Manda wrapped her arm around Jim's waist. They were both drenched in sweat and smelled like hell, and she fancied that the air was already going sour. All her muscles had turned to putty; she was shaking and could barely stand.

They weren't out of trouble yet. But they were a lot better off than they'd been a few minutes earlier. Thanks in large measure to the alien.

"Thank you," she echoed, with great feeling.

At a command from the alien, the starmonsters released them. The submersible settled gently to the floor of the chamber, with Jim and Manda hanging from their seat belts at an incline and *Octo* mostly beneath *Trieste*. The big, slow boomspeak started again. She wondered if the alien was telling its distant counterpart what had happened here.

"What now?" Jim asked. "Without a propeller, we're stuck. Those renegade waldos are going to wake up in another hour. Unless we can get out of here right now, we'll be back where we started, and immobile to boot."

Manda winced. "It's worse than that. We've lost three air Recyclers. We only have another seventeen hours of air."

"Aw, shit." Jim lowered his head onto his arms.

"We'll think of something," she said.

He didn't respond for a moment. Then he straightened. "You're right." He pulled her close. She rested her head against his chest, and listened to his heartbeat. Beneath the brave words, she too was sick with fear.

"We need to—get to the surface," Manda said, pausing between booms.

"How?"

"*Duo* has ballast balloons for—emergency ascent. But we have to—get out of this enclosed space first."

"Surface through the ice?"

Manda shrugged. "If need be. *Duo* can hammer—and drill.

And there are breaks, slushy spots. We can find—them with echo-location."

A thoughtful expression came onto Jim's face. "A seismicity-monitoring—site is on a volcanic island chain, due west—of here. Much closer than the drill hole, and—it has a homing beacon—plus shelter, a radio—possibly even a transport. We—could hike across the floes to it—if we could—surface."

"The surface is only an hour—or two away, straight up."

"So we might be—able to make it."

Manda nodded. "We—have to find a way to take *Octo* out with us. Or—at the very least, convince our alien—friend not to tamper—with it, till we can do something more permanent about—the crèche-born."

"Do you think," Manda asked after a moment, "you could find—a way to tell our alien friend—our situation?"

"I'll see what I can do."

While Jim was setting things up on his liveface, she heard a skritching sound, and caught motion in her peripheral vision. She looked down. *Octo* was moving. Or part of it was.

"I don't believe it," Manda whispered, staring. She gripped Jim's arm. "It can't be." But she wasn't imagining it—*Octo*'s forward manipulator attachments were now reaching back into the housing on the opened section.

The crèche-born were at it again.

She unbuckled herself and sprang to the wall by Jim's speaker, enraged. "No! Those *bastards!*"

Jim saw what she saw, and his face registered shock. She pounded on the glass wall. The attachment was *right there*, within easy reach—on the other side of the metaglass. She called up the disabler and she-*Duo* transmitted it once more, but she already knew it wouldn't work: *Octo*'s sonar link had been dead since long before they'd come down here. If it hadn't been, *Octo* would have been disabled in the same transmission that had disabled *Unus* and *Quinque*. And the crèche-born wouldn't let her use that trick again anyway.

Manda grabbed Jim by the arms. "We've got to let the alien know what's going on! Tell it to stop them!"

He ran trembling fingers through his hair. "Right. Right. What do I say?" His hands ran over invisible controls. "We have to be careful, or we'll simply confuse it. Help me out, here, Manda. What do we say? How do we say it?"

"Let me think." She took a deep breath. Her heart raged in her chest. *Calm down, calm down.* Ignore the fact that they could be blown to atoms any second now. Right.

"I could show that *Octo* is being tampered with," Jim said. "Show the waldo blowing up."

"Yes. Good."

Hanging at an angle, his face contorted, he pumped his hands and arms furiously. Meanwhile Manda crouched on the wall that was now the floor, and watched the attachments probing *Octo's* containment.

For their enemy's purposes, the angle of *Octo's* attachments wasn't ideal. The enemy was having difficulty grasping the clamp screw that held the final containment barrier in place. More than once, it withdrew the arm, bent it using a different attachment, then tried again.

She heard Jim's speakers make noises, and glanced at his projection. He had taken an actual image of the chamber they were in, and superimposed on it a crude but identifiable simulation of *Octo* blowing up. He played it several times.

"How much time do we have?" he asked Manda. She worried at a cuticle, studying the enemy's efforts. The opened housing with the antimatter container was less than a meter from her feet.

She remembered what UrsulaTomas had said about the submersible. *As long as you're not at ground zero,* he'd told her. Her body hurt with the need to run away.

"They're having difficulty getting hold of the final clamp screw. I'm guessing they'll have it soon—say five minutes, maybe six. Then it will only be a few minutes before magnetic containment is breached. After that we'll have a few seconds before the inner wall of the vacuum chamber that houses the antimatter nugget collapses from the pressure."

"So, eight to ten minutes."

For some reason his cool estimation infuriated her. She managed to control herself—perhaps more out of exhaustion than self-restraint. A moment later she was embarrassed at herself, and glad she hadn't said anything.

He went back to work trying to tell the alien what was happening. Pacing restlessly, Manda ran through various possible mental scenarios on how to hijack or disable *Octo*'s.

"*Octo*'s systems have shut out sonar, so we can't reach it that way. It doesn't have laser-link. And *I* don't have any way to use an omnilink. *Goddammit!*" She went to her knees and pounded on the glass again. "There's no way!"

"Um, could you hold it down?" Jim said.

"Sorry. I'm sorry." She slumped over her knees, breathing through her nose, trying not to hyperventilate. Her body was one big knot of strung-tight sinew. *Hold it together. Don't panic.*

The alien had broken off its deep boomspeak once more. Now Jim was telling it with pictograms, video, and sonar that their enemies were attacking *Octo*. Then he showed *Octo* blowing up again. Then he gave the parasol distress cry. *Urgent—help!*

It must be confusing to the alien, for them to declare that their enemies were attacking *Octo*, since they and the alien and its starmonsters were the only ones present in the chamber.

But the alien figured it out. After a long pause, it replied, *rising moan-whistling shriek*, and the starmonsters descended once more. Unfortunately, they fell on *Aculeus Duo* instead of *Aculeus Octo*. After a moment it called them off again.

"The starmonsters aren't smart enough to understand which

disabled waldo is the threat," Manda said. "Shit!"

"Hard to find good help these days," Jim muttered. He clasped her hand. Her laugh had a ragged edge to it.

The alien's lightstalks went out suddenly, and Manda saw behind and to the right that on one of the alien's imaging panels, some sort of picture was forming. It created a pictogram of a partly-disassembled waldo in little spots of light, and then showed it expanding and brightening. *Rising moan-whistling shriek!* Jim broadcast. *True!*

Then it showed the following pictogram:

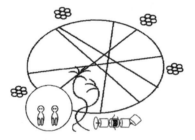

—and released sonar song. At the same time, the marine-waldo glyph moved away from the alien toward the right, and the symbol for Manda and Jim in *Trieste* moved toward the left:

"What does it say?" Manda asked.

Jim listened, frowning. "It looks like it's mostly just repeating what I said, but it's also making sound symbols we haven't used yet."

Manda looked back at Octo. Her stomach gave another sick lurch: the attachment now had hold of the clamp screw. She gasped.

"We don't have much time, Jim. Tell the alien to get *Octo* out of here. *Now.*"

Jim stared at her. "Oh, my God—that's what it was saying!" His hands flew, and the speakers blared—*True! True! Urgent! Urgent! Urgent!*—while on his own projection, *Octo* was moved away from them and the alien, far and fast, as the alien had done a moment before.

The alien sang again, and two starmonsters closed in. One grabbed *Octo* and the other grabbed *Duo*, and then—apparently in response to further instructions from the alien—the one holding *Aculeus Duo* released it and helped the other starmonster carry *Octo* up and away.

Faster, Manda thought. *Faster.*

There was no way they could carry it far enough, fast enough, before it blew. And there were three other waldos down here, whose antimatter batteries would go when the concussion of the blast hit them.

This was ground zero, times four. The alien was going to die, and so were they.

Somehow Manda couldn't wrap her mind around this. There was a chance . . . a chance the bubble would hold, and that the impact of the shock wave wouldn't turn them to instant sushi.

Manda looked at Jim. He sat still now, face blank, head bowed over his knees, shaking his head mutely.

I love you, she thought. She reached out and twined her fingers through his, and kissed his knuckles. His hands were cold.

Something in her rebelled. Her hand tightened on his.

Her life had been one big fight. She couldn't stop now.

"We need to move the speakers and remount the handholds," Manda said, standing. Her voice shook; her heart was knocking around again. "We'll need to strap in if we want even a chance of surviving the blast. Come on, Jim. I need you. Get off your butt."

He looked up at her.

"You're right," he replied. "We should try."

They moved the speakers and wiring and secured the setup further back and to the top of the bubble, which was now on the starboard side. Then they remounted the cushions and hand-holds, and got out additional straps.

"We're going to secure ourselves by our chests and legs," Manda said. "There's less likelihood of tearing muscles or knocking our heads against flying equipment that way."

Jim glanced back at the alien, and wore a baffled frown. "Can you work on your own for a minute? Our friend is trying to tell us something else."

She started to argue—but what was the point? She broke off. "All right."

Manda worked quickly, getting all materials tucked into cabinets, latching doors, and ensuring all their equipment's vacuum suction-cups were secure against the walls of the bubble. Meanwhile two starmonsters positioned themselves around the submersible, grasping different parts of *Duo* and the lashings.

"Let's strap in," she said, locking the harness clasps across her thighs and preparing to lie down and strap a second harness across her chest. She eyed the starmonsters. They only had a few minutes left. "What are they waiting for? We need to get the hell out of here!"

"Wait," Jim gasped, and pointed. "Look."

A series of sphincters were opening up in the wall near the narrowest part of the horn, and Jim-*Duo* shone his-its floodlights into the small chamber beyond. Inside were clusters, about six or seven of them, that held what looked like quartz balls. Parasols came in and began harvesting them.

"What's going on?" Manda asked.

Jim shook his head. He gestured at the panel of lights the

alien had been using to communicate. "It keeps showing us those four images."

On the alien's display panel, first a ball moved onto the end of a curving tube that was part of a small complex of tubes. Parasols attached it there. Then the system of tubes and strands got bigger. And yet again bigger. Then the process started over again. They watched it two or three times. An image formed in Manda's head of her twin siblings, floating in their vat, back before the cave-in. She stiffened.

"Jim, the balls are those eggs, or whatever they are in there. It's trying to tell us that those are its babies!"

Jim looked dubious. "Where do you get that?"

Meanwhile one of the parasols brought them a ball, clutching it in some sort of biologically extruded net. The globe glistened in their floodlights. It was about a meter in diameter. Its interior sparkled, filled with a complex of crystalline planes and lines. The rest of the parasols darted away through one of the tunnels, carrying other balls like it.

"Beautiful," Jim murmured.

"It wants us to take one of its babies," Manda whispered. "In case—"

"In case it doesn't survive the blast," Jim finished, his eyes widening. "I believe you're right!" He focused in using *Duo*'s magnifying camera. "It's even more than that. Those look like crystal matrices, like what people used to use to store data in. I think that's some kind of memory storage."

"Memory storage—?"

"Yes! Think about it. These aliens have a lot in common with computers. Their brains consist of semiconductors, probably using some sort of chemical system for memory storage. It makes sense that it could create copies of itself. It sends its parasol fleet out to new areas of volcanic or geothermal activity to build the basic structures, and when they're ready, it sends these memory-seeding stones to be planted."

We don't have time for this! "Jim—"

"I know I'm right." In-face, he called up a map of the alien, and gestured. "Look at how amorphous its large structures are—"

"*Not now, Jim!*"

"Sorry."

"Manda took the controls. She-*Duo* extended a manipulating arm and took the netting with the egg, or whatever it was, from the parasol holding it out for them. Then she opened one of *Duo*'s sampling compartments—one designed for handling fragile specimens—and lowered the egg-like thing inside. Then she-*Duo* filled the compartment with protective foam.

The panels went blank, and the alien sang again. The two starmonsters lifted them up as they strapped themselves in. "I wish we had some of that foam in here," Manda remarked.

The starmonsters were none too gentle as they dragged the submersible up toward a different tube than the others had taken *Aculeus Octo*. But at least they were fast. Manda looked back at the alien, as they exited the chamber.

"Good-bye." The word choked her.

Jim took her hand. They interlocked fingers and waited, while their starmonster escort dragged them upward, bumping and scraping, through a winding tunnel. The deep, slow boomspeak followed them out, giving them added propulsion.

This set of tunnels led mostly straight up, and in a minute or two they were in open water again. Manda-*Duo* scanned the waters. There was no sign of *Aculei Tres*, *Quatuor*, or *Sexis*. But she did spot *Octo*. It was still being dragged by its two kamikazi starmonsters, almost straight up, heading for the lip of the trench. They were just over two kilometers away. They just might make it.

And if they do, maybe we all have a chance of surviving. If the explosion doesn't trigger an avalanche that buries us.

Some analytical part of her mind noted that their starmonster escort was taking them back through the bacto-weed forest toward the volcano. With her imaging equipment she caught a glimpse of the volcano in the distance. Then she-*Duo* picked up *Octo*'s automated distress call.

Too soon. They'd gotten *Octo* up above the wall of the trench, but not—quite—beyond its lip.

"Containment's been breached," she said. Her throat threatened to close but she felt numb. She looked at Jim, whose eyes were shining with tears. He kissed her hand. "Here we go, then. See you on the other side."

"I'm afraid." Her voice cracked. She gripped his hand in both of hers.

"Me too," he whispered. "Me too."

She'd always liked his hands. They were strong and able. Competent; gentle too. She squeezed her eyes shut.

Was it an accident that she was here—in the wrong place at the wrong time, as Teresa had been? Or had she, like Paul, secretly hoped to follow her own twin into oblivion?

The explosion burned her eyes even through her eyelids. Mercifully, she didn't truly feel the shock wave that hit a second later.

Someone was shaking her. ". . . Manda? Please. Please wake up."

"Not yet, Arlene," she muttered, and tried to roll over. The movement drove spikes of pain through her temples and neck. *I'm not home in bed. What's going on?*

She opened her eyes. The world spun in a lazy circle and Manda retched. Hands rolled her onto her side as she emptied the contents of her stomach.

Finally the spasms stopped. She looked up. Jim knelt there, holding her up with his right hand twisted in her long-john top, concern graven on his dirty face. He held his left arm clutched to his chest, and his neck and shoulder were covered in blood.

Overhead, the straps of their harness hung down. Jim must have gotten her down.

Manda wiped her mouth. Bile stung her throat. Every muscle cried out in agony, as though she'd had a series of prolonged seizures, and her ears were ringing.

She remembered. *We didn't implode.* Trieste *held!*

The thought floated up, bubble-like, from her subconscious. It took her a minute to fully understand what it meant. Everything seemed to be happening in slow motion.

"We're alive," she said finally. The words felt detached from context. She was all frozen inside: balled up, still, in a psychic clench.

Jim grabbed her in a painfully tight hug. His voice came out oddly constricted. She had a hard time hearing him over the chimes in her ears.

"I thought you were dead," he whispered, over and over. "I thought you were dead."

She tangled her fingers in his long, knotted hair. The strands dragged against the calluses on her fingers. The mundane sensation seemed, somehow, remarkable. His lips slid gently across hers. She wiped bloody smudges off his cheeks and nose. *What a wonderful organ skin is,* she thought. *So smooth and pliable.* She smiled. "You're a mess."

He ran a light thumb across her cheekbone. "Beats the alternative."

Manda got a whiff of herself as she shifted, and made a face. "*I'm* a mess. We need a bath."

Jim started to guffaw—then clutched his midsection with a grimace. "It only hurts when I laugh." After catching his breath, he said, "We're both at least mobile. We'd better see what shape the ship is in. Make sure nothing's critical. Then first aid."

"Right."

"I'll check *Trieste,*" he said. "You see what you can do with *Duo.*"

Manda crawled over to the edge of the bubble. Beyond the metaglass, all was black, except for the volcano's faint orange glow over the rise. She could also see bits of luminescence here and there, defining the ocean floor. The lashings that held *Duo* and *Trieste* together had come loose, and lay in large loops of steel cable around *Trieste's* base.

She searched and finally spotted Aculeus Duo about four or five meters away, snagged on one end of the cable. *Trieste's* interior lighting wasn't good enough to tell her much about *Duo's* condition, other than the fact that the connection between the front two modules and the back two had been sheared off—the two sections were lying at odd angles a short distance apart. Not a good sign.

A band of muscles tightened across her chest and her hand went to her mouth. Tears sprang to her eyes. She'd been junked on adrenaline for too long. She couldn't keep holding it together. Then she lowered her head, wiped away the tears. *Come on. Stop being a priss. Finish assessing things. We might still have some options.*

It took several tries and finally a hard reboot, but her liveface blossomed around her. She straightened, more hopeful. It worked. *Trieste* was live. She raced through the basic checks. *Systems nominal. Let me see if I can contact* Aculeus Duo.

To her surprise, she could—the unit's modularity had given it enough redundancy that its smart systems had patched together something resembling an interface, and with Manda aiming the laser manually at *Duo*, its laserlink still worked.

But it was in sorry shape. Its detecting, sonar, imaging, and sampling systems were all down. Only three of its twelve manipulating arms were even marginally functional, and major sections of its commandface were trashed. It could only respond to very simple commands.

Worst of all, its ballast systems didn't respond.

Manda turned to face Jim, who had just come forward from the rear of the submersible. He sank onto the cushions, cradling his arm. He didn't look so good.

"Well?"

"*Trieste* itself appears to be intact," he replied. "No sign of impending leaks or structural stress. Not that we'd know till it went, but . . ." He shared a look with Manda, and shrugged. "We're not too bad off."

Manda at the debris around them. "That's hard to believe."

"I know the damage looks extensive, but it's mostly superficial. The food storage cabinet that was there"—he pointed; she hadn't noticed in all the clutter and chaos—"came loose in the blast."

The debris scattered across the inside of the submersible bespoke just how much force they'd been under: multicolored rations mottled the interior surfaces in a fine spray, like paint released from a high-gee centrifuge. Burst food and drink packets—and many other materials that had been in cabinets—clung to the walls and littered the floor.

"And we've lost one of our data collectors," he went on, pointing at one of the computer cabinets, now smashed. He gripped his arm. "I think that must have been what hit me."

"What are those buzzing and dripping sounds?"

He shook his head. "I don't know what the buzzing is yet but it's coming from the Recyclers." He paused to draw some breaths. "Emergency lights and heaters working," he went on. "Primary life support control systems seem OK. I think the head is ruined. It's sprung a leak but is contained inside the lavatory cabinet for the moment."

"Charming. Is that what that smell is? I thought maybe I'd shit my pants."

Jim tried to laugh again, and again winced.

She hesitated. "And our air?"

He shook his head. "Haven't had a chance to check it yet."

She noticed blood staining on the cushions beneath where he kneeled. "Well, we know we've got air enough to do first aid. Are you bleeding?"

"Yeah," he grunted. "Feels like I'm pissing from the chest down."

"Right, we'll do you first." She tore back his long-john top at the neck and inspected his injury. "Ouch." She bit her lip. He kept a stoic expression as she pulled bits of fabric away.

Something big, heavy, and pointy had hit him. His livesuit had been shredded at the shoulder, and the muscle-nanomachines inside its mesh had shriveled on exposure to oxygen, turning to tiny, lime-green pellets. These beads were all over inside his shirt, and many were also lodged in a deep gash that stretched from the base of his neck halfway to his shoulder. Blood with green dead-muscle-nano beads floating in it trickled out of the wound in a sluggish stream. Blood had soaked into his clothes and more was trickling down his torso. How the hell had he managed to get her down from the ceiling, in his condition?

She fingered the mesh of his livesuit. It was stiff and unresponsive.

"I'm afraid your livesuit has bled to death," she told him. "Let's get it off you."

"I think my collarbone is broken," he said. "And maybe a rib or two. It hurts like hell to breathe and I can't really use my left arm much. I think I sprained it or tore a ligament or something."

She dug a first-aid kit out of their emergency supplies, and used the scissors to cut him out of the suit. He jumped with a yelp when she helped him pull his left arm out of the suit, and she could feel things moving around in there that shouldn't be. "Your arm is broken. We'll need to splint it."

Manda had done all the first-aid similes, and had kept up with the annual recerts; it was mandatory. The gash she could handle—they had the right supplies and she'd done it before, for their herd animals if not for humans. Setting a bone wasn't something she'd ever done for real, though.

"How about let's stop the bleeding first, and then I'll give you a full exam."

"Suits me."

She washed the gash with distilled water and disinfected it. He bore all this with no reaction.

"I've only ever treated animals before," she said, as she got out the wound sealant and sprayed it on the gash. "You have the honor of being my first human patient, ex-face."

"Ah?" His tone stayed light, but his face drained of color and he clenched his jaw as she pressed the edges of the wound together.

"Back when I was an adolescent," she went on, holding the edges closed till they stuck, "I helped out a lot with the herds. . . .

Sorry. I'd never make a good doctor, I'm afraid." Then she applied Second Skin on top to protect it.

" 'S all right," he grunted, but when she was finished he had to bend over his knees and take deep breaths.

"Lie down," she said. "I want to finish checking you."

Manda ran through the other basic checks you were supposed to do. His pulse was a bit fast. She guessed that might be due to blood loss.

"Any pain here?" she asked, feeling around his skull and neck. He shook his head.

She felt of his collarbone. He grimaced. "I think you're right that it's broken. There's not much we can do till we get back to the colony."

She checked his ribs. But she didn't know how she would tell if they were broken anyway, unless they were poking out of the skin. She didn't remember what to do about rib injuries. At least none seemed to be jutting into his lungs or heart or liver.

Next she poked around his abdomen to make sure he hadn't sustained a blow to some internal organ. No sign of injury. The skin of his scrotum crawled when she ran a nail across his inner thigh, just as it was supposed to—he made a feeble attempt to leer as she did so—and his legs and right arm were also fine. Then she checked his spine from top to bottom, and laid him on his back again.

"I'm going to go ahead and see if I can get your bones realigned," she told him, "and then we'll splint it. OK?"

He drew a deep, readying breath. "Go ahead."

Manda rechecked the position of the bones, then took hold of the elbow and wrist and gave a pull and a twist. Jim grunted.

"Sorry," she said again. She felt it. "It feels like it's back in place, or at least close. Without imaging equipment I can't be sure. But let's go with that, shall we?"

"Yes, let's," Jim said breathlessly, through his teeth.

She splinted the arm, rigged him a sling from pieces of his

440

long-john bottoms, helped him change into clean long johns, and gave him some pain medicine and a Defender tab to fight infection.

"Your turn," he said. "Lie down."

Clumsily, one-handed, he ran through the same check with her that she had with him. Other than some lingering nausea and dizziness, she'd escaped with nothing more than a wrenched lower back and lots of bruises and scrapes.

"I got off lucky, didn't I?" she asked, sitting up—then steadied him, alarmed, as he wobbled and his eyes went crossed.

"Jim, I think you'd better lie down for a bit. I'll finish checking the Recyclers."

She got up and headed back.

"What about . . . what about *Duo*?" he asked after a moment. "Is it usable? You never said."

Manda looked back at him.

"I'm afraid not," she said finally, and gave him the rundown of her assessment. He eyed her without saying anything.

Without the ballast balloons, they were dead. They had no way of surfacing.

"Let me mess with it for a bit," she said. "Maybe it's the programming module and not a hardware problem. And even if it *is* hardware, a minor problem might be fixable with the working manipulator arms. . . ."

In her heart, she didn't hold out a lot of hope. *Duo* was in pieces—all but nonfunctional.

But first, the Recyclers. She needed to know how much time they had. She drew a breath, crossed her fingers, and opened the Recycler cabinet. The single remaining functional canister remained the right color, a rosy pink, and air and nutrients were still bubbling through it. The CO_2 readouts at top and bottom showed the nanomachines still hard at work separating carbon from oxygen, and while CO_2 levels in the submersible were starting to climb, they were still well within acceptable limits. The intake fan had picked up a buzz. That was the noise she'd heard earlier.

So we have a little time to come up with something. Manda rocked back onto her heals, releasing the breath she'd been holding.

Make sure the buzz isn't something serious. She shut off the airflow and opened the casing. A bolt had penetrated the housing and the blades were scraping it as they rotated past. She got a pair of pliers, removed it, and turned it over. It was a big one, two centimeters thick and almost ten centimeters long.

That bolt could have been thrown into one of their bodies instead. Like their skulls, or an artery somewhere. Or it could have struck the submersible wall and cracked it. It struck home then just how very, very lucky they'd been.

Jim had propped himself up and was watching her.

"How much more air do we have?" he asked. She had to do the calculation over again; the crash had wiped out her earlier estimates.

"Seven or eight hours, maybe," she said finally. "We were out for quite a while."

"I guess we don't have a lot of alternatives," he replied heavily. "Certainly none of the other waldos in the vicinity would have survived the blast, even if we could somehow get them out of the crèche-born's control. They were right in the middle of the blast zone."

It occurred to her then that the three renegade waldos that had left the area already—*Tres, Quatuor,* and *Sexis*—could still be a danger to them. She opened her mouth to say as much, but Jim was already responding, "They can't hurt us now. You locked them out of our systems, and they must certainly believe we're dead."

This reminded her of the alien egg-stone they had, and of the alien on the far side of the world, who was still in danger. "We have to make it out, Jim. We have to! They have to be stopped."

He only looked at her with weary despair in his gaze. He still looked very pale, and his eyes were sunken and dark. Then he laid back down with an arm across his eyes.

"I just need to rest for a minute," he said. Manda eyed Jim, scared for him. Scared for them both. She pressed a hand over his brow. It felt too warm.

While he rested, she mopped up the bloody water and cleaned up the bodily fluids and other mess on the bubble's floor, as best she could. She hurt all over and she stank and she was shocky and weak. But they were alive. That simple fact gave her the energy to do what needed to be done.

Next, swallowing despair, she pulled up her liveface to see what she could do with *Duo*. But things were just too damaged. *Duo* had no propeller and she couldn't even access the ballast icons. They weren't anywhere to be found. All she could do was make a couple of its attachment arms flap.

We're fucked, she thought, after a bit, and sank back on her heels. There was simply no way *Duo* was going to get them to the surface.

And then she remembered *Aculeus Septimus*, trapped in the lava not so very far away.

Septimus had sonar but no laserlink, and she couldn't route through *Duo*'s, since its sonar was down, so Manda had to jury-rig a setup with materials they had in the submersible.

Jim's speaker still worked. She mounted it on the wall, pointed in the direction of the orange glow. Then she had to recode her commandface to route signals out through the speaker, and in through her livesuit's throat mic, which she'd taped to the metaglass next to the speaker.

What a ridiculous setup, she thought, eyeing the arrangement.

Jim by this time had fallen asleep. She checked his breathing and pulse once more. His pulse was still rapid, but not excessively so, it seemed to her. She pressed a hand to his forehead.

Too warm. She wondered if he had an infection. *Wish we had a doctor in the house. Wish I knew what I was doing.*

"Hang in there," she whispered, and kissed him on the cheek. Then she brought up *Septimus's* commandface.

And it responded! There were gaps, and static, and she was forced to repeat things a lot, but the images came through.

Immediately she shut down the connection. The crèche-born still had full access to *Septimus,* and could detect and infiltrate them through its systems. She doubted they were paying it much attention, but the risk remained.

She spent some time modifying her disabler program so it would only shut out omni signals, not sonar, and made the shut-out a permanent rather than temporary state. If they bothered to check the waldo after she ran this, they would find it didn't respond and would likely assume it had been destroyed in the blast. Then she transmitted the disabler.

Once *Septimus* had received and auto-executed the com-mandfile, she verified that its omnilink was dead through the sonar link, and then ran through a series of systems checks. The marine-waldo seemed unaffected by the blast. All systems were functional. She-*Septimus* turned on her-its floodlights, and she strained to make out detail from the broken, strobe-like, low-rez images that flickered around her.

The ocean floor around *Aculeus Septimus* was littered with bodies—mostly parasols, or parts of them; perhaps a few star-monster bits. That's what the flecks of luminescence must have been that she'd seen from inside *Trieste.* Many of the geothermal chimneys had also been shattered by the antimatter blast—or blasts. (She still wondered whether *Unus* and *Quinque* had gone up too. They must have.)

But not all. Not even most. The majority of the geothermal chimneys were still standing, spewing out their fluid and heat and smoke. She-*Septimus* couldn't make out much detail on the earlier biomineralizing efforts of the parasols. She thought she-waldo could make out some movement out there, though. Maybe there were other survivors.

The bag Jim-*Duo* had dropped beside *Septimus* on their way to the alien had been on the lee side of the antimatter blast, and was still—barely—within *Aculeus Septimus's* reach. She-waldo extended a manipulator, and after several tries managed to pull the bag over and open it. First she-waldo attached the laser-link fittings and made sure they worked. She'd need them later. Then she-waldo installed the laser-saw and mirrors, and then took the next hour or so cutting, whacking, and tugging her-itself out of the lava.

Finally she-waldo rose up into the dark waters of Omi-Kami on a wave of sheer glee. Back inside *Trieste*, she laughed out loud.

She-*Septimus* would need to hurry, though. Until she switched over to laserlink, there was still a chance the crèche-born could detect her sonar signals.

Transmissions improved rapidly as she-*Septimus* closed on *Trieste*. With her own eyes Manda caught a glimpse of her-*Septimus's* floodlights coming over the rise; at the same instant she-waldo could make out the soft white glow of the submersible. She-waldo saw the figures of herself and Jim inside, their upturned faces staring at her-*Septimus*.

Surprised, she looked over at Jim, who had awakened and was watching her-*Septimus* approach.

"I knew you could do it," he said.

anda first installed one of Duo's backup laserlink fittings onto *Septimus* and switched over to laserlink control—with Jim in charge of aiming the laserlink gun at *Septimus's* receptors; a sloppy way to do it, but their best option, for the moment—so they could cease sonar transmissions. Then she-*Septimus* extracted the alien egg-stone from *Duo's* storage bin, painstakingly peeled the layers of hardened foam away, and held the thing up for their scrutiny, just beyond the metaglass.

"It's still intact!" Jim exclaimed, after a moment or two.

Manda broke into a smile. "I think you're right."

She-waldo set it inside *Septimus*'s sample container, repacked with the foam padding they'd stripped off of it. Next she-*Septimus* rolled *Trieste* carefully over onto its side, and held *Septimus* in position on the side that would be the top when they were done. Then Jim remounted the laserlink to communicate with *Septimus*, and they started the lashing process, Manda controlling *Aculeus Septimus*'s forward eight manipulators and Jim, using his still-intact livegloves and-hood, one-handedly controlling the aft four.

The work went slowly. They had many flubs and frustrations; the cables slipped off time and again, and *Trieste* kept rolling onto its bottom, causing Manda to lose laser contact with *Septimus*. Finally Manda-*Septimus* dragged *Duo* over and used the latter's broken body to prop Trieste in the right orientation. Jim took over *Duo*, using its three working manipulators to secure the cable on the side that would be *Trieste*'s bottom, while Manda-*Septimus* passed the cabling up her-its back or through her-its belly clamps, and then tossed the end to Jim-*Duo*, who scrabbled for it and tossed the end back over to Manda-*Septimus*.

Six times they managed to get the cable around *Trieste*'s belly before it got too short to make another circuit. She-*Septimus* secured its end with a final set of clamps, and then Manda put away her liveface and slumped, exhausted.

It was nowhere near as secure as the original lashings. If they slipped loose from their cradle sometime during their ascent, they wouldn't have enough air left to redo the lashings and try again.

"It should hold," she told him. "It'll hold."

They had maybe two or three hours, now, before the CO_2 content became too high for them to tolerate. It was almost time.

But they had one more errand, before they ascended. *Manda-Septimus-Trieste* lifted off the ocean floor.

"We're going to check out the alien first," she told Jim. She couldn't leave without knowing what had happened to it. Manda-*Septimus* steered over toward the alien and fired a series of flares. The water was choked with particulates, but echolocation and image enhancers told her much more than she really wanted to know.

The devastation was complete. The alien's gorgeous towers, its graceful hectares of tubes and coils and arches and glowing strands, had been levelled. That beauty, that ancient, articulated structure, all that deep and unknown knowledge, now dust and ash. Before they'd even had a chance to discover what—who—the alien really was.

She'd known it would be. But seeing it made it all too real. She couldn't even tell where the alien's horn-chamber had been, anymore.

Perhaps where that large crater is. Must have been where the two captive waldos blew.

Manda pressed her hands against the metaglass as *Septimus* carried them over the wasteland.

"I'm sorry," she whispered.

Jim came up beside her and gripped her shoulder. "It's not your fault, you know," he said. She bowed her head and cried.

Too much loss, too quickly. First her siblings, and now this. Too much pain.

Jim took over *Septimus*'s interface for her, flying one-handed, till she could recover herself. His struggles to master his own pain, just to give her those few moments, helped bring her back. She plugged back into *Septimus*'s controls.

"Thanks," she said, wiping her face. "I'll take it from here."

Jim gave her a look, and she nodded reassurance. He lay gratefully back down beside her on the cushions.

The destruction diminished gradually as they moved away

from the alien's atomized remains toward the volcano—though the "improvement" actually made the scene more grisly. Masses and clots of blasted bactoweed, and the corpses of many parasols, starmonsters, and other bioluminescent creatures, lay strewn about in sprays that pointed away from the blast's epicenter.

"There went our miracle food source. Looks like the colony is back in starvation-rations mode."

Once they made it over the final rise and the volcano and its attendant chimneys hove into view, the level of destruction dropped. Clumps and clusters of living bactoweed began to appear, here and there, and in the shallow valley before them Manda-*Septimus* could see several parasols and even a couple of starmonsters moving about.

"What do you propose we do with the egg-stone?" Jim asked.

Manda gave him a sidelong look.

She wanted to take it back to Amaterasu. Perhaps it could be studied—carefully, without harm to it—before it was returned here. It would certainly tell them a great deal about the alien.

But she wasn't sure they were going to make it back. And even if they did, how could she be sure it wouldn't be harmed in transit, or during analysis? Its best chance to survive and grow was with its natural caregivers: the parasols, starmonsters, and rotoshells.

"We're going give it to them," she said, gesturing. "And hope they know what to do with it."

"Do we have time for this?" he asked. But before she could even reply, he was shaking his head. "We can't not, can we?"

"We can't not," she agreed.

As they neared, Manda could see that the parasols' biomineral chimneys had sustained damage. They and the tiny rotoshells were hard at work repairing it. A starmonster was harvesting bactoweed, and two other starmonsters had conjoined and were extruding a large coiling tunnel. Rotoshells created gossamer strands of silicone that hung between the different tubes and points like spider's silk. The structure that the new alien would inhabit was slowly taking shape.

As before, the parasols and starmonsters ignored them—until they set the egg-stone down near a chimney where a parasol pair was attached. Then a parasol darted up and grasped the egg-stone, and extruded netting over it. Several others gathered around: chittering, squeaking, quivering. The first parasol lifted the egg-stone up and hauled it over to the nearby mating pair, and the outward-facing partner opened its center aperture wider than Manda would have imagined possible, and sucked the egg-stone into the cavity its body created with its mate's.

Jim squinted. "They're going to attach it to the tube, aren't they?"

Manda nodded after a moment. "I think so. That's what the alien told us." She sighed. "Talk about birth trauma. I wonder if it will ever know what has happened here."

Jim nodded soberly. "It will. We'll tell it in time to come."

He wiped away a few tears of his own. Manda thought again how much she loved him. "Come on. Time for us to go."

For once, things went right. *Aculeus Septimus*'s ballast systems were in excellent working order, and when Manda triggered them, white bladders exploded out of the marine-waldo's interior compartments and swelled to great size, obscuring their view on both sides of the submersible. Manda incongruously thought of being buried in a set of enormous breasts—a child clutched in its elder sisters' bosoms—and giggled. Not that her elder sisters had ever had much in the way of bosoms, much less maternal leanings.

The boiling chaos of the volcano's mouth receded beneath them. Jim, resting on the cushions, cocked an eyebrow at her. Manda shook her head.

"Just getting a little punchy." She did some quick calculations. "We'll reach the ice shelf near your islands in an hour and a half. The blast would have loosened things up, up there. And it's later in the spring. We'll have an easier time of it than JebMeri did, I think." With that, she slumped over her knees. Exhaustion was catching up with her.

Jim gestured. "Come here and rest with me."

"I was going to make some preliminary soundings of the ice cap."

"That can wait. You'll be more effective once you've had a rest."

His reasonable tone annoyed her. "We don't have time! If we don't get it right the first time, we'll *suffocate*, goddammit!"

He only looked at her. The gaunt look on his face made her

ashamed. He was right. She was shaky and ill from fatigue. She passed a hand over her eyes.

"I'm sorry, Jim. I'm sorry."

"Forget it," he said.

Manda set up *Trieste*'s systems to do some preliminary processing of the ice-cap scans it had begun, and set an alarm to wake her when they were within a hundred meters of the surface ice. Gratefully she slipped into the crook of Jim's arm, rested her head on his uninjured shoulder, and almost instantly, it seemed, fell asleep.

The rest was only an hour: far less than either needed. Manda awoke feeling groggy and irritable. She shut off the alarm, splashed water on her face, and took a quick spritz-bath to rid her body of the smell of fear. It helped, a little.

The air was sour. CO_2 levels were way up. Her breathing felt labored.

She woke Jim and gave him a quick report.

"We can probably go another hour," she said. "As long as we stay calm."

"No adrenaline surges, eh?"

"Absolutely not. No laughing, either. You take up all the air when you laugh." She'd meant it as a joke, but neither smiled.

They both looked at the image-enhanced scene overhead. *Septimus-Trieste* had brought them to the eastern edge of the island chain Jim had told Manda about. They now hovered near one of those islands, just beneath the inverted spears and crags of the ice cap. Groans, crashes, and squeals reverberated all around as the massive ice mountains overhead slammed together and pulled apart in Omi-Kami's powerful currents and tides. Water bubbled, swirled, and coursed beneath and between the passes and crevices.

We could be squished like a bug up there, Manda thought. Her heart lurched. But the only way out was up.

Jim still looked pale; his face had stress lines. He was weak. Very weak. She worried a nail, eyeing him. He was a large man; how would she get him out, if he collapsed?

Then Manda caught a glimpse of sunlight: a narrow shaft that filtered briefly through a crack. She gasped.

"Look!" She pointed. Jim grinned feebly when he saw it. Then the glimpse was gone.

"*Trieste* survived an antimatter blast," he said. "Surely she's up to a little iceberg chicken."

While Jim studied the scans and maps *Trieste* had made, Manda got out all their cold-weather gear and packed it in waterproof bags. They had about fifteen meters of climbing rope, thirty-two D-rings, and a piton gun with sixteen pitons. She eyed them, thinking back to her conversation with Charles and Bart, remembering how she'd teased them for including climbing and cold-weather-hiking gear.

Thank you for being paranoid, brothers, she thought. *Thank you. If we're lucky we'll even get a chance to use it.*

She got out a can of lubricating grease and held it up. "Insulation."

Jim nodded. "Good idea."

Once they reached the water-ice boundary, they'd have to climb the rest of the way out on foot. Here on the equator the ice was thin and didn't rest on the continental shelf. So it shouldn't be too far a climb. But they'd be getting wet, and without protection they could only survive a few moments in water this cold.

Manda removed her livesuit and put it in one of the waterproof, insulated bags. It probably wouldn't survive the cold, but it was a valuable piece of equipment—it had seen her through all of this—she wanted to try. She also packed food, the first-aid kit, life vests, and other emergency supplies. As she started applying grease in a thick layer over her long johns, Jim leaned forward with a pensive frown.

"Here's the deal. The sea floor in this area has a lot of volcanic and geothermal activity, and the water is shallow enough to create plenty of wave action from the tides. There's so much turbulence and so many ensonified zones and pockets up there that I can't tell from these readings exactly how thick the ice is. I only have guesses."

"What's your guess, then?"

He squinted at his data once more. "If there are no major errors in this data, I'd say we have about two or three hundred meters of ice overhead. This area here"—he gestured at an area on the livemap with many crevices and pockets in it—"appears to be a heavily pocketed fissure between two bergs. I believe it represents our best shot at surfacing.

"The shifting will be our greatest risk. I'll be on sonar and giving you continual updates. We'll take it as it comes."

"Right."

Manda handed Jim the grease and helped him apply a thick layer to himself, all over. He helped her apply more to herself. Carefully—to avoid smearing them with grease—they donned sturdy control-gloves and goggles, and began their ascent.

They rose through ice canyons whose surfaces reflected *Septimus*'s floodlights like giant diamonds and blue topazes. Bubbles effervesced around them, and currents buffeted them. Despite Omi-Kami's noisy complaints, for some time they had no difficulties.

But the air was getting harder to breathe. Manda had to resist drawing great breaths of the sour, dead air, and she saw Jim's breathing was growing more labored too. Her heart hammered, trying to pull more oxygen through her system.

It was time to break out the emergency supply. She pulled out the pony bottles. They had six. She strapped one to Jim's back and took one for herself. The four others she threw into a bag for later.

Hurry, surface, she thought. As she sucked fresh air through her teeth, she fantasized that they would come up in a quiet pool somewhere, and not have to climb at all.

Finally they entered a large, pressurized pocket half full of air. *Septimus* surfaced inside the chamber. Manda-*Septimus* took some samples of the outside air and ran screenings on them while Jim was doing soundings.

"It's breathable!" she reported, and ran back to open the hatch.

She had a hard time getting it open. It took several kicks. There was a *whooosh!* and her ears popped, and sweet, fresh, ice-cold air rushed in. Manda turned on the fans and helped Jim over to the entrance. They removed their respirators, and filled their lungs again and again with clean, oxygen-rich air, getting sprayed with freezing, briny water as waves struck the submersible below the hatch. She'd lost track of just how foul the submersible smelled, until she drew fresh air into her lungs.

Next, hatch open, Manda-*Septimus* circled the chamber, looking for a way out—a tunnel or fissure—so they could continue their ascent. But they were trapped in a cul-de-sac whose only opening was below. She didn't fancy having to retrace their steps.

Jim did soundings, then sat back with a grunt and pointed up at the top of the cul-de-sac, about twenty meters overhead. "Overhead is a network of crevices and tunnels. They're completely dry. I think they lead right to the surface. You can even see a bit of light through the ceiling. I don't think it's very thick."

Manda stared upward. They were so close! "If only we could reach the top of the cul-de-sac somehow."

"Well, I have a thought about that. That wall"—he pointed toward the wall nearest them—"is maybe four to five meters thick. Beyond it is another pocket, higher up than this one, completely full of water. If you can drill through the wall all the way up as the water levels equalize"—he pointed up the wall—"most of the air in this pocket will bleed into the other one, because its roof is higher than ours. That will lift us up. When we get close enough, we can try to punch through this ceiling, reach those crevices overhead, and climb out the rest of the way." He hesitated. "I think we're less than a hundred meters from the surface," he said. "Maybe a lot less."

"I don't know . . ." Manda said doubtfully. "Four meters of solid ice, maybe more, and I have to cut through all the way up? Maybe I could do it—*maybe*. But then the water levels will rise into the crevices above us too, won't they?"

"A ways, probably." Jim winced. "We'll just have to stay ahead of it."

"We have some air now. Couldn't we go back down and try to enter the other chamber from below?"

Jim shook his head. "Best I can tell, there's no entry from below into the other chamber. At least nothing large enough for the submersible to fit through. And I can't be certain that the crevices are reachable from there, as they are from here. We're in a partially frozen interface between two different bergs. The other chamber is deeper into one of the bergs and there are fewer fissures there."

"So we drill." Manda adjusted *Septimus*'s fittings and attachments. Jim showed her where the wall was thinnest. Manda-*Septimus* got started digging into the ice.

Before she'd gotten far, a loud groan and crack made them both jump. The crack turned to rumbling, like thunder, as the cul-de-sac's wall began to collapse, on the side where she-*Septimus* was digging. Water cascaded into their chamber, which was shrinking and moving in too many directions at once.

"*Holy fuck!*" Manda scrambled over and slammed the hatch shut, as the opposite wall and the ceiling also began to collapse, shedding ice daggers into the water. The ice pinged and clanged in a raucous chorus as it struck *Septimus-Trieste*.

The icebergs between which they had ascended were shifting

suddenly, closing in on each other. Manda shone *Septimus*'s lights upward. Sunlight trickled down through the cracks in the ceiling now. Ice continued to rain all around them. There was nothing they could do for the moment but ride it out; Manda took Jim's hand and they waited, as the walls closed inward and sideways, grinding and screaming. Meanwhile they rose closer and closer to the ice tunnels that led to the surface.

The water lifted them up above the big pocket and with Jim's cues, Manda-*Septimus* steered toward the largest nearby crevice Jim could find. They shot up into a narrow space on a fountain of water.

"We're going to jam in a couple of minutes," she shouted over the roaring, as she-*Septimus* struggled to turn them into a better orientation for further ascent. The ice walls around them ground together like giant teeth; slushy ice water tossed them around. Manda struggled with the controls, her heart thundering louder than Omi-Kami's ice mountains.

It was all happening too fast.

Don't let me be crushed, she thought, remembering Teresa, as the walls closed in on both sides. . . . *Nor drowned,* remembering Paul. They only had a couple of seconds' margin for error. *Keep it together. Come on.*

"I'm tipping us so the hatch is higher up. Hang on!"

Jim nodded. "Good thinking." He gripped his handholds and they went over on their side.

Then *Septimus-Trieste* jammed against a promontory. The waters were still rising around them, though not as quickly as before. Manda grabbed Jim. "Come on!"

Jim gasped in pain as his arm and shoulder were moved. The water level was nearing the hatch—they didn't have much time. While Manda tossed the rest of her liveware into the bag and sealed it, Jim climbed awkwardly up through the equipment and threw the hatch open. Icy water began trickling in from the hatch's lower edge, and quickly became a stream, a heavy flow, as the water continued to rise around the tightly wedged submersible. Manda's bare feet went numb, despite the insulating grease, then her ankles.

As she was reaching for the packs, the ice walls lurched sharply sideways, in opposite directions, rolling *Septimus-Trieste* between them like a marble. Manda slipped and belly-flopped into the water collecting in the floor of the bubble.

She gasped—she'd forgotten how cold the water could get.

Manda tossed the packs up and Jim took them. She scrambled up through the hatch as the waters rose inside the submersible. They both scrambled up along *Septimus*'s spine out of the freezing water, to the highest point.

The ice had ceased shifting, for the moment. But the water was still rising, several centimeters a minute.

Manda pulled out a piton gun and a coil of rope, shivering violently.

They quickly pulled on a couple more layers of insulated clothing—including their boots, which had retractable spikes in the soles and toes—but it wasn't enough to abate the chill. Her feet felt like frozen blocks. They swapped out their pony bottles with fresh ones, secured themselves to the rope with D-clamps and jury-rigged rope harnesses, and started up.

Manda went first, using a pick and the spikes in the toes of her boots. Every five meters she set a piton in the ice and attached the rope to it. The water crept up behind them, splashing at their heels. Light beckoned to them from perhaps thirty meters or so overhead; its many-colored shadows lay in strips along the white-and-aquamarine swirls of ice.

Thirty meters, she told herself. *It's only thirty meters. The climb up from the baths is nearly twenty. You can do this.*

The water on Manda's clothes turned to ice, and her hands and face grew numb with cold; her throat and sinuses grew raw as she climbed, centimeter by centimeter. But the rest of her body quickly overheated: every muscle had to remain tight, to maintain balance and position. It was an enormous strain. Every so often she'd glance down at Jim. He was inching up after her, his face a garish mask of pain.

She tried to keep from overusing the pony bottle; she wanted it last till they reached the top. For one thing, she didn't want to try to change bottles in mid-climb—and for another, they'd need their other ones for the trek across the ice. But it was hard to force herself not to suck great, deep breaths out of the bottle with every step upward.

I can do this. I can do this. I can do this.

She distracted herself with thoughts of baby Terence. *Seizures. Neurological damage.*

Oh, God, don't think about that now. Think of getting back to him, and to the others, my CarliPablo others—they'll rejoice when they see me alive. She imagined Teresa at the top, urging her on, scolding and chiding when she faltered. She didn't dare look down, not even to see how Jim was faring. It took all she had to keep going.

The ice shifted once more and she slipped loose, and slammed into the wall a meter or so down from the piton she'd just set. Slowly—painfully—she regained the ground she'd lost, and kept climbing.

Finally, about an eon later, she came to a ledge wide enough to stand and turn around on. She set a piton and secured herself, and then leaned out to check on Jim once more.

He clung to the surface a few meters below her: unmoving, one arm outspread, clinging to the ice face, the broken one pressed against his chest. The water was only centimeters below him.

"Jim," she called. "Come on!"

A long pause. He looked up at her. The grimace on his face scared the shit out of her. It made him almost unrecognizable.

"Water's stopped moving," he panted. "Let me rest."

"You've got to keep moving. Don't stop."

He didn't respond, just hugged the wall.

"Get up here. Move your butt!" she shrieked. The words tore at her throat.

"Can't," he said hoarsely. "Go on. I'll be along."

"The hell you say," Manda snarled. "You get your ass up here or I'm coming down for you."

No response. Manda gritted her teeth, looking up. She wasn't sure she could make it back up again. And she certainly couldn't carry him all the way to the top of the crevice.

I'm not leaving him down there.

"Here I come, then," she said, despair sinking deep into her belly, and leaned out over the precipice, preparing to rappelle down.

For the first time, Jim really reacted: he gaped up at her in alarm. "*No!* Don't. I'm coming."

The ice walls shifted again, cutting off his words. With a terrible grinding sound, *Trieste*—weakened by the antimatter blast, no longer protected by tens of thousands of metric tons of evenly dispersed water pressure—cracked, with a sound like cannon fire. Metaglass shards flew. Manda ducked, covering her head. *Aculeus Septimus* was slowly crushed. When the motion stopped, the opposite wall was only a meter or so away. At most. One more major shift would finish them. Or the crushing would breach *Septimus*'s antimatter containment.

Shit—and we're so close.

"The crevice is closing, Jim! Hurry!"

She tugged on the rope using the piton for leverage, hauling for all she was worth. Her arms shook with exhaustion. Jim scrambled up, scraping for purchase with one hand and two feet as the walls started to shift once more, screaming. Jim got hold of the ledge and Manda pulled him up onto it—at least up to his belly—and held him there. It must have been agony on his arm and collarbone and ribs. She hated to imagine what kind of pain he must be in.

Laura J. Mixon

They both drew many breaths from their pony bottles. With Manda's help he got up over the lip. The ice had stopped shifting, for the moment. Jim's color was ashen and sweat was pouring off his brow and cheeks, drizzling into his beard, where it was turning to tiny icicles.

They checked each others' air gauges. The bottles were almost empty. Manda swapped them each for new ones. She looked up at the light. They had maybe another ten meters. Ten meters she could do in her sleep. If not for everything that had come before.

Jim looked up, too. He gave her a grimace that tried to be a grin. Manda tried to return it.

"Not much farther," she said.

And then what had been a threat became a blessing: the opposite wall was near enough now that they could chimney-walk up the rest of the way, using mostly just their legs. The climb went much more quickly.

Finally Manda scrambled out onto the surface, using her pick and spikes, and once more helped pull Jim up over the slippery edge.

"We did it," Manda gasped.

Jim nodded, but didn't try to speak. His breathing was ragged, his teeth clenched on the pony-bottle respirator, and his face still contorted in a terrible, pallid mask.

They crawled a short distance from the edge and threw off their packs, then flopped down in the garnet- and-lavender-tipped snow and lay there, side by side, fingertips touching, and stared up at the early morning sky. Both panted, bleeding from a myriad tiny metaglass cuts neither had felt, shaking and fragile as ice sprites. Manda had gotten so overheated from exertion that—except for her feet, which had gotten so cold from the water that they still ached—she couldn't feel the cold. Her head hurt and her sinuses burned.

The air tasted so crisp and fresh! Uma had just risen, making the rough ice and pools of melt sparkle all around them, and fairy dust glittered past in a gentle breeze. Fire was nowhere to be seen but its ring, a gold band crossed with its own shadow on the far side, looped above the horizon to the west. The sky, empty of clouds and—for once—of moons, went on forever. She caught the salt scent of sulfur on the air: there must be a geothermal vent or hot-spring nearby. The ice floes' moans and rumblings seemed like a song once more—a wistful lament. Not a threat.

Omi-Kami had spared them.

It seemed impossible. Manda remained half-convinced she was still trapped down there somewhere, inside *Trieste*'s belly: dreaming of freedom while the air went bad and they slowly suffocated.

But no. The air was too pure—the sights, sounds, and smells all too vivid. This couldn't be merely a dream. She lifted up on her elbow to look over at Jim. He returned her gaze, wearing a strained expression as if he had something to say.

"What is it?" she asked.

Jim drew a deep, slow, obviously painful breath, gripping her forearm so tightly it hurt. "You sure know how to show a guy a good time."

It had to be the most inane thing he could have said. They both collapsed in helpless giggles.

33

Ice Calves and Inspiration

The iceberg shuddered and lurched once more, and the crevice ground further shut, sending a spray of slush into the air. Manda and Jim looked at each other.

"We can't stay here," Jim said. "It's not stable. The antimatter battery could go any time."

Manda nodded. "You're right."

But Jim looked bad. He tried to mask it, but his face was flushed and the muscles in his neck and jaw were drawn taut, as if it were difficult for him to remain upright. When she'd handed him his cup, the skin of his hand felt too hot.

She was pretty sure he'd gotten an infection.

They crawled well away from the edge, and there they took a while to rest and eat, sitting on their blankets in the snow. Manda worked on their feet, which had been damaged by the ice water, and put chemical heat packs in their boots to keep them warm.

Next she got out the first-aid kit. Jim jerked away when she tried to check his wound and take his temperature—"I'm fine. Leave me alone"—but she gave him a ferocious scowl (much like the ones Teresa had always used on her) and he subsided. She slapped the thermopatch on his forehead. Within seconds it reported his temperature as over thirty-nine degrees C.

The wound, beneath its protective coating of medicated polymer, had swollen up, angry and red like two sullen lips, straining at the wound's seal. She touched the Second Skin she'd applied over it. It was hot. Red streaks splayed out from the site.

The Defenders I gave him aren't working.

With a baffled frown she dug the packet of Defender tabs out of the first-aid kit and checked it, then tossed it angrily back into the kit. It was dated four weeks ago—before the alien microbes had been discovered and the colony's Defender Templates updated to recognize and fight them. They hadn't upgraded the first-aid kit.

Stupid, stupid, stupid!

But she should have caught it during her inspection. It was as much her fault as anyone's.

He'd had one infusion of the upgraded Defenders already, right after his exposure to the parasol creature. But Defenders were programmed to break down and be excreted within forty-eight hours. Still, perhaps he'd receive some lingering benefit, some boost to his immune system.

She prayed it would be so.

Manda pulled out their homing device, built into a wristband she'd tossed into one of the packs, and checked it. The station lay twenty-eight kilometers west-by-northwest. She doubted Jim could walk that far.

She paced, thinking, while Jim tried to force a couple bites of food down. Her livesuit had a radio transmitter. The livesuit would be useless in this cold, though. Its muscle-nanos might already have frozen. And she didn't have any other equipment she could use to jury-rig a different set of controls for the radio.

Manda dug around in the supplies, looking for something else she could use—anything. Finally she rocked back on her heels, eyeing Jim.

"We've got to get to the hut," she said. "We can radio for help from there."

He only nodded, hunched over his knees.

anda repacked the bags and placed them on the blanket. Their packs had aluminum support bars; she emptied the packs, stripped out the bars with a knife, and used them, the blankets, and the ropes to rig a travois. She pulled the travois, and Jim trudged along beside her, over terrain now rough, now slushy and pocked with pools, following the homing beacon. Numerous times they had to detour around ice karst, and they had to stop often to rest, given Jim's weakened state. It was slow going, and even slower once they'd depleted their oxygen supplies.

The sun crawled across the sky as they threaded their way across the ice floes, dogged by a changing wreath of Fire's moons. At one point during a rest, they watched a storm system gather on Archangel: a spiral of white storm clouds that raced across the moon's dark, fractured face. Another time, she saw a rare triple eclipse: Demon eclipsed God's Wrath, and as quick-moving Demon moved away, they both passed across distant, giant Heaven's Gate, looking like eyes against a mottled, pale blue face—one amber, one coal-dark.

The floes trembled underfoot as they walked, and occasionally lurched or cracked. Manda was terrified that the ground would open up under their feet any moment. They had a couple of close calls—enough to keep their adrenaline levels up and keep them going.

She also worried about the antimatter battery going. If they were out on the ice when it went (if it went), they wouldn't survive. But they couldn't move any faster than they already were, and after a while her fear dulled. There was no point in worrying when there was nothing she could do about it.

Mostly, though, she was scared for Jim. Bloodied, stiff, one arm bound to his chest, dripping sweat: he walked like the undead.

But somehow he managed to keep going. And if he could, Manda was determined to as well. She kept her feet moving even when they felt like dead stumps, stumbled another few steps, heaving her rickety, makeshift travois across the quivering ice, though her lungs were on fire and oxygen deprivation caused the sparks dancing in front of her eyes to outnumber the ice crystals that stung her cheeks. It began to feel like a journey that had no end.

U ma was peering out through the loop of Fire's ring, a muted orange through a layer of high-lying cirrus clouds, by the time they reached the tiny volcanic island among whose cliffs Jim's seismic station lay.

At first Manda didn't believe it. She had so many times scanned the horizon, looking for signs of land, for a structure of bamboo and mud, that she thought now it was a hallucination. She wiped at her burning eyes and looked, and saw it again. Beyond the churning surf, a low range of black, volcanic crags and rocks, draped with ice stalactites and stalagmites, rose above a layer of fog into the violet-blue sky. Atop the tallest of them was a reed-thin radio antenna. A little later a breeze swept the fog away, and in a crevice partway up a wash between two cliffs worm-eaten by lava tunnels and caves, she spotted with her binocs the hut itself.

She grabbed Jim, who had long since fallen silent.

"There it is! We've made it!"

Jim raised his head, briefly, and squinted into the sun setting behind the island's rocks. Clearly he had nothing to spare for words.

"Almost there," she said. He nodded once, then went to his knees. Manda eyed Jim and then, regretfully, their travois, with its spare equipment and supplies. There was no way she could get all that across the surging, uneven surface that lay ahead. She'd need the travois to transport Jim.

I'll come back for it, she thought. *If I can,* and knew she would not.

She untied her harness and shrugged off the straps. From the travois she took the first-aid kit, some food and water, her live-suit, and the last four D-clamps. These she tucked into one of the backpacks, which she put on. Then she gestured.

"Lie down," she said.

He gave her another nod. She could feel the heat radiating from him as she helped him onto the travois. And then she pulled him across the treacherous last hundred meters toward land.

Finally there was no other way: she shoved the travois holding Jim onto an ice calf that bumped up against the berg they were on. She jumped into the knee-deep, desperately cold, slushy surf, and dragged him the last few meters toward shore, bumped and dunked by chunks of ice.

The tide was going out; his ice calf slid down the slopes on the receding water and Manda planted herself, pulling Jim off it. The travois crashed onto the shore. Jim moaned. Manda staggered up the slope, dragging him a few meters further away from the worst assaults of water and the crashing and lurching of the ice calves. Then she released his collar and curled up against his back. She couldn't feel her legs.

After a moment she saw that the tide was moving steadily down the slope, dragging its rowdy herd of ice calves with it. She didn't know what they would have done if it had been coming in instead, or if they'd arrived at low tide instead of high. Brimstone's tides were quite a bit higher than Earth's, as well as more chaotic. Unpredictable. And faster. They'd have likely been doused and drowned before they could reach the cliffs, if they'd been here twelve hours earlier.

They were still at grave risk. She had stopped shivering. Temperatures were dropping and the wind was coming up as twilight spread across the sky. The ground shuddered in bursts and fits, as though the world were having seizures—she didn't know whether it was the ice calves slamming against the shore below, nearby volcanic activity, or a tectonic quake. Maybe all three.

It scared her. She lowered her head and cried, weakly. *I can't do this all by myself. Jim, I need you. Please.*

She laid a hand on his back. His coughing spasms had subsided; now he lay curled on the broken ice with a palm under his cheek, his face slack, as if sleeping.

He's dying.

The thought gave her a burst of panicked energy. She crawled over and tugged at him. "Come on, we're almost there. You can do it." When he didn't respond, she hit him hard on the back.

"Goddam you!" she shrieked. She grabbed handfuls of his parka and shook him. "You're not going to die on me! Get up. Get up, *get up, GET UP!"*

No response. Manda collapsed on top of him, crying more tears. The heat of his fever soaked into her, warming her cheek and chest. Gradually, a calm settled like snowfall over her. If he was going to die on this slope—if she was—so be it. They needed a rest. So she opened his parka and hers, pressed herself against his bloody chest, and they rested together.

For how long they remained there, she didn't know. It couldn't have been long, because the sky above the cliffs had not yet gone completely dark, when a loud noise roused them both. Out across the floes came a brilliant flash.

"Antimatter," Jim muttered, and his hands clutched her spasmodically. She couldn't think clearly and didn't understand him; she thought he meant it didn't matter.

Far out on the floes the ice bucked as if some great creature were bursting through its shell. A boom struck—a blast of wind—a tsunami of ice rose up. It bore down on the island, whip-fast. Manda watched, filled with awe. The fact that it was headed right for them seemed somehow irrelevant.

"Fuck." Jim grabbed her arm and hauled. "Move your ass, woman! Let's go!"

Confused, Manda struggled to sit up. With her as a counterbalance, Jim staggered to his feet. Manda managed to stand. Supporting each other, they stumbled across the igneous rock and cracking ice of the beach, up the black sandy rise in the center of the crevice, trying to outrun the blast front. The briny, frigid waters were now dropping far down the slopes, moving much faster than the tides had.

They ran. House-sized, fist-sized, head-sized chunks of ice crashed all around them. Then the icewater wave struck like a second explosion and flooded up the hill toward them.

When it had passed, they were only meters above the flood's apex. If they'd stayed where they were, they would have drowned. And if not for the blast and the tidal wave, they'd never have found the energy to move: they would have died of exposure.

Somehow, with the rising night winds whipping ice crystals and frigid salt spray against their backs, they made it up the wash to the hut.

The door was frozen shut. Manda hurled herself against it, kicked at the ice built up on the jamb, and then found an ax lying against the wall, to break the ice with. Finally she got the door open and a dark interior greeted her: one very similar to the other shack they'd shared. She helped Jim inside, laid him on the bunk, and piled furs on top of him, and then crawled in with him. When she felt strong enough, she got up again, lit a fire in the stove with cold-clumsy hands, and turned on the lantern.

A radio unit lay on the shelf. She set it on the bamboo-and-acrylic table and flipped it on. It spat nothing but static until she tuned it to a channel the pilots used. She heard a pair of voices fading in and out with the static, chattering about weather and landing-strip conditions. *Yes!*

Manda looked back at Jim. He was tossing feebly, muttering, in the grip of some hallucination.

During their hike across the ice, she'd toyed with all sorts of ploys to get people out here without revealing to the crèche-born that they'd survived. But they didn't have time for that. Jim needed help right away.

She flipped the emergency toggle, and an automated SOS began to play, the ancient distress call—*dit-dit-dit, dah-dah-dah, dit-dit-dit; dit-dit-dit, dah-dah-dah, dit-dit-dit.*

The two voices on the radio didn't immediately respond. Manda wasn't surprised. This island lay about four hours southeast of Amaterasu by jet-waldo: pretty far for the radio's signal to carry, even with the tower up on the cliffs to boost it. It was possible too, that Uma had kicked up a solar flare that was interfering with radio transmissions. She left the distress call going and made some bean soup, *mana*-bamboo-shoot rolls, and tea. First she ate, and warmth spread grudgingly through her, dispelling the chill. Then she fed Jim. Most of the soup she spooned into his mouth dribbled down his chin.

" 'anks, Bella," he muttered.

She laid a hand on his forehead again. His fever seemed worse. She cleaned the Second Skin off his wound and drained as much pus as she could out of it. He moaned and thrashed. Then she resealed the wound, gave him more painkiller, and treated his frostbite. His fever seemed to have staved off any serious problems with frozen limbs. He seemed a little more comfortable afterward.

Next she treated her own frostbitten feet, hands, and face. *I'm probably going to lose a toe or two before I'm through,* she thought ruefully, eyeing her sore, bandaged feet. *And possibly a finger.* They were in pretty bad shape. With her bandaged finger she touched her nose, which had gotten a freeze-burn too. Then she wrapped up again and went out to the supply shed, in the howling, subzero night winds for another canister of natural gas for the stove, and found a power sled.

She fired it up. *Yes!* It still worked and was fully charged.

But an overland journey home on this would take a good twelve to fourteen hours to make, and expose them to radiation: possibly more than a little, if conditions weren't optimal. And while they could probably both fit on the sled's seat, Jim wasn't up to such a long, rough ride. Best to wait for air rescue, if they could get a signal through.

When she went back inside, someone was responding to their SOS, trying to raise them on the radio.

"This is Amaterasu," they said. "Who is this? What is your emergency; come back?"

She thought she recognized the voice as KaliMarshall's. Maybe even her old nemesis Abraham, himself. She never thought she'd be glad to hear *his* voice. And perhaps it was that tiny hesitation over having to ask him for help that sparked an inspiration.

What if they only found Jim here? They'd assume I was dead. And so would the crèche-born.

So instead of answering, she carried the radio over to Jim and knelt, holding the microphone next to his mouth.

"Say your name," she told him, pressing the *transmit* toggle.

"Huh?" He blinked blearily at her.

She released it. "Say 'Jim LuisMichael here.'"

"Wha'?"

"Say 'Jim here.'" She flipped the toggle.

"Jim here," he muttered.

The radio spattered and squawked. "Come back? Who?"

"Say it again," Manda urged, shaking him. "Say 'Jim Luis-Michael.'"

"Jim LuisMichael," he muttered obediently as she pressed the toggle down. "Tha's me."

"LuisMichael—oh my God—is that you, Jim? We thought you were dead! Where are you?—Wait, I have it on my screen. We have you. We're sending someone right away. Hang tight."

In the supply shed she also found a warmsuit that hooked up to the power sled's battery. It would make the ride a good deal more bearable, and maybe she wouldn't lose fingers and toes, after all. The station was also well stocked with food and water.

Her top priority was to warn the colonists of the danger they were in—without alerting the crèche-born. Jim in particular was in danger; he knew too much about their true intent. The colony needed to know to guard against clandestine attacks on him. And they needed to begin preparing themselves for the major attack that would soon come.

She had little time to prepare a secret message before the rescuers arrived—and anything the rescuers saw or heard, the crèche-born would see or hear. Wouldn't they? But she had an idea.

The crèche-born had access to everything that happened in the colony, yes. But they weren't blind, and she was willing to bet they couldn't read Braille.

She found a coat made of a stiff, water-resistant fabric and cut a square from it. Then she donned her yoke, hood, and livegloves, brought it up offline, and called up her personal library, which still had the Braille translator guide on it. Dot by painstaking dot, she used her livegloves to transcribe a brief message onto the cloth:

Manda here, in hiding. Crèche-born tried to kill us underwater. They see and hear everything—do not read this message aloud. Jim is in danger! Seal him away from all liveware right away. Tell Derek to meet me tomorrow night at the place I showed him before.

—M.

This message she folded up and put in a packet made of the same material, on which she'd written in Braille:

URGENT! READ ONLY ABSENT ALL LIVEWARE!

She sealed the makeshift envelope with duct tape and wrote PROPERTY OF URSAMERI—PLEASE RETURN in block letters above

471

the Braille, and thrust it into the outside pocket of Jim's parka.

They'd certainly check his pockets when they checked him into the medical center, and someone would make sure the packet got to one of the UrsaMeri sisters. It might make the crèche-born suspicious, but if UrsaMeri were careful, the crèche-born wouldn't find out exactly what the message said until too late for them to harm Jim, and that was all that mattered.

Then she packed—carefully, making notes to herself so she wouldn't forget anything important in her fatigue. Meanwhile, Amaterasu made several attempts to reach them again. Manda simply didn't answer. The automated distress call and Jim's voice on the radio had been response enough.

By the time she had everything ready, almost four hours had passed. Manda fed Jim some more soup, and then kissed his fever-swollen lips. She comforted herself that his condition didn't seem to be worsening. But he was still delirious, and didn't seem to recognize her or remember where he was.

"Jim, can you understand me?" she asked. "You must tell them I'm dead—that I fell into the water and drowned. You came here alone. Can you remember that?"

He smiled lazily, and touched her cheek. "Bu' you didn' drown, Bella. You blew up."

She sighed in mild exasperation. "I'm not Bella. I'm Manda. Just remember, Manda's dead. Drowned. Remember. OK?"

"Manna's dead," he repeated agreeably, and rolled over to face the wall with a muffled grunt.

Oh well. Best I can do, without leaving a suicide note. They'll certainly assume I'm dead if they find no sign of me here. She tucked the radio between him and the wall, and put the mic in his hand. Then she spread the first-aid materials out around him, to make it look as if he had treated himself.

She checked the time again. *They'll be here any time,* she thought. The idea of being back in her own bed, safe back in Amaterasu, pulled at her like siren song.

But how safe would I be, with the crèche-born out there? And how safe will the other alien be, with no one to help it fight off the crèche-born's attack?

I'll be home soon. Soon. Finish the job first.

She donned the warmsuit, bundled up once more, and then picked up the last of her supplies and ducked out the door into the terrible cold of Brimstone's night.

The wind had died down some. Stars shone down like glittering chips of dry ice. The Host cast feeble, silver fragments of light into the canyon down which she slid. Below her, beyond the rocky ledge that had been their beach, a steep slope fell away, coated in frothy, gleaming ice, broken by black volcanic mounds, holes, and ridges, where only a few hours ago ice calves had crashed in a soup of slush. She heard them slamming against the slope farther down.

Even as she limped up the rise to hide with the powered sled and the rest of her supplies, which she'd secreted in a cave midway up the wash, she heard the engines of the jet waldos in the distance.

anda crouched next to the power sled at the tiny cave's mouth, snug to the point of drowsiness now in her warmsuit, and watched them arrive. Her binocs had a night-vision setting but she hardly needed it: Archangel and Heaven's Gate, Fire's two largest moons, shone down from opposite ends of the sky, lighting up the snowy landscape almost as brightly as daylight.

Up on the cliff top, two jet-waldos alighted, dragonfly-deft, sending a fountain of snow and ice shooting into the night sky. They skidded to a halt, jets blazing fire. The plateau up there was barely big enough; they stopped awfully close to the edge. A dangerous trick—Manda was impressed at their skill. Four figures emerged, carrying flashlights. From the cargo holds they unloaded backpacks and two stretchers.

She could tell instantly that two of them were Farrah and Janice. They must have been the flyers.

Her heart gave a hard thump. *They came for me.* She guessed that the other two were Amy and Brian; they moved like Jim.

Manda could tell by the smooth, gleaming bulk of their outlines, as they picked their way among the boulders, that they had drysuits on. And they probably had warmsuits on under those. At least they wouldn't risk hypothermia.

She had to quell an urge to call out to them as they passed her hiding place and descended into the wash. They'd be live-wired; whatever they saw and heard, the crèche-born would see and hear. Manda's only real hope against the crèche-born, if she wanted to save the other alien, was the element of surprise. She couldn't sacrifice that advantage. Not even to spare her loved ones the anguish of believing her dead.

They reached the hut and Manda caught a glimpse of their worry-marred faces. They were indeed Amy, Brian, Janice, and Farrah. The echoes as they stamped their boots and scraped off the snow carried to Manda's ears on the wind. Then they pulled the stretchers inside. Manda sat for some time, listening to the low-pitched whistling of the wind across the mouths of the lava tubes, before they emerged with Jim on a stretcher.

Amy, Brian, and Janice half-carried, half-dragged Jim's stretcher up the slope, stumbling and slipping. A few moments later Farrah too, came out of the now-darkened hut. She looked around, and her glance halted right at the dark cave mouth where Manda crouched.

She knows, Manda thought, with a shiver of twin delight and fear.

"Manda!" Farrah called. "Manda! Manda-a-*a-ah!*"

She *didn't* know. The despairing tone of her cry made it clear. Manda hunched over her gut with a gasp of sympathetic pain, as did Janice up on the cliff top. The cry blended with the wind's howling and faded away beneath Omi-Kami's thundering cacophony. Farrah turned to follow the others, dragging the second, empty stretcher.

I'm sorry, Manda thought after her, watching her climb the slope. *I'm so sorry.*

Farrah caught up with the others, who were lifting Jim's stretcher into one of the jets. Manda caught her breath, watching them struggle with it. Finally, together, they maneuvered it inside. Through the binocs Manda watched them strap him in. His head lolled. Her heart lurched again.

You'll be home soon, she promised him silently, *and they'll heal you. And I'll return to you as soon as I can. I promise.*

Part IV

A Dead Reckoning

Dead reckoning. *Naut.* [Dead *a.* V: Unrelieved, unbroken] The estimation of a ship's position from the distance run by the log and the courses steered by the compass, with corrections for current, leeway, etc., but without astronomical observations.

1866 LOWELL *Witchcraft* Prose Wks. 1892 II. 372: The mind, when it sails by dead reckoning . . . will sometimes bring up in strange latitudes.

—from the Compact Edition of the Oxford English Dictionary (copyright 2065): United Nations Interstellar Ship Exodus *archives, logged 01/31/2067.*

34

What We Become

Despite the howling of the deadly-cold winds across the mouth of her tiny cave—and despite all her worries—Manda was so exhausted that sleep fell on her almost instantly. She slept hard and long, snug in the heated comfort of her warmsuit (which warmed everything except a strip of exposed skin around the eyes, and she had tinted goggles to protect those). She awoke just before sunrise.

Manda emptied her bladder and bowels in the miserable cold and slammed down a hurried, frozen breakfast. Then she wrapped her torso and legs against the water's fatal sting and got underway.

The power sled rode on three float-skis and had brief but powerful pneumatic lift capabilities. It could handle snow, ice, slush, or water. She wove down the wash among the volcanic rocks and lava tubes toward the surf—and nearly lost control of the unfamiliar vehicle as it picked up speed on the ice-coated hill. It veered wildly back and forth, threatening to spin out. Somehow she managed to keep her seat and bring the sled back under control.

The tide was coming up once more, roiling into the lava tubes and over the icy rocks. As she neared the surf, she slowed way down and eased the sled into the rising water, and lifted her legs onto the seat, frog-like, to keep them from getting too wet. Then she sped up again, skipping the sled across the churning, ice-laden chaos, and dodged ice calves till she neared a low-floating iceberg. She tacked, getting a sense of the iceberg's motion. As the berg's nearest edge began to drop, she put on a burst of speed and hit the lift button—the power sled surged upward in a blast of freezing air and spray whose sour salts stung her lips and nose, and skipped up over the edge of the berg.

The sun had crept above the horizon, and blazed right into her eyes as she descended onto the berg. The sled's float-skis barked against the rough ice—Manda spun out and smacked onto the ice, knocking the wind out of herself. The power sled scooted sideways across the ice and finally stopped some distance away.

Probably won't be the last time, Manda thought ruefully, and sat up, rubbing her throbbing elbow. When she'd caught her breath she trudged over and remounted.

"Now, behave!" she told the sled. Breathlessly, ridiculously pleased with herself, she sped off across the bucking-swaying-crackling floes, northward. Homeward.

Fire's curve crept above Brimstone's horizon during the day's journey, first baring the white thunderheads of its upper atmosphere, then the planet-sized, crimson and yellow and fire-blue cyclones that coiled past each other in broad bands deeper in, with faint, pale orange threads winding among them.

Fire's changing position was the only real indicator of Manda's progress; the icy landscape all around her remained unchanging: endless white and pale blue stretches of ice and snow, marred here and there by patches of raspberry-colored snow moss; brown, lavender, and black dust; shallow pools; ice ridges and snowdrifts; and tunnels and crevices that wandered down into darkness within the ice.

She thought again about radiation exposure. They'd been outside without dosimeters all day yesterday, and now she'd be out all today as well. But there was nothing to be done about it, so there was no point in worrying.

She had a couple of close calls with karst and shifting bergs too, and took a few more high-speed tumbles, till she got the hang of driving the sled. She ached all over from yesterday's abuses. But all in all, she decided, travelling by power sled was the way to go, for a long trek across the ice.

Manda took a break to eat and rest in mid-morning, and a second break in the afternoon. She also checked her compass bearings. She wished badly she had a real map. She was navigating by dead reckoning: by angles and trajectories, but with no reliable landmarks to correct her course by. She'd calculated the angles carefully, and had drawn a rough trajectory for herself that she was marking as she went. But she'd had to make several detours to avoid crevasses and mounds. Even a little bit of unmeasured deviation and she'd miss Amaterasu altogether. She could be wandering in the wilderness for days.

While she was eating lunch, she heard the engines of a jet-waldo and scrambled in a panic to mount her sled and drive it into the shady overhang of a nearby snowdrift. Then it occurred to her that the waldo must have originated at Amaterasu. She crawled back out and, using her binocs, backtracked and visually marked its origin on the horizon. Then she crawled back into hiding in the lee of the drift.

Once the waldo had disappeared over the horizon, she checked the location against her map's prediction of Amaterasu's location. She made some minor corrections to her position, but overall she was reassured. She hadn't gone very far off-course.

Manda also spent plenty of time worrying about the transition she'd soon have to make once more, from floes to land. Not having recovered yet from yesterday's dreadful, freezing trek, she wasn't looking forward to repeating the experience of wading through an icy surf with enormous slabs of ice crashing into each other all around. She didn't know Arcas's southern coastline at all.

Fortunately, as she neared land, she happened across a mostly thawed bay. The bay's tides surged as high and low as the island's had, of course, but were much less tumultuous in this protected area. The bay was visibly draining as she entered it; the icebergs' motion was gentler and the ice-calf-filled surf much better behaved. Manda managed to skip off the floes and onto the water with only a minor splashing, and reached land with no further complications.

Travel overland was safer but slower than it had been on the ice floes. Thirteen hours after she'd left Jim's island—by the time Uma had crawled all the way up the sky and halfway back down again—she spotted Amaterasu's radio towers with their bright strobes far away, above the ice fog.

The cave-colony lay in the southern quadrant of the curved range of mountains known as the Scimitars. The main entrance faced northwest, into the range's curved interior. Manda was approaching the Scimitars from the south, outside their curve. On the inward edge their slopes were sharp and craggy, but they rose more gradually on the southward side. Still, she had to abandon the power sled three-quarters of the way up and make her way slowly, with scrapes and tumbles, and stops every few minutes to catch her breath once she'd depleted the last of her reserve air, the last stretch of the way up onto the ridge of the Scimitars' crest.

It was dusk by the time she reached the metal pyramid of Carli's old astronomical observatory. The evening winds buffeted her, nearly knocking her off the ledge as she worked loose the pins of one of the pyramid's hinges. Her warmsuit's chemical batteries had run down earlier, and a chill was settling into her bones through the suit and parka and inner layers. Finally she got the triangular panel open, and streamers of light flowed into the twilit sky. The lights were already up, down in the main lab area. Someone was there.

Heart suddenly pounding—*it must be Derek; he got my mes-*

sage; or could the crèche-born have intercepted?—Manda dropped her pack inside the observatory, scrambled up over the edge and dropped into the shack that held Carli's massive, handmade telescope. Then she headed down into the main area, half-afraid it would be some kind of trap.

Partway down the spiral staircase she paused. Derek stood on the thatching below, along with Arlene, Charles, Bart, Farrah, and Janice, crowded in among the old broken-down machinewaldos by the lab bench. Derek grinned wryly at her surprised expression.

"We couldn't keep it from them," he said. Arlene added, "Believe us, we tried."

The others swarmed her as she came off the stairs, with scolds and hugs and exclamations of relief. Farrah shook her, saying, "Don't you ever scare us like that again!"

While they spoke, Bart climbed up and closed and latched the trapdoor to the observatory. She noticed then that the room was warmer than it had been the last time she was here: Amaterasuwarm. With a grateful sigh, she set down her pack, and shrugged off her parka and outer gloves. She'd be able to use her livesuit in here—if it still worked, and if there were a way to plug it in.

"Tell me what's happened," she demanded. "Is Jim OK?"

Arlene pulled her over to the desk, where they'd set food and drink out for her.

"Eat," she said. "We'll fill you in."

"We found your packet just after we arrived back here," Farrah told her as Manda stuffed food and drink into her mouth. Janice added, "We delivered it to UrsaMeri ourselves."

Derek went on, "Helen and Rachel came to us," he said, gesturing at Arlene, "as soon as they read the note—" "—and asked me-us to accompany them down to the hot springs."

Manda swallowed, pleased. "Very clever!"

"Indeed. Once we'd gotten undressed and they'd made sure my liveware was off, they told us about your note." "That was good thinking, by the way, sending them a Braille message."

Manda grinned. "Thanks."

"And of course," Arlene went on, "when the rest of the clone saw us shortly thereafter—" "—we couldn't mask our relief that you were all right, so—"

"—here we all are," everyone else said in unison.

At this, Manda shot a worried look at Derek.

"Relax," he said. "We were extremely careful." "Downright paranoid," Arlene assured her.

"Some surreptitious preparations are being made even as we speak," Bart said.

"But what about Jim?" Manda asked again. The rest exchanged looks. Manda sprang out of her seat. "*Shit!* They got to him!"

Derek said, "We don't know—" and Arlene went on, "—but we don't think so." "His vat-mates have gone missing too."

"All three disappeared within a half hour of our arrival," Janice said, "before we'd had a chance to act on your note." "And we found the monitoring systems for that area had been tampered with," Bart finished.

"But the crèche-born might have done that!" Manda snapped. She snarled fingers in her hair. "It's my fault! I should never have left him."

"Whoa." Derek took hold of her hands. "Stop. That doesn't help."

"He was improving by the time he got back here," Janice told her. "We *think*," Farrah said, "he must have regained consciousness and told them what was happening—" and Janice finished, "—and they took him someplace safe."

"But you don't know for sure!"

"We'll find out," Derek replied. "The rest of us can't stay here long, though."

"We have to get back," Arlene said, "before they notice we're missing and start looking for us."

Manda noticed as the others headed for the exit tunnel that a body wrapped in strips and layers of sheeting lay there. Her heart gave a lurch. She pointed. "Carli?" she asked.

Arlene nodded.

"But—the crèche-born—"

All her older siblings smiled at her: a little sad; a little fey.

"Meet your corpse," Bart said with a sweep of his hand. Manda's scalp tingled as she eyed Carli's long-frozen body.

Janice went on, "ByronDalia did the hack for us. The crèche-born think we located your body and are heading down to pick it up."

Manda remembered ur-Carli's request that the corpse not be moved. She grimaced. "I'm not sure this is such a good idea."

Arlene laid a hand on Manda's shoulder. "We need the protein. And it's time her spirit be freed. I know she'd approve. She designed our Recycling systems, and she was the first to perform the *mana*-sharing rituals."

Manda gaped. "I didn't know that."

Derek and Arlene nodded, twin gestures. "She herself taught us to accept the gift of flesh," said Derek, and Arlene added, "She showed us how to make this final gift of our bodies as a gesture of commitment to the colony." "We know she would want this."

Then why, Manda wondered, *didn't she let her body be taken to the Recyclers back then, and why did ur-Carli want the body to remain hidden?*

But perhaps Carli had died up here without being able to summon for help. And maybe ur-Carli had simply been trying to protect the existence of the room for a little while longer, to aid them against the crèche-born. If the body had showed up, the room's existence couldn't have stayed a secret.

"We'll have the body held for a while before it's processed," Arlene added. "We'll hold a special ceremony for her, as soon as we can." *If we can.* They all shared the unspoken amendment.

"Everyone should be able to share her *mana*," Charles said softly. "She'd want it that way."

Manda watched them lower the body through the hole.

Good-bye, Carli, she thought. *Good-bye.*

A wave of grief caught her by surprise. She heard other sniffs and coughs, but didn't meet anyone's eyes as she swiped her own tears off her cheeks.

Arlene was the last of the others to depart, leaving Manda alone with Derek.

"I need to find out what happened to Jim," she told Derek. "I can't just sit around doing nothing—"

"Let us worry about Jim," he said. "For now you're our wild card. Our secret weapon. You need to stay hidden till we figure out how best to use you."

Manda paced to the tall window, filled with anxiety and guilt. *I shouldn't have left him.*

But Derek was right. Jim was smart, and strong. If they'd given him an upgraded infusion of Defenders at the seismograph station, he might well have recovered from his delirium by the time he reached Amaterasu, enough to realize he was in danger, and he would have taken measures to protect himself. She clung to that hope.

I can't throw away this one best chance to catch the crèche-born by surprise, she thought. *I've got to trust my siblings.*

She turned. "Derek, you have to find him. Make sure he's all right."

Derek eyed her, and she sensed in him that anxiety: *one of ours has an exo-bond.*

"If anything were to happen to him I could never forgive myself," Manda said. "Please."

He nodded, gruffly. "We'll spare no effort. I swear it."

"Thank you. And tell him I'm OK. He's probably worried about me—or worse, convinced I'm dead."

"Of course."

Derek gave her shoulder a comforting pat. She wiped away a few last tears and turned her thoughts back to what Derek had just said about her being their wild card.

"I have a thought about how you might use me against the crèche-born. But it'll take some explaining." And she told him what had happened to them under the sea.

Derek's eyes went very round as she described the alien and their communication with it. "But that's incredible! That 'city' was a silicon-based *brain*? Are you sure?"

"Well, I *think* it was silicon-based. I'm positive it was sapient. The smaller creatures are symbionts with it. I wish you could have seen the recordings!" She grabbed his hands. "Derek, it was *amazingly* smart! It correctly guessed all kinds of things about us and our situation from only a couple of clues—" The muscles of her throat tightened. "It saved our lives when the crèche-born took over my *Aculeus* waldos and attacked us. But we couldn't save it in return. We rescued its child, though. Or a copy of its memories . . . or something. At least, we think we did."

She described everything else that had happened, including the strange message their secret crèche-born contact had delivered. At this Derek growled, with a ferocious frown.

"They're monsters. *Monsters!* See what I told you? Destroying an alien intelligence as if it were nothing—less than nothing!—to them. Everything is a game." He made fists as old memories played behind his eyes. "Sick bastards," he hissed. "We should have fought them to the death years ago."

Manda eyed him, disturbed by this glimpse of a violence, a deadly anger, in him that she'd never seen before.

What are we becoming?

After a hesitation, she told him about the cache of weapons and knowledge Carli had supposedly hidden. "I think it's here," she finished, spreading her arms to gesture around them. "And

I think maybe I can use what's here to get at them without them knowing what's coming."

He lowered his head. Manda sensed a struggle. When he looked up at her again his gaze glittered, hard and cold, green-tinged ice.

"Manda, you do whatever you have to, to stop them," he said. "Show no mercy. You've glimpsed now just what they're capable of."

Manda stared. "Um, I can't believe I'm saying this, but . . . shouldn't you clear this with the rest of the council first?"

"No. I'm *not* going to let us get bogged down in coup games and protocol again—arguments over whether what you've said is accurate, whether we should negotiate with them—all the power brokering, arguments, cowardice—*stupidities!* We don't have time for that. The cost of waiting is far too high."

Manda eyed him. She knew how coup worked. This was either political suicide—for both of them—or it was another kind of coup game: a coup d'état. Either way, things would never be the same again.

"Are you *sure* about all this. . . . ?"

Derek answered her troubled gaze, his own creased face unyielding. "Do *you* want to be remembered as one of those who let our own kind wipe out an intelligent alien species, and let our own colony be enslaved?"

They're not my *kind,* Manda thought, annoyed. "Of course not. I wouldn't have risked my life down there if I had."

"Well, then." He spread his hands. "I'll worry about the council. *You* deal with the crèche-born."

Manda thought of what they'd done to the alien, of what they'd tried to do to her and Jim. She nodded. "I will."

"I've arranged for this tunnel to be sealed from below. We've stocked some food and water." He pointed at a shadowed corner of the large room, where packages and carboys sat. "Get us word on your progress, when you can. We'll communicate in Braille; it gives us a little better security, at least till they figure out what we're doing. I've checked Carli's systems—they're completely sealed off and clean. We installed a Braille reader and writer for you on her system. UrsaMeri will be our reader down in the caves, till we can secure the local-area systems."

"But how do I get the messages to you?"

"The herder clones. I've already alerted them; they don't wear much liveware out there anyway so they won't be suspect."

Manda nodded slowly. "Very good."

"You'll find a pile of six lichened stones at the wash a hundred fifty meters from the main entrance. Just follow the ridge; you'll see it easily."

"I know the place."

"They'll drop messages into the center of the pile. Send a waldo to check the drop-off every four hours, at a minimum."

"I will."

"There'll always be something there for you. You needn't prepare a message unless you have something to report. If you miss getting a drop-off I'll assume you're in trouble, and I'll send help."

Manda grabbed him in a hug hard and long. She breathed in Derek's musky, old-man's-scent—a scent that went back with her before conscious memory. They were all changing, in unpredictable ways. In her mind the future was falling away from her, a void as dark and fathomless as Omi-Kami's depths.

The crèche-born were the colony's parents, *and* their boogeymen. They'd bred them, raised them, and then had cast them like so much trash—or perhaps like seeds; seeds they'd created but had had no use for—onto the winds of chance. Now they were coming back. And they weren't playing nice.

No one—not Manda; not any of the colonists—knew how much damage the crèche-born might be able to wreak, nor how quickly. They had to assume the worst: that the crèche-born were aware of the movements and capabilities of every single individual in the colony, and that they could commandeer any and all of the colony's liveware systems.

For the crèche-born, though, this place didn't exist, and neither did Manda anymore. Which meant she could safely hide here for as long as it would take to find and familiarize herself with Carli's cache of weapons, and then to strike on their blind side.

And they had allies, of a sort: they had ur-Carli and they had their unknown friend among the crèche-born. Uncertain allies, to be sure—but it beat having nothing.

But she was afraid. She didn't want to kill, and she didn't want to die.

They heard a sound; both turned as Charles stuck his head up from within the ice tunnel, breathless and wild-eyed.

"Derek, the refinery has been cut off from the network. We think they're under attack."

Manda gasped, grabbing Derek's arm. "It's Jim. That's why they attacked. It must be!"

Derek gave Manda a sharp glance, and a nod. "Did they cut themselves off," he asked Charles, "or were they cut off by the crèche-born?"

"We don't know. They sent an odd message to the council first, but—" He shrugged.

Derek looked at Manda. *It's begun.* "Any sign of overt attack here yet?"

"I don't know. Things are confused. Everything's going crazy down below. Word is, *Exodus* is headed this way at high acceleration—the council is demanding to know where you are—PabloJeb is fit to be tied—"

"I'll be right there," Derek told Charles.

Derek pointed at an ice-patch tank with a hose attachment sitting by the tunnel exit. They were used to create temporary partitions inside Amaterasu, and outdoor shelter for the herders; they blew a super-cold, directed blast of wet ice that rapidly froze into a solid block.

"Manda, when I give you the signal from below, start spraying ice down the tunnel. We've set up another ice patcher that Bart will use to blow ice up and block off entry from below. Don't worry—" he said, at her expression "—we removed the units' liveware systems first. Both are set up to be only operable manually." At Manda's lifted eyebrows, he explained, "We've been identifying and creating safe areas and equipment ever since you first warned us that the crèche-born were spying on us. I would have liked more time, but . . ." He shrugged. "We're not completely unprepared for this."

Manda gave him, and then Charles, each a last good-bye kiss and hug. Charles disappeared below, and Derek lowered himself into the tunnel. He paused to look at Manda.

"Good luck," they told each other.

Once she'd sealed herself in, Manda looked around. The room was much the same as the first time she'd seen it. Was that really only seven weeks ago? Less than two months. Hard to believe. *Everything* had changed, since then. Teresa and Paul gone, and their singleton baby brother in the nursery now, no doubt lost and forgotten in this confusion. She felt a pang of remorse.

I'll come for you, Terence, she thought, *if I live through this. I won't leave you alone in there the way I was left. I swear it.*

She wandered through the room. Things were so quiet, now, with everyone gone. It was hard to believe a war had started. She peered into Carli's chambers. Manda's siblings had cleaned up for her. The dust had been swept away. Fresh linens and comforters had been piled high on the bed and she saw they'd added one of her own outfits to the items hanging in the closet.

Can I really sleep in her *bed?* Manda wondered. But she doubted she'd be sleeping much over the next few days.

She went back into the main area and got out her livesuit, stripped, put it on, and pulled a couple of layers on over it. Then she plugged her yoke's leads into the ports on Carli's computer.

Might as well start with the obvious, she thought, and brought up her liveface. She booted up Carli's computer and opened the main communications queue ball for messages.

And ur-Carli stood there, waiting for her.

"Greetings," it said. "I've been monitoring events. I'm here to show you around."

Manda gasped. "So you *do* have access to this room!"

"Of course. I'm housed in this room," ur-Carli replied. "I wasn't allowed to contact you directly till you plugged into my system."

"But—but you said you were housed in DMiTRI—"

The syntellect nodded. "Ah. That is my other copy, Version One-Point-Three. That copy is slaved to the crèche-born and has been rather seriously corrupted."

"And you are not?"

"Correct. I'm an upgrade. To differentiate us, you may refer to me as Version-Two-Point-Oh, or simply Two-Oh, if you prefer. Come." It crooked a finger, as above it a door appeared and opened, revealing a blaze of light. "I'm here to help you halt the crèche-borns' attack."

Manda donned her cat avatar and moved forward into livespace behind the syntellect. The perspective shifted till the door was on a horizontal plane. Other interfaces and icons receded as Manda moved forward; she passed through the doorway and stood at the brink of chaos. Icons and fragmented infostreams stormed all around her, in a dazzling roar of incomplete numbers, equations, words, tones, and imagery. Two-Oh took Manda's hand and pulled her off the ledge, into the fray. Around them formed a bubble that approximated their shape, with about five or six centimeters to spare.

"I'm guiding you out of Carli's systems and into the wider network," the syntellect explained, speaking over the din as they raced through streaming info, dodging back and forth to avoid collision. She-cat saw over its shoulder that the syntellect was using some sort of control console to guide them.

"Is this safe?"

"We've built a series of encrypted tunnels through their hardware and software, disguised as old archives and bad sectors. But things are always changing and the paths aren't always reliable. Stay alert. Don't make any sudden gestures."

"I will. I mean, I won't." Manda-cat hesitated. "You said 'we.' "

"Carli and I together set up some initial pathways. I've carried on with them since her death. Careful—don't deviate," ur-Carli said, steering Manda-cat away from a stream that veered suddenly toward them. The bubble bowed inward, and the stream just barely missed striking it. "If you disturb even a single data bit we might be detected. They are on full alert now."

"Where are you taking me?" Manda-cat asked, dodging yet another chunk of errant code. As it passed her she heard an oddly distorted voice speaking something that might or might not have been English. Another chunk flashed past, nearly smacking her-avatar in the face—she-cat dodged, catching a glimpse of a face made of squirming algorithms. It bared numeric teeth and opened white-black eyes made of zeros and ones.

Too long in here and I'll go a bit mad, she thought.

"We're headed to *Exodus,*" the syntellect replied, in answer to the question she'd already forgotten she'd asked.

Ohmigod.

"Wait! I mean—" she-avatar stammered, as the syntellect disconcertingly duplicated its face on the back side of its head to look at her-avatar while steering them onward, "shouldn't we take a few moments to plan things? I don't know what I need to do!"

"It's quite straightforward. The plans have been all laid out. Carli and I developed it years ago. *Stop!*" it said sharply, as Manda-cat's momentum started to carry her-avatar past the syntellect. She realized then that ur-Carli had stopped moving.

Around them chaos still raged in many shades and hues, but it had all shifted somehow. The information was flowing differently. She saw many jagged fragments of commands and data files hanging or sliding among complete ones, to and from which clots and gobs and flashes of data streamed. She'd nearly stumbled right into one such fragment.

The sounds and imagery confused her. It made her dizzy, how everything shifted in size and shape as it all whirled and spasmed around her. The world looked way too big and too small, simultaneously, and sounds echoed strangely all about. She couldn't tell what things were, much less how far away they lay.

From this she guessed that she was inside a fourth-dimensional—or higher—raw livespace, with no real iconic interface developed to accommodate the human user. These were crèche-born constructs, and she knew about them but had no experience navigating in them.

She could tell, though, that the info turnover here was staggeringly fast. It was like being in a garbage heap being churned in a vast mixer, or standing in a tornado.

"We're in DMiTRI now. Please don't move. My twin mustn't detect us. I've secreted numerous blind spots and friendly subroutines in its code, but they're not always reliable—the crèche-born keep stumbling across them, and I've had to be careful to avoid detection. One-Three is under orders to report to them any tampering with its primary systems and to destroy the intruding code."

"I hate when that happens," Manda-avatar remarked. To avoid transmitting an unintended movement, she removed her arms from her avatar's shell, disabling her livesuit's motion-responder. Her virtual avatar now stood before her, an empty, transparent suit, and the real world of Carli's secret room reappeared, with the datascope a faint overlay on her vision. Her motion icons disappeared from her faceware display, though her other commandshapes remained.

The syntellect went on: "It'll be a moment before my subroutines can clear a space for us on the omnilink to *Exodus*. Meanwhile I can answer some of your questions."

"OK." Manda could think of several: what did the crèche-born have planned? What was happening at the refinery? Was Jim still alive?

"Is there any way," she-avatar asked, "that I can see what's happening back at the colony, or at the refinery?"

"The refinery is beyond my reach. The crèche-born commandeered all faceware systems approximately one hundred eighty-four seconds ago and it's a complete lockdown. But the colony systems are still mostly up for grabs. Here."

It placed its hands just so, and between them appeared a hole with strange crystalline distortions, which made it look like the inside of a face. Manda slipped her arms back into her avatar and the avatar refitted itself to her. The *virtu*scape appeared again. Manda-avatar stuck her face into the hole.

Suddenly she-avatar floated inside a soccer ball–shaped room. Each panel—including those underfoot—contained a different view of Amaterasu's caverns and corridors. Whenever she-avatar looked in a given direction, the ball shifted, moving the panels she was gazing at toward her.

Numerous panels—perhaps third—were blank. In all the remaining images, pandemonium reigned. People were running, screaming—fighting the machine-waldos that chased them through the corridors, slashing and smashing as if the humans were bugs—or netting them, as though they were wild animals. Elsewhere, in growing numbers, people began to march like marionettes into small rooms and chambers, where waiting machines locked them in. Others collapsed, clawing at their arms and faces. Inexorably, one by one, more panels blacked out as she watched.

"What's happening?" she-avatar gasped, pointing at the people falling to the floor.

"Their livesuits have been hijacked," came the voice of Two-Oh. "Those with full suits are being rounded up. Those with only partial liveware are being tortured, to render them harmless. It's a liveworm program. They beta-tested it on you earlier."

Those fucks, she thought savagely. She-avatar bounded here and there through the programball's center, pressing her-cat's paws against the different screens. She-avatar couldn't see her siblings anywhere.

Fleets, not only of machines, but of empty livesuits carrying metal poles and saws and chains, began pouring down stairways and through halls in ever larger numbers, chasing waves of terrified people before them. They had to be coming from the CarliPablo workshop and the spare equipment hangar. Waldos in Amaterasu vastly outnumbered colonists.

One panel showed the nursery, from the corridor outside. It was under attack. A piece of heavy machinery—her own mole-waldo!—whaled on the door and pounded on the walls, cracking rocks loose. Clouds of dust drifted down with each blow.

Great—bring the whole ceiling down, why don't you? Morons.

She-avatar could find no image of the nursery's interior. *Terence!* "What about the babies? The children?"

Two-Oh materialized beside her-avatar. "The nursery has no liveware. They're sealed in and heavily defended. Safe, for now. But not for long. Amaterasu will stand perhaps another seven hundred seconds. By that time, all colonists will be either captured or killed."

"Seven hundred, that's—" Manda did the mental math. "Less than twelve minutes! Get us that line to *Exodus*, would you?"

"Patience, Memsahib. I'm hurrying."

"Memsahib?" Manda-avatar repeated, with an incredulous stare.

"I'm a Kipling fan," Two-Oh replied. Was that a smile on its artificial lips? She gave the syntellect a suspicious look. Had Two-Oh somehow escaped its design constraints and achieved sapience?

"Where are my siblings?" she-avatar asked.

A pause. "Out of range."

Manda paced, checking the different panels. The crèche-borns' renegade waldos were being careful not to damage any of Amaterasu's critical systems. The robotic arms and movers in the Recycling area, for instance, were careful to avoid damaging the vats and reactors and nutrient baths, as they captured and dragged and herded colonists into the refrigerated storage areas. It was only people they were attacking. And Manda-cat saw some casualties, but most of the crèche-born seemed bent on capture.

Naturally—they're saving us to be their slaves. Manda felt sick to her stomach.

She thought about the alien on the far side of the world.

"Can you see where my *Aculeus* waldos are?" she-avatar asked the syntellect. "Are they headed for the creature on the far side of Brimstone?"

"They are," the syntellect confirmed; "they reached the farside creature about six thousand two hundred twenty-two seconds ago," and it showed her-avatar the images on three panels.

Through two of her marine-waldos' commandfaces she could see different false-color views of an alien structure. The structure was much the same as the one she'd seen with her own eyes— and yet intriguingly different as well, with its arches and enormous curving tubes and coiling strands.

Wildlife darted before the cameras, with differences from the nearside wildlife that begged to be studied. Surrounding everything was a streaming scarlet forest of bactoweed, lush and vast.

The third waldo's camera was focused tightly on its own midsection, she-avatar saw, and its mechanical arms were in the process of dismantling the armature around its antimatter battery, as the other two waldos towed it forward amid the majestic towers and spirals and arches of the second alien, toward the creature's center.

A terrible anger surged up in her. *You sick bastards. You don't have to kill this creature. It doesn't matter whether we know about it anymore.*

She-avatar spun to face Two-Oh—and spotted a transparent avatar in the shape of a pyramid on a rectangular base, floating overhead in the ball-shaped room's center. She-avatar leapt back, jabbing a claw upward. "Intruder!"

The syntellect spun, then saw what Manda-cat was pointing at. "No, that's merely a subroutine I stole from the crèche-born to override others' waldo control."

"Then let's turn the tables on them!" she-cat cried, and bounded toward the figure, but ur-Carli V2.0 rose up to block her. "No!"

Manda-cat sank to the floor. "Why not, goddammit?"

"You are one; they are many. There is a much better way."

"*How?*"

"I'll show you. It's very easy," Two-Oh said. "Come, it's time to move," and suddenly the syntellect was using its commandface to guide her among immense, terrifying blasts of digital process flows again. Almost instantly, it seemed, Two-Oh brought them to another dazzling, swarming, high-dimensional infoscape. Manda-cat squinted against the vertigo.

"Welcome to *Exodus*," it said. "Be very careful. *Exodus*'s smartware is even more paranoid than my twin."

"So how do we—"

"I only know of one way to stop the crèche-born," Two-Oh replied. "Carli designed an infobomb. Over the years I have completed it, and have been inserting pieces of it in nooks and crannies in *Exodus*'s systems."

"An infobomb. OK. What will it do?"

"Once assembled, if it functions as it should, it will bring down all their higher-order computer systems. The ship will no longer have a brain. They won't have any maneuvering capabilities. Life support will shut down. They will all die."

Manda remembered Derek's words. *Do whatever it takes.* "But I know we have at least one friend in there. And there may be others. The one we talked to implied that there were. We'd be killing them, too."

"Yes. It's unavoidable."

Manda chewed her lip, and her avatar tried to mimic the motion with its fangs. "There's got to be another way."

"I know of none. And there is little time," Two-Oh said.

"*Why me*, goddammit? Why haven't you acted before now?"

The syntellect shook its head. "I can't perform this act. I'm not allowed to harm humans. It was hard enough for me work around my constraints long enough to build some of the components. *You* must trigger the mechanism that assembles and detonates the bomb."

Manda-cat shook her-its head. *Not fair. I don't want to do this. Who else, then?*

Manda stalled. "Is there anyone else onboard, besides the crèche-born?"

"Yes," it said. "They have been breeding a new generation of clones."

"So I'll be killing the innocent as well. Young people. Children. Babies."

"Yes."

"I can't do this." She swept off her livehood and disconnected, and sat alone in Carli's old lab, face in her hands.

It was dead quiet. Hard to believe people were fighting and dying down below her.

A message every four hours, Derek had said. What a joke that had turned out to be. This war would be over in another few minutes. The crèche-born had been planning it for years. The colony never had a chance. Except this one.

Every second you hesitate means another colonist dies. Innocent people are dying here too, and they *are the aggressors.*

Do what it takes, Manda. Do what you must.

Numbly, she pulled her livehood back on and reconnected,

and stood again in *Exodus*, in the midst of seething, blinding digital tumult, with ur-Carli V2.0 at her side.

"Are you ready?" it asked. Beside it was a big red button on a pedestal. On the button it said *PUSH ME*.

"A little melodramatic, don't you think?" asked Manda-avatar. The syntellect shrugged. "I'm not the designer."

"Just following orders, eh?" She-avatar eyed the button with great distaste. *I'm responsible for the death of innocents, either way*, she thought. *Just push the damn button.*

But a thought was niggling at her.

"Ur-Carli," she-cat said—"excuse me; Two-Oh—their omni field generator needs to be within a certain range of a large gravitational pull, does it not?"

"Yes," the syntellect replied.

"And they're currently moving away from the sun."

"Yes."

"Then—won't their omni generator be useless shortly?"

"Yes. However, the crèche-born have planned their attack so as to entrap most of the colonists in the next six hundred twenty-three seconds, while they are still close enough to Uma for their omnilink to work. They'll then wipe out whoever remains uncaptured, so as not to permit them to attempt the release of prisoners before they arrive."

She-avatar gnawed a claw; the tang of her livesuit's meta-plastic mesh spread onto her tongue. "How much time do we have before they start wiping out the ones who have eluded capture?—in minutes, please."

"Approximately eleven."

"Once the infobomb goes off, could you commandeer their systems, as they have ours, instead of destroying it?"

Two-Oh shook its head. "No. Part of the infobomb's job is to send a massive power surge through their systems that destroys crucial hardware. It leaves no place for me to go."

"Well—suppose we *didn't* set off the bomb, then? Could you copy yourself onto *Exodus*'s systems? Could you infiltrate?—Suppose you stole from them a copy of what they're using against our systems?"

"There's an interesting thought." It looked pensive again. "If they activated it from DMiTRI I could sneak a copy from my twin. . . ."

Manda-cat waited.

"I could do it," the syntellect said finally. "It will be complicated. I don't have all the subroutines I'd need."

"How long will it take you to develop them?"

"A while. I'll need a good two hundred forty-three seconds—excuse me! Six minutes—to modify the code, and another minute to load it."

"So we have about a five-minute margin for error, would you say?"

"A bit more, if I go right now. But I'll be forced to intrude into their systems at several points, and my activities are likely to be detected and traced back to the computer where my source code is housed."

"Shit." Manda-cat eyed the button. *The ship's systems are bound to be under a heavy strain.* "We'll chance it."

"I feel obliged to point out that if I succeed in this, eventually they might find a way to overwrite or corrupt the copy I leave aboard *Exodus*, in which case they'll merely return here and finish the job they started. Or, if they don't succeed in taking back control, you'll be stranding them in interplanetary space, where eventually they'll die anyway. And if I fail, you will have doomed your people, when you could easily have saved them."

Manda growled. "I know, dammit! Stop arguing! *Just go.*—But wait!" she-avatar cried, as the syntellect started to fade. It paused. "When your copy gets into their systems," Manda-cat said, "take *Exodus* out of the plane of the ecliptic as far and fast as you can. Once you're well into interstellar space, you delete that copy of yourself—and any backups they might have of you or of *Exodus*'s smart systems—so they have to rebuild it all from scratch. Leave their life-support alone; just paralyze the ship. Can you do that?"

"Ah! That would strand them in interstellar space for a long time. Several fire-years, even. During which time they'd be completely cut off from you, and harmless." The syntellect paused. "A much better option for your people. They might eventually regain control of the ship and make their way back, but it's more likely that they'll end up permanently stranded in interstellar space."

And end up dying of starvation. Manda lowered her head. *OK, it's not a great alternative.*

But she couldn't just push a button and murder people outright. Not if she had another choice. This choice won the war for her people, while leaving *Exodus*'s clones at least a chance at survival.

"Very well."

"And before you go—" Two-Oh paused again. Manda asked, "Can you send me back to the video monitoring station, back on DMiTRI, while I wait?" She wanted to know what was happening to her people.

"Of course." Ur-Carli V2.0 vanished, and in that same instant Manda-cat was back in the soccer ball–shaped monitoring room. An icon hung before her, its face a countdown clock showing the time left till the crèche-born started killing her people. 10:10:22:01, it said. Ten minutes, ten seconds, and counting. It was clear from the many images that things weren't going well for her people.

She looked up at the waldo-hijacking pyramid in the room's center, and couldn't think of one good reason why she shouldn't.

You are one; they are many.

But that wasn't a reason not to act; it simply meant she'd better work smart, and work fast.

She bounded up into the waldo-commandeering avatar. Her cat avatar vanished and a view sphere sprang up. The hijack software itself may have been complex, but its user interface was quite simple: the sphere was a miniature version of the room she was in. A message appeared across her vision in glowing red letters:

CHOOSE LOCATION.

Manda saw that she had arms, hands, and fingers that responded to her movements; she touched a thumbnail image on the miniature sphere, and it opened out into a larger image.

CHOOSE TAKEOVER CANDIDATE, the message now read.

She knew right where this particular image came from; she'd seen the view before through her own faceware. A series of cameras were mounted along the big spiral equipment ramps that led down from the storage hangar into the populated areas, and this was one of them.

Down the ramp in a clattering and rumbling mass came a small fleet of housekeeping and construction waldos. The waldo in the lead was a cleaner, about half the size of a human, brandishing its foam spray hose. Its tank of steaming suds sloshed along behind it. It was followed by a big dirt-tamper, three wall-builders, and a grouter. Lagging behind, a giant mole waldo brought up the rear, lumbering down the stone ramp on its tractor treads, the titanium drill blades on its nose extended to their full diameter.

In about seven more turns they'd emerge into Hydroponics. She switched views. A small group of colonists there was fighting off two large waldos. It was the KaliMarshall fiveclone—including Abraham and Robert, she realized—defending the UrsaMeri sisters. Abraham and Robert were fighting a bamboo-harvesting waldo, a twenty-meter-long caterpillar-like construct with several dozen blades attached to its mechanical arms. Their elder brothers sought to tie down the second waldo, a crane, with steel cables and crane hooks. Abraham and Robert managed to make their way through the gauntlet of slashing blades to the harvester-waldo's back, where they were now attempting to open its maintenance control box.

It looked like the KaliMarshalls were about to win their skirmish and get the UrsaMeris to safety. But the waldo reinforcements on the way down from the hangar would overwhelm them.

Manda switched back to the ramp cameras and found the waldos again. She touched the waldo in the lead. Its control shapes and forward views sprang up around her—she-waldo flailed as she tried to familiarize herself with the controls.

"Spray foam—ah!" She-cleaner activated her-its foam disperser, spun around and, steering backward down the ramp, used one of her-its spray tubes to coat the floor behind her-it in warm sudsy water. Those following skidded in the suds, crashed against the walls, and began careening down the ramp, out of control. The others bowled her-waldo over, and all six slid out the bottom and slammed up against a rail in Hydroponics.

Then someone wrenched control back, and Manda found herself back in the control pyramid inside the video soccer ball. The other waldos were starting to disentangle themselves, and the mole waldo was lumbering down the ramp toward them.

Move fast!

Manda commandeered the mole, and—as she-mole accelerated down the ramp; the suds presented no challenge to the mole's tractor treads—she-mole used her-its pincer claw to open the processor housing on its back. As the unit rolled past a camera view, she was able to zoom in on the precise point she needed. She-mole groped—grabbed it with her-its pincer, and waited—accelerating—waited more—till, as she-mole barrelled toward the waldos below, she-mole yanked the bus loose that carried the processor's commands to the waldo's body. The disabled mole's momentum sent it crashing into the other waldos, knocking them down like bowling pins and pinning them against the rail with a horrible grinding sound.

She caught a quick view of the wreckage, and smiled. Reparable, eventually, but they weren't going anywhere soon. And she saw the KaliMarshalls escorting the UrsaMeris into the bamboo forest. *They're heading for the Honeycombs.* That must be where CarliPablo and company had set up the command base for their resistance. *Good.* With its multitude of winding tunnels and hidden crannies, and its limited technology, it was an excellent choice.

She pulled up another screen, and gasped. The RoxannaTomases and a cluster of others were trapped in the Bio-Med complex. A horde of medical waldos and robots was attacking them in waves, trying to drive them from the hallway into a small isolation unit. Several colonists were holding off the waldos while others were evacuating patients. One of the defenders stumbled backward, screaming and swatting at himself, as a mass of tiny algae-harvester waldos swarmed up him—he knocked over a stretcher and sent an injured woman sprawling. Jeannelle helped her up while Vance came to the other man's aid. Manda saw that another of those damned bamboo harvesters was just around the corner, coming in the direction they were headed, bearing down fast.

Manda tried to hijack the harvester—and failed. They'd figured out what she was doing! They'd come up with a hack to keep her out. She could only watch helplessly as they came around the corner to meet the bamboo harvester's forest of slashing blades. The harvester forced them back, back, back, into the isolation room. The RoxannaTomases made a concerted rush—blood went everywhere—Vance was down! And one of his older sisters. And another. *Shit.*

Then the rest of the clone, all four remaining, were on top of the harvester, and it went dead. They gathered their wounded and headed for the freight elevators.

So much blood. They left a trail of it.

Manda couldn't stand to watch anymore. She moved out of the hijacker pyramid—her cat avatar sealed itself around her—and she checked her clock. 06:03:44:02 and counting. Six more minutes. Two-Oh mustn't fail, or Manda had doomed her own people. Weary and frightened, sick over the carnage she'd just witnessed—*I could have prevented it; I could have just pushed that fucking button*—she-cat closed her-avatar's eyes.

If it hadn't been for that, she might never have heard the small sound, amid the din and commotion around her-avatar. It was a scraping, a rusty jagged noise that grated on her ears in a peculiarly *real* way.

With a gasp of realization she pulled off her livehood and ripped out her liveplugs—and saw a motion in the shadows. The broken-down waldos behind the work benches were stirring.

Something brushed her foot. With a shriek she jumped: several small waldos—about the mass of a cat, but with numerous long arm-legs—were scuttling up the legs of Carli's desk. She knocked them away. More kept coming. Meanwhile the two bigger ones were nearing too. Manda edged away from the desk, but the waldos didn't track her. Their cameras remained trained on the desk.

They're after Carli's computer! They're trying to stop Two-Oh.

At all costs, she had to keep them away. She didn't dare unplug the unit and remove it—the instant she did she immobilized ur-Carli and doomed the colonists.

Manda looked around for a weapon. Nearby stood a heavy push broom: a homemade, industrial-sized one with a metal pipe handle. One of her siblings must have left it. She dashed over, grabbed it, and swatted at the insect-like waldos, sending one—then another—flying across the room.

It'll do, she thought.

The third waldo, a multisegmented one bristling with sampling and monitoring gear, got hold of the broom bristles and she couldn't shake it loose—but that only gave her a little more leverage when she smashed it up into the camera platforms of the larger hulk now lumbering forward. She slammed the broom against the big waldo's face a second time, and the mini-waldo made a satisfying crunch and fell to the floor in pieces, while a camera fitting on the big one cracked. One of its top attachments broke off, spitting sparks and having seizures. Two more insect-waldos crawled up, and some miniature tank waldos with treads and attachment arms were shimmying up the legs of the desk.

How many of those fucking things are there?

While she was fighting these off, the second big waldo rolled up, screeing and clanking, littering parts across the floor as it came around the first big one. One of the small ones was now crawling across the desk, ports extended to insert into Carli's computer. Manda sent it flying with the broom, aiming it at the new big one. The insect-waldo ricocheted off the big waldo's midsection, and the next one smashed through the window slit in a shower of glass shards. Freezing air blasted into the room in a cloud of ice crystals.

Manda jumped up on the desk and crouched there, broom handle and feet flying at the fleet of assorted tiny waldos now assaulting her. The first big one got her arm as she took a swipe—it was old and rusty and crotchety, trailing wires and parts, and its clamp couldn't quite close on her—but she only just managed to worm free as two spiders reached Carli's computer and were starting to plug themselves in.

Manda began to panic. She was tiring and couldn't keep track of them all. *I can't do this alone!*

She yanked the mini-waldos away from the computer port, receiving slashes on her hand that disabled one of her livegloves. Blood and nano-muscles spattered the desk and floor as she hurled the waldos—two at one go, then another three—across the room. She didn't feel the pain yet, but it was a bad cut.

The second big waldo moved in, grabbing her ankle. It backed, pulling her off the desk as more spiders and mini-tanks swarmed over her back to the computer. Instead of resisting, Manda sat and shoved herself off the desk, *toward* the massive waldo, raining mini-waldos onto the floor. Manda grabbed its camera platform to lever herself and jammed the broom handle into the crook of its grip.

If these hadn't been ancient, decrepit machines she wouldn't have stood a chance. But the clamp entrapping her ankle was rusted. She heaved and pulled—and half of its grip snapped off. Manda tumbled to the floor, and scrambled up onto the desk again.

The spiders were swarming across the face of the computer housing. Three were already plugged in. She yanked their cords out of the computer ports—praying they hadn't been able to do any damage—the syntellect must be as heavily defended as its digital enemies were; she clung to that hope—and swept the army of miniature robots away once more.

A third large, equipment-hauling waldo was now rolling toward her from the shadows. She stared in dismay.

"Hurry up, ur-Carli!" she yelled, praying the syntellect could hear her, wherever it was and whatever it was doing. "I can't hold them!"

Then she gaped in amazement as the third large waldo, which had finally reached them, grappled the first waldo and pulled it away with a horrible grinding, blatting noise.

An ally!

"Ur-Carli?" she asked. "Is that you?"

No answer.

Her enemies abruptly switched tactics. The small waldos swarmed all around Manda and up her legs, cutting and jabbing, while the big one whose grip she'd just snapped off—which had been trying clumsily to club her—turned to help its compatriot waldo, now locked in combat with Manda's unknown ally.

Swearing, Manda dropped the broom in her effort to get the small, biting and stinging machines off her. She fell off the desk, still swatting at them, and tried to scramble away. But they were all over her, cutting and pinching.

Then she spotted the ice patcher. She crawled toward it—reached—grabbed the hose, and used its nozzle to sweep them off her. Then she toed the pedal and, as they started to rush her again, buried them all in a blast of icy slush.

Next she dragged the ice-patcher over to the big waldos. The two enemy waldos together were smashing at Manda's ally. It was slowly losing the fight, being ripped up and disassembled part by part. Manda dodged flying debris, closing. One of them started to turn toward her, but she opened the hose nozzle and cemented them all to the floor with several hundred kilos of ice, and then covered their upper attachments with a thick glaze of ice sheeting as well.

Eat snow, assholes, she thought.

She pulled her livehood back on, limped over, bleeding from about a thousand tiny cuts and punctures, and plugged back into Carli's computer.

There was no sign of ur-Carli V2.0. Manda's connection to the networks had been severed.

She sat down—hurting, panting, both in-face and ex-face. *Shit. What do I do now?*

Then a tall, piebald woman-avatar appeared before her. Her-avatar's body was covered in chocolate-dark patterns against ivory-white.

"I'm Dane Elisa Cae," she said. "We met on the ocean floor."

"You're the one who helped us!"

"Yes, then and just now. It looks as though they found and severed your link to *Exodus*, I'm afraid," she-avatar said, surveying the digital surroundings, "and they've wiped out the local copy of ur-Carli. But I've got a link of my own to the ship. Hurry—follow me. We'll find out if ur-Carli completed its work before it was wiped."

Manda's heart sank at the other's words. Ur-Carli was gone. Another casualty of her unwillingness to kill the crèche-born.

But it might have completed its mission first. Or there might be another way to stop them.

"Thanks for your help," Manda-cat said, as the other woman dragged her, dodging back and forth, among the dataflows. Her livesuit was a wreck: one paw was completely nonresponsive, and the rest of the avatar had gone sluggish and twitchy, as the main portion of her livesuit slowly bled its muscle-nanos away. "How did you know I needed help?"

"I buried a software tracer in your liveface, back in the submersible," the other replied. "I'd been monitoring you till you disengaged your liveware, and picked you up again when you started using the waldo-hijacking software. I kept them from using the liveworm bug on your suit while you were commandeering their waldos. It took me a while to hack in and figure out what they were doing in here."

"Thanks," Manda-cat said.

They materialized together by the pedestal with the big red button. Ur-Carli V2.0 was waiting there. Manda-avatar gaped.

"You're all right!" she-cat exclaimed. "I was afraid you'd been destroyed.

"I had a backup hidden away," V2.0 replied, with a modest shrug. "I updated my backups before I exposed myself to them. SOP. When they found and wiped the original, I automatically came back online and finished the task while they were fighting you.

"Dane Elisa Cae," the syntellect said to the other. "What are you doing here?"

"She helped me defeat the attackers back in Carli's room," Manda-cat said.

"Which version are you?" Dane-avatar asked the syntellect.
"Two-Oh."

"I didn't know she'd gotten that far with you."

"Just before she died," the syntellect replied. "Are you here to try to stop us?"

"That depends. What's this?" and Dane-avatar gestured at the button on the red pedestal. Manda's heart was thumping again. Tell the truth, or lie? This woman had saved her life at least twice. Manda couldn't bring herself to lie.

"I've ordered ur-Carli to commandeer *Exodus*," Manda said, "to take your ship out into interstellar space and strand you there."

Dane-avatar turned to the syntellect. "True?"

"Confirmed." Two-Oh turned to Manda-cat. "We've only got a few more seconds. They're about to start their 'cleanup' campaign."

"Move out of the way, please," Manda-cat said to Dane-avatar, who was blocking her access to the button on the pedestal. "I need to push that button, *now*."

Dane-avatar looked beyond Manda-cat at ur-Carli. "And what is the risk of death or injury to my people?"

"The risk of immediate death is minimal. I can't predict every exigency, but it seems unlikely you will be put in serious danger, as long as no one does anything stupid. However, your people *will* be stranded in interstellar space, once my copy deletes itself, and according to my calculations you are highly likely to die there."

Manda realized with a sick feeling that she was going to have figure out a way to attack and disarm her. But she turned to Manda. "I'll let you do this, on one condition."

Manda looked at the clock. They were running out of time. "What condition?"

"That you order this syntellect to return control of the ship to me, if I and my allies are able to overcome the others."

"How can I trust you?" Manda asked, anguished.

"I give you my word that I will not let them have control of the ship again. I'll have you build a dead man's switch, before you release control. I'll destroy us myself, before I'll let them have control again." At Manda's skeptical look, she smiled. "My dear, I am almost one hundred seventy years old. I've lived a very long life and I'm in no hurry to die, but I don't hold the fear of it that you younger ones do. In any event, you don't really have a choice, do you?"

Manda sighed. "I guess not." She turned to ur-Carli V2.0. "Will you do this?"

Two-Oh spoke instead to Dane-avatar. "Carli loved and trusted you. Will you be true to her? To the colonists?"

Dane-avatar lowered her-avatar's head. "I will try. She knew how complicated it is for me. But I won't allow the colonists to be betrayed again. If that means we must die, so be it. Give me a little time to try to save the young ones, is all I ask."

"I agree to your terms."

"That's all I can ask." Dane-avatar stepped out of the way. "You may push the button."

"Go," ur-Carli told Manda-cat. "The massacre has started."

Heart pounding, Manda-cat leapt onto the pedestal and shoved her-its working paw onto the big, glowing button.

Dane Elisa Cae's piebald avatar vanished in a burst of light. Datastreams began to explode—shredding, fragmenting—all around in a cascade of color and sound like nothing she had ever seen: a digital death spasm. She was watching a highly sophisticated syntellect—*Exodus*—die. It was a stunning and horribly beautiful process.

As this was happening, Two-Oh split in two. One copy dove into the imploding tumult, as the other copy pulled her-avatar away, back the way they had come before. Suddenly she-cat and Two-Oh stood back in the midst of DMiTRI's high-dimensional systems, watching one of its major datastreams—its omnilink to

Exodus—come apart, whiplashing as it strewed meaningless symbols throughout livespace.

"Confirming the hit," V2.0 said, and brought up a viewsphere. Through DMiTRI's powerful lenses they saw the approaching starship begin to veer away from its planned encounter with Brimstone. An orbital overlay showed them its new trajectory. It was leaving the plane of the ecliptic, moving away from any of the system's gravitational bodies. Its current acceleration was well over three gees.

Happy trails, Manda thought. *And good riddance.*

"There's karmic backlash for you," V2.0 murmured. Manda-cat twitched her-its whiskers at the syntellect, which was watching the image with a strange expression.

"What are you talking about?"

The syntellect shook its head, smiling, in a very human-like gesture, and didn't answer for a moment.

"I borrowed a technique they used back on Earth, a long time ago," it explained finally. "When they first set out."

"You're talking as if you wrote the code. I thought you said you only implemented it."

"That's correct. In a manner of speaking."

Manda-cat frowned at the syntellect. She considered asking it to elaborate, but she had more immediate concerns.

"Status?"

"A few of them are trying to carry on with the battle on Brimstone," Two-Oh replied, "But most are trying to deal with my takeover. Ineffectually, I might add," it added with a smug expression. "And they'll be out of omnilink range," the syntellect reported, "in ten seconds. Eight . . . five . . . two . . . one . . . and they're out of range."

"Show me the colony," Manda-cat demanded.

The transparent facehole appeared in front of her again, and she-avatar faced into the programball and looked around at the panels.

In the first image, Manda saw a machine just as it froze in the act of bringing a metal beam down on Amadeo PabloJeb's wrinkled, white-haired crown. He scooted backward away from the beam, face pallid. Then, in every scene, the battle was over. All machine-waldos had frozen. People were just beginning to pick themselves up and shy away from the machines, looking shell-shocked, baffled, grim.

From hidden corners and shadows, those in hiding began to emerge. Some aided the wounded and others began to pry at doors and blockades, attempting to set free those trapped in closed rooms and sealed chambers. Among these early rescuers Manda-cat finally spotted three of her siblings—Arlene, with Bart and Charles, emerging from the Honeycombs. They used their own strength as well as that of a construction-waldo to rescue some people pinned inside a metal Hydroponics trench in the partly-rebuilt gardens.

"The refinery is sending a voice communication by radio," V2.0 told her-avatar. "Shall I patch it through?"

"Yes, please," she-avatar said, and heard Jim—she was sure it was Jim—say breathlessly, "—peat, this is LuisMichael. The refinery fell under attack by the crèche-born at twenty-five forty this evening, but we appear to have defeated them. We have casualties and are urgently in need of medical assistance. Are you receiving this? Come in, Amaterasu, over!"

"Give me a line!" Manda-cat ordered, as he was finishing his transmission.

"Done."

"Jim, is that you?" she-avatar asked the air.

"Manda? Thank God!" His laugh boomed around her-avatar. "I *knew* you were still alive! What happened?"

"We've had a bit of a ruckus too, but the crèche-born are out of the picture. I'll fill you in later, in private."

"In private, eh? I like the sound of that."

"I do too," a third voice broke in, "since this is the official communications channel. Get off the line, CarliPablo, and let us do our job."

A spike of annoyance shot through her; *I just saved your ass, you idiot.* But she somehow resisted saying it.

"I'll call you, Jim," Manda-cat promised.

"You'd better!"

Smiling, she-cat withdrew from the conversation.

When she-avatar returned to DMiTRI's main commandface, yet another copy of ur-Carli had appeared beside the first. The two copies were pressed together, face to face, ensnarled in a web of flowing datastreams. It reminded her enough of love-making to embarrass her. On the other hand, it might have been a battle.

"Excuse me," she-avatar said. Neither responded. "*Hey!* What's going on?"

Still no answer. Then she realized that the two copies were merging, with strange reflections and distortions, into a single copy.

"Two-oh?" she asked, tentatively. "Are you okay?"

"Two-one, now, actually." The syntellect pursed its wrinkled, pale lips. It looked a little different, somehow. Manda couldn't put her finger on exactly what had changed. "Two-Oh was doing an upgrade on One-Three—the one you called ur-Carli. We're both, now. Or rather, I'm both. One-Three's corrupted systems have been deleted and its memories have been integrated with Two-Oh's. Then I did a little file cleanup, made some quick improvements, and deleted the extra copy. We are one."

"How lovely for you." Manda cleared her throat. "What about the alien? Did we also manage to stop them from blowing it up?"

In answer, the syntellect lifted Manda's cat-avatar off her point of consciousness, then grabbed handfuls of code and shaped them around the spot of Manda's awareness, till she stood inside the glacine contours of one of her marine-waldos: *Aculeus Tres.*

It was pitch-black. Manda-*Tres* turned on her-its floodlights, but her question was answered even before she saw the graceful arches and towers and lush forests and sea creatures that surrounded her-it. For she could hear the alien's boomspeak from the moment she plugged in.

Mingled relief and sorrow flooded her. This being had survived; yes—but was now alone, bereft of its only companion, after millions of years of partnership.

We'll make contact with this one, she decided. *As soon as we can. We'll let it know what happened. And its partner's child will grow up, eventually. Till then, perhaps we can be its voice in the dark.*

"Listen," she said, turning off her marine-waldo's command-face and returning to her cat-avatar, "I've got to get back to the colony. Thanks for everything, ur-Carli. I *can* call you that now, can't I, now that you're a single copy again?"

"Of course. But before you go, there were a couple other things Carli wanted you to know—"

"Is it urgent?"

The syntellect hesitated, then shook its head. "Not really."

"Then it can wait. I'll be in touch."

She stripped off her livehood and unplugged. A little wistfully, she removed her ruined, stiffening livesuit and laid it on the desk by the computer. Somehow it seemed the death of a friend; the end of an era. Henceforward she'd be facing the world in a new skin.

She checked her livehood, mic, and the one working glove. They were all still intact; to carry on her work with the aliens, she'd have to get a replacement for the rest. Under the circumstances she doubted if she'd have much difficulty. She'd just bought herself a whole tankerload of coup tonight. A world's worth.

She knew, though, at what cost she'd bought it.

Manda bundled up her working bits of liveware and clothes again, tucked the liveware next to her skin where it would stay warm, and slipped into her parka. She climbed the spiral stair-case and scrambled painfully over the observatory's ledge, out into the stabbing, midnight-cold of the ridge and down to help her people.

Derek knew at what cost she'd bought it too. When she told him what had happened, Derek yelled in her face, there in front of all their siblings, in their sleeping chamber. "*Goddam* you, Manda—can't you ever do what you're supposed to?"

All seven of them were in sorry shape: slicked over with polymer-coated cuts and bruises. Farrah was using a cane, and Bart was propping Charles up; his leg had been broken at three points and he was in a hip cast. Arlene had a deep gash down the side of her face, and the left side of Derek's jaw was swollen.

Manda just stared at her eldest brother. Her other siblings exchanged looks. Janice touched Derek's arm. "She just saved the colony, Derek. For Christ's sake, warm it up."

But Derek's gaze didn't waver. "They're coming back," he told all the others. "It's only a matter of time." To Manda he said, "They haven't changed *in a hundred-fifty seasons*—you think a few more is going to make a difference? Do you?" He shook his head, with a heavy sigh. "You've changed, Manda. A month ago you wouldn't have hesitated to do what was necessary. Whatever the price."

Manda's skin tingled. "Yes, I have changed. And I like who I've become. Can you say the same about yourself?"

"How many of our people *died* while you jury-rigged your clever alternative? How much pain would you have saved us if you hadn't hesitated to push the button? How much more pain will your squeamishness cause, if they return and attack us again?"

She didn't allow herself to react, but the image of those blades slashing into Vance RoxannaTomas—and all the bodies lined up neatly outside the Recycler rooms—flashed before her.

"Nobody knows the future," she said, softly. "You don't know what's going to happen."

Arlene said, laying a hand on Derek's shoulder, "We know them, Manda. Better than you." She sighed. "They'll figure out a way to hack ur-Carli and defeat Dane Elisa Cae, and they'll be back. We'll have to fight them eventually. Derek's way . . . well, it would have been cleaner. It would have been over quicker. With less loss and risk. I understand why you chose to do what you did, but . . ." She shook her head. "We've only bought a little time. They'll be back, and it'll be ugly."

Manda replied, "Do our cousins aboard *Exodus* not matter? Their captive children, their undecanted babies? Does Dane, who saved Jim's and my lives down below the ice, not matter?" Manda shook her head with a frown. "I wasn't willing to kill them all. Not when there was an alternative."

"But you didn't know whether your alternative would even work!" Derek burst out. "You risk all our lives on a gambit that might have failed!"

Charles stepped forward with Bart. "But she didn't fail, Derek."

"Forty-seven died, Charles. Forty-seven."

Janice and Farrah stepped up too. "You're being too hard on her," all four said together.

Derek looked them all over. Farrah, Janice, Charles, and Bart had gathered around Manda, close enough that she could feel their body heat. After a moment of staring at all of them, Derek turned on his heel and left. With a backward, discomfited glance, Arlene followed.

"Sorry," they said. "Don't let him get to you, Manda." "I-we don't know—" "—what's gotten into him."

But Manda didn't need Derek to remind her about those forty-seven. She thought of them every night when she went to sleep. She lit candles for them at the memorial ceremony held the next day, and she thought of them as their vat-mates began dying or disappearing, a day or two after that.

It was after Jeannelle attempted to kill herself—and very nearly succeeded—that Manda realized how she might make some small amends for the choice she'd made.

"I want to start a program to help my fellow singles," she told the council, and she laid out her equipment and personnel needs. They let her do it.

If anyone could help them, she could.

Four nights later, just before the town meeting in which Carli's room would be revealed to the colony, Manda went to the secret room for one last visit. She crunched through the debris from her fight with the waldos, thinking how empty the place felt, now that Carli's body and her digital clone, ur-Carli, were gone.

Manda limped painfully up to the observatory and opened the ceiling petals. She leaned on the ledge, gazing upward, captivated once again by the beauty of Brimstone's night sky. The stars and moons were all blazing their many colors, and the far edge of Fire's ring glowed white, all these nighttime lights making the snowy plateau below shine softly. For a moment, it was as if she pierced all the ambiguity and contingency, saw through the fog to some great, glorious dance of life: some pattern of birth and death and rebirth. On that scale—somehow—things really *would* be all right. It wasn't just a lie.

As this fleeting vision, this comforting certainty faded, Manda took a breath of the searing-cold air. She wondered where the crèche-born were now: whether one of those tiny points of light out there might be them, racing toward their own oblivion.

She would be grieving those forty-seven colonists for a very long time.

Do right by me, Dane Elisa Cae, she thought fiercely. *Do right by me. Don't make those lives that I sacrificed for you wasted lives.*

And she bent her head and cried.

The crèche-born were unused to unilateral defeat, and they didn't take it well. Especially Pablo. No one could find him.

Dane knew what had happened. He'd retreated far inside their mind—as Buddy had so long ago, back when they'd left Earth; as she herself had recently done; as Pablito had done.

The others coped as best they could. They tried to hack back into the ship's systems, but ur-Carli version 2.0 had them quite thoroughly shut out. So everyone wandered around in a posttraumatic daze, not knowing what to do next, as they raced faster and faster from 47 Ursae Majoris, toward a distant star that they didn't have enough fuel to reach.

Dane knew what what would happen. Someday soon Pablo would recover. His ego was insurmountable. He'd be back, and with his will and brilliance driving them, the crèche-born would find a way to hack into Two-Oh's systems and take Exodus *back. They'd return to Brimstone and try to take it over again. She knew now that she could never change her crèche-mates. The damage in them went too deep. Too many people had suffered and died at their hands, over the years.*

When she realized this, Dane knew what she had to do. It just took her a while to work up the courage to decide to act, and a while longer to find a way to make it work.

Once she had a plan worked out, she tried to talk to the ship clones, let them know what she was about to do and what it would mean for them. But the poor young things were too terrified and filled with hate to listen; they cringed and ran back into their own spaces. So instead she got in touch with Two-Oh.

"There's enough fuel to get to 70 Virginis," she said, "if you shed sixty percent of the ship's mass and reprogram the nanotemplates thus." She input the plan for the reworking of the ship, and waited while Two-Oh considered it.

"It works," Two-Oh said finally. "I note that there will be insufficient supplies."

"There'll be enough for those who remain," Dane said, and transmitted the second part of her plan to Two-Oh. "I'll need your help with this as well."

"I'll help," Two-Oh said.

The crèche-borns' flesh lay in the very heart of the ship: twenty-four inert bodies sealed in metal, hooked to their interfaces, cared for by automated servants. Two-Oh found and deactivated the security systems one by one, and shut down the servants, so finally Dane in her proxy body entered the chambers where the twenty-four crèches lay: hers and her companions—her family, her enemies, for the past hundred and seventy years.

She could have just let it go at that, but alarms were already going off, warning them that their life-support systems had shut down. She wanted to make absolutely sure.

So she injected a poison into each crèche's IV. The crèches were old technology, and easy to circumvent. As she killed her crèche-mates, they appeared in virtu, panicked—screaming at her—trying to save their flesh. It was too late—there was nothing they could do—and they faded, sad-eyed, one by one, like the sour old ghosts they were.

Last she came to the crèche she shared with Buddy and Pablo. She wanted to open it—to say good-bye to their flesh—but knew she didn't dare: she'd falter if she looked now.

Buddy appeared in virtu as she reached into her pouch for the last IV, and put out a hand to stop her, horror and fear on his face—but she was in proxy and he was in virtu; he couldn't stop her.

"It's time, Buddy," she said softly. "We're old and mean and ruined. We've outlived our time. It's time to turn the world over to the young."

He covered his face, acquiescing.

Pablo appeared with a roar of rage. "Stop! I'll kill you! Cunt!"

"Cunt," she said, with a sudden laugh. "Don't I wish. My only cunt exists in our imagination. Come on, Pablo," she said, and to her surprise, she even felt affection for him, and for Buddy too. "Come, brothers. It's time to give up the ghost." With a smooth motion, she put the poison in their own IV.

Pablo screamed, terrified. As sensation began to bleed away, she took him in her arms in virtu, and Buddy. Little Pablito—the baby boy, long hidden deep within, father to them all—came last, whimpering, holding out his arms. Dane comforted him.

Slowly they joined, and were one again after a lifetime apart. As the anger and terror ebbed, first forgiveness, and then wonder, filled the being they became. And for that brief moment before life ended, Dane/Pablo/Buddy/Pablito knew joy.

Manda got her Singles Club up and running in that first week after the Ten-Minute War, as they'd dubbed it. They were forced to use drastic measures with the survivors: physical restraints, locks, even drugs, as well as lots of counselling and trips to the hot springs and meditative retreats and the like. They and some of their clone-siblings fought Manda's methods at first, but she'd held her ground and the remaining UrsaMeri sisters backed her up. Ultimately the council had endorsed her plan.

Manda made Jeannelle her personal crusade, fighting the fight she'd fought herself for many years: the fight she wished she'd fought for Paul. Jeannelle hated her for it. It would be a long time, Manda realized, before she'd forgive her for not allowing her to die. But Manda knew how to endure the scorn and hatred of her peers, and she wasn't going to let Jeannelle go without a fight.

"Why are you doing this to me?" Jeannelle shrieked once, and Manda said simply, "Because I love you, Jeannelle. You're my friend and I don't want you to die."

Jeannelle laid back on her hospital mat. "If you loved me, you'd let me end the pain."

Manda sighed. She thought for a moment. "Remember after the cave-in, when you found me on the floor in NICU?"

Jeannelle merely looked at her, sullen.

"You helped me, at a time when I was in pain." She paused. "I've known a lot of pain in my life. I've lived what you're going through. If you stick around, at some point you'll get past it and find as I did that life is worth living, even with Vance gone. So." She shrugged. "I'm not going to let you take the easy way out."

"Get out!" Jeannelle hissed. *"Get out."*

Manda shook her head. "You're stuck with me, I'm afraid."

Jeannelle broke down and sobbed. Manda sat with her. After a few moments Jeannelle laid her head in Manda's lap.

It was also a time for rejoicing. Not only had they banished their long-feared parent-enemies, but shortly after the war ended, UrsaMeri brought a small section of Hydroponics online. The section was not large enough to provide a lot of food, and certainly not anytime soon; still, it was good for morale. (Manda wondered if that might be UrsaMeri's intent.) A couple weeks after the war, Manda's *Aculeus* waldos brought in the first bactoweed shipments from Rima Longinquum, the deep-sea trench that housed the far-side alien and its symbionts, and the colony food stores were augmented and replenished by the new xeno-*mana*.

The days flew past: repairs, healing and convalence, rebuilding. Everyone worked at a brisk pace. People burst out in song at odd times. Laughter could be heard echoing through the tunnels and caverns.

Manda's status as hero had been sealed by her defeat of the crèche-born. People sought her out, asked her opinions about things. Even KaliMarshall, PatriciaJoe, and PabloJeb were behaving civilly toward her. New elections were planned, and ironically Derek was benefiting from Manda's actions, despite his disapproval. He was easy-coup to displace Jack PabloJeb as head of council. Manda had already received permission to mount at least two more peopled undersea expeditions: one to Rima Longinquum during the summer, to establish contact with the adult alien, and a second to Rima Optabile in three or four seasons, to check on the near-side baby alien's progress.

*   *   *

One evening after second watch ended, they held Carli's recycling ceremony. Manda sat in the Majestic with her baby brother Terence cradled in a sling on her chest and Jim by her side. He and his siblings had come in for the ceremony; in fact, the whole colony was there. She heard someone nearby say to her companion, "Did you hear those odd rumors about Carli's corpse?"

"No, what?"

"Apparently her brain was missing. Everything but the *medulla oblongata*. It was the strangest thing. They think it was surgically removed, somehow. They're looking for it now."

"How odd," someone else said. "Do you suppose she had it removed and preserved for some reason?"

"There was no sign of incision or intrusion," the first one said.

"Maybe the crèche-born used some weird weapon on her."

"Are we sure her *mana* is clean?" someone else asked. "What if it was some strange disease?"

"No disease could do that!"

"We screened the tissues thoroughly," yet a fourth whispered. Manda recognized Jeannelle's elder sister Tania's voice. "We found no evidence of pathogens. The *mana* is clean."

Manda thought of ur-Carli, and was certain. "Carli had a download done. A destructive download. She had her memories and personality digitized."

Others—including Jim—gaped at her.

"But how?" he asked in a low voice. Others leaned close, straining to hear.

Manda shook her head. "I don't know. Maybe she got her hands on a different kind of nanomachines. Or maybe she had a way to reprogram Defenders."

"Defenders aren't made to do that kind of work," Tania said. "They have a very constrained structure and purpose. I just— can't picture it."

But there was no further time for reflection because the ceremony was starting. The drummers and flutists started their introductory music while a line of robed and hooded celebrants filed up in front of the crowd, carrying pitchers. They stood in two rows before the carved stone faces. The leader was Arlene.

The celebrants passed out small cups and beeswax candles. Tapers passed from hand to hand. The main lights went down. Manda sat in the darkness with her lit candle in one hand, the fingers of her other hand enmeshed in Jim's, looking out over the flickering sea of flames, catching glimpses of people's faces. A thousand whispers echoed against the cavern walls, blended with the distant calls of cat and owl, and the clanks of automated machinery.

Then Arlene stood, and a hush fell over them.

"We come here tonight to celebrate the life of Carli D'Auber," she said, lifting her pitcher, "and to share among ourselves what remains of her, remembering each who she was and what she meant to us.

"Because Carli meant so much to all of us, and we wanted to make sure everyone could share a small part of her *mana*, GeorgJean has prepared liquid *mana* for us tonight, sweetened with honeyed mead, instead of the usual *mana* loaves."

The celebrants passed among the attendees, passing out tiny sips of Carli's *mana* from their pitchers. So many were there that everyone got only a few milliliters.

Finally the celebrants returned to the front. Arlene lifted her own cup with one hand, and her candle with the other. "We are all stardust, and to dust we return at the end of our time. Eat—I mean drink—now, and remember Carli."

Everyone raised their candles over their heads. Jim touched Manda's cup's rim with his own, and spoke the traditional words as a toast: "To those who have passed on," and Manda said, "To those who remain."

A rustling, as cups were tilted up. Manda drained her own

cup of sweet liquor and purified proteins, and then smiled down at Terence, who'd made a cooing noise.

"You want some too, don't you, Ter?" she said.

Jim raised his eyebrows at Manda. She shrugged. "I know he won't remember, but I'd like him to be a part of this too."

She dribbled the last of her drink onto his lips. He smacked hungrily and then rooted, seeking more nourishment; she pulled his bottle of infant formula from her belt and he sucked greedily. Then she and Jim kissed, and the taste of *mana* and liquor was sweet on his lips.

Everyone doused their flames at Arlene's cue, and they were submerged in cool, breezy darkness. With a slow release of breath, Manda leaned her forehead on Jim's chin. He wrapped his arm about her shoulders, with Terence a warm, shifting bundle between them. Manda shed a few tears onto the bone-white rock: a libation of farewell to the past and a greeting to the future.

The colony was still technology-poor, hungry, and oxygen-starved. Their struggles to survive weren't over. The crèche-born might be back sometime. Maybe they'd be friendly, and maybe not. Forty-seven of her people's lives had been snuffed out while she'd sought a way to save her enemies' lives. She would never forget that; for the rest of her life she'd mourn her comrades who had fallen. She had begun collecting mementos from their clones, and had placed them in a cubby in her sleeping nook. Every night she would touch the knickknacks and remember those who might still be here if not for the choice she'd made. The alien bacteria were becoming a problem, contaminating their algae, infecting their people and livestock, attacking their bamboo. The sapient alien on the far side might not be as sanguine as its near-side twin about humans' presence on its world. All in all—while it beat extinction—this meeting of human and alien intelligence would not be without its price.

And on the personal side, things were equally uncertain. Terence might or might not have brain damage. Jim's sister Amy still hated Manda, Brian distrusted her, and the anxiety Manda's clone felt over Jim could explode into open hostility anytime. He was resisting a covalence ceremony, and she knew well that this would result in trouble soon. Exo-bonds rarely lasted more than a few weeks; a month or two at most.

We'll be different, she vowed, *Jim and I,* and willed it to be so. Despite all these uncertainties, Manda couldn't help but feel happy. The future, which had seemed so dark only a short time before, seemed now hold promise, as a tulip or a sprig of edelweiss pushes stubbornly up through the spring snows.

Life wasn't so fragile, after all, she'd decided. Hold on through the hard times, carry on in the face of pain and loss, and birth—or rebirth—followed death just as surely as death followed birth. The whole somehow remained: an entity somehow greater than the sum of its flawed and faltering parts.

Jim stayed with her that night, and so did the baby. While the baby slept at their feet, she and Jim made love, quietly and tenderly—not an easy feat; though his bones were knitting, they were both still banged-up and sore. Later when Terence fussed, she brought him up between herself and Jim to share their body warmth.

Jim soon drifted off to sleep. The baby fell sound asleep too. But Manda was restless despite her deep fatigue, so she donned her liveware and enough layers to keep warm, and went for a walk, sorting and answering the many messages that had stacked up in her queues, and organizing tomorrow's tasks.

The colony seemed quieter than usual, despite the crowding due to all the refinery people and herders coming in for Carli's ceremony. She passed many dark cubbies and nooks wherein she heard the sound of people asleep. In the nursery, the caregivers lay slumped in their chairs, asleep with their charges.

A spell of restfulness had fallen over the weary colonists. Only the animals in the stables stirred, and the wildlife in the forests and gardens of the lowermost levels.

Everyone is asleep but me, she thought whimsically.

Her wanderings brought her to the bamboo forest, where she found a clearing and a bench. There she finished organizing her files and icons, and tucked them away. She started to turn off her liveface, but a mother cat passed through, distracting her. The cat carried a kitten in her mouth. Two more kittens tumbled along behind, scuffling. One of them, with his orange-and-brown stripes and his one white paw, looked exactly like her old half-grown Terrible Tom. Perhaps he *had* survived the beating he'd gotten when young, and this was a descendant of his. It seemed fitting.

And finally Manda felt drowsy. It was a pleasant feeling, to finally relax. Her body felt light, airy, even tingly, as though a gentle breeze were blowing across, somehow even through, her. She yawned so hard her jaw cracked, and then slouched in her seat. She might have even dozed off right then, if not for the interruption.

"Manda—" said a voice.

She turned, startled, to see a *virtu*-projection of ur-Carli standing at the edge of the clearing.

"Excuse the intrusion," it said, "but this is the first time I've been able to find you unoccupied and alone while wearing your liveware."

"Yes, of course. I know you wanted to speak with me further, but things have been hectic—"

"I quite understand. But there are some things it's becoming critical you should know."

Manda yawned again. "Excuse me. Sure. What is it?"

The syntellect sat down next to her, and laid a faux-arm across the back of the bench. "There were additional items Carli wanted me to make sure you knew about. She hid other things besides the infobombware in her room."

Manda grew more alert. "More weapons?"

"No. Something else." The syntellect paused. "First of all, I should tell you that I'm partly made up of Carli."

Manda stared thoughtfully at the syntellect. "I'd already figured that out, actually. You did a download on her, didn't you? With nanotech."

The syntellect blinked at her. "Yes. Naturally it required destruction of the organic matter, in order to read the chemical information there and translate it to digital. Most of the memories and traits are still in storage. I haven't translated or integrated all of them yet—only bits and pieces throughout her life, and most of the last twenty-five years of her life by Earth reckoning. There is too much, and I haven't had access to sufficient processing cycles yet. But at least in part, I am a digital version of her."

"Why are you telling me this?" Manda asked finally. She suppressed the urge to use her fingers to prop her eyes open, which stubbornly tried to keep closing.

Ur-Carli ignored the question. "We did it using technology I brought with me from *Exodus*." Manda detected a subtle shift in the avatar's tone and expression; she realized with a sudden shiver that—in a sense—this was Carli herself talking now. "The crèche-born cheated you in so many ways. They gave you barely enough to scrape out a life here."

Manda really was getting too tired to think very clearly. She frowned. "What are you talking about?"

"They could have given you so much more—all the tools you'd need to make your lives plentiful and comfortable. A paradise. The older members of the colony have some inkling of this— though even when you were on the ship, the crèche-born hid much from you."

Manda shook her head. "Why?"

Ur-Carli shrugged. "Partly revenge. Their leader, Pablo, was angry. There were other reasons too. They didn't want you to grow too powerful. They wanted you grateful—indebted—when and if they returned, for all that they would bring with them. And they wanted to be able to control you. You'd have been able to put up some serious resistance if they'd fully equipped you. So they gave you enough to sustain yourselves and begin to lay down the infrastructure they would need, but no more." Ur-Carli bent her head. "I tried, but couldn't persuade them differently. So I decided to smuggle out some of those tools and provide them to you."

"What nasty shits!"

"It was nasty, what they did, yes." Ur-Carli sighed. "I loved them, you know. I tried to help them. When I failed, I knew that I had to come here and protect their children from their worst intentions." She paused. "I honestly can't hate them for what they've done—I understand too well why they are what they are. But I understand how *you* could. I'm glad that despite your anger, you found a way to save yourselves without destroying them.

"I had given up on them, you see. They're nearing two centuries old now, and they seem to me to have only gotten worse with time. That's why I designed the infobomb. Now that Dane Elisa Cae finally found the courage to revolt outright, maybe there will be others. Perhaps there's hope for them. Or for some of them. I don't hold out a great deal of hope for that—but I still think you made the right choice, not to destroy them."

Manda lowered her head. "If I'd pushed the button, more of my own people might have lived."

"True."

Manda lowered her head. "But I just couldn't do it."

Ur-Carli sighed. "You didn't kill your fellow colonists, Manda. The crèche-born did. War forces brutal choices. There is often no clean win. You made the choice you had to make. Perhaps the mercy you showed will cause some of the crèche-born to set aside their destructive natures. You may have helped Dane Elisa Cae in her cause. We can't know the future, but I am hopeful that good will come of it, somehow."

"I hope you're right."

"I believe I am. Sometimes destruction is necessary, but I have observed that it often sets off further cycles of destruction that propagate themselves long after the original dispute has been forgotten. I believe you have averted this fate for your people. You have dampened a destructive cycle, instead of feeding it."

Manda digested all this. "Why are you telling me all this now, after so long?" she asked. "And what tools are you talking about? I didn't see anything unusual up there in that room."

But ur-Carli was still playing back old memories. "They were afraid of me. And I think they loved me too, after their fashion. They wouldn't dare harm me. But I'm afraid my actions sparked violence back then, between them and you. People died and I felt badly. I wasn't sure I'd done the right thing."

Finally the syntellect looked at Manda. Its gaze burned as hot as a human's would. Manda was sure then that ur-Carli was as sapient as the alien they'd found under the sea.

"The tools I stole from them are very powerful. Useful, yes— but extremely dangerous, if not handled properly. Worse than anything you can imagine." It paused again. "When it came down to it, I just couldn't face releasing them to you. I should have given you the choice, I suppose, but—I shrank from that decision. I struggled with it for a while after we arrived—but I just—couldn't bring myself to act. So hid myself and the tools away." Ur-Carli sighed. "I was old, Manda. Very old, and un-speakably tired. I'd been contending with the crèche-born for so long. I was ready to die. So I had ur-Carli—back then we weren't one—I had it collect and preserve my memories for its use, to help protect you all until it decided the time was right."

"I still don't—"

"I hid the tools inside my body, Manda," the syntellect said. "Nanomachines. Far more powerful than the crippled forms the crèche-born provided you with. You took them in with my *mana*. They're changing you already. That's why everyone is sleeping."

A shock exploded through Manda, core to skin. She gaped down at herself and suppressed a gag. "You mean they're already inside us? But they said your *mana* was clean!"

Ur-Carli gave a little shrug. "They read as residual Defenders," she said. "Harmless. In their dormant state they're not much different from what you're used to. But they're infinitely self-perpetuating, and much, much more versatile. I call them Partners."

"Partners." Manda's head was spinning.

"The machines have been multiplying inside the bodies of everyone who participated in the *mana* ceremony tonight. The templates for reprogramming them are in DMiTRI now. You'll all wake up ravenous, I'm afraid. That was unavoidable."

"What—what will they do to us?"

"Their default programming is to simply make your bodies better adapted to this world's parameters: larger lungs, higher oxygen exchange and efficiency, greater resistance to radiation. They can be programmed to do other things, if you wish them to, such as allowing you to consume cellulose—which I think would be a good change; it'll make food production much easier. You can extract samples and breed them. Once you learn how to program them, you will eventually be able to build anything you have the raw materials for. Buildings, equipment, topsoil, whatever.

"Ultimately they will be able to produce greenhouse gases and warm this world for you, if you so choose. They're not *quite* capable of generating the seeds of life for you, but they can be used to build just about anything else. Everything you need to make this world a paradise.

"Of course," she said, "now that you've discovered life here, that becomes more problematic. But I'm sure you'll find a way to work with the native entities to find a mutually agreeable arrangement. If you don't wipe each other out first."

Manda gasped. It turned into another jaw-cracking yawn.

"*What?*"

"Just a little gallows humor."

"Why—excuse me—why didn't you go to the council with this?" Manda's speech slurred with fatigue despite herself.

Ur-Carli looked sheepish. "I have some of Carli's memories and personality traits, but my programming has certain—limitations. I've observed that you handle conflict better than most—"

"I seem to get lots of practice."

"—so you seemed a natural choice."

"You were afraid, in other words, so you dumped the burden on me. Thanks loads." Another big yawn. She was having difficulty keeping her eyes open.

"You're getting very sleepy, aren't you?" ur-Carli said. "*Cease amanuensis!* That will slow the process for a bit, till I can finish showing you what I need to show you."

Manda held up her hands like stop signs and lowered her head, shaking it the way a bull reindeer does when it's plagued by gnats. The shock inside was fading along with the drowsiness, but fear was swelling up to fill its place.

"I'm not ready for more," she said. "This is too much already. Please."

"I think you'll like this one," ur-Carli replied.

"Like what?"

"I'll show you."

With that Manda's surroundings melted away and she was Manda-cat, inside DMiTRI's main high-dimensional raw-process platform, with its digital sea of dataflows and algorithms swirling and flashing and jittering around them. Ur-Carli spread its hands and turned—and moved—and turned again, in strangely complex ways that Manda did not understand and could never have replicated on her own. And then before them was a *nothingness*: a stretch of featureless black, as if livespace came to an end here. This void extended as far up and down and to both sides as she-avatar could see. Though up close its boundary appeared straight and flat, it gave a sense of some subtle curvature or arc in the far distance. Though how a void could curve Manda wasn't sure.

"Careful!" ur-Carli warned, too late: as Manda-cat touched it, the wall seemed to drain the life from Manda-cat's paw. She-avatar snatched the paw back and rubbed the numb appendage. "I'll help you repair that, but if you try to push into this, it will destroy your avatar. It's impenetrable and absolutely deadly to digital lifeforms."

Manda-cat cocked her-its head at the syntellect. *"Digital lifeforms,"* eh? *Hmmm.* "I thought it was just—a big nothing. What is it?"

"A firewall to end all firewalls. While we were en route here—early on, when the ship reached relativistic speeds and our omni generator went online—an infowar broke out between the crèche-born and Earth. Earth and the crèche-born locked each other out. Both sides have tried to break through each others' defenses over the years, occasionally, with no sustained success. But I've been experimenting and I believe that there might be a way to open up a bridge. A thread of communication. It will take a while, but—"

The implications of ur-Carli's words finally sank in through the wadding of Manda's fatigue and shock. "My God—that's right! We have an omni field generator of our own!"

The absurdity of the situation suddenly struck Manda, and she-cat burst into laughter loud and long—in that glassware-rattling way Jim always did—clutching her-its tawny belly with her-its enormous paws, shrieking and snorting with the hilarity of it all, till tears squeezed out of her own eyes and her sides ached.

"Why are you laughing?" ur-Carli asked, looking mildly miffed. Manda-cat shook her-avatar's head.

"It's nothing. It's just—I can hardly wait to see the council-members' expressions tomorrow when I break this news to them."

"Well, now you know everything," ur-Carli said. "I have work to do and you need rest. We'll talk again soon."

With that, ur-Carli vanished, and Manda found herself in corpus, back in the bamboo caverns on the bench.

"Holy shit!" she breathed.

What do I do? Who do I tell? Should I wake everyone up?

Manda tried to call Derek. No answer. She tried each of the councilmembers in turn, and when no one answered, she left them all an urgent message telling them what had just happened. Then she headed back to her cubby, pushing against the leaden sleepiness that crept back over her, and scrambled across the bed to shake Jim, trying not to disturb the sleeping baby.

"Wake up, Jim! *Wake up.*" But Jim was hard asleep.

What was that phrase?

"*Cease amanuensis,*" she hissed. Her own drowsiness once more lifted a little. She shook Jim some more. "Wake up!"

"Huh—?" He sat up, tousle-haired, wild-eyed, looking confused.

"Jim, I need to tell you something important. Come on—pay attention, damn it!"

"All right. All right." He rubbed at his eyes and yawned. "I'm awake. What's wrong?"

"I just found out that we've got a new kind of nanomachine inside us—ur-Carli told me only a few minutes ago. It's changing everyone right now."

He gaped, alarmed. "*What?* What are you talking about?"

"It was in Carli's tissues. We took it in at her funeral tonight. Just imagine what this is going to mean!"

"Biotech? Nanotech?"

"Exactly!"

He shook his head, wild-eyed and drowsy. "Are you serious?"

"Yes! And there's more. Ur-Carli does have Carli's personalities and memory! I was right about that. Not only that; we've got our own omnilink, now! It showed me the firewall between us and Earthspace—"

Jim raised a hand. "Slow down. Is all this true, or are you waking me up to tell me about a dream?"

Manda opened her mouth, and closed it again. It all seemed so incredible—she half wondered if perhaps it *had* been something from a dream. "No—no! I'm serious, Jim! Not five minutes ago I was standing *right there*. Ur-Carli thinks there might be a way through the firewall—"

"Firewall?" He twitched, finally getting it. "Holy shit—we *do* have instantaneous access to Earthspace! I hadn't thought of that." He paused, mulling over what she'd said. "But there's a firewall." He nodded. "Makes sense. Manda, this is incredible!"

"Yes." She gave him a quick kiss. "This will turn everything upside down."

She leaned back against Jim's propped-up knees and eyed sleeping Terence. "And what about the babies?" She took Terence's tiny hand, and stroked it. "He had Carli's *mana* too. I wouldn't have done it—but I didn't know—"

"Of course not." He yawned again, and so did she. The drowsiness was sweeping back over her, tugging at her eyelids and her limbs. It wasn't just the nanochanges; she had been working hard and it was getting very late. She fought it.

"Look," Jim asked, "should we try to stop this—this nanochange? Is it bad?"

Manda frowned, then yawned and stretched. She shook her head. "I don't think so. Ur-Carli made it sound benign—at least in its current form. Better than benign, even: a positive good. Apparently the crèche-born have been using it for years, so ur-Carli would know the risks. It's adapting us to this world. And from what ur-Carli said, if we don't like it we can change ourselves back to the way we were. It's as if we'll be able to work the best parts of PabloJeb's plan *and* ours.

"It can be reprogrammed to do almost anything we can imagine, Jim! Give this world topsoil, add carbon dioxide and methane to the air, build us cities. Think of it!"

"That's a relief."

"But"—cavernous yawn—"she did say it's *extremely* dangerous, if it's misused."

He twiddled thoughtfully with his beard. "Can't misuse it much when we're sleeping, though."

Manda shook her head. "True. But—"

"And this firewall—is there anything you need to do about it right away?"

Manda started to speak, then smiled. "I get the message." She squirmed under the covers between Jim and Terence, pillowed her head on Jim's muscled bicep. He was smiling sleepily back at her.

"See you on the other side," he said, and closed his eyes. Just like that, he was asleep again.

He believed her. That was something. She was having a hard time believing it all, herself.

Oh, I love you. She pressed her buttocks against his hip, tucked her cold feet between his warm calves, and pulled the baby close, inhaling his heady-sweet baby smell.

As sleep came for her, she remembered standing up on that ridge the night of the war. She remembered that glimpse she'd gotten of a great pattern that wove itself whole from the dark and light threads of causality. She recalled her realization that, briefly, she'd played an important role in some immense tapestry of meaning.

She'd often wondered why she'd survived and her brother hadn't. She'd always felt like a mistake. A freak. She'd been wrong.

Her life had purpose. All the events in her life that for so long had seemed merely random—painful snarls of complexity—now made some kind of sense, in a way that was impossible to put into words. In her life a pattern had formed, whose meaning emerged even as the events that shaped it occurred. She might not like all the threads of pain, hatred, love, betrayal, and conflicting loyalties that molded her life—she might not necessarily understand them. But she took comfort from knowing that beneath all the confusion, there were some fundamental truths.

Life mattered. Doing right—when you could figure out what was right—mattered. And when you couldn't, doing the best you could was good enough.

She took comfort from knowing who she was, where her limits were, where her own loyalties lay. If the crèche-born died out there, in space, she'd grieve for the innocent; if they returned to blight the colonists, they'd find the colony ready. But along with ur-Carli and Dane Elisa Cae, Manda had opened a door to a third, life-affirming possibility. She was glad of that.

It seemed to her, too, that life was a work in progress: untidy, not predisposed to clear-cut beginnings and endings. Till the moment when life and consciousness ended, there would always be work more to do—issues left unresolved—risks unfaced, questions left unanswered. Threads left dangling. She'd make time for those threads later. She'd find time to learn what this new technology in their blood would mean; she'd find out more about their new omnilink to Earthspace; she'd discover whatever other secrets old Carli might have hidden when she died. She'd find time to grieve her losses and mistakes, and to figure out how to make this scary and wonderful new thing with Jim work. To help Terence learn and grow.

But for now, to sleep in the warm dark with a partner she loved and a baby she cherished—for now, it was enough.

Acknowledgments

This story owes a huge debt to Ursula K. Le Guin, whose works over the years have inspired me and taught me what it means to be human. In particular, her powerful and haunting story "Nine Lives" moved me when I read it long ago, and eventually became a vital seed at the core of this story.

Chris Crawford is also due a truckload of gratitude, for assisting me with xenobiology and planetary and orbital physics, for the education he has given me in computer interface and interactivity design, and for letting me borrow his fascinating variable-roles theory of human consciousness.

I owe thanks as well to Kate Wilhelm, whose work has also moved me deeply, and whose novella *Where Late the Sweet Birds Sang* increased my desire to write about the secret lives of clones. Thanks to Kim Stanley Robinson for his novel *Icehenge* and his *Mars* trilogy, which made me want to write about cold worlds and terraforming.

Thanks are also due Joe Haideman, for his help with orbital calculations, and Dr. George Somero, for advice both biological and ecological. Dr. Rebecca Rogers gave me useful information on premie babies and their health problems; John Sigda helped me with geology and geophysics. Sage Walker saw my book's ties to Le Guin's "Nine Lives" when I'd been unable to extract the title or author from my junkyard of a memory; Melinda Snodgrass pulled out the scalpel and pressure bandages and helped me surgically separate this book from its abortive sibling, when both were in danger of dying the death of a thousand subplots. Pati Nagle, Terry Boren, Fred Ragsdale, Daniel Abraham, Sally Gwylan, MaryAnn Shore, and Holly Gilster all gave me a plenitude of helpful suggestions. And as always, I'm grateful to Stevie Chuck, who helped in too many ways to recount.

Whatever flaws remain, naturally, are mine alone.